QUEEN OF VAMPIRE HEARTS

BOOK ONE
IN THE
FATED LOVES
SERIES

JEANETTE ROSE

ROSE & STAR

ROSE & STAR PUBLISHING

To Mom & Dad

I was truly lucky to have such a supportive pair of parents throughout this whole thing. My dad who shamelessly pushed this book on his patients, marketing it as "Twilight meets Fifty Shades" and my mom who read this book…Which I'm not sure how you ever looked me in the face after. I love you both.

Love,
Your daughter

I

*THE REALM OF TÍR NAILL.
THE UNSEELIE COURT.*

I NEEDED SOMETHING TO RELIEVE THIS MONOTONY, something to draw my interest, anything at this point to fill this hole inside me. Gods, I sounded so pathetic. I hated this part of me. Well, live for ten thousand fucking years, and tell me you don't get fucking *bored*. By then, you've seen it all, done it all, fucked it all. And given that I was amid a massive immortal orgy, that was saying something.

To my left, three nymphs serviced a massive ogre. To my right, two lycans filled a gorgon as she screamed in ecstasy. Ambrosia, a potent fermented alcohol for immortals, flowed as every sensual delight imaginable was at my disposal, just waiting. But I couldn't summon even the slightest interest in any of them. I didn't quirk a brow at the sight of the blindfolded gorgon being bent over by two wolf-shifters. Even her snakes had little blindfolds to keep from turning her partners to stone.

My eyes glazed over when faced with all these hedonistic spectacles. Maybe Tir nAill wasn't the right choice for me. I needed a different realm to draw my eye, something more *exciting*.

Gods, I've only been here for a couple of hours, and already I'm over this place.

Fuck. The boredom was worse than normal, almost like a rut. Could an immortal get stuck in a rut? I was tired of doing the same thing over and over again, but the party should have worked. I was in another realm at an erotic immortal ball. It had my name all over it, but there I was, and I was fucking bored.

Something was wrong. It had to be. Ten thousand years of using sex to distract couldn't just suddenly stop working, could it? I'd dressed for the occasion, only a pair of leather pants and boots on, leaving my chest bare. One tug at the ties on my pants, and I would be ready to participate in any of the assorted delights. But not even a twitch of interest down south.

Fuck. I came to the Fae realm because I needed to get away from Romania. There were too many vampire sycophants trying to court my favor. Plus, the cold, obsidian walls of my castle made me weary. *Alone.* Like always. There had to be another realm out there that could stir my interests, if only it were this one. I needed something to distract from my own thoughts, my own company. Without distraction, I was only left with self-reflection, which was a fucking bad idea for me.

Tír nAill, the home of the Fae, was a magical realm only accessible through specific rifts—tears in reality—from the mortal plane. There were millions of host realms with thousands of species, and over time, they had leaked into the mortal realm. Though they remained hidden from humanity, all the creatures and monsters that were reduced to legend and myth were real, and roughly sixty percent of them were represented at this erotic ball. Immortality was nothing more than a constant battle against eternal boredom. That's something they didn't tell you in the stories. Immortality, the ability to live forever, immune to sickness and able to regenerate from all but the most fatal of injuries, was a curse. At least to me.

A dryad sidled up next to me. Her transparent green dress left absolutely nothing to the imagination, her body supple in all the ways a female should be. "Looking to play?" She boldly reached for my cock, frowning when her touch did nothing to rouse me.

I forced a chuckle at her presumptive grab and pulled her hand away. "Seems I need someone more gorgeous than you to make my shaft stir."

My head turned with the resounding slap she delivered, my lip splitting slightly from the force. My healing kicked in almost immediately, leaving only a dot of my own blood on my lip. The older the immortal, the faster the regeneration. At ten thousand, most of my wounds healed the minute they formed. Her steps sounded in the sudden silence as she stormed away from me.

The entire room paused with bated breath, waiting to see my reaction. I was *really* not in the mood for a fight. I flashed a wicked smile and shrugged at the audience. They saw I was not going to pursue the matter and dismissed me, turning back to their partners. Free of their gaze, I let my smile fade and swiped a large goblet of blood-laced ambrosia from a passing tray. It bobbed on its way through the event without a waiter, hovering and moving around on its own. I tossed it back, slamming the empty glass down on another table. I strode through the room by rote, with no intended destination. Not even the potent alcohol and the welcome taste of blood could infringe on my disinterest.

6

When I'd grown bored with sexual delights in the past, though admittedly never to this extent, I rallied my vampires into a war. When it wasn't sex for me, it was war. So around and around I went, from war to sex and sex to war, repeatedly for ten thousand years. I was seeking anything to pull me out of this fog. Desperate to forget the lack I felt, the loneliness that pursued me tirelessly, I was looking for anything to distract.

No, I couldn't go there. I forced myself to think about war and forget the yawning emptiness inside. I envisioned the bloodlust overcoming me on the battlefield. My opponents changed as I imagined the various species of immortals that had been pitted against my army. The list of immortal opponents, each with their own kings and queens, their own armies, was endless. A warrior could go mad listing them all. Still, I attempted to consider each one.

Lycans? No, we still had that peace treaty after that last skirmish, and it had lasted over a thousand years at last count. Lycans were wolf shifters, touched by the god Odin. They were formidable adversaries, able to shift into massive wolves at will. For ten years, the vampire and lycan war was a suitable distraction. It came to a rather sudden end when I beheaded the King of the Lycans, installing his much more level-headed son, Erik Wulfric, on the throne. The truce was tenuous and, with just a spark, could turn into another all-out war, but I actually *liked* Erik, even considering him to be a friend. So, the lycans were out.

There were hundreds of different species of immortals to choose from and no shortage of enemies. I just needed to pick the right opponent. I glanced around at the other species present for inspiration and pondered the possibilities.

The Fae were out of the question. Fae were, to put it mildly, fucking insane. They were a strictly hierarchical society. *Fae* was more of a general classification, which included everything from faeries to sprites, banshees, and brownies. The Fae were divided into dark and light, Unseelie and Seelie. Their ruling class were the faeries and their Queen Titania. Titania and I had…a history. But that was before she met Oberon. If I even thought about rallying my armies against the Fae, Oberon would assume I was attempting to reclaim Titania. Oberon would unleash a jealous rage that would make even me pause. As a Dark Faerie, Oberon's skin emitted a deadly poison, and his gossamer wings would turn black when enraged. I bit back a sigh. You would think having fucked Titania and discarded her, Oberon would get the message that I was *not* interested. I didn't go back for seconds, *ever*. Seconds usually turned into them wanting a commitment, something I'd *never* been interested in.

I sensed Titania as she approached. In the world of immortals, you must always be prepared for an attack from any corner, something I'd always resented. Why couldn't we just get along? I supposed that was a bit fucking rich since I was planning a war in my head, but I never said I was perfect.

Titania rested her hand on my arm, drawing my full attention as she said, "Nothing to interest your varied tastes, Lucien?"

Titania topped out at just over five and a half feet and was tall for a full-blooded Light Faerie. Oberon was just over six feet, and it was usual for Dark Faeries to tower over their light counterparts. Their bright, almost glowing, silver eyes and gossamer wings easily distinguish them from other immortals. Their wings appeared delicate as if a single breath could tear them but were deceptively strong and capable of cutting the throat of an enemy. Like everything regarding the Fae, appearances deceive. You took things at face value at your own peril. When I first met Titania, I asked her about the human's erroneous interpretation of faeries. Titania had furiously muttered, "If I ever get my hands on that Disney fucker, I will show him just what a faerie really looks like."

"Nothing yet, love," I said. "Give it time."

Her dark eyebrows rose, knowing I usually would have burned through several partners by now. That was the thing that fucking sucked about people knowing you for more than a century. They could tell when you were just going through the motions.

Why couldn't I be attracted to Titania? She was gorgeous, with dark hair and silver eyes. She haunted many males' dreams, but I hadn't thought of her that way in years. Plus, her new husband barely let me breathe in the same direction as her.

"Your male approaches, no doubt enraged at you for speaking to me in such a setting," I said, gesturing toward the ongoing orgy, then to the furious Fae king storming toward us.

Titania smothered a smile, winking at me. "I'll admit to using you, Lucien. I enjoy Oberon's jealousy too much."

Oberon's eyes were dark with rage, his tall frame stomping towards them, the veins in his wings beginning to turn black. Weaker immortals would have cowered at the sight. I sighed, glancing away from the approaching opponent as if he was beneath my notice. Which, in all honesty, he was. Age meant strength in our world, and I was almost twice his.

"My love!" Titania called out, and Oberon's look of murderous intent morphed to one of tenderness at the sight of his queen. Titania was the heiress of the Light Fae and Oberon, the heir to the Dark. Their arranged marriage united the two courts under a single banner. Yet the arrangement morphed into a love match, though it was touch and go there for a while. Most of which had a little more to do with me than I was willing to admit.

With the Fae king momentarily distracted, I slipped away, darting through more writhing bodies. Fuck, coming to this was a mistake. I thought coming here would distract from the echoing emptiness of Romania, but the crush of bodies had the opposite effect.

I noticed the only empty balcony and headed toward it. Maybe I needed a moment alone to reinvigorate my desire or to pick a new opponent in my planned war. I needed something, anything, to keep from retreating into myself.

The doors to the balcony remained open as I stormed past them. I came to the edge of the marble balustrade and rested my hands against the cool stone, staring out over the exterior courtyards. The skies of Tír nAill were lit up with colored streaks from its various inhabitants' fabled dust. It drifted into the sky when it fell from their wings. I supposed the sight would cause most immortals to sigh in wonderment, but such sights became commonplace over the years.

When was the last time I sat in awe of something? I bowed my head, and the ache that plagued me, that hole inside me, seemed to grow bigger for a moment. For ten thousand years, I'd tossed everything I could think of into it, hoping to stem the icy loneliness creeping up my spine. I needed something to relieve this monotony. I tried to force my thoughts to battle, to war, anything but this emptiness.

I took a deep inhale of the wind whistling by, the ambrosia and perfume of sex almost negating my enhanced sense of smell. Usually, I could scent an immortal from afar, but with so many present in the room, my nose was overwhelmed, unable to differentiate one from another.

Maybe I should stop looking for a challenge and settle for a fight instead. There was a reason I maintained my rule over my volatile, blood-hungry subjects for so many millennia. I was indomitable, or at least I acted like I was, and attitude was everything. I should really keep track of how many wars and skirmishes were put down by word of mouth. Rumor and reputation puts down more insurrection than a massacre once a millennium.

I lost my focus on the scenery, no longer interested in the silver trees with golden leaves lining the palace courtyard. Instead, I stared sightlessly beyond them, forcing myself to consider more opponents for my war. Maybe the witches? *No.* Not enough had survived the years of persecution to be a threat to my army. The witches were immortal spell-casters and one of the physically weaker species. With their magic, they could have been a formidable opponent, but constant infighting and treachery tore them apart. Their governing body, the Council, was more dangerous than any other immortal court.

The demons held promise. They were always good for a fight. When Pandora released all the evils of the world, she created the daemons, the first of the lineage of demons. Each daemon lineage was unique. Descendants of the daemon Lyssa became almost invincible when enraged. Whereas, descendants of Thanatos could travel all realms to gather souls. All demons appeared human until it was too late. In their natural form, their eyes turned black, horns sprouted from their heads, and their mottled skin changed colors depending on their daemon lineage.

In the mortal realm, there were a plethora of demons, each faction holding different root powers. Some grew wings, and others could manipulate emotions, while others were poisonous. All demons were rumored to bow only to one being—their queen. Though no one had ever actually *met* her, and I was starting to think she was only a figment of their imaginations.

Once, in a fit of boredom, I tortured a high-level demon to get him to reveal her location. But after almost a decade, I realized that the demon *literally* could not reveal anything about his queen. My interest waned, and I finally granted the demon's pleas for death with a short beheading, one of the few ways you can truly kill an immortal.

I was reflecting on which demons would present the most intriguing battle when a female's voice carried across the balcony to me. My back snapped straight at the realization that my guard had slipped. That hadn't happened in thousands of years.

"The only immortal not taking part in a Fae orgy. How could I resist my natural curiosity?" she asked. People didn't *surprise* me. Yet, now I'd been taken off-guard by a being of, as yet, undetermined species. Was she cloaked?

There was something about her voice. Even without turning around to face the unknown female, her rolling lilt sent a shiver down my spine, a reaction I barely managed to conceal. Her voice pulled at something deep within my chest, yet I made sure not to let on that she affected me. I slowly turned to face her. An intruder surprising me was one thing. It was quite another to let them *know* about it.

I could not cover my sharp inhale of breath when I caught sight of her. I wasn't sure what to expect, but she…she wasn't it. Her eyes locked on me, and I froze. Even in the muted light, they appeared to glow a vibrant shade of purple. I'd never seen such uniquely colored eyes. I summoned more willpower than I could have suspected I would need and pulled my gaze from hers.

Red hair, the color of burning embers, spilled from the golden comb she'd used to keep the mass up. A few rebellious locks played against her bare shoulder, and I wanted to snatch the clip from her hair and unleash it. I imagined the length of the fiery mane splayed across silk sheets—my sheets. I could almost feel it wrapped around my fist and sticking to her sweaty back as her arms were locked above her head. She would pant and beg for me to let her come.

Her heart-shaped face was clear of the freckles that often plagued beings with her hair color. Her pink lips were full, and her cheekbones slashed high on her face. I could imagine that mouth around my cock, sucking me dry and whispering all the words I wanted to hear from her.

Clad in a Grecian-style gown pulled tight over one shoulder, her dress lingered on her form, though the flowy material and the slight light concealed most of her from view. My mind short-circuited the longer I looked at her, too busy imagining all the ways I wanted to lay this female out for my pleasure, taking her to new heights.

Had she said something? I couldn't recall.

"I don't see you taking part either," I croaked. My answer seemed to amuse her, drawing her further into the colored lights of the Fae sky.

I finally saw her body in the light, no longer hidden by the shadows cast by the ballroom, and my mouth went dry. The cock I'd bemoaned for being unresponsive went rock hard. I could barely process how quickly my shaft became like steel in my pants, and I shuffled my feet to cover it. I needed to bend this beauty over until she begged for relief. My mouth watered at the thought of tying her up and see her pale skin flush with my handprints.

Her breasts were pert and full, her nipples becoming hard little buds as I watched. My hands ached to squeeze them. Her petite waist flowed into generous hips, enough for a male to grab and hold while fucking her for dear life, enough for *me* to grab.

I must not scare her and let her come closer. For the first time, I wished my reputation didn't precede me. I just wanted her here with me, or not here. I wanted her under me and above me, anyway I could get her. What the fuck was that? I wanted to turn my gaze back to the courtyard, to feign nonchalance, but I couldn't force my eyes away from her for a moment. I had a feeling that if I let her out of my sight, she might disappear.

She sidled closer to me, appraising me as I had her. I didn't want anything between us and was thankful I was shirtless, though I wished I'd forgone pants. I craved to have her skin against mine and could barely stop myself from yanking her against me. At my height, I towered over her petite frame, covering a relieved exhale when I failed to sense any fear in her. Most women and men came to my bed for two reasons. They either liked my face, or they got off on the fear they felt at being with someone of my reputation, and sometimes it was both. When did that start to annoy me?

The mysterious female continued her approach, rolling her hips seductively as she closed the distance. Who was this woman? I bit my tongue until it bled to keep from panting. I didn't think I had ever been so affected by someone. She stopped an inch away and jumped to sit next to my hand on the marble railing, facing the open doors to the ballroom.

The slit in her gown revealed one toned thigh, and her scent hit me like a freight train. I closed my eyes, trying to inhale more of the cherry blossom smell. I turned back to the courtyard, hoping she didn't notice my hands were clutching the marble banister. My nails darkened and became claws, digging in to keep from reaching for her.

"Would you like to know a secret?" her throaty voice whispered, her breath teasing my ear. I couldn't stop the shiver this time, and I half-expected her to gloat at having brought me so low.

"Anything from you." Was that desperate voice mine?

I planted my feet to prevent myself from rocking my hips, imagining I was plunging inside her. The confusing cloud of aromas nearly obscured the scent of her arousal. I didn't know why I hadn't grabbed her yet and kissed her. Desire was usually so simple. Yet, I didn't want to rush this, to rush *her*.

Her lips came closer to my ear, her breath ruffling the wisps of my hair. "I've never been to an event like this."

Slowly, I turned my head toward her. Her face was even closer to mine than I'd thought. My gaze locked on those magnificent lilac eyes of hers before dropping to her lips.

I knew what she wanted, what she's asking for without using words. "So, you chose me to introduce you to it?" What if she hadn't chosen me? What if she'd asked some other male to enter her lithe little body? I fought to control my rage.

I turned to face forward again, hoping to conceal some of this riotous desire and anger. Her lips were back at my ear, her teasing voice making me ache and forget my irritation. "I noticed you inside, and something told me to come out here."

She felt it, too. It was all the confirmation I needed. Unable to contain my need, my movements blurred as I shoved her legs apart with my hips. My arms caged her in, preventing escape, but I stopped myself just inches from her lips.

"Oh? And have you had your fill of amateurs tonight?" My voice was harsh, and one of her fiery brows went up in response.

Her husky voice remained low, mesmerizing me even more. "Would it bother you? If I'd been with someone else tonight?"

I clutched her nape roughly, unable to gentle my touch, but the savagery I was barely keeping in check seemed to arouse her. "I don't relish being someone's second choice." It had actually never bothered me before, but it did now.

She bit her lip, making my mind go blank. "There's no one else. I saw only you."

Her answer rang with sincerity, and I lost control. Control was a myth, a joke at that point, and I yanked her closer for a bruising kiss. Gods, the taste of her! I could become addicted to it and to the sounds she made when she mewled into my mouth. She wrapped her arms around me, drawing me closer, biting my lip hard enough to draw blood.

I always tempered my strength during sex. I could kill my partner if I weren't careful, but this female pushed me to unleash. She wanted everything. The tangy scent of blood only inflamed me more, my tongue plundering her sweet mouth with even more force. I wanted to meld into her, leaving no part of her unexplored.

She broke the kiss with a rough inhale. "Shouldn't we head up to a bedroom?" Her breaths were coming in small pants, her luscious breasts shaking. It was obvious she was feeling this pull, too.

I could barely think or process her question. I doubted I could make it upstairs without pushing her against a wall and slamming myself inside her. But my voice was smooth as I responded, covering my inner turmoil. "I'll take you where I please."

II

THE FEMALE'S EYES WIDENED at my words but hooded almost immediately in interest. It seemed she liked it when I sounded more controlling. Gods, it was as if she were made for me. If we were in Romania, I'd have her thrown over my lap, my hand making her ass red before fucking her. Though she'd have to beg for it first.

I yanked the gold clip from her hair, the fiery length falling down her back. The sight of it far surpassed what I'd imagined earlier. I broke the clip, tossing it away. Her hair would never be bound again. I grabbed it in my fist, forcing her to meet my eyes. "You like being fucked here on the balcony where anyone could look out and see us, don't you?"

She bit her lip in response, her eyes burning with desire. Oh, the things I was going to do to her. If she knew the fantasies running through my mind, she'd run screaming. I wanted her tied against the wall in my castle, her tits rubbing against the cool stone and her nipples tight with the bite of pain, while I turned her ass red with a crop.

However, her next statement cut through my erotic fantasies and nearly knocked on my ass. "Just so we're clear, I'm not having sex with you."

I nearly fell back a step as I yelled hoarsely, "What?!"

Her body was arching toward me, desperate for my touch, her arousal sharp in the air and clouding my mind. But she didn't want me to fuck her? People *begged* me to fuck them! Yet she threw this limit out as if it was some kind of obvious conclusion? I couldn't deny her. We didn't have the relationship necessary for me to tell her to obey me, to submit to me, that required conversation, exploring rules, not a chance meeting on the balcony.

Still biting her lip, her nipples beading, she didn't relent. "I'm saying that we can do absolutely anything except have sex."

Why come to an event such as this if one didn't intend to get fucked? This close to her, any kind of rational thought was *gone*. My voice was unrecognizable, even to me. "I'll take you any way I can get you."

She took that as confirmation of her ridiculous stipulation, and I will not admit, even to myself, that I capitulated to her demands. Without waiting for her to add more qualifications, I plundered her mouth again, her cry of arousal at my aggression smothered by my lips. Her cries were for me alone.

With minor consideration of her dress, I ripped the shoulder, letting her breasts bounce free. The gown cinched beneath them, preventing the move from revealing more of her. But her breasts… I hissed at the sight. They were perfect pale globes. A full handful tipped with blush nipples begging for my mouth. I teased the very tip of one hardened bud with the pad of my forefinger. I kept her on edge, close to relief, but not providing it to her.

She released her lip from between her teeth to form a pout, thrusting her breasts toward me, trying to get more of my touch. Her hips rocked slightly against the marble banister, hungry for more. I pulled my finger away, bending my head to blow cold air on her aching nipples, teasing them even tighter. The sensation made her jerk, and she reached up to dig her fingers into my hair, trying to force me to put my lips on her. She was such a naughty girl.

Slowly untangling her hands from my hair, I placed them over the curved marble behind her back, forcing her breasts to jut forward. Her pink nipples made my mouth water, and yet I resisted. I needed to get back under control. That was something I'd never struggled with before, yet with a single whisper from this woman, I was grappling for even the illusion of it.

"You're to keep your hands there until I tell you to move them. Is that understood?"

She just moaned, panting at the sight of my length silhouetted in my pants. Her violet gaze was locked on it, her lip finding its way back between her teeth and her pupils blown with desire. The way she gripped the marble tighter made me realize she was restraining herself from reaching forward and touching me.

"You'll submit to my orders, or I won't let you come."

She paused for a moment, her teeth practically splitting her own lip. Her eyes glowed slightly in the light while I waited for her decision. I wouldn't move forward until she consented. When she nodded, I bit off a groan. Finally, I took her nipple into my mouth, and my eyes rolled back at her taste, stunned anew.

Gods!

I suckled her hard, bringing my other hand up to play with the other nipple, pinching it roughly, and slapping it as the blood returned. Her tits should be pierced for me, a secret I alone would get to see. When I had her fully, I'd demand it. I'd be able to roll the piercing on my tongue or hook a delicate chain to it.

"Gods!" she yelled, giving voice to my secret exclamation. Her head fell back, her hands tightening on the marble, her breasts shaking from her pants. I moved to her other breast, sucking hard before remembering to gentle myself. She immediately protested, her voice a whimper as she demanded, "Harder!" She couldn't please me more.

Everything I held back in my normal liaisons shattered with her, she wanted everything, and I'd give her *everything*. I sucked harder than before, nibbling on the sensitive peak. I expected her to wince, to pull away, yet she didn't. Instead, she only moaned at my roughness, her hips pushing forward again. She was such a wicked, exquisite female.

I claimed to want eyes on her. Yet the closer she got to coming, the more I wished I had taken her upstairs to a private room, where she could be mine alone. Not to mention that the rooms would be outfitted with some of the tools I preferred. But it was too late, and I'd have to make do.

I used my speed to lift her off the railing, twisting her, so her back aligned with my front. Her bare breasts jutted forward, defenseless against the cold winds of Tír nAill. She moved to cover them with her hands, but I tsked, causing her to freeze. As she awaited my direction, I made sure she felt my rock-hard shaft against her ass as I rocked against her.

"Place your hands around my neck," I growled into her ear.

She reached back, locking her hands behind my neck, leaving her even more vulnerable, even more at my mercy. I rubbed against her ass more frantically, enjoying the way her tits bounced in response. They were still wet and swollen from my ministrations. They would be mine soon. I'd brand them as mine, a nice little chain from nipple to nipple, attached to a delicate collar around her neck. I shook my head at the thought. I hadn't given a collar to anyone permanently, ever. My middle name was *temporary,* and a collar was commitment. She moaned again, breaking through my musings.

"You like feeling my shaft against you?" She nodded, going to her tiptoes, molding against me. "The words, female."

She complied, her voice half moan, half whisper. "I like feeling your cock against my ass."

I spanked her ass, enjoying how she leaned into my light strike. Where had this perfect female been hiding? I found the part in her gown, the slight slit enabling those maddening flashes of her thighs. I ripped it higher to where the gown tightened under her breasts.

The new tear allowed me to part the gown, draping it over the railing in front of her, keeping it from falling back to conceal her curves. I stifled a groan at the sight of her bared ass. The only underwear she wore was a slight white thong. I immediately tore it from her, stuffing the soaked lace into my pocket. I never considered myself an *ass* man, but hers had me going weak in the knees. She wiggled her hips, feeling my gaze on her, rocking slightly.

"Gods, woman, your body drives me mad," I moaned, unlacing my pants.

She jerked when she felt the hot skin of my shaft against her, and I sought to comfort her. "I remember."

It just felt too fucking good rocking against her bare ass. She relaxed again, and I succumbed to the call of her intoxicating sex. I reached down, gripping one toned thigh, and forced her leg up onto the railing, spreading her wide. The cold air made her shiver as it met her heated flesh.

A voyeur would only see my back from the ballroom, with her pale leg spread on the marble. I dragged my hand down her front, pinching her nipples again before palming her sex and hissing, "You're drenched for me. Was some other male to enjoy this tonight?"

Is that jealousy ringing in *my* tone? My motto? Always be the leaver. Yet, the thought of leaving her even for a moment filled me with such a frenzy it almost muted my desire. The keyword there was, *almost*.

"Only you, only you," she muttered, desperate to come, unknowingly soothing my anger and panic.

"Feel how wet and ready you are." I cupped her sex, not rubbing her clit or entering her, just hovering. She tried to thrust herself into my hand to create some friction. "You want them inside you, don't you? You want me to fuck you with my fingers. Feed them into your greedy little pussy."

24

She nodded breathlessly. I slapped my palm against her drenched sex, making her jump. "The words," I growled.

"I want you to fuck me with your fingers, and I want them in my pussy so bad, I ache. I want you to touch my clit as you pound them inside me." Her voice was drugged with desire. She felt it. This...this need, this desire, I could barely think. Absently, I realized I didn't even know her name. There would be time for that later. There would be time for everything later.

I moaned, biting her earlobe. "I'm going to work your luscious body until you scream."

My fangs sharpened at the smell of her blood. I barely resisted the urge to sink my fangs into her along with my fingers. I stretched her leg higher so she almost couldn't touch the ground. Her stability depended on my hands, which I moved from her front to glide over her ass. I reached for her from behind, slamming a single digit into her. I felt and heard her lose her breath at the intrusion, and it was as if I'd never even heard of control.

From her high hold, she had no choice but to endure my movements, her bouncing tits keeping time. *She was at my mercy, where she belonged*, I thought absently. I slammed my finger inside her, timing it with every thrust of my hips against her ass, imagining I'm plunging my shaft between her thighs.

I add another finger and whisper, "I'd kill to replace these with my cock."

Every time I pounded my fingers inside her, her breasts shook. I set a punishing pace, and the harder the thrust, the more she drenched my fingers. I used my spare hand to collar her throat. "You're soaking my fingers, so desperate to come." More of her excitement wet my palm, and she mewled. "You like when I tell you what to do, don't you?"

To my shock, she shook her head. I instantly stopped my fingers and prevented her from rocking on them to get herself off.

"No! Don't stop! Please don't stop!" she begged. I pulled my glistening fingers from her, and she cried out at the loss.

"Tell me you like it when I command you, and I'll let you come." I was torturing us both by keeping us on edge. Yet, I needed her admission, her submission to me, more than I could recall ever needing anything before.

She paused, so my hand moved from covering her wet sex to her ass, delivering a punishing slap. "What was that?"

She let out a gasp at the first slap, purring when I massaged away the sting. "I like when you tell me what to do." Her voice was a whisper, almost lost on the wind. *Slap!* Another punishing hit to her ass. "I like when you tell me what to do!" she screamed. "Please make me come!"

"Only because you begged." I smirked, feeding three of my fingers into her this time.

"Oh, my gods!" she yelled, and I resumed my punishing rhythm.

"Tell me your greedy little pussy needs to come. Beg me for your orgasm," I ordered, my voice guttural.

"Please let me come! Please!"

I twisted my fingers inside her. "You ready to come?" I asked, and she nodded, her face glazed with desire.

I used my other hand to reach around her front, rubbing her clit at the same time my fingers pounded into her. She came with a scream, and I let out a hoarse yell as her inner walls clamped down. I came on her ass, my hot cum marking her, and damned if that sight didn't satisfy me. Just the ability to have her at my mercy made me orgasm, which had never happened before, not once in my entire immortal life. It was another thing to analyze later. Everything would make sense later, but at that moment, I needed to feed.

If she'd been facing me, she would have seen my eyes change from enigmatic green to a dark glowing red, as they always did when I was about to drink. I inched toward her neck, my fangs lengthening in my mouth. They ached for this female's blood, and I needed it. The pulse in her throat was hammering, still coming down from her orgasm, and I could imagine the taste flooding my mouth. I almost panted in anticipation. How would she taste? Would it show me answers as to why I was so affected by her? Why did the things that mattered to me, once intrigued me, seem pointless?

Answers. Blood had answers. I leaned closer to her neck and was a breath away from piercing her when a fresh voice made me freeze, and my fangs retract. I gently pulled my fingers from inside her.

"Lucien? Wulfric is here. He says he needs to speak to you."

Titania. Gods, the fae queen had the worst timing.

I whipped around, concealing the female behind me, not even bothering to lace my pants up. I was not even sure I remembered how at that point. My control was still on shaky ground. However, the sight of Titania's knowing smirk made my teeth grind, and a muscle in my jaw twitch. Reality slowly inched its way back into my mind.

"Looks like you found something to interest your varied tastes," Titania said.

Tatiana tried to lean around me to catch a glimpse of the being who had captured my attention, but I refused to budge. I even hissed, my fangs returning as Titania continued. The queen paled in surprise and fear. I never bared my fangs at anyone unless I intended to use them. I didn't believe in idle threats. Titania froze, though she regained her equilibrium fast. Her gaze took a slow tour of me, from my boots to my head. Her smirk returned, and my control flooded back.

Finally, Titania turned away from us, mentioning as she departed, "He said it's urgent."

I whipped around, delighted that the female did not move but covered herself. The only trace of our interaction was the tear in her gown, easily dismissed in this crowd.

"I have to go."

Her face was still flushed, which reminded me. I brought my fingers to my mouth, licking them clean. "Gods, you taste fucking amazing. Will you wait here for me?"

28

That sounded a bit too much like pleading. Any of the control I'd just regained vanished as I connected with her eyes again.

She bit her lip but nodded. "Hurry back." She glanced down and pulled my pants closed, deftly knotting the ties. "I don't like anyone else seeing that." She smiled shyly, but her show of possession struck a chord in me. I liked her jealousy, something I had never enjoyed before. When my partners became possessive was when I usually left.

I charged back into the ballroom, determined to find the wolf shifter, and then return to the intoxicating female.

III

THE REALM OF MORTALS.
NEW ORLEANS, LOUISIANA.

*F*UCK, FUCK, FUCK, FUCK, FUCK! It was a constant litany from the moment I snuck away from Lucien. I didn't *technically* lie when I said I would wait for him. I waited for him to leave, so I could rift away. But wait for him to return? *Yeah, no.* How the actual fuck did things go wrong? I wasn't even supposed to be at that gathering! Yet, like fucking *always*, I managed to colossally fuck things up.

I wasn't supposed to even be seen! Get in, get the information, get out! That was the plan. Yet, the second I saw him from across the room, it was like I was spelled into following him. As a witch, it was a little offensive. I did the casting! The entrancing! I didn't get entranced! All those plans, carefully laid out schemes, slipped away like water through my hands.

Lucien. Nice name. It suited him, strong and uncompromising. My lips formed his name over and over. Without even trying, I could hear myself moaning it, screaming it. *Fuck, Phoebe! Focus! You were there for a reason, remember?*

I needed to find a strife demon who could track down my ex-boyfriend, but one glimpse of Lucien's face and all my carefully laid plans were shot. Like some invisible tie yanked me to that balcony, keeping me in a state of suspension as long as he touched me, as long as he spoke.

His voice held me spellbound. It held *me*, a witch, spellbound. As I said, it was borderline offensive.

It took the fae queen's interruption and his disappearance to snap me out of it. Free of his *allure*, I rifted back to the mortal realm from the balcony, not even bothering to say goodbye. I needed to get away. He'd already scrambled my mind too much in such a short period. If I'd waited, I didn't know what would have happened. Absently, I touched my lips, remembering the plea in his voice when he asked me to wait for him.

The way his body tensed, brimming with barely contained malice, the way his eyes roamed my body with such...*possession.* If he knew the truth about my powers, he wouldn't have left me alone. If I'd stayed, I didn't know if I would have been able to leave. So I took a major risk and opened a rift, a decision that would likely bite me in the ass sooner rather than later.

I should only be using my power to rift in case of emergencies. Otherwise, it painted a big trackable target on my back. *Hello! Escaping from immortal males who look like they could fuck me into the next century definitely qualifies.*

Rifts, little tears in reality, allow immortals, and mortals if they are unlucky enough to stumble into one, to travel to all the mystical realms connected to this one. *Most* rifts were specifically designated *rift zones* created at the beginning of time. These zones were regulated, like the one in and out of Tír nAill, but some witches, usually a group of six or more powerful ones, could create temporary ones. Together, they would pool their power and create a tear in our reality, opening a doorway to a place of their choosing. Temporary rifts required a massive amount of energy and magic to create, and the power of multiple witches was a necessity. A witch could kill themself exerting the energy necessary to slam two realities together. Then there was me, the exception, the *freak.*

My hand dropped from my lips, and I unlocked the front door of my shotgun apartment. It was close enough to Tulane's campus for raucous sounds to filter through the thin walls. The paint on the front door was peeling, and I reached out to trace the biggest crack. The tip of my finger caught at the apex, and suddenly it was a different door with a distinct crack. My touch cut a trail through blood, dark crimson spilling down the white paint. It slid down my finger, joining the blood covering my palm. Then the screams started, my screams.

Several drunken fraternity boys called out to me, yanking me back into the present. I gave them a small smile and, under my breath, cursed them with a vicious hangover the next morning. What could I say? I was a bitch like that.

It took three very precise jiggles of my key and a slam with my shoulder to get the door open. Though my apartment was an absolute dump, not even a broke college student would consider renting, and my landlord asked no questions. He never asked why I paid in cash every month, why strange energy pulsed from the walls, why my black cat appeared to be in multiple places at once. Hells, in this city, it was just another Tuesday for him.

New Orleans was a city of strange. Most locals shrugged off the weird daily occurrences as merely another aspect of the city. None guessed at the many immortals hiding in their midst, or maybe they were just too drunk to care. Immortals flocked to cities like New Orleans. It was easier to blend in when you could hide in plain sight. I'd seen several death demons in full demon form walking down Bourbon Street the other day. Not a single person batted an eye even with their chalk skin, massive horns, and tails. Later, I saw them taking shots with some tourists at the Bourbon Cowboy. Some sought the notoriety, a city full of their kind, others, like me, the anonymity to be just another in their number. With the sheer amount of witches calling this city their home, on top of the Voodoo practitioners, I was just another face in the crowd. Which didn't mean I was completely safe here or anywhere.

My familiar, a small black cat, greeted me as the door opened. It took me another three tries to get the key out of the lock, and I made a mental note to get my landlord to fix that. I cooed to the animal, setting down my keys and closing the door before striding to my closet. It was really a garment rod, and a sheet held up by a wire attached to the ceiling. I removed my now ruined gown, shivering as I unzipped the back. I attempted to distract myself from the memory of Lucien as I walked to my bathroom. The familiar creaking of the old floorboards beneath me did nothing to ground me in the present. Maybe after a cold shower, or three, I would be able to forget his touch.

Beneath the icy spray, I tried not to feel Lucien's hands on me. I bit back a groan at the memory of his mouth against my ear and the rumble of his voice as he whispered into my ear. His hands were rougher than I expected, gliding over my curves. He'd demanded my obedience, and I'd surrendered, helpless not to. My eyes closed as my hands followed the path his had taken. I could almost smell him. My eyes flashed open, and I slammed my hand against the shower wall. I had to stop this! My libido was what got me into this mess in the first place.

It was harsh but true. My taste in men was not exactly what you would call *spectacular*. Usually, when I found a guy *hot,* it meant, *will betray me in the immediate future.* Even males of undetermined origins who acted like their life depended on pleasuring me.

I stepped from the shower, shivering in the cooler temperature. I changed into sweatpants and a t-shirt before falling spread eagle onto my pitiful bed, the cheap metal frame creaking loudly. Another night wasted, no leads on my target, and my grimoires even further out of reach.

Nothing was more sacred to a witch than their family's grimoire. All part of our Great Initiation into the world of immortality, when we are brought before the Council and gifted our full powers and immortality. A blessing handed down from the first witch touched by Hekate. The Witches Council had a big ceremony for each new witch. Idly, my hand traced down my stomach, remembering the formal robes, the chanting, and the feeling of pride, of *unity*. I remembered my aunt's eyes sparkling as she placed the two massive tomes in my hands.

Aunt Caroline. A pang of despair slammed through me, making me sit up. *Not going there, nope.* I shook my head hard, forcing away the sensation of smoke-filled lungs. Instead, I focused on the familiar creak the ancient tomes made when I first opened them, the whispers of spells and curses calling to me. Grimoires were everything to witches. So much so that losing one, or even showing it to a non-witch, was a crime. Three guesses what I'd done. Yes, I'd shown it to my boyfriend, and worse, he was a vampire.

Apparently, being an immortal witch didn't preclude you from becoming the most dreaded of forms—*a Karen.* I'd hidden the relationship from the Witches Council. They tended to execute first and ask questions never. Though dating outside our species wasn't *technically* against their archaic laws, I had been cautious. The Karens were relentless. They tended to judge a witch for dating outside of the coven with the intensity of demanding to speak to the manager. It was a decision that bit me on the ass when I was dragged before the Council to account for my crimes. Not only had I hidden the relationship, but I'd shown him my treasured grimoires.

There had been all of that, which was bad enough, but then there was my...other crime.

How was I supposed to know he was going to steal them and disappear? At first, I'd thought someone had kidnapped him, that he'd stumbled across someone trying to steal the books and intervened, but there were too many signs pointing to his betrayal. And then,

I couldn't track him down because of my own fucking idiocy.

The Witches Council had ignored my pleas for leniency. Loss or theft of a grimoire was a major crime, with no exceptions, but losing two grimoires meant death. They'd sentenced me to burn at the stake, despite such a punishment not being enforced since the witch trials.

Lucky Me.

Well, if I were honest with myself, the *other crime* would have justified the execution, but I hadn't committed it yet. They had charged me with it, anyway, and somewhere, someplace, John Adams was rolling in his grave. Yet, I refused to stop trying to undo the damage I'd done. I needed to get the grimoires back before being executed. It would be delusional to think it would erase what happened, but maybe, *just* maybe, things could go back to normal. I had to try.

I couldn't just run and run and run for eternity. There had to be hope on the horizon that one day I could *rest,* and it had already been almost a decade. I let out a long sigh at the thought. It had been ten years with no friends, no family, no roots. I rarely stayed longer than three months in any place before moving to a new city. I searched out the places I knew had a large immortal presence, such as NOLA.

Rule No. 5: Abandon everything at a moment's notice.

No one noticed when I moved. I existed as a ghost, keeping everyone at a distance, never feeling connected anywhere. No friends, no familiarity, no community, all the things I took for granted when I was a part of the Council. I'd learned my lessons well.

Rule No. 1: Trust no one.

The Council hounded me, sending immortals and mortals after me, hoping to make me pay for my crimes. I'm their enemy number one—please hold your applause, and autographs are by appointment only. However, if I knew anything about the Council, it was that they would never, ever, think I would be hiding in their own backyard. They would never believe that I dared to take shelter in immortal rich cities with big Council presences.

Rule No. 2: Use your enemy's strengths against them.

The Council was arrogant, assuming their intimidating posturing would have me cowering in fear in some hole across the world. I did so love proving them wrong. They could scry for me with their crystals every day for the rest of eternity and never find me. I had ensured that I was protected from magical tracking, which meant I only had to keep an eye out for *non-magical* tracking. Also known as, *don't be fucking stupid, and you live another day*.

I stayed away from people who might be out to betray me. I didn't get attached to anyone. My interactions with the opposite sex were to scratch an itch and nothing more. *Except...* I trailed the back of my fingers down my breasts and thighs, feeling Lucien's touch all over again. I'd never felt such pleasure, and just imagining it... I shook myself before I got carried away again.

My small black cat approached, launching herself onto the bed. Even her diminutive weight made the rusty springs creak. I pushed the hair back from my face, looking at the familiar. "I might have done something really fucking stupid tonight, Bast."

The cat surveyed me with unblinking lilac eyes, identical to my own, and tilted her small head. "I didn't get any information on someone who might be able to track down He-Who-Must-Not-Be-Named." The cat appeared disappointed, curling into my side. "I got distracted."

Bast lifted her head, giving me a loaded look.

My cheeks burned at the memory of Lucien, and I exhaled loudly. "Don't worry, I'll never see him again, and I'm sure he's forgotten all about me already."

Why did that feel like a lie? I literally met him at an orgy, and not even a mortal orgy, but an *immortal* one. Some would say that immortal lust was a perk of being immortal. It was not a bonus, but a fucking curse. You thought mortals fantasize about sex a lot? Imagine having the need of an immortal. It was like a cat in heat, rubbing against any available surface just to get off.

Lucien would move on to another conquest. The chances of someone that gorgeous trying to find me were somewhere around, never to never in a million years. I didn't give my name or any other information. He couldn't track me down even if he wanted to, not that he would.

Rule No. 3: Don't tell anyone anything, ever.

I only knew his name because the fae queen had called it. *Lucien.* I flicked my hand, and all the lights in my apartment went out, my door and window locks snapping shut. He tasted like lemons and olive oil. I trailed my hand over my lips in the dark. Immortals were more hedonistic, never wasting time in hunting for pleasure when it was there for the taking. His presence at such an event showed his lustful nature. Yet, when paired with his boredom at the surrounding orgy, it hinted that such scenes were common for him. It was impossible that he would seek me out.

Would he have even bothered to return for me in Tír nAill, or would he have simply moved on to someone who would have sex with him? I'd surprised myself when I'd told him I wouldn't. I was not a prude by any means, but something had held me back with Lucien. Infrequent one-night stands were my standard fare when I needed that momentary release, but when Lucien first touched me, a warning whispered through my mind that one night would never be enough.

Forget about him. He's probably forgotten all about you already. With that sobering and disheartening thought, I forced myself to sleep.

I only know the dark, the fathomless abyss of blackness. It's comforting, soothing, almost familiar. I can smell my mother's perfume, the scent of Georgia peaches stinging my nose. My father's hands are heavy on my shoulders, the palms, calloused and rough from work. I look up to see his familiar face, only to find nothing but the unwavering twilight. I drop to my knees, my eyes watering as I start to choke, unable to breathe. Why can't I breathe?

The lack of air forces me awake, and my eyes flash open. My back arches as I try to breathe, rolling to my side. I cough, trying to clear my lungs of whatever is choking me. Spittle sprays from my lips, dropping onto the black floor, disturbing the mound of ash beneath me.

My vision is blurred, everything just shapes and traces of colors, but I can't focus on one. My hand forms a fist, and I slam it into my stomach, dislodging more. The black dust chokes me more on its way out of my system. My hands shake, and my arms tremble as I try to push myself to my feet. I barely get to my knees before black spots invade my vision, trying to force me back into the darkness. I don't know how long it takes for the black dots to stop. It feels like hours but could have only been minutes.

When I'm confident I'm not about to pass out, I slowly sit back on my heels, shaking my head to dislodge the film of ash over my eyes. My hands touch the side of my head, trying to recall where I am. What do I remember?

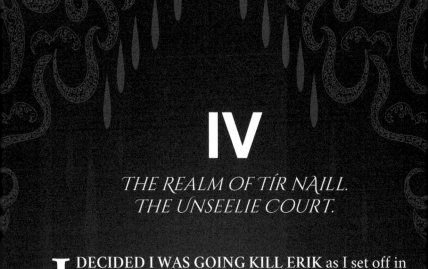

IV

THE REALM OF TÍR NAILL.
THE UNSEELIE COURT.

I DECIDED I WAS GOING KILL ERIK as I set off in search of the werewolf.

It took less than a minute to find the lycan in one of the private rooms upstairs. Unsurprisingly, two of his wolves were escorting him. Some of his most trusted followers always surrounded the Lycan King, something I knew irritated Erik to no end. They acted as pseudo bodyguards for the werewolf. Protection Erik insisted he neither wanted nor needed. The King of the Lycans was more than capable of taking care of himself, and he was not in danger from me. Strangely enough, we were *friends*, something neither wolves nor vampires seemed to understand. Though, I wasn't quite sure I understood it either.

The two sentries sneered at my appearance, shifting to glare at me. Their eyes glowed amber, a sign that their wolf was close to the surface and warning me to get the fuck away. I rolled my eyes. When would the wolves understand I had no intention of killing their king? A thousand years since I beheaded Erik's father, and they still expected me to betray Erik at any moment.

"Titania said you needed to speak to me? That it was urgent?" I whipped out, impatient to get back, already imagining the depraved things I was going to do to the female downstairs. Why the hells was Erik even here? That kind of event was always more my thing than his. Not that Erik was a monk by any means, just more *discreet*.

His light eyebrows shot up in surprise at my tone, tugging at the three slashing scars that tracked down one side of his face. "Why, *hello*, Lucien. Nice to see you, too."

"Urgent was the word. *Urgent*. Does that mean something different in Norwegian?" I snapped, my voice still hoarse from shouting earlier.

Erik just stared at me, his blue eyes sparkling with humor despite the millennia he'd lived. He was a former Viking and light where I was dark. Though we were close in height, Erik was broader, more like a brawler. He'd shaved his long braids sometime over the years, leaving his cropped blonde hair slightly longer on top. The three faded scars that reached from the corner of one eye into his hairline were a gift from his deceased father. They were testimonies of an injury he'd received from before he gained the immortal ability to regenerate. Wolves only became truly immortal on their first full shift, like most shifters, though some never achieved the final shift. The scars only made him more attractive to females, his dangerous edge alluring to many.

I grumbled out the usual niceties. I regretted my harsh tone, but my mind remained on the female I'd left alone on the balcony. What if someone approaches her she likes more? I needed to get back to her.

Gods, that female. I didn't think I'd ever been so consumed by someone, so desperate to own them, to make them mine, to have their submission, to *need* their submission. I could already imagine her on her knees before me, her stunning eyes gazing up at me, begging to be rewarded for behaving. My mouth watered at the thought, but right now, the wolf demanded my attention.

"It just might," he said, then his face turned serious. "The witches approached me." I quirked a surprised brow at the announcement. The witches never sought other species. They were usually too busy grappling for power and control. "They want a favor."

I crossed my arms over my chest, trying not to shift my weight from foot to foot in impatience. "A favor? From us?"

Very unusual, and any other day, I would have been all over this intriguing little mystery. The witches were usually above *interspecies* mingling. They saw themselves as above most other immortals. So them coming to a wolf and a vampire for *help* was fucking rich. Normally, I would be peppering Erik with questions and demanding details, but I could barely think past my need to get back downstairs. I grasped for control, forcing myself to focus on Erik.

Erik nodded. "They want our help to kill a witch."

"The *Witches Council* wants *our* help with killing a witch?"

The Council was renowned for tracking and executing their wrongdoers with a vengeance, even going so far as claiming that no one could escape their magic. Their definition of *no one* clearly differed from mine.

Erik smirked, his sky-blue eyes sparkling. "Now you see why I showed up here."

In my entire immortal life, all *ten thousand years* of it, I could count my interactions with the Council on one hand. They predated even the creation of vampires and wolves, and by the time I was born, their Council had already turned their attention inward.

"Any details about the witch?" I inquired. Once I got this woman out of my system, I was going to want to pursue this lead. Though, it might take a couple of months to pull my head out from between her pale thighs.

Erik snapped his fingers impatiently, prompting one of his wolves to hand a scroll of parchment to me with a disgusted snarl. I read the bounty out loud. *"Last lineal descendent of the Atreus & Margaux House of Witches. Wanted for treason, murder, and other capital crimes. Last sighting: Her would-be execution, where she murdered the witches present and escaped."* My eyes returned to Erik, and I raised a brow. "A little light on physical description, isn't it?"

Immortal bounties were mystical contracts, *utterly* binding on the parties involved. If I agreed to the bounty, it would *require* me to fulfill it. We often took on bounties for other species, collecting the rewards. Though we often entered them separately, there were incidents when we went after targets together. There was nothing more horrific than hearing the two kings were on your tail.

The wolf smirked again. "They believe she's likely glamoured her appearance so many times that no one could recognize her."

How intriguing. Any description they could offer would be useless. She could change her appearance in the next breath if she chose.

"Is there anything they gave us that might actually help?" I snapped, handing the parchment off to the wolf. I'd take on the mystifying bounty. Other than the female waiting for me, it was the first thing to pique my interest in years.

Erik didn't drop his smile. "Yes, their only lead on her is that she's searching for her family grimoires."

That had both of my eyebrows rising. "She lost her grimoires?"

Witches were young when they received them, and it often took them years to master the litanies of spells within. Each lineage specialized in a certain magic, and they guarded their ancestral tomes viciously, not even sharing with their own kind. They were *very valuable* on the black market simply because of their rarity. A collector would be set for life with just one.

"That is another interesting point. She is apparently powerful enough to avoid the Council without them. They gave me the distinct impression that she is *creating* her own spells."

That rocked me back on my heels. Witches hadn't branched outside their specified lineage magic to create or experiment with new magic since before even I was born. To do so, she must be monstrously powerful. No wonder the Council was so desperate to locate her. She was a walking example that the oligarchical group of immortal spell casters didn't know shit.

"Tell the Witches Council we'll take the bounty. Is there anything else, Erik? Not that I'm not honored by the visit, but I was *busy* before this," I said, impatient and unable to stop myself from shifting my weight from foot to foot. I needed to get back. She was there alone. What if another male approached her? Their blood would coat the walls of the Unseelie Court if they dared.

Erik's smile dropped, though a single tawny brow shot up. "Oh? And I drew you away?" He paused, looked me up and down. "You seem a bit *frantic* to get back. I never knew you to be so clingy."

Erik hurled the word as an insult, and normally I would have a cutting remark about the *frequency* of my partners. But the words died on my tongue. I had never been this desperate to get back to anyone. It felt like my skin was too tight, my muscles locking down on my bones, making me tense and agitated.

Instead of dignifying Erik's comment with a response, I spun on my heel. I knew the wolf would follow. His animal curiosity about my behavior forced him to. It didn't mean I didn't want to punch my fist through his ribcage for doing so.

Get back to her, my mind ordered, *make her yours.* What the fuck was happening to me? I'd definitely never had that thought before. Maybe something was wrong with me.

I bypassed Titania, practically sprinting toward the balcony, only to find it empty. *Fuck!* I whirled around, checking that I hadn't overlooked her, making sure she wasn't hiding behind some balustrade. I glanced inside, catching no trace of her, knowing I'd lost her. My skin tightened even more, and I couldn't relax my muscles. Rage burned in my belly before flooding my entire body. I'd never struggled to control my emotions. Often it was as easy for me as flipping a switch. At that moment, I couldn't even find the fucking room the switch was in.

I turned on Erik in a killing rage, my voice guttural, shredding through my vocal cords. "This is your fault, wolf! If you hadn't arrived with your *urgent* message, she wouldn't have left!" My nails were black claws, my fangs filling my mouth, emotion surging through me as my eyes turned red. I snatched my friend up by his throat, slamming him against the wall of the Unseelie Court.

Titania intervened before I could go too far, shooting a handful of faerie dust into my eyes. The sticky crap forced me to drop Erik, allowing the wolf to breathe. The dust was a powerful toxin. Erik hit the ground. His knees buckled, making him land hard on his ass. His choking breaths slowly eased before turning into...*laughter?*

"Damn, I never thought I'd see the day," Erik choked out, tears welling in his eyes as he struggled to his feet.

Titania held up another handful of dust when I almost charged him again. "Never see what day?" I snapped.

Erik wiped the tears from his eyes and smirked evilly at me. "The day you met your mate."

V

THE REALM OF MORTALS.
NEW ORLEANS, LOUISIANA.

My head is pounding, and I vaguely recall something about the Witches Council. Is that where I am? When I try to focus, a deafening hum echoes through my head. I cover my ears in reflex to mute it. I force a steadying breath into my lungs, struggling to my feet. The blurs and shapes persist, making me dizzy. I reach out to support myself against what I hope is a wall, but I stumble when my hand meets nothing but air.

The movement makes me register the tearing pain in my side. I blink away the tears that spring to my eyes, and my hands drop to push the heavy velvet robes to the side. A cry breaks free from my lips, though it's soundless to me. A piece of wood impales my side, stopping regeneration from starting. I wrap my hand around the wood and yank it out.

I hear my scream this time.

I CLOSED THE FRONT DOOR OF MY apartment, forced to slam it three times before it finally locked into place. The rickety A/C unit in my window and the two fans were off, and the sticky weather made my clothes cling to my skin. Dressed for my bartending job at Tulane's campus bar, the black short-sleeved shirt, and matching pants felt more like a parka with the humidity. One downside to the swamp city was that it felt like you were walking through hot soup some days.

I sighed heavily, my steps trudging toward work, preparing for the night ahead. I would rather be heading anywhere else. Well, I guess not *anywhere*, but *close* to anywhere. I was not looking forward to the grabby hands of frat brothers, spilled drinks, aching feet, and long hours of pounding music.

Temporary, this is temporary, I reminded myself again, probably for the seventeenth time since I'd dragged my shapely ass out of bed and into my work clothes. I didn't know why that phrase reassured me. My entire life was temporary. Every city I was in, I had a new name, new background, new face, and I was gone before anyone could ever come close to discovering the truth. My current fake ID said I was *Serena Carmichael*, born and raised in Lafayette. My hair and eyes were their normal color. Sometimes, I needed to see *my* face in the mirror. It could be too easy to lose myself in these identities. I needed to remember who I was.

I sighed again and dragged my feet the several blocks to work, ducking into the air-conditioned building with a relieved exhale. The air was arctic in the bar to combat the humidity, and soon I'd be shivering. One of my coworkers called out to me as I stepped through the door, his voice way too cheerful. "Hey, Serena!"

I waved my hand in acknowledgment, moving to the register to clock in and prepare for the night. I felt Luis come up next to me, knowing it was him without having to look. He bumped his hip playfully against mine. When would he get the message that I *didn't* want to be friends? "You ready for tonight, *chica?*"

"As always," I answered wearily, trying to maintain some distance between us. He'd wanted to be friends with me since I started working at the bar. I couldn't have friends. Friends were the roots of the tree that I could never grow. Friends required trust, and that was something I couldn't afford. Most days, I couldn't even trust myself. I'd made so many mistakes on the run, some very, *very* recently. Rule number one was number one for a reason.

"What's that blush about?" Luis asked as we stocked the bar with alcohol, making sure we replaced all the empty bottles and the various cups were ready to go. "You get laid?"

I barely stopped myself from choking at how close he was to the truth. I covered it with a wistful exhale. "If only, Luis. If only."

Luis shook his head and mimicked a dramatic sigh as he leaned on the bar. "How someone so hot never gets laid is the second biggest mystery since the disappearance of Osama Bin Laden."

I couldn't stop my laugh, covering my mouth in surprise. Luis's eyes sparked, and I could practically hear him think, *look at us, bonding and shit.* Fuck, he was going to think we're friends now. I needed to throw my walls back up, push him away.

Rule No. 3: Don't tell anyone anything, ever.

It looked like I was doomed to one-night stands and non-existent friends for the foreseeable future. So I kept everyone at a distance. Everyone was a bounty hunter waiting to betray me. A feeling of despair settled on my shoulders, and I tried to suppress the way my mood plummeted. I shook my head, trying to clear my thoughts. I needed to get the grimoires, and then maybe I could figure a way out of this. Yeah, I could make up spells. Being on the run had forced me to explore spells once forbidden to me, but for the *really* powerful stuff, I needed my grimoires to pull it off.

If I had them, maybe I could permanently alter the memory of the survivors. Memory spells were tricky. The longer someone knew something, the harder it was to erase. But maybe, if I could erase the Council's memories, I could finally rest, put down roots, and move on. Maybe I could have a real relationship.

It was the reason I didn't have sex with Lucien. Something had told me once would never be enough, and once was all I could offer. I was still thinking about him days later, and I had flicked the bean to the memory of us together more times than I could count. Honestly, I needed to give the old gal a break.

Students began filtering in, and the raucous nature of the young mortals distracted me from my inner turmoil. We were busier than normal. The newest freshman had engaged in the recruitment process for Greek Life, and the bar was crammed full with them, each vibrating with frenetic energy.

Wistfully, I reminisced about the same process at UT, the excitement, the parties, the drama. I had been so naïve. I'd met he-who-shall-be-castrated at one of those parties. It was the beginning of the end for me. My eyes glazed as the orders came in, and I filled them by rote without conscious effort.

An asshole snapped his fingers at me multiple times from down the bar. His shirt was a blinding salmon, and his khaki screamed *douche on daddy's money*. What a dickwad. I wasn't blind. I was busy. Finally, I made my way to him, seeing a young girl, likely just a freshman, standing next to him. She appeared to be trying to inch away from him but seemed unsure if she should. It was like she was feeling pressure to stand there with him.

"What can I get you?" I asked, narrowing my eyes at the boy.

"Two hand grenades," he answered, tossing his credit card and fake ID at me. It wasn't my business, and I wasn't going to get involved.

Rule No. 4: Never draw attention, mortal or otherwise.

"I just want water—" the girl tried to speak up.

"Come on. You can't come to the Boot without having a hand grenade."

"I don't know—"

"Trust me," he interrupted her again, and I barely suppressed a loud scoff. In my experience, any man who said *trust me* was full of shit.

I turned away to mix the drinks, making one light on alcohol. When I returned to hand them off, the girl had vanished, so I handed both drinks over to the douche. If I hadn't been suspicious as fuck about him

52

already, I would have turned away without a thought, but I watched him from the corner of my eye. When he thought I wasn't looking, he pulled a pill from his pocket. He dropped it into the young girl's drink before carrying it over to their little group of friends and handing it off to the skittish girl.

It wasn't my business. I should stay out of it. *Fuck!* I couldn't keep out of it. I hid my hand beneath the bar as it began to glow with magic. With a flick of my fingers, I switched the drug from her drink to his. Have fun with that asshole.

Satisfied, I turned back to my other customers, mixing more drinks with a slight smile on my face. At least one girl was going to be safe from a fucking asshole trying to take advantage. The rest of the shift dragged, but at least there were no further incidents. I noticed with a vicious smirk that three frat brothers were forced to carry the douche home.

The doors finally shuttered at six in the morning, the slight rays of sunrise glowing through the glass windows. Luis cleaned tables as I scrubbed down the bar. Our boss waved as he exited, leaving just the two of us. Very typical, the one who cut the checks got to leave before the actual work was done.

With him gone, my focus returned to the bar, a comforting monotony in the task. Each time the rag I used went over the surface of the scarred wood, I imagined the last ten years of my life disappearing, rubbed away with the stains left behind by the patrons. Instead, I was standing in the Council's chambers, and they—

I hit Luis in the chest as he suddenly appeared next to me. How had he moved so fast? "Holy shit! You scared me!" I exclaimed, a shiver of unease going through me.

"I saw what you did," he muttered.

There was no way he saw me do that spell. I was just going to play it cool. "You mean scrub down this bar like it's my life goal?" I joked. My voice trembled slightly, but I hoped to distract him by gesturing to the still dirty bar. I was going to act like nothing was wrong, and maybe nothing would be.

"You're the witch."

Well, there went that hope.

"I don't know what you're talking about," I asserted, trying again to keep my voice neutral. He gripped my wrist hard, moving faster than humanly possible. Shit! He was an immortal!

I flinched as he grabbed me, his grip tightening as I attempted to yank my hand away. He didn't even react, and my wrist remained locked in his. A little fun tidbit about witches? We were among the physically weakest species of immortals. We didn't have super strength, eyesight, smell, or any of the other fun abilities that most other immortals had. So I was kind of fucked. His tight hold on my wrist heated, and the stench of sulfur escalated. Okay, scratch that, I was really fucked.

"Who are you?" I snapped, pulling a ball of battle magic into my free hand. I chanted the spell I'd invented in my head and slammed my hand into his chest, throwing him into the wall behind us. His body hit with a thud, but he recovered quickly, too quickly for me to power up another spell. His dark complexion flickered, a flash of flame playing beneath his tanned skin. The sulfur scent I'd noticed before became distinct and identifiable as brimstone.

On his feet again, he snarled, displaying the jagged fangs filling his mouth. "There's a big bounty on you, witch. It will be mine."

Witch Enemy Number One. Thanks again, Council!

His form rippled, and the flames beneath his skin grew brighter. His veins glowed, and the attribute finally allowed me to identify his species as a Cherufe. I brought more magic into my palms, desperately trying to recall what I knew about Cherufe as I did. They were evil humanoids, man-eaters, native to Chile.

He lunged at me, and I yelped, throwing myself over the wooden bar. Bottles crashed as he hit the bar behind me. *Shit! Shit, shit!* What else did I know about them? It was a little difficult to think about obscure Chilean lore when my life was on the line.

He regained his feet and, instead of circling around the bar, he reached out to touch the wooden fixture with a smoking hand. I gaped as he reduced it to ash within a couple of moments. *Shit! Think!* Okay, Chilean, mountains, volcanoes, lava. *Lava! That's it!* Some enchanted magma core powered Cherufe, making them virtually invulnerable to harm and able to reform limbs almost instantly. However, without the core, they crumbled.

The floor smoked as he stepped through the molten remains of the bar. I was forced to stumble back, frantically trying to recall a spell that might help me. Lava had to be molten to move, so I needed ice. I could think of several spells that could work, but none were powerful enough alone to stop him. I needed to do what I did best, which was make shit the fuck up.

The power built in me as I muttered under my breath, pulling from several spells and merging them together before throwing the magic at him. No one could ever say that I couldn't think on the fly.

The second the magic left my fingertips, I collapsed to my knees, the sound of them hitting the scarred wood floor making me wince. Every spell required my energy, my very essence, to power it. The more powerful the spell, the more energy it took and throwing six spells into a super powerful one to take out a mythical beast took quite the toll. Black spots were already swimming in my eyes, and exhaustion settled on my shoulders, trying to force me to the ground.

The amalgamation of magic hit Luis square in the chest, causing the magma in his veins to freeze. His steps forward slowed before coming to a stop.

"You *bitch*," he growled out before the spell hit his mouth, preventing him from speaking.

I let out a shaky laugh, tears of exhaustion wetting my face. Hate burned in his eyes, and I realized he still wasn't dead. Did no one die anymore? It took me three tries to get to my feet and stumble to the remains of the bar. I rummaged around for a weapon, finally grabbing the short paring knife we used to cut up limes and lemons.

I gripped the handle of the knife tightly and tripped back to his frozen form, fumbling as I plunged the small blade into his chest. His eyes glowed with pain, twining with the hatred, yet I kept eye contact with him even as I carved out his enchanted core. It was him or me, just like before.

Luis crumbled without his core. His form changed from the tanned visage I'd worked beside for the last couple of months to a cold lava rock in the shape of a man. I yelped when the enchanted core dropped into my hands. The heat made me drop it, and it burned a perfect circle in the wood floor before falling to the grass below. The sight of it smoldering filled me with rage and pain, tears filling my eyes. I screamed and slammed my fists against down on either side of the hole.

Rule No. 1: Don't Trust Anyone.

VI

*E***RIK IS AN ASSHOLE AND A MORON,** I told myself again. The strange female from that night in Tír nAill was not my mate, or *consort*, as was the formal vampiric term. She couldn't be. I could not possibly have met the one person deemed by fate to be mine. The one person destined to rule beside me, the one woman I could sire children with, and the de facto Queen of the Vampires because of our connection. It couldn't have been her. I could not have made an utter ass out of myself in front of my queen. I could not have been utterly *ghosted* by my queen.

Erik was delusional because I'd cut off his air supply. It must have been the hypoxia. Of course, that was it! Erik suffered brain damage, and that was why he thought the female was my mate. There was no other reason.

That logic worked for about eight hours, and then I tried to feed.

My fangs hovered over the throat of a willing donor, but they refused to extend. Even when I pricked her soft skin, allowing the blood to spill and drip down her neck, nothing happened. My fangs were useless in my mouth. I was forced to scarf down a blood bag, almost hurling in disgust. It was foul and left a bitter aftertaste. If I weren't already low, I wouldn't have been able to manage it.

Maybe I was having a slow day or something, or I'd caught some kind of immortal flu. My fangs were lifeless, but the rest of my body was primed for action. My cock had been hard as steel since the night I met *her.* No matter how many times I stroked myself, my cock would spring back to life almost instantly after spilling my seed. I considered finding another female to screw, hoping to relieve some of the building tension, but the thought made me almost physically ill.

Fuck me. She's my mate.

The delayed recognition had hit me like a ton of bricks when I first pulled out her panties and caught her scent again. My body had shot tight with hunger, the smell of her wiring me with need yet soothing my mind at the same time.

I'd heard the legends, though I thought them *slightly* exaggerated, and I'd never thought to experience it. According to *myth*, vampires recognized their predestined mate by the scent of their blood. The clouding scents of the fae realm must have muted the call, even when she stood in front of me. I'd wondered about my fascination with her, but I was in such deep denial that I couldn't see the obvious.

The obsession and jealousy now made sense. I was such a fucking moron. I pinched the bridge of my nose and slumped on my throne, struggling to recall the rest of the myths and legends surrounding the fated mates of my species. *A mated* vampire could not take the blood of others, not that I ever understood *why*.

What if, say, a fucking dumbass vampire never got his mate's name, and she vanished? What then? Did he starve to death? Mother would never have considered that when she cursed us. No one could be that stupid. Well, surprise! Her only child was, in fact, that stupid.

The curse was a never-ending spring of delights. It wasn't enough that vampires were bound by fate to a *single* person. She had to add all the extra stuff, too. *Thanks, Mom!* As I was fast finding out, the longer I went without claiming my mate, the weaker I would become. The bloodlust, which plagued all of my kind, required me to feed on the blood of others in order to survive. The hunger was chipping away at my sanity. I was already experiencing fits of rage and unexplainable blackouts, and it was only going to get worse.

Two weeks, it had been two weeks and not a *trace* of her. What would happen if I didn't find her? Would my grip on reality finally slip? Would I be wandering the streets of Budapest, irretrievably mad? Already, I was more unpredictable, and soon I wouldn't be able to tell reality from fantasy. Had I once thought the yawning emptiness inside me was bad? I would take that isolating loneliness, that *void*, over this. I was an immortal accustomed to control in all things, and after the slightest taste of her, I was struggling for even a glimmer.

Two. Fucking. Weeks.

In Tír nAill, Titania controlled and policed the one stationary rift in and out of the realm, but when my mate vanished, the rift was inoperable. Titania wanted to ensure that no one would stumble in or out of her ball without her say. That news had given me a flare of hope at first. If there was no other way in and out of the realm, she had to be somewhere in the area. *Right?*

Wrong. A week wasted scouring every inch of the fae plane without even the scantiest scent of cherry blossoms. She was gone. It was almost as if she'd never existed. In the beginning, I'd entertained the thought that she was some conjuring from my mind. But Titania saw her. Even Erik was able to catch a slight trace of her scent. So she was not an illusion.

There were a few spirit shifters, shapeshifters between life and death, who had the power to become intangible, even invisible. My mate must be one of their ilk. It was the only way she could have slipped through the fingers of so many powerful immortals.

With that realization, I returned to the human realm, back to my castle in Romania, sending servants to post bounties in every known realm. Shame filled me as I recalled my answers when Erik asked what I wanted on the bounty.

Name & Species: Unknown
Physical: 5'5", red hair like the embers of a dying fire,
eyes lilac like the freshest blooms.
Last Seen: Tlachd Ball, Unseelie Court, Tír nAill
Offered by: King Lucien of the Vampires
Reward: Absolutely Anything

Erik shook his head in amusement, not bothering to ask why I couldn't offer any further information about my fated mate. Erik knew me well enough to guess why, and even though the wolf didn't say anything, I could practically feel his judgment.

All of my old contacts were on the lookout, but it was impossible to even know where to begin without a name or species. Every moment that passed without news of her, I lost a little more hope and a lot more sanity.

I needed help, or maybe—

"A little divine intervention?" a voice called.

My eyes flashed open, and my hand dropped to the arm of my throne. I could barely believe my eyes. The previously empty throne room now contained a small child with flaxen hair tied into braids and swirling white eyes. She was licking a rainbow lollipop and was the very image of innocence.

I was on my feet in a flash but wavered as spots formed in my vision. Fuck, I was far weaker than I thought. Instead of rushing forward to embrace her, I was, instead, forced to place a steadying hand back on the onyx throne behind me.

"Cassie, welcome home," I croaked. When was the last time I'd spoken out loud? My throat felt raw from lack of use. "You don't need the guise. We're alone."

Known throughout history by various names, often Pythia, the Norn, Ma'at, Matres, and more, Cassandra of the Sibylline steered immortals and mortals alike for almost two thousand years. She used her foresight to shape and change the future, altering her glamour to suit her needs.

Though many versions of her were littered throughout history, no one realized they were the same person. Few knew of our connection, something I ensured. None knew that once upon a time, I'd found a squalling babe and gave the child shelter in this very castle. Her foresight was a gift, a terrible curse, and something I *never* exploited. Her visions came at far too high a cost to me.

Cassie departed this very castle for the first time well over two millennia prior. She reappeared sporadically, sometimes staying for a day, sometimes for a month. But like clockwork, she sent me a letter every week. Most often, it was an *I'm fine* message, but occasionally I did receive an *I need your help* message. Fuck, I just realized I didn't get one last week. I hadn't even noticed. I was such a fucking asshole.

The glamour melted from her, a flicker of white glowing over her body before revealing her true form. In place of the small child with a lollipop stood an ethereal blonde, appearing to be in her mid-twenties. Her hair was in two high lopsided pigtails, and she was absently sucking on a blow pop. The enchanted amulet I had given her on her sixteenth birthday hung around her neck. Her eyes were a bright blue but lucid. I'd heard the rumors of her losing touch with reality over the centuries. Every time she changed someone's fate, even slightly, she paid with her sanity. It was a heavy price, and the toll added up.

It was often the fate of Oracles, many unable to handle the pressure of steering the future or losing their grip on reality. Cassandra was the oldest living Oracle in memory, by far the most powerful and definitely the most mad. When she had left the safety of Întuneric almost two thousand years ago, she mentioned it was her destiny to be *the person who prevented immortals from constantly fucking shit up.*

I hadn't envied her that mission, but apparently, I'd made the list of immortals fucking shit up.

"Do you have something to say for yourself? Or are you just planning to stand there gaping at me like an idiot?" she said, reveling in my discomfort. She always lacked a filter with me, enjoying her immunity to the rage and reputation that sent other immortals cowering.

"You could have given me a heads up, you know? A little *Hey, dad, you're about to meet your mate, don't cock it up!*" I snapped, my eyes narrowing on my pseudo-adopted daughter. "Would a phone call have been too much to ask for?"

Cassie reached into her bag, one I hadn't noticed she was carrying until that very instant, and pulled out a banana. She gazed at the fruit with extreme concentration before miming dialing on the fruit as if it were a cellphone and holding it up to her ear.

"Ring! Ring! Hey, Dad! It's Cassie. That's right, your adopted daughter and legendary Oracle! I just wanted to let you know, and I know it sounds insane that I have to spell this out for you, but probably ask a woman her name before trying to screw her. Just a thought. Okay, love you, bye!"

She tapped the banana as if hanging up and shot me a lethal glare. I *hated* when she did that. Her reprimands were more pointed because she knew me so well. I faltered under her gaze, falling back onto my throne with a sigh.

"You know this takes thinking with your *downstairs* brain to a whole new level," she added with a shrug, twirling her lollipop.

Cassie gaily skipped forward and settled into the queen's throne. Like mine, it was cut from obsidian, and the back was far too straight and rigid. But, unlike mine, it had sat empty for the last ten thousand years. If I could find my mate, it would finally have an owner. I was so fucked.

I shifted toward Cassie, who was idly surveying me while lounging in the queen's chair. I couldn't ask her. It was fucking unfair to ask for her help. I'd gone two thousand years without needing her visions, and I knew the price she paid for them. I. Wouldn't. Ask.

"Can you give me any clue where to look?" I blurted out.

Even as the question slipped out, I noticed how *tired* Cassie looked. Cassandra always appeared youthful, but I could see the shadows under her eyes. Something was weighing on her, and I wondered what horrors she saw. What steps did she take to prevent wars or even cause them? Did all immortals merely dance to her tune, or did every prophecy she extolled only prevent a worse fate?

She smiled, her blue eyes going vacant. A milky white fell like a film over them, as they did when she experienced the future. Her mind was somewhere realms away as she rose to leave. She headed toward her old room, which remained much the same as it had when she'd left it. As she walked away from me, I experienced a pang of loss. I missed the little girl who had once sought the shelter of my arms when the storms rocked the castle. The child who listened to my fanciful tales of myth and mystery until her eyes slowly closed was lost to me forever.

In her place, an oracle stood, an immortal able to change the world with only a handful of words. Yet, she couldn't help me. If she could have, she would have told me where to go, where my mate was, even *who* she was. I knew it was fucking wrong to have asked her.

With her departure, I glared down at my useless hands. Then, out of nowhere, an object hurtled at me.

It beaned me in the temple and dropping to the floor with a clatter. I narrowed my eyes on Cassandra's back, knowing she'd done it on purpose, waiting for me to become distracted before chucking it. I glanced down at what she'd thrown, recognizing it as a string of cheap plastic beads. The necklace was the kind you could buy at any party store, but this one had a small plastic pendant that read *Krewe of Endymion*. Welcome realization flooded me as I called, "You're my favorite daughter, Cassandra!"

"I'm your only daughter!!" she responded.

I smothered a smile as I pulled out my phone to dial my pilot, ensuring the jet was prepared for immediate departure to New Orleans.

VII

THE REALM OF MORTALS.
NEW ORLEANS, LOUISIANA.

I LANDED IN NEW ORLEANS ALMOST fifteen hours later, just as the sun was rising. It had taken less than an hour to collect the things I needed from the castle. I wasn't a person attached to very much. My home was spartan by this century's standards, as I despised most modern technology, except for the most basic necessities. I had just recently agreed to a cellphone, and I was prone to crushing it beneath my heel when it rang too much. The small bag I packed was full of well-worn jeans and various band t-shirts I'd collected over the years. I had also remembered to pack the dreaded bagged blood. Though, I wanted to hurl every time I looked at it.

Throughout the flight, my thoughts tortured me with *what-ifs. What if someone figured out her tie to me and got to her first? What if someone hurt her? What if someone claimed her? What if? What if? What if?* At least, the horrors in my imagination kept me from speculating more about the actual source of my bone-chilling panic. *What if I find her? What the fuck do I do then?* My silver tongue did me little favors past the actual seduction part.

Always be the leaver. Something my mother taught me when I was barely old enough to have fangs. I'd never kept another woman around for longer than was necessary to get off. If a partner was after seduction, they need to look no further, but I had zero experience in keeping someone around. Even Cassie had left to fulfill her calling, leaving me behind as well.

I raked my hand through my hair for likely the millionth time since boarding the plane. At least I was able to keep the bagged blood down for the flight. Although, it was close. My clothes no longer hung off me, but every extra drop of blood I consumed was pooling in my cock. I swear my downstairs brain only cared about getting inside my mate, not whether I survived getting to there.

As we taxied along the small private airstrip outside Metairie, I mentally prepared myself. I had no fucking idea how to convince my mate that we were destined to be together, so I kept my plan simple. I would get to her first and then figure everything else out after.

We finally stopped, and I twisted one way, then the other, my long limbs protesting the cramped flight. Even on a private plane, I was not a fan of closed spaces. I struggled to conceal my impatience, waiting for the flight attendants to lower the steps for me. It took them longer than usual, and I suppressed the urge to snap at them. As I descended from the jet, I pulled the sunglasses from my pocket and strode to the car idling patiently for me on the tarmac.

My lips twisted before I donned the bored facade I usually wore. I didn't need enhanced vision to know that several of my subjects were sitting inside the limo behind the sun-proofed glass. The sun's normally deadly rays warmed the skin exposed by my short-sleeved band t-shirt, black jeans, and scuffed combat boots. Everything about me was meant to disarm. They expected me to step off the plane in a six-figure tailored suit, but I enjoyed being comfortable. I would take a cotton t-shirt and jeans over a suit any day. One of the few modern allowances I enjoy.

Their envy was palpable as I strolled through the warmth of the morning. Sunlight was lethal to vampires, one of the few things mortals got right, but I was an exception. As the firstborn vampire, I was immune to the damage of the sun's rays, but there were other ways for vampires to become day-walkers. I was wearing a sunlight charm on my right ring finger. The magic of the charms was extremely rare, and I had yet to decide who deserved such a gift. The ring was merely decorative on me.

My ability to move about during the day added to the myths of my savagery. The reputation helped to keep my subjects in line. They knew I could strike against them while they were sleeping and vulnerable. Plus, I was vain enough to admit that I looked much better with a natural golden tan. I didn't pull off *pasty* well.

I slid into the town car and slammed the door shut, facing the four vampires who fancied themselves the rulers of this area of North America. Vampires were notoriously territorial, even with our own kind. When I'd called ahead to let them know I was arriving, purely as a courtesy—I was still their *king*—they'd sounded less than pleased.

Often I would let little territorial vampires declare themselves leaders of certain geographical areas, mostly so I didn't have to police the area myself. I stepped in only if they thought to call themselves *royal*. Over the centuries, I'd made examples of those who had overstepped. A whisper of my interest in an area's activities was usually enough for them to stand down. Words could be more powerful than weapons, my fearsome reputation quelling more rebellions than my fangs. But I enjoyed showing up every once in a while, just to make them uncomfortable. If I wasn't so panicked about seeing my mate, I would have laughed at the sight the group of posturing vampires made. It was the little things in life.

A sharply dressed, dark-skinned man was the first to speak. He placed a hand over his heart and bowed his head. "Your majesty, it is an honor to have you in the Crescent City."

Elijah Jackson, former slave and American Civil war hero had been a friend since the aftermath of the Battle of New Orleans. Elijah had been turned by William Anderson, a vampire who had patrolled the dead for worthy soldiers. Elijah's thousand-dollar suits and shoes, along with his cultured tones, made many believe he'd always lived a life of luxury. The assumption was far from the truth.

I smiled brightly at him, making sure my fangs joined in my showing of teeth at the other three, who seemed less than happy with my appearance. Two males and one female completed the little ensemble. I glanced at the female, noting that her tight red curls were brassy and dull compared to my mate's luxurious mane of fire. I recoiled from her in distaste, forced to recall the last time I saw my mate. Gods, I was such an asshole. I was about to fuck her in the middle of the pleasure ball without even getting her name.

I refocused, pulling away from my recollection of that night. I glared at each of the other three vampires, waiting for them to introduce themselves. The subpar redhead mimicked Elijah's pose. She placed her hand over her heart and bowed her head. "Your Majesty, my name is Evangeline Bisset—"

"Born 1512, turned 1530 by Heath Artoix in Paris, France," I finished for her, entertained when her mouth dropped open. I gestured to the first of the other two males in the car, my tone lazy and a bit bored. "Akhiro Tashiro, born 1298 in Kaminokuni, Japan. Turned in 1345 by Xiao Tau." I pointed to the youngest member. "Stefan Michaels, born 1910, turned 1929 in New York City by Daniel Arturo." I lowered the sunglasses from my eyes, relishing how all their mouths dropped open in astonishment. I added with a wicked smirk, "You don't really think I've been king this long without knowing every single thing about my vampires?"

It was an uncomfortably quiet car ride after that. They were uncomfortable because they'd underestimated me. I was uncomfortable because the quiet left me time to reflect on all the ways I could fuck up with my mate. I barely noticed as we exited the freeway into the Garden District, my mind miles away, even as we pulled up to a large mansion.

The town car entered the garage, and my companions waited with bated breath for the garage door to close, sheltering them from the lethal rays of the sun. My lips twitched in amusement when a hiss of relief came from one of them when the light vanished.

Evangeline exited the car first, straightening her pencil skirt and brushing a rebellious lock back over her shoulder. "King Lucien. We have several factions of immortal species inside, hoping to meet with you, along with some of your loyal subjects. When the sun sets, we can give you a tour of the territory."

Akhiro and Stefan both nodded in agreement, all three turning and heading into the house. It did not escape my notice that they expected me to follow meekly behind them. Elijah sent me a droll look, and my lips twitched again. I stepped close and whispered, "Did you find out anything about the woman I asked about?"

As far as Elijah knew, I was looking for information about a potential threat to the lycans for Erik. No need to advertise my idiocy with my fated queen. As long as she was out there without me to protect her, she was vulnerable. If my enemies discovered her connection to me, they could strike at me through her. Fate did not give second chances.

"There was a strange woman of undetermined origin spotted in the Howard-Tilton Library at Tulane." Elijah pulled his phone from his pocket. "I thought she was close enough to your description to flag it. Here's the security footage we pulled from campus PD."

My heart thudded at the sight of my mate striding through the halls of Tulane's library on the small screen. She was just as stunning as I remembered, clad in skintight jeans and a baggy sweatshirt that concealed some of her curves. Her hips swayed to some unheard beat, and men's eyes lingered on them as she passed. I kept myself from crushing the phone, but I did memorize the mortal's faces for possible *unwilling* blood donors.

She was perusing the rare books section on the top floor of the library, a floor rarely visited by the students attending the university. She bit her lip as she had in Tír nAill, this time deep in thought. Her pale fingers trailed along the spines of the ancient tomes, her lilac eyes distant. A door slammed over her shoulder, making her jump at the sound, and for a moment, she appeared terrified. Her fear fell like a lash against my skin. She was running from something, and if I didn't find her soon, she was going to disappear again. The need to keep her safe was overwhelming. She was mine.

"When was this taken?" I asked, my voice a little hoarse.

"Yesterday," Elijah answered, putting away his phone. I barely stopped myself from snatching it back so I could watch the small clip again. Elijah glanced surreptitiously again at me. He no doubt heard my racing heart but had the grace or the wisdom not to comment.

"It's essential that I find her with all speed." I pulled the gold ring off my finger, flicking it to the other vampire. Elijah caught it in a blur of speed. "You're coming with me."

Without waiting for his reply, I threw open the door leading to the street, letting the light flood the garage. The other vampire hissed and recoiled, not making it to cover before the lethal bolts of sun hit him. Elijah futilely tried to block it with his arms.

It took a few moments, but eventually, Elijah opened his eyes and gaped at me. I stood in the doorway, my arms crossed over my chest as I waited for him to process the reality. The realization of what was happening was slow to sink in, his smile bright as he slid the gold sun charm onto his finger.

Elijah stepped outside into the sun for the first time in almost two hundred years. He lifted his head and closed his eyes, embracing the warmth. I heard the gasp of outrage and shouts of astonishment from the three other vampires as they watched us from behind the filtered glass. Evangeline's hands were pressed against the window, her eyes filled with longing. Various other immortals, mostly vampires, were standing behind her, their expressions stunned and amazed.

I sent them a sarcastic salute, a smirk curving my lips. The sunglasses I pulled from my pocket were identical to mine. I passed them to Elijah, and I could tell my message was as clear as the morning sun they could not enjoy.

Never cross the king.

VIII

THE REALM OF MORTALS.
NEW ORLEANS, LOUISIANA.

The blood-soaked spike of wood falls from my fingers, the sound of it hitting the ground too quiet for my hearing. Witches have healing powers like almost all immortals, though the healing is almost more painful than receiving the injury. You can feel your skin crawl back together, your organs regenerating, and your muscles knitting.

My fingers fumble as I part my robe to grip the sundress underneath. I rip a piece off and lift it to cover my nose and mouth, tying it into a knot behind my head. It allows me to breathe a bit easier.

The blurs in my vision are more circular, enough for me to see the flash of red, giving me a direction to limp. Each step makes my teeth dig deeper into my lip until blood drips down my chin.

NIGHT IN THE FRENCH QUARTER WAS A magical time of revelry and debauchery, clouding the senses, consuming most people's sense of logic and morality with the chaotic atmosphere. Tourists and locals alike took part, stumbling from bar to bar, their colorful attire and state of inebriation contributing to the mystical nature of the city.

I hunched my shoulders, making myself as small as possible to avoid attention. I wished it was cool enough to wear a hoodie, so my hair would draw less notice, but it was still too humid. Unless I wanted to melt into a puddle of sweat, I didn't have much of a choice in attire. Drunken mortals and immortals called out to me, hoping to envelop me in their aura of chaos and pull me into their world. The one I never got to be a part of, not truly. I never got to be free or enjoy life. I'd started dating a vampire at eighteen and was sentenced a few years later.

Rule No. 1: Trust no one. Everyone was a bounty hunter out to kill me. Luis just enforced that rule number one was *necessary.*

I rubbed my shoulders, suddenly aware of the presence of eyes on me, tracking me as I hurried down Frenchmen Street. The feeling of being watched was like another layer of unseen humidity pressing down upon me. Usually, I could easily dart between the numerous bodies of the French Quarter, both mortal and immortal, drawing no attention to myself. But something had locked onto me and was following me.

When the sensation became overwhelming, I slipped into an empty alleyway and waited for my pursuer to catch up. Sure enough, three witches appeared, blocking my exit. They probably sensed the lingering magic on me from destroying the cherufe the day before. Magic, especially powerful magic, left a scent on the witch. It was why I usually only hid in towns with large magical populations, so my aura of magic mixed in with all the others.

With the massive spell I'd performed yesterday, I positively *reeked* of magic. I shouldn't have left my apartment, but I needed to tie up some loose ends before I disappeared again.

"You didn't report to the local coven upon your arrival in NOLA, stranger," one witch called out.

It was considered common courtesy to announce your presence to the local coven when you arrived in a new city, three guesses why I hadn't.

"I didn't feel the need to check-in, just passing through," I bluffed as I straightened, hoping they would just leave and forget they ever saw me.

I sent a silent probe toward the three witches to judge their power levels and knew they were not a serious threat. Hopefully, I could avoid a fight. I really didn't want to kill them, but sometimes they left me no choice, like Luis. I tried not to lose sleep over it, but the truth was, I still did.

The witches in front of me were *young*. They were new to their powers and their role in the Council, not to mention in the world. They were new initiates, barely immortal. Silently, I urged the baby witches to run, to get the chance I never did. The newest members of the coven, often from the weakest magical lines, were tasked with patrolling the city, looking for rule breakers. My mother once told me it was because they were more expendable. It was easier for the less powerful lineages to reproduce than the more powerful ones like mine.

Which was pretty fucked up if you thought about it. At the time, I'd asked why we judged them by lineage instead of on their own merits. Couldn't a weaker magical lineage become more? Or is our birth everything? My mother had no response to the question, never having thought about it. But it altered the course of my life, and no matter who I asked, they couldn't explain why things were the way they were.

Some of the most dangerous words in the English language were: *we've always done it that way.*

Your lineage should not define your life.

The witches fanned out, coming closer to me, but I refused to back down. With my powers, most witches weren't an *actual* threat. It was when they were in a large group that I might break a sweat. The three witches surveyed me, and I tried not to shift my weight from foot to foot. The sooner I got away from these sentries, the better.

Run and live to fight another day. I'm not the one you want to mess with, baby witches. I should have known it wouldn't be that simple. Things in my life never are. In a blink, the three witches fell before me. One by one, their drained bodies collapsed, discarded into the filth on the ground.

Fuck! Magical blood called to vampires, and a group of five of them had taken out the three witches, draining them in less than a second. Red eyes locked on me, and despite the meal they'd just consumed, their leader sniffed the air. His eyes *glowed* when he caught my scent. Powerful witch meant smelly blood, as if I didn't have enough problems.

"You really don't want to do this, guys," I warned. If they didn't back off, the death toll had the potential to increase in the immediate future. *Did it really count if they were not witches?* As soon as the thought entered my mind, I rejected it. What kind of thought process was that? I respected all species! Just because I had a history with vampires didn't mean they were all seeking to fuck me over.

The leader stood in the middle and smiled viciously, his teeth still stained with blood. "Oh no, little witch. We really do."

There goes the high ground.

We couldn't always be Obi-Wan. Sometimes we had to be Anakin.

"You underestimate my power," I challenged, waving them forward, battle magic glowing in my palms.

Their eyes went dark at the insult, and I saw their bodies tense, preparing to lunge forward. They stopped when two more beings dropped down behind me in the alley from the roofs. Couldn't I catch a fucking break? I slammed my back against the brick wall, one glowing palm held toward the vampires and the other at the new threat.

It took a moment for me to see past the magic glowing in my hand to make out the shapes of the two other beings. When I saw the enigmatic emerald eyes, my knees threatened to buckle. Lucien was here, and I was unequivocally *fucked*.

His dark hair was windswept, his eyes glittering. Instead of the leather I last saw him in, he wore comfortable jeans, biker boots, and a Nine Inch Nails t-shirt. Fuck, did he have to look even hotter in casual clothes? He vibrated with an aura that screamed *death to all who approached*, and I couldn't help the hunger and need that rose in me.

When I didn't lower my hand, he raised a dark eyebrow at me, though his body language said that he did not take the threat seriously. His hands were down at his sides, his hip cocked. If I didn't know better, I would think he found himself at the end of lethal magic every day.

"I pose no threat to you, female," he murmured as if such words would inspire the utmost faith. I barely covered my shiver at the sound of his voice. It was too easy to recall that night, too easy to feel his hands on me, and too fucking easy to let my guard down.

His eyes drifted away from mine, and pure menace radiated from him. I sucked in a slight breath at how different his aura was when he looked at me before he looked down the alley at the vampires. I thought him intimidating before? *Try terrifying.*

"The female is mine," he said, even his voice shifting. His tone left no room for disagreement. It was a statement of fact, as obvious as the moon and the sun. It took me a moment to remember that he didn't know my name, and *I* was the female in question, but I didn't belong to anyone. I was on my own, always alone. I wasn't his, could never be his.

The leader of the vampires didn't have the sense to back down at the aggression rolling off Lucien, but several of the other vampires paled even more beneath their chalky complexions. It took just a look at his face for three of the five to speed off in terror.

I would love to know why his very appearance could make bloodlust frenzied vampires flee. Only two remained, snarling at Lucien, seeming to have forgotten about their desire to drain me. I was surprised when the magic flickered in my palms before going out. Confusion furrowed my brow as I looked down at my hands. Why did I do that? The frantic energy inside me was fading.

"Who the fuck do you think you are?" the leader spat.

Lucien moved in between heartbeats. One beat, he was down the alley from me. The next, he was in between the two vampires, his hands buried in their chests.

"Alec Jeffreys, born 1974, turned 2005 by Mohammad Al-Shiekah in Afghanistan," Lucien said, then turning to the beta of the two. "Frank London, born 1991, turned 2019 by Alec Jeffreys."

Both vampires' eyes widened at Lucien's dossier on them. The beta whispered, trying not to move, as Lucien still had a locked hold on his heart, "Who are you?"

Lucien let out a harsh laugh, "Your *king*."

The vampires released a harsh exhale, and Lucien yanked out their still-beating hearts. He dropped them, and they rolled on the moist cement, making a gut-wrenching sound as they hit. The vampires' eyes went dull before they collapsed to the ground. My stomach rolled, my eyes locked on the hearts, unable to look away.

Lucien turned away from the bodies, dark blood drenching his hands. Regeneration could regrow a heart, but it took days, and the rising sun would finish the vampires off before they healed. He spoke to his equally gorgeous, dark-skinned associate calmly, as if he hadn't just ripped out the hearts of two vampires.

"Leave them for the sun. Let someone on the Witches Council know about their lost members and that justice was served to those responsible," he said to the other man, who nodded and was already typing away on his phone.

Lucien held his hand out, and the other immortal passed by me swiftly, ruffling my hair slightly with his speed. He handed Lucien a snowy white handkerchief. Lucien took the offering and callously cleaned the dark blood from his fingers.

I covered my mouth with my hand, trying to keep my breathing normal. I couldn't pull my gaze from the two discarded hearts on the pavement, barely able to keep my gag reflex in check. Slowly, I edged toward the other end of the alley, my back plastered against the brick wall. I could still escape before he noticed me. I hit a trash bag with my foot, and I almost cursed out loud when his attention snapped to me.

"Don't run," he ordered, making my hackles go up in response. I bit off a reply, my eyes returning to the discarded hearts on the ground. If I disobeyed, would I be next?

Lucien's feet shuffled, and I looked at him. The traces of a flush rose up his neck as our eyes locked. He took a stuttering step forward with his hands held out in supplication. He opened his mouth to speak, but in a moment of blurring speed, his companion's arms wrapped around me from behind. My panic ratcheted up even higher, my breaths coming in shallow gasps.

"We will not hurt you," he whispered in my ear, his creole accented voice soothing. Though he was trying to reassure me, I couldn't stop glaring at the two vampires lying in the muck. My heart raced, my breath shallow. It was him or me, fight or flight. I was a witch. I had magic and was not helpless! It was time to focus and save myself because no one else would.

My mind scrambled for the spell, but the icy terror sliding down my spine made focusing nearly impossible. Lucien moved like a blur before I could launch the spell, his hand landing on his companion's shoulder. He launched him away from me, his eyes flashing dark red in the dim lights from the Quarter.

"Never touch her!" Lucien's voice was a guttural growl, his fangs bared.

I didn't know what the fuck that was all about, but I didn't wait to ask questions. Instead, I bolted out of the alley, shoving my way through the crowded street. Survival was all that mattered, and to do that, I had to get away from them. Some part of me was struggling to process the events of the last ten minutes. I needed focus to rift, but that was in short supply. My mind was a maze of chaotic, half-formed thoughts, nothing that would help me escape.

I ducked through another alleyway to cut through the Quarter, barely out of sight of a group of mortals. I let out a small yelp when a hand of iron caught my upper arm, yanking me back. Lucien pressed me against the brick wall, looming over me. The lines of his jaw looked as if they were cut from granite, and his eyes flashed red as he commanded, "Do not run from me!"

Blood-red eyes were a signature of the vampiric species. Their eyes would change when their emotions were high or when they were about to feed. My instincts were screaming at me, but still, I prayed he was not a vampire.

"Let me go!" I hissed, though I wanted to scream. There was *one* tenet all immortals abided by, *never risk exposure.* Terrible, unspeakable things happened to immortals who risked exposure to the mortals.

"Never. I will *never* let you go," he snarled. A moment of silence passed between us, and his expression shifted from the hard lines of fury to his brows furrowing in what looked like *confusion.* But that made little sense. Why was he confused? I was confused, not him! He'd just killed two people in front of me after declaring...

"Wait, did you say you're their king? Are you a vampire?" I blurted out. Why did I care? Once I got away, he was going to be a distant memory, but I desperately wanted him to say no. The last vampire I trusted took everything from me. I would not be making the same mistake. In my experience, vampire equals betrayal.

He pulled his gaze from my throat. I met his eyes, watching as the color flickered between a dark, maddening red and bright enigmatic green. "I am Lucien Silvano, King of Vampires."

King? King of Vampires? It took a moment for my brain to connect, but once I did, I struggled against his hold. He pressed hard against me, forcing my hips to connect with his. I bit my lip to keep from moaning as I felt how hard he was. I forced myself to stop wiggling when I realized the action only brought me closer to him.

"Let me go," I said, my voice a tad too breathy. I wanted it to be firm and resolved, but it was impossible with him this close.

He trailed his thumb across my lower lip, and it took way more concentration than I expected not to nip his thumb with my teeth. "What's your name?"

My mind went blank, and I felt dazed. "Serena," I said, answering automatically.

My imagination was supplying the sound of *Phoebe* on his lips, not *Serena*. I hadn't gone by my real name in years, not since my sentencing, often discarding names and identities with each new city. It had become a habit to dig up the roots before they had time to grow, never allowing them to sink into the earth and bind me to one spot.

Rule No. 5: Abandon Everything at a Moment's Notice.

He shook his head, leaning closer, the maddening scent of lemons and olive oil clouding even more of my mind. I arched away from the wall, pressing myself against him without conscious thought. My nipples hardened, and I squeezed my thighs together, trying to ease the ache between them.

"I don't think so. Your true name," he said, dragging his mouth along my throat. How could he tell I'd lied, but more importantly, why wasn't he fucking me? Wait, what had he asked?

"Why?" I whispered, rather impressed that I could speak at all.

Lucien moved even closer, trapping me against the hard bricks. He slid his hands down over my curves to the hem of my sundress, dragging it up so he could grip my bare hips. I expected him to rip my underwear away, but he stopped. His fingers splayed against my skin, holding me tight. I was under his control. Every shift of my body was his to command.

Desire swept through me, my body instinctively submitting to his will. I murmured between heavy pants for air, "Phoebe."

I didn't know why I'd given him my real name, but it seemed imperative that he knew it.

"Phoebe," he said, dragging out my name as if it was a drug. *Oh, that's why.* The way he said it sent chills down my spine, putting my imagination to shame. "I've been searching for you since that night. I couldn't stop thinking about you, about…" He trailed off as he struck like a viper, his fangs planting into my neck.

A scream caught in my throat, turning to a moan as a flood of lust ripped through me. The second I felt the strong draw of his mouth, utter *need* bolted through me. My body was no longer under my control.

"Lucien."

The acute pain turned into an all-consuming pleasure as he sipped on me. It made me desperate for more of him, for his cock, his touch, just *everything.* I'd never let a vampire feed on me, so I wasn't prepared for the tsunami of lust crashing through me. No one told me it was like this.

I grappled for his pants, yanking at his fly in desperation. I freed his cock from his jeans, the long, thick length landing in my hand. Was he possibly as frantic as I was? I wrapped my hand around his length, and he jerked. Still feeding hungrily at my neck, he roughly slammed against me, pressing me hard against the wall. Brick dust cascaded from the force, but I wanted more, *needed* more. I felt his muscles flex as he lifted me, forcing me to wrap my legs around him. I mindlessly obeyed. This strong immortal was as desperate for me as I was for him. I could feel his hot length rubbing against the soaked cotton of my panties, and I shifted, trying to get him right where I needed him.

Lucien thrust his hips, grinding against me, the friction making me come apart at the seams. His cock was hitting right against my clit, and the sensation twined with the bite made it enough. It took several jarring thrusts before I came, screaming into his neck to muffle the sound. His body jerked as he followed, and his cum fell to the ground. For a moment, I froze. I didn't want him to ruin this moment, but he would. I wanted this afterglow for as long as possible. He gently withdrew his fangs from my neck, licking at the punctures lovingly, as if he couldn't get enough of my taste. I shivered at the feel of his tongue over my pounding pulse, keeping me in a daze of lust.

"Gods, I never thought...never knew..." he muttered, nuzzling his face against my neck, almost praising me.

When the shaking aftermath of my orgasm subsided, I realized what we'd just done. I eased my legs from around Lucien and lowered my feet to the ground. I was unsteady from the lingering force of my climax and held tight to his shirt. Who knew a vampire's bite could do that?

Lucien's hands released my waist, gently cupping my face. His eyes were back to their sparkling green and seared me as they locked with mine. His thumbs traced along my cheeks, and he mumbled something in a language lost to me.

"What are you doing here?" I whispered to him.

He licked his lips before saying, "I'm here for you."

He placed a gentle, lingering kiss on my lips, stopping me from asking more. I couldn't remember the last time someone acted with such tenderness toward me. He pulled back to study me intently as if he was memorizing my features. He pinched a lock of my hair, seeming to explore its softness before tucking it behind my ear.

Wait, did he say he was here for me? I stiffened, panic weaving through the bliss of my post-orgasmic bliss. People who came looking for me either wanted to kill me or hand me over to the Witches Council so they could kill me.

Lucien seemed to sense my sudden discomfort and stepped back, putting a bit of distance between us. He dropped his hand to tuck himself away and right his clothing. That done, he linked our fingers and led me toward the entrance of the alleyway. I followed him for a few slightly shaking steps, my brain still not fully online yet. I tried to disentangle my hand at the mouth of the alley, but he refused to relinquish it.

The well-dressed man from earlier had returned and was waiting a respectable distance from us. I blushed when I realized he'd probably heard me moaning when Lucien had bitten me. I needed to focus and forget about the feel of his bite. No one came for me unless they meant to harm me. I trusted no one, and no one trusted me. That was for the best and how it needed to remain. There were fewer surprises that way. It was rule number one for a very good reason.

"What do you mean you're here for me?" I asked, yanking on Lucien's hand until he turned back to face me.

Lucien wasn't paying attention. Instead, his eyes became hooded, staring at the already healing marks on my neck, looking like he couldn't wait to mark me again. He licked his lips as if he was already picturing it. Unfortunately, so was I.

I cupped my hand around the mark, forcing him to break his gaze. "Lucien, what do you mean?"

"Come with me. I'll keep you safe." Again, he tried to tug me toward the entrance of the alleyway. I resisted, finally managing to pull my hand from his.

It was tempting to let this man, this *king*, keep me safe from my enemies. Too tempting, if I were honest. My mental walls snapped up. I'd learned the hard way never to put my faith in anyone. Rule number one had been lesson number one, the first thing I'd learned on the run. I muttered a spell under my breath, creating an invisible barrier between us. I made a wide circular gesture with my other hand, opening a rift behind me, the tear in reality appearing as a fission of air.

Lucien's eyes widened in alarm, and he reached for me, but my shield stopped him. His brows furrowed, his hand pressing against the barrier. His eyes glimmered with what looked like hurt.

I knew I couldn't weaken, forcing myself to turn away and step toward my rift. I glanced back at Lucien as he began pounding against the shield. His eyes widened, and I backed away as I saw the possessive determination in his gaze. I shook my head and said, "Goodbye, Lucien."

He banged harder against the barrier, his eyes flashing bright red, not seeming to hear me. "Phoebe!" he yelled, but whatever else he might have said was cut off as the rift snapped shut.

IX

THE REALM OF MORTALS.
NEW ORLEANS, LOUISIANA.

THE SHIELD DISAPPEARED when the rift closed and sent me pitching forward at the sudden release of her magic. I'd found her and lost her again. I whirled, looking for an outlet to rid myself of this coiled rage and madness banging against the inside of my skull. Mercilessly, I pummeled the brick wall of the alleyway. I barely felt my knuckles split from the strike, heal a moment later, and rip open again with the next punch. The russet-colored dust swirled in clouds around me. Elijah wisely did not try to stop me. Not even I was sure what I would do in this state. I kept fucking this up.

The control I was famous for was absent. Without my mate present, the bloodlust was already working to destroy my sanity. I wondered if that was what Cassandra felt. I knew her name was Phoebe, and I used it as a talisman, just thinking it enabled me to stop and take a shuddering, stabilizing breath. Phoebe and the lingering taste of her blood on my lips were all that was holding me together.

Fuck, her blood had been life-changing. My mouth felt like it was on an electrical line, sipping at the power contained within her. Even now, what I had consumed was making my nerve endings come alive, my entire body awakening to a feminine strength that tasted of her, my mate. My fangs lengthened, and I shook my head, trying to forget about her blood. I needed more. I needed her!

She'd run from me *again*. I shook my head to clear my thoughts, trying to focus on the new things I'd learned about her. I'd heard her chant something when she pulled the shield up. She had barrier magic. She was a fucking witch! The Queen of the Vampires was a fucking *witch*. The Elders would *love* that.

Phoebe had the power to open rifts. That was some heady magic. I hadn't heard of an immortal with such a handy ability since they established the first stationary rifts, and that was before even I was born. It was a coveted and dangerous gift. As a witch who could open and close them at will, her enemies, and now *my* enemies, must be legion.

She could sneak entire armies into unsuspecting realms, could appear in impenetrable fortresses, could seal off realms from reinforcements. In my head, I listed the factions who would want to kidnap or even kill my queen. I lost count somewhere in the thousands. I had to find her and keep her safe.

Elijah broke the silence, sensing my disquiet. "We got a hit from the parish DMV. She's going by the name Serena Carmichael. I have an address for an apartment in Uptown."

"DMV?" I asked. I was a little out of touch with most mortal terminology and technology. My castle in Romania only had the barest of modern amenities, just enough to keep me in touch with my businesses.

"Department of Motor Vehicles," Elijah answered, holding out his phone to show me.

I would have never thought I would need to resort to *mortal* means to track her down. Yet, without them, tracking her would have taken much longer. I suppose there are some benefits to mortal technology.

I'll find her, and this time she won't escape.

"Go there. Monitor her house and tell me if she returns. Stay hidden. If she sees you, she'll run."

Elijah nodded, bowing slightly before taking off into the night.

She ran from me. I was her mate. Did she not understand the tie between us? I pinched the bridge of my nose, fighting the pounding in my skull. I recognized her, but she didn't recognize me. As if I didn't already have enough problems with her.

My queen was an extremely powerful witch with the ability to tear reality with a swirl of her hand, who seems to have the fun quirk of running away from me. With her magic, she could vanish into any of the million realms that existed every time I got close. She would, too. If the last two interactions with her were any indicator, she wouldn't stick around to get to know me. Fuck, how did I get her to stay in one place long enough for her to understand her new life?

I needed help, and there was only one person in the entire city of New Orleans who might have the mystical artifacts necessary. I took off without a second thought, heading deeper into the Quarter toward the Lower Ninth Ward. The Ninth Ward had been devastated by Katrina and was the slowest to come back from the hurricane. Over a decade later, it was just returning to its former glory.

The hurricane had destroyed most of the parish. Only a single building had been untouched by the storm—a hair salon. From the exterior, it appeared no different from the dilapidated buildings surrounding it.

But if you looked long enough, you would notice the variety of oddities around the structure. Like the alligator wearing a feather boa climbing the back steps or how the yellow eyes watching you from the second-story window were not exactly human. Many speculated on how it had survived the devastation, but none guessed at the thrumming power contained inside.

The slight sounds of a bell ringing echoed through the small structure when I pushed the door open. It was as if I'd dropped a bomb. Every chair was full, varying hairstyles being meticulously executed while hip-hop music blared from the speakers. All conversation stopped, and the bass was the only sound in the salon the moment the door closed behind me. Each of the hairdressers turned to face me in the doorway, their glares deadly, several of them reaching for the charms at their stations.

One of the women took a step forward. She was outrageously tall and wearing a pair of white boots and a floral dress. The hoops in her ears were large enough for me to put my fist through. She hissed at me before calling out, "Ain't nothing for you here, *leech*."

The insult made my hackles rise, my hands clenching into fists at my sides. The priestesses immediately took the small action as a threat of violence and moved to shield their clients, their charms out and ready. I took a slow breath, forcing myself to calm down and bow to show my respect. "I need to speak with Mambo."

Unlike witches, Voodoo practitioners were mortal, requiring the aid of charms or enchantments called *gris-gris.* Every millennium, a Voodoo priestess was born who would become the high priestess, or mambo. She would drain the life from the previous high priestess and become the leader of them all. Any practitioner of Voodoo could come to the mambo for protection. If you crossed one practitioner, then you crossed them all. You never, ever, ever wanted to cross the current mambo.

None of the priestesses moved or relaxed their defensive postures. I crossed my arms over my chest, waiting for someone to make another move. Whatever might have happened was interrupted by the sound of beads clanking together as a curtain was parted. The mambo stepped into the room, her dark brown eyes locking on me. A smile that held an evil, malicious tint spread across her flawless ebony face. I felt a momentary flash of regret for even thinking of coming here. She tilted her head at me. The beads at the ends of her tight black braids clicked together as they shifted along her back.

Marie Laveau, mambo, and Voodoo Queen smirked at the sight of me. She was always a striking woman, and often she used her beauty as a weapon, delighting when people underestimated her. They often never lived to correct the mistake.

"Mambo."

She rolled her hips seductively as she stalked forward, like a cheetah cornering a gazelle. Her voice was husky. "Now, as I live and breathe, that cannot be Lucien Silvano coming to pay me a visit."

As she spoke, she closed the distance between us, standing on her tiptoes to kiss both of my cheeks. It took everything in me not to recoil at her show of familiarity. The leopard-print jumpsuit showcased Marie's curves, and her heels made her only a couple of inches shorter than me.

"It's been too long." *Not long enough.* "Unfortunately, I'm here for business, not pleasure. Can we speak? Privately?" I gestured to the back and her office with my hand, my eyes drifting pointedly to the other priestesses who were waiting with bated breath to attack.

She smiled invitingly, taking my hand to lead me back the way she'd come. I gritted my teeth to stop myself from yanking it away. Marie had always been overly familiar with me, and I'd once made the mistake of spending the night with her. She had taken it to mean that she could manipulate me with sex. There was a reason I hadn't been back to New Orleans in the last fifty years.

I reminded myself that I needed her. As we passed together through the bead curtain into the back room, the ripple of illusion came down. A clean, modern office appeared, and when I glanced over my shoulder, the salon was also suddenly upscale.

"What can I do for you, *cherie?*" she asked, her accent making her words sing. She slipped into the plush white chair on the other side of her massive black marble desk. I took one of the open chairs in front of the desk, faking a casualness I didn't feel, putting on a show for Marie. Her dark eyes watched my every move.

"I need something to bind a powerful witch." I tried to keep my tone bored, but a tremor came through. I could only hope she hadn't noticed. Her eyes flashed. *Fuck.* Marie was always looking to make a deal, and they always, *always,* went bad. I'd just handed her a glaring vulnerability that she could use to manipulate me.

Marie tapped her chin in thought, her long dark fingernail making the action menacing. She clicked her tongue after a moment, gesturing to the shadows. "I have just the thing."

At the snap of her fingers, a massive anaconda slithered out from behind her, its eyes locking on me. A matching pair of silver cuffs adorned its neck. They were made of thin, flexible metal, the chain between them delicate, but even I felt the power humming from them. They were made to deceive. The snake lifted its head high enough to meet Marie's eyes and tilted its body, depositing the bracelets on the desktop. Marie affectionately stroked and cooed to the huge reptile, giving it one last pat before it slithered its hulking body away to lurk in the darkness. Its yellow eyes remained locked on me.

"How much do I owe you?" I asked, reaching into my pocket, prepared with various charms and mystical artifacts, to exchange for the cuffs. With Marie, you paid immediately, never dealing in any form of an IOU.

"Well, I'm running a special for handsome vampire kings. These cuffs are all yours for the fantastic price of a single, tiny kiss."

My head snapped up, and I gaped in shock. Marie, at her core, was a cold-hearted businesswoman. Despite our history, she displayed no type of favoritism with her deals. She always demanded the same from me as she would from a stranger.

My jaw ached as I gritted my teeth. I should have known that Marie wouldn't make this easy. "I can't give you that."

"That's my price, *cherie.* Take it or leave it." She smiled with malice, relishing my struggle.

My eyes locked on the cuffs, focusing on the way they glinted in the light of her office, trying to figure out a way that I could get them without kissing Marie. I could snatch them and run, but I would make an eternal enemy of the Voodoo community. So that was out. I could find another way to bind Phoebe's powers. But the only other people who would have the power necessary to do so would be another witch. Witches didn't like to create things that bound them. Plus, I didn't know a witch powerful enough to spell something that would keep Phoebe powerless. There was no other option. I had to make the deal with Marie.

"Marie, I have many valuable charms and artifacts. Are you sure you don't want those instead?" I asked, not even bothering this time to hide the tinge of desperation in my voice.

"I'm a woman who knows what she wants. A single kiss and they're yours."

My teeth were almost ground into dust from clenching my jaw. I gritted out, "Fine."

Unable to see any other option, I stood and circled her desk, pulling her to her feet. As I leaned down to kiss her, her eyes slid closed, and she puckered her lips. The scent of oranges gagged me, and I was forced to hold my breath to stop myself from jerking away.

I'd kissed her before, and I could kiss her again. I just had to imagine it was Phoebe. Phoebe, my queen, my mate. I was doing this for her, right? Surely one brief kiss was meaningless if it gave me my queen. Less than a breath separated our lips now, but I couldn't force myself to press my mouth to hers, wrenching away at the last second.

"I can't," I whispered, my voice breaking. Phoebe was already inside me, and I would not betray my mate.

Marie didn't appear upset, only smug. "And why can't you?" she asked archly, though she knew the answer.

I turned my back on the Voodoo Queen, my shoulders slumping slightly. "How did you know, Marie?"

She returned to her seat with a knowing smirk. "I could see her aura tied with yours the second you walked through my door, *cherie*. Your queen is a slippery one."

I let out a deep sigh and returned to my chair. "How much for the cuffs?"

A witch revered their magic above all things. If I went through with this and bound Phoebe's, I wasn't sure she would ever forgive me. Yet without them, I could turn my back, and she could be in any of the millions of realms, lost to me forever. I had no choice. She'd leave me, just like everyone else.

"I want a meeting with your Oracle." It was a decent exchange, but I hesitated. I didn't speak for Cassie. Few even knew of our connection, and I liked to keep it that way. I didn't want my enemies knowing they could use her to exploit me.

"I have no control over her, but I'll talk to her," I said, knowing she likely already agreed to the meeting, or she would have told me not to transact with Marie.

The priestess nodded, accepting the terms. I swiped the silver cuffs from the desk, rising to exit the shop.

As I strode toward the door, Marie said to my back, "Your queen has many enemies. Best keep her close, vampire."

I lifted a hand in acknowledgment but didn't look back as I left the shop.

Next, I just had to get close enough to capture my queen.

X

THE REALM OF MORTALS.
NEW ORLEANS, LOUISIANA.

My feet hit the side of something hard as I shuffle forward. I can't rebalance myself in time and fall with a loud thud. If there are still enemies waiting to pick them off, I just made it extremely easy for them.

Thankfully, the mask stays in place, and my mouth remains free of the cloying, choking dust that continues to fall from the sky. At least, I think it's still falling from the sky. I see something falling from the sky. But I'm also blind, so there's a pretty good chance I'm seeing things.

I **WAS STILL MYSTIFIED BY THE** strange interaction with Lucien as I shoved my clothes into my threadbare rucksack. My go bag was already waiting by the door, filled with the cash I had squirreled away and my stack of fake ids. *Rule No. 5* was coming in handy. I couldn't stop thinking about the expression on his face when he tried to protect me. He had lunged forward, trying to put himself between the threat and me. Why? Why did he care? I was nothing to him. Why come looking for me?

Outside of the witches, I was no one. I avoided other species of immortals unless I was forced to fight them. *Rule No. 4: Never Draw Attention, Mortal or Otherwise.* Yet, I had the vampire *king* on my ass. Almost all immortals swore fealty to a royal family, often a lineage traced back to the first touched by the deity who created their species.

Lucien was coming for me. There was no doubt about it, not after the way he reacted in the alley. I shuddered, remembering his blood-red eyes, his fists pounding on the shield, almost cracking it with his strength. He'd been desperate to get to me, but why? Why me?

Maybe it originated from his shock that a female could *ever* want nothing to do with him. Maybe he was like all other immortal males when faced with a challenge, a dog with a bone, refusing to relinquish his prize, no matter the cost. Men, immortal or otherwise, were all the same.

How the fuck did he even find me in the first place? Was the Council going to show up on my door next? Was Lucien going to find me again? I knew I had to disappear again, existing as a ghost in a new city. I would leave no trail, nothing to follow. My heart clenched as I thought about running again, leaving nothing behind and putting down no roots ever again.

With my clothes packed, I sat on the sad little cot in my apartment, trailing my hand over the blanket. I was already missing the familiarity and hated that I always ended up getting attached. Some part of me hated running, hated every aspect of what I was forced to do to survive.

The lazy tendrils of the rising sun were emerging from the horizon. Once the sun was up, it would be time to go. Vampires couldn't withstand the sun, and I needed the time to put distance between Lucien and me. I couldn't summon the energy for another rift for a while, so I had to run the old-fashioned way.

I glanced down at Bast, who was pacing through my legs. Idly, I scratched her head, and she emitted a loud purring sound that would normally relax me. Now, it only made me more anxious. My knee was bouncing up and down as I watched the ever-creeping sunrise. When enough light bathed my front door, I scooped the feline into her travel carrier and threw my pitiful rucksack over my shoulder.

Rule No. 5: Abandon Everything at a Moment's Notice.

I paused at the door, turning back to cast one last wistful glance at my pitiful little apartment, unable to stop the tears from filling my eyes. I hated this part. This little apartment was home, even with its too-thin walls, the landlord with several missing teeth, and the reverberating noises from the nearby campus. At least for a little while.

The longing to stay in one place was a tangible force inside me. I wanted to make friends, to form a community, to feel safe. I didn't know if I knew what it felt like to be safe. I didn't remember what it was like to sleep through the night without waking in a cold sweat, haunted by the faces of the people I'd killed?

There was a moment, a single moment when I felt safe. When Lucien shielded me from the fae queen, there had been a glimmer of safety. It was just an illusion, one that I desperately wished to cling to, but he was a vampire. I had learned my lesson, once bitten, twice shy, and all that.

Rule No. 1: Trust No One.

Maybe I should change rule number one to include, *especially a vampire.* It might be a good idea. I swung the door open, my jaw dropping at the sight of Lucien. He was leaning against the door jam, the sunlight warming his face. My eyes went round, and I sputtered, "H-how?" I couldn't comprehend how he was standing there on my doorstep rather than being reduced to a smoking pile of ash. My mouth opened and closed.

Lucien's smile died as he took me in. His eyes trailed down my body, and he frowned when he noticed the bags in my hands. After a moment of stunned silence on my part, he crowded forward, forcing me back into the apartment. He took the bags from my hands and set them off to the side. I couldn't summon the focus to fight against him.

With my hands-free, he spun me around, pulling me back against his chest. He pressed close, fitting his body against mine as his arms wrapped like steel bands around my waist.

"Were you planning to run from me?" His voice was deadly soft, which shot an involuntary shiver down my spine. My body immediately responded to him. His scent, his touch, his voice were overwhelming. A sensory overload from just a simple moment with him, and I needed more.

I knew I had to resist him, but that was easier said than done. All the reasons I needed to run vanished at his touch, logic nothing but a whisper in the wind.

"Yes," I whispered huskily, wishing I could have made my voice cold and unfeeling, but it was impossible when his hands were on me.

My heart slammed against my ribs, and he chuckled darkly, no doubt able to hear the racing beat. My breath was short, even more so as he kicked the door shut and walked us further into my apartment.

"I must punish you for your attempt," he growled into my ear. His comment slid across my skin, making my nipples tighten in want, already imagining his touch.

The flash of his claws was the only warning I had before he cut my shirt down the middle, leaving me exposed. He pushed the ruined fabric off my shoulders and tossed it aside. My translucent demi-cup bra did nothing to hide my nipples as they budded under his gaze.

"Look at you. You missed me."

"No—"

My protest was cut off when his large hands cupped my breasts. He cradled their weight, and I moaned as he squeezed the soft weight, my head falling back against his chest. Slowly, he traced his thumb around each peak. The sensations made my hips rock, and I arched my back, seeking more of his addicting touch. His fingers evaded my nipples, not giving the pressure where I needed, teasing my desire higher and higher. Gods, all he had to do was touch me, and I forgot everything I'd learned on the run.

Finally, he took my nipples between his thumbs and forefingers, roughly pinching one then the other. "The things I want to do to your luscious little body," he said against the sensitive skin of my neck.

"Like what?" I whispered to him. My determination to resist him vanished, replaced by the same hunger that had taken me over the night of the ball.

"You want to know all the ways I want to fuck you?" My knees hit the edge of the cot, and I held my breath. "Then I'll tell you all about it after your punishment is over." Even the word *punishment* made me shiver with desire. Wait, punishment?

Lucien leaned down, and I felt the smooth edge of his claws along my hips and legs as he sliced my jeans, shredding them. A shudder rippled through me, not of fear but excitement. I briefly wondered if he could smell my arousal as I grew even wetter. He crouched behind me as my pants fell to the floor between my feet. I squealed when he gripped my hips and nipped my ass with his teeth.

Lucien hooked his fingers into my panties and tugged them down my legs. I moaned low and deep as he trailed hot, open-mouthed kisses in their wake. He took his time, the heat of his breath making goosebumps rise on my skin. His hands followed my curves as he stood, catching a claw under my bra strap and slipping it down my arms. I leaned back against his solid strength, naked and trembling with need for him.

Lucien pushed me onto my hands and knees on the bed and stepped back. I looked back at him over my shoulder. His eyes flashed, and I squirmed in response. "Grab your knees and spread your legs. Show me your pussy."

I bit my lip and rested my head on the bed to do as ordered. I reached to grab the backs of my knees, spreading my legs wide for him. His sharp intake of breath was a reward for my bravery, and I felt myself drip in response.

"Lucien, please…"

In answer, his hands landed on my ass, massaging my curves and eliciting another moan from me. The soft sound turned to a shocked gasp when his palm came down hard in a punishing slap. I flinched at the sting, relaxing when he massaged it away a moment later.

"You should not have run from me." His voice was guttural, showing his own tenuous hold on his control.

He raised his hand again, landing another hard slap to my ass before massaging away the ache. The heat between my legs built with every strike, arousing me further and making me frantic. I rocked back on my knees, eagerly meeting each spank.

"That's my good little witch, eager for her discipline," he praised.

My need to come was making me crazy. My skin felt unfamiliar, and I ached with need. I tightened my hold on my knees and gasped as both his palms came down hard on my abused ass.

"Should not have run from me…" he murmured, still sounding crazed as he rubbed his hardness against my overly sensitive flesh. It was as if spanking me relieved none of the tension within him. I ground back against him, seeking the release that was just out of my reach. He growled, low and deep. I felt the prick of his claws against my hips as he flipped me onto my back, and I finally caught sight of his madness. His eyes glowed red, and he looked deadly.

Lucien dropped to his knees and hooked my legs over his shoulders, bringing my pussy closer. His fiery breath bathed my needy flesh, and I undulated toward him, begging for his mouth and the press of his tongue. He groaned his approval and slowly licked me with one long swipe of his tongue, a move that nearly made me come out of my skin. I panted, my hips twisting in his grip, trying to catch his tongue when it retreated. He brought it back across me, and I moaned at the sensation. "Please, Lucien! I need more! Give me more."

I felt him smile against me. "You don't deserve it," he teased, then set upon me.

His tongue laved my clit, and I fisted my hands to keep from grinding against his mouth. With my legs resting against his broad shoulders and his tight grip on my hips, he was in control and could do whatever he wanted to my body. Instead of fear, the knowledge only increased my arousal.

Lucien locked his mouth over my core, stiffened his tongue inside me, and began to fuck me with it. My belly clenched, and I screamed as my climax rushed through me. My thighs squeezed his head, my muscles shaking. He swallowed my orgasm, growling against me, his glowing eyes locked on me. He continued to lick my sensitive folds, ignoring when I protested it was too soon to come again.

Lucien pulled back to snarl, "You are *mine.* You'll come as many times as I tell you to."

I could only moan in response, trying to pull away from him, but he focused his attention on my swollen, sensitive clit, and soon I was climaxing again. Lucien stood, dropping me back on the bed. Sweat misted my skin, my eyes glazed, my breasts shaking from my quick breaths. It took a moment for me to focus on him standing above me, hovering like a predator about to pounce. I couldn't remember why I was determined to run from him.

His hard shaft was outlined in his jeans, and I licked my lips at the sight. I quickly sat up, reaching for him and cupping him through the material. I clawed at his pants, ripping them open, desperate to get my hands on his cock. My lips parted, and I gasped at my first sight of him. He was huge and pierced. I trailed my fingers lovingly along the four barbells at the underside of his shaft. Jealousy seared me at the thought of anyone marking him in such a way. He was mine! I blinked, shocked at the thought. What was happening to me?

His swollen crown jutted towards me, practically begging for my mouth. Heat pulsed at my core as I looked up and saw him watching with hooded eyes as I explored him. I dropped my gaze and tightened my hand around his cock. Gods, he was huge. The dark head was like marble, pre-cum lingering on the tip, more forming as I watched. I moaned in sympathy, feeling his pain, and his cock jerked in response. "Poor Lucien." I nuzzled my face against the side of his shaft, delighting in his groan as his eyes flashed brighter.

"Suck on it. Now."

He loved ordering me, but I wanted him weak in the knees, out of control, like how I felt every time he was near. So, I ignored him, torturing him with short little licks of the crown, enjoying how the pre-cum was pearling for me.

"I love your taste, Lucien," I moaned, still unbearably aroused.

I scooted to the edge of the bed, my legs hanging over the side. I pumped my fist up and down the silken shaft and swirled my tongue over the head of his cock before wrapping my lips over it.

"Gods! Your fucking mouth."

I looked up at him as he threw his head back in pleasure, but he snapped it back within a few seconds, his eyes locked on me as if he didn't want to miss a second of this. Lucien's hands tangled in my hair as I took more of him, hollowing my cheeks as I sucked on him. My fist continued pumping him, my lips and hand meeting then retreating, both working together to make him come. With my eyes locked on his, I felt him stiffen, and his release climb his shaft.

"You're going to take my cum into your mouth. Swallow me down, every drop," he ordered, and I moaned in assent.

He came with a shout, his semen shooting down my throat, and I swallowed him, savoring the salty taste left behind. I continued licking him clean, trying to get more of him. He pulled me off him with a pop, his breathing ragged. He leaned down to kiss me hard and easily swept me up in his kiss. I was consumed by his touch, his scent, his taste. I reached for him, about to pull him on top of me so we could finish what we had only just begun.

The unfamiliar feeling of cold metal around my wrist made me pull back in surprise. The shock remained for long enough for the identical sensation to encircle my other wrist. I shoved Lucien away, glancing down at my hands. Cuffs? He wouldn't dare. As I watched, they shrank and grew to mid-forearm, adjusting to fit snugly around my wrists, leaving no space between the metal and my skin. I tried to claw them off, but there was no give in the spelled metal.

He'd trapped me. Why did I ever trust anyone? Lucien, the one person I had felt even slightly safe with, had betrayed me. When would I ever learn?

Fucking rule number fucking one.

"You asshole!" I screamed, jumping up, desperately trying to pry them off.

I let my fury roll over me, storming over to rifle through my rucksack, yanking on jeans along with another t-shirt. My body still felt wrong. Unfulfilled desire simmered in me, making my anger and sense of betrayal burn even brighter. Fully dressed, I whirled around, unleashing my anger, finding he had corrected his own clothes.

"So, what? You just had to get off one more time before turning me over?" I asked, my bitterness betrayed by my rough tone.

He reached out for me. "I had to make sure you couldn't run from me again. This was the only way."

I flinched and backed away, reaching for my magic, needing to escape. The familiar comfort of my powers had vanished. *No!* The worst thing you could do to a witch without killing them was to cut them off from their magic. For Lucien to seduce me just to do so...the blow was devastating. "I think I understand perfectly. You distracted me with sex, just so you could cuff me."

Lucien dropped his hand to his side as I shrank away from him. His voice was a deep growl when he said, "That wasn't originally my intention."

I whirled away from him, my fury heightened to dangerous levels. If he hadn't cuffed me, I would likely have leveled the building with my anger. "When will I learn that I can't trust anyone?"

First Malcolm, now Lucien. When would I realize that *vampire* meant betrayal?

New Rule No. 1: Trust No One, especially a vampire.

"Phoebe." He tugged me around to face him, but I shoved away from him again.

"Don't touch me! You really think I'm still going to sleep with you when you're about to turn me over for execution!!" I couldn't have survived all these years on the run just for another vampire to trick me. Not. Again.

His dumbstruck expression made me pause, even more so when he snarled, "Any attempt on your life is an act of war."

His eyes went bright red with his rage at the thought, cooling my anger a bit. He lurched forward, digging his hands into my arms as if he needed to make sure I was still alive. I was confused. None of this made any sense. He yanked me into his arms, even as I resisted, wrapping them tightly around me, kissing the top of my head. "I won't let anything happen to you, Phoebe. *Ever.*"

What exactly is going on here? I stood rigid in his arms and blurted, "What are you talking about? You *bound* my powers." Some part of me wanted him to have a good reason, but I knew *nothing* could justify it. Betrayal was betrayal, no matter the reason.

He stepped back, looking down at me. There was still a trace of madness in his eyes, barely held at bay. "I had to make sure you wouldn't run from me again."

I wrenched away from him, forcing his hands to drop. "Why me?"

I couldn't read the emotions in his eyes as he said, "Because it has to be you." He tried to take me in his arms again, but I dodged him, ignoring the flush of delight at his answer.

"What does that mean? Who am I to you?" I yelled at him. As much as I hated the thought of him with someone else, I couldn't be with Lucien. Despite how much I wanted him.

He thrust his hands forward, shouting, "My mate! You're my mate."

My mouth gaped for a second in total surprise. That was the absolute last thing I expected him to say. I hope I misunderstood.

"Please, *please,* tell me where you are from, that is a cute little term for someone you want to nail."

"It is not. You are her. The one I've waited millennia for. You are my queen."

"You're wrong. I'm not her. I'm just…not."

He frowned at me, his eyes narrowing as they returned to a bright green. "I am not wrong. You are my mate."

I glared down at my wrists, shaking the cuffs binding me. "These cuffs don't really vibe with what I've heard about immortal mates."

He covered the cuffs with his hands, forcing my eyes to his. "Tell me true. If I took them off, would you run? Even knowing what you are to me?"

If the legends I'd heard were, in fact, true, his health and power would steadily decline until he claimed me. I couldn't soften at the thought. My eyes drifted from his, and he had his answer.

His hands dropped, fisting in anger. "Then they remain. You're coming with me, Phoebe. I can keep you safe from whoever is after you."

Lucien didn't give me a chance to answer. He reached down to swipe my go-bag, rucksack, and Bast's carrier from the floor before grasping my arm in an unyielding grip and forcing me to follow him. My familiar had been strangely quiet during the entire encounter, probably not sensing an actual threat from Lucien. That made one of us. Lucien was a bigger threat than even the Council.

The sun hit me full force in the face, blinding me for a moment as he pushed me into a darkened SUV. The well-dressed man from earlier was in the driver's seat. How were all of these vampires suddenly able to walk around during the day?

"Hi." I waved awkwardly, unsure of what I should be doing. How did one react when you were forced into a car against your will after your powers had been bound?

Lucien climbed in next to me and pulled me onto his lap. I put my hands on his chest and leaned back, desperate to create space between us. I needed to marshal my chaotic thoughts. "Where are you taking me?"

The cuffs glinted on my wrists, and I frowned again at the bindings. He lifted my chin with his finger, forcing me to look him in the eyes.

"Somewhere you'll be safe. Tell me who's after you."

Rule No. 3: Don't Tell Anyone Anything Ever. Especially assholes who kidnap you.

I remained mulishly silent, refusing to answer. Just because I might have been submissive to him sexually didn't mean I was normally or at all. I wasn't going to reward him with more information about me, not after he bound my powers, making me as helpless as a mortal.

I got off of his lap and moved away from him, finding my own seat. Anger filled me that he *let* me. We both knew he could have easily stopped me. Then I was disgusted with myself that I cared. My emotions were all over the place. I snapped, "Why should I tell you anything?"

He looked at me with a single raised brow, green eyes sparkling. "Tell me who's after you."

I snarled, "You know what, someone is after me."

His eyes narrowed. "Tell me."

I crossed my arms over my chest, glaring at him. "Some controlling, high-handed *asshole* who can't take a hint."

His lips curled back from his teeth in distaste, and he turned away from me to glare out the window.

With his focus off of me, I scoured my memory for anything I might know about vampire mates. The information was spotty. In my defense, why would I have ever devoted time to studying a vampire's mate when I was struggling to survive? I knew immortal species with predestined mates, like lycans, demons, and vampires would never leave them in danger. That didn't mean I could trust Lucien. I glared down at the cuffs in renewed fury.

"I'm taking you home. *Our* home," he said, breaking the silence between us. His arms were crossed in anger, frustration simmering from him as if it were my fault he'd kidnapped me and bound my powers.

I didn't respond or ask more questions. I opened Bast's carrier and placed the familiar in my lap. The black cat purred, curled into a ball, and immediately went to sleep. Lucien turned toward me multiple times, opened his mouth repeatedly before closing it and facing out the window. I ignored him.

The cab of the SUV remained silent until we reached the private airstrip outside of Metairie. We came to a stop on the tarmac next to a small private jet. The well-dressed vampire turned off the car and got out, waiting patiently outside of the car. Lucien stepped out and turned back, holding his hand out for me, waiting for me to take it.

I shot his hand a withering look and allowed Bast to jump down first. I stepped down after her, dodging Lucien's hand and gripping my go bag and rucksack. Lucien shoved his hand into his pocket and glanced over my shoulder at the well-dressed man with narrowed eyes. "I'll join you in a moment, Phoebe."

I scoffed at him and followed Bast as she bounded up the steps of the plane. The private jet was luxurious, but I kept my gaze down. I found the farthest seat in the back and threw my bags into the plush leather seat next to me. I crossed my arms over my chest and waited for takeoff.

XI

THE REALM OF MORTALS.
OUTSIDE NEW ORLEANS, LOUISIANA.

I SPOKE WITH ELIJAH, inviting him back to Romania. Although, I was sure that he heard my invitation more as a command. It was clear from the way Elijah noted my possessive actions toward Phoebe that he knew she was my mate. The other vampire had always been observant. I should have known he would eventually figure it out. What I had not counted on was my reaction to Phoebe. I hadn't expected such a loss of my otherwise infallible control.

If I was honest with myself, some part of my motivation in strong-arming Elijah into accompanying us was because I was *slightly* concerned about being alone with Phoebe. I was fucking up at every turn. I knew the look of devastation on Phoebe's face when she realized what I had done would haunt me for years to come. Maybe Elijah's presence would stop me from being a complete ass.

Yet, you don't truly regret it, do you? Without the cuffs, she wouldn't be here.

Stupid conscience, pointing out the lies I told myself. My stomach rolled when I recalled how Phoebe wouldn't let me touch her, avoiding it at all costs and struggling out of my arms. Our bond demanded I be near her, touch her, hold her, kiss her. Yet, she wanted nothing to do with me. The one woman to resist me would be my mate. Of. Fucking. Course.

With her ability to tear reality, she could vanish the second I turned my back, just like my mother. I had turned toward her during my coronation, hoping to see her luminescent with pride. I had longed to see something other than the cold face of indifference I'd known my entire childhood. Instead, there had been nothing but an empty space. I'd turned my back, and she had vanished. It seemed history wanted to repeat itself. My mate hates me, and she wants to leave me.

I shuddered, recalling the way her eyes had blazed with fury and disgust. I doubted any other vampire had ever struggled like this with their mates. All the fated bondings I'd heard about over the millennia were always of the same species. A female vampire would feel the pull like I did. But Phoebe wasn't a vampire, and I was forced to bind her powers just to keep her in the same room with me. It was an act I doubted she would ever forgive. I was so fucked.

I spoke briefly to the two mortal pilots as they prepared for takeoff. The stewardess pulled the stairs in, and the sight made a small breath of relief hiss through my clenched teeth. I could just see Phoebe's red hair out of the corner of my eye, and once the doors were closed, she was trapped. Fuck, that sounded so wrong. Once we got home, I would start my campaign of convincing her to stay with me.

Do you really think she's going to want to stay with you? After what you did? She wants to leave you, just like Mother. Just like Cassandra. I couldn't stop the self-recriminations and the thoughts that threatened to steal my sanity.

Elijah stretched out on one couch, throwing an arm over his eyes, attempting to give us some modicum of privacy in the small aircraft. I was thankful but had no idea how to proceed. I needed to work on defusing Phoebe's rage. There had to be a way to draw her mind away from the loss of her magic and toward what she could gain if she gave me a chance. I just had to figure out what that was.

It wasn't like I was planning to keep her powerless forever, just until I could trust she wouldn't leave me. But with a power like hers, could I ever truly trust her not to leave? I hated how tempted I was to listen to the insidious voice in my head, even as I strode to the back of the plane.

I could not let Phoebe's anger dissuade me. She had put her bag on the open chair next to her, practically a neon sign of *back off, fucker*. Fortunately, she didn't have enough belongings to take up each of the four seats, so I sat across from her. Her cat jumped onto my lap the moment I sat down, curling into a ball for a nap. I knew her mistress would be as easily won over.

The grinding of machinery echoed from outside as the plane was prepared for flight. Within the small cabin, it sounded louder than what you would normally hear on a large aircraft. My eyes landed on Phoebe, my brows furrowing in confusion when I saw how pale her face was and the way she clutched the armrests. I focused my hearing on her racing heartbeat. It took me a minute to realize her heart slammed in time to the noises from outside.

"Those are normal sounds. It's just the pilots preparing for takeoff," I assured her.

Another loud bang made her heart jump with fear. I froze for a moment, unsure of how to comfort her. Everything within me was ordering me to soothe her, but I was lost at how to do so. No one had ever comforted me before. I nudged the familiar into the open seat next to me. The cat hissed and glared at me as I reached out and unbuckled Phoebe's seat belt. I pulled my mate into my lap and wrapped my arms around her, locking her against me.

"Are you afraid to fly?" I asked.

Her eyes were slightly wild, but she didn't try to move away. I counted that as a small win.

"I've never needed to fly before, have I?" she snapped.

There had to be a way to close the gulf between us. It wasn't a chasm I alone had created. She had run before I cuffed her, but I made it wider.

I tucked a stray lock of hair behind her ear, relieved when she didn't pull away from me this time. I couldn't seem to stop touching her. Even now, with her heart racing in fear, her anger with me simmering, I still needed to make sure she was *here*. I needed to assure myself that she wasn't some fevered figment from my dreams.

We needed to be a unit by the time the Elders arrived at Întuneric. News traveled fast in the world of immortals, and the Elders would flock to our home once they heard of my mating. If we weren't *together* by then, the Elders would create a rift between us, one I doubted could ever be healed. The Elders comprised a pseudo-council of sorts, but they usually only met once a century or before a *Great Event.* A new queen would definitely classify as a Great Event. I tightened my hold on Phoebe, my heart pounding at the feel of her in my arms.

I was already at a disadvantage having a non-vampire as my queen. The Elders made no secret that they hoped my queen would be from one of their lines. I doubted they ever considered she would be anything but a vampire. I couldn't predict how they would react to Phoebe, especially if they discovered her power. So many unpredictable variables in my future. Two weeks ago, I was complaining about the monotony of immortality. *Fate clearly took that as a fucking challenge.*

Phoebe needed a distraction to take her mind off of her fear. I scrambled to think of various points of discussion. Her favorite poet? Philosopher? Food? Color? Musician? Instead, I blurted out, "Were you always able to create rifts?"

Her eyes met mine. "No, not until I was a teenager. I could only go a couple of blocks at first, but the more I practiced, the farther I could go." She smiled softly, and I felt some of the tension leave her body. I brushed a tendril of her hair back from her face. She didn't seem to notice, not moving away from my touch as she continued, "I got stuck in Tír nAill once when I was eighteen. It took me two days to figure out how to return."

My breath caught in my chest, my mind creating the image of a young Phoebe wandering the treacherous realm. I pushed away the panic. She was safe and in my arms.

"A witch child stuck in the realm of the fae. What could have gone wrong?" I murmured, partly to myself and partly to her.

Tír nAill was such a treacherous realm. The fae enjoyed tricking and trapping immortals and mortals alike into slavery. Titania reformed the realm when she took the throne, outlawing the practice of slavery. Since their marriage, Oberon followed suit, persuaded by his new queen. Now both the Seelie and Unseelie Courts were pushing for the abolishment, though many fought against the change.

"My mother really let me have it when I finally made it back." Her face dropped slightly, her vivid eyes dimming. My arms tightened around her. I wished I could absorb some of her pain into my body. I'd never connected like that with my mother. She was always the ethereal, untouchable goddess, never the warm, comforting maternal figure.

I covered my flash of discontent, murmuring, "I'm trying to imagine having a teenager able to rift off to another realm when upset with me."

I couldn't help but smile, imagining Cassie with such a power. Her foresight was already a major pain in the ass. It was a challenge having a daughter who could predict the exact moment you would discover she'd painted the halls of Întuneric Castel pink. She had made herself scarce until my temper cooled, and I could find the humor in the situation. Instead of berating her, I'd scooped the young Oracle into my arms and told her I never was a fan of all the dark walls, anyway. I could still hear her laughter as we spent the rest of the day painting other walls in the castle bright colors. Perhaps she'd known that was how I would react.

The plane ascended, and Phoebe clutched me tighter. I really shouldn't have felt such delight that she clung to me when she was afraid. I was so pathetic, enjoying that small moment with her.

"Tell me about your parents," I cajoled, attempting to distract her again. I wanted to comfort her, soothe her, and make sure that she had no desire to leave my lap. She smiled softly at me, and I kissed her forehead before she could pull away.

"My mother and father were both powerful witches and Council members. They were my best friends. They were my everything." Her eyes dulled, and she looked unseeing over my shoulder. "Someone murdered them when I was nineteen."

"How?" I asked, again pulling her tight as if I could physically ease the remembered pain of her parents' deaths. I was shocked when she rested her head on my shoulder, pressing her face into my neck. A part of me wanted to push about accepting me as her mate, as her future, but I knew it would break this fragile truce. It was like a gossamer thread shroud of a truce surrounded us. I knew it was temporary, but I wanted it to last as long as possible.

She snuggled closer and yawned, allowing me to comfort her. "I came home one day and found them dead. The Council looked into it, but they had no leads on who would want to harm them."

Her voice broke, and I stroked her hair, humming soothingly to her. I silently vowed to find out more about her parents later. I had resources the Witches

Council could only dream of, like a two-thousand-year-old Oracle.

"I never met my father," I said, "and my mother is…complicated." Phoebe's breath was warm against me as she waited for me to continue. I hoped that if I shared more of my past, this moment wouldn't have to end. "My mother told me nothing about my father, only that he was the first vampire. Whenever I pressed for more, she would claim to have forgotten the conversation." I didn't know if she actually forgot or just didn't want to speak of him. Eventually, I'd discovered more about my father through one of the Vampire Elders, my father's brother, Ambrogio.

"Does she still live with you?"

The more she was involved with my life, the easier it would be to convince her to stay, at least in theory. I had to draw her in, force the bond. I didn't have any actual experience with mates, and I needed time to prepare her before we had to face the Elders.

"She lives in the Ethereal Realm."

The Ethereal was the realm of the gods, colloquially known as the land of slumber or Ether. Most pantheons slept to conserve their power. Few knew the truth of my past, or my parentage, outside of the Elders, but this was *my mate*. I had already revealed more to her in this small interaction than I ever shared with another.

"My mother is the Goddess of Vampires," I confessed. "She created the first vampire by accident during the first days of her life. She often felt responsible for the chaos the vampires caused after their creation. As Goddess of the Moon, she had stumbled upon a mortal dying after being set upon by bandits. She felt pity for him and fed him her blood, believing it would heal him. It did, but it also bound him to her, making him vulnerable to the sun. He craved the blood that had changed him, giving him immortal strength and speed. She watched in horror as the now immortal, Endymion, discovered he had the ability to change other mortals. Rage filled her at his sloppiness, and she cursed him and all vampires twice."

Phoebe shifted against me, her body relaxing further into my embrace. "Curses?" she asked, her voice drowsy.

I brushed my lips against her forehead and nodded. "The first curse was the frenzy. Endymion would lose control if he went without blood for several days, setting upon any mortal who crossed his path. His eyes would turn red when the frenzy was high. My mother had done so as revenge against him for changing other mortals so recklessly. The second curse was more of an afterthought on her part. The curse of the ταίρι prevented vampires from reproducing with anyone except for their predestined mate. She feared that a born vampire would be infinitely more powerful than a made one, so she had to cut off the possibility of a world of born vampires. Though, if I am honest, mates might be fate's way of keeping the immortal population under control. Almost all immortal species can only have children with their fated mate."

Phoebe yawned again, her voice softer and slower with sleep. "Your father was a vampire and your mother, a goddess? Is that how you became king?"

Most immortal species had designated royal lines, established when they were first brought to life, often after interference by the divine. Royals brought order to a world filled with constant war. Unlike mortals, immortals had the benefit of an eternal amount of time. They would argue a single issue for eternity. Monarchs prevented that kind of indecision.

"My mother was ashamed of what monsters the creatures had become. They rampaged through the realm, killing indiscriminately, but she couldn't bring herself to kill them. As the goddess of a species, certain responsibilities fell to her, such as instituting a royal line. So, she had me."

She later confessed to me that Endymion was my father, the first of her vampires. Zeus later cursed him to eternal sleep, keeping them apart forever. Endymion was my mother's mate, but that mattered little to the spiteful Olympian.

I felt Phoebe frown against my shoulder. "That sounds cold. My mother always made sure that I knew how loved I was and that I was their greatest joy," she admitted.

I envied her that. Unfortunately, despite my many partners, there were very few I would call genuine friends. I never had someone I trusted, at least not completely.

"My mother loved me, in her own way," I hedged. "But, I was a means to an end."

To my surprise, Phoebe tightened her arms around me. My initial instinct was to shift away from her, but I stopped myself. My lovers never sought to comfort me, always taking pleasure where they could before departing. But Phoebe's soft, warm body filled me with contentment.

I kissed the top of her head softly and stroked her hair. The fiery mass played through my fingers, and her breathing evened out as she fell asleep. I doubted she had slept the night before, planning to run from me. My mate was such a mystery. She was running from something but refused my protection. She had to know I could shelter her better than any other immortal in the realm.

Her scent flooded me when she shifted in her sleep, soothing my mind, the frenzy absent in her presence. *Why now?* Why was Fate finally giving me a mate *now?* Ten thousand years of fighting and never-ending boredom. I'd spent millennia trying to fill the yawning emptiness inside me, and Fate, the vengeful bitch, waited until I could not recognize her in Tír nAill.

Boredom would be the furthest thing from my mind with Phoebe in my life. Instead of the bland future I dreaded, I would spend my days and nights making love to her. I doubted I would ever tire of her body. When I could *finally* share her, we would have children. Princes and princesses who would likely raise all kinds of hells if they inherited even a fraction of their mother's power. I just had to convince her to stay.

My first priority was to find out who was after her. I hated that my mate felt even a second of fear and wanted to wipe any threat to her from the earth. Any who dared to harm her would serve as a cautionary tale for all. I was desperate to know every secret she hid behind her violet eyes and wished she trusted me enough to reveal all. I still knew so little about her and would need to proceed with caution and patience.

Unlike lycans, vampires didn't actively pursue their mates, believing fate would provide. Matches between different species were *extremely* rare, and as I was learning, fraught with problems. If Phoebe was a vampire, she would have recognized me as her mate and would not be resisting so aggressively. But then, if that were the case, I wouldn't have *Phoebe*.

A huge yawn interrupted my musings, and I recalled that I had barely slept since first meeting her. I closed my eyes for a couple of minutes and considered carrying her to the segmented bedroom at the back of the plane but decided against it, worried that any movement might wake her. I clutched her more tightly to me and allowed myself to drift off.

XII

THE REALM OF MORTALS.
OUTSIDE OF BUCHAREST, ROMANIA.

But I am not imagining that I hit something on the floor. I sit back on my ass and hiss out another cry as I try to avoid pressing against my injured leg. As I blink again, my vision sharpens a little more, healing from whatever had decimated the Council chambers.

It's enough for me to see what I tripped over.

MY EYES SNAPPED OPEN to the feeling of being tossed around in a sardine can. On instinct, I tightened my arms around the seat, slamming my eyes shut again and burying my face into its warmth. It took me a moment to realize my seat was *breathing*. I opened my eyes slowly this time, surprised to see Lucien still held me, his brows furrowed in sleep. Yet Lucien never moved and hadn't let go of me. There was no way he could be comfortable with me in his lap like this. I was not exactly light, and I would never be model skinny, not with tits and ass that no amount of dieting could get rid of. As a kid, I became very familiar with belts because pants that fit my outrageous ass gaped at my waist.

I shouldn't have let him hold me. I should have fought to get out of his lap, but I was weak and wanted comfort. Despite my better judgment, I'd let him soothe my fears. I tried to wiggle out of his arms, but his hold only tightened around me. It was clear I wasn't going anywhere at the moment. I huffed and disentangled my arms from around him, shifting to look out the window.

A beautiful countryside swam into view once we pierced the cloud cover. We could be anywhere. The plane flattened, the human pilot yelling back to alert us of our impending landing. I thought again of trying to get out of Lucien's lap, but the plane bounced and skidded as we hit the ground. I gave up trying to look brave and clung to him for dear life, my heart slamming against my chest. Once the commotion eased, the well-dressed man appeared next to us. An amused smile quirked his lips when he noticed me clinging to Lucien.

"I don't think he's been sleeping," he commented in his creole-accented voice, gesturing to Lucien with a nod of his head. I refused to feel bad.

This was getting too confusing. I needed to distance myself from him and reached out for my magick out of reflex. I needed its comforting presence, the feeling of the world breathing in and out with me. But there was nothing. My senses felt as if they were wrapped in wool. *Quite the reality check.* I shoved hard against Lucien this time, falling out of his arms and tumbling to the ground in front of him.

The other man made no move to help me up, staring at me with a smirk. I'm sure he was recalling Lucien's reaction the last time he touched me. I huffed and flicked a lock of my rebellious hair out of my face, glaring at the other vampire. He merely shrugged, never dropping his smirk. It was obvious that his fear of Lucien's reprisal was greater than the pull of his Southern manners.

I rose and looked out the small window again. "Where are we?"

The airplane taxied to a full stop, making Lucien come awake with a jolt. His fangs were exposed and his eyes red, ready to attack at a moment's notice. I started in surprise at how absolutely *vicious* he looked. At that moment, I understood why those vampires had run from the alley rather than face him. I gulped, not taking my eyes off of him, tempted to back away.

He remained on edge until his wild eyes locked on me. The tension dissipated from his face, the mad red fading from his eyes. He leaned his head back and reached for my hand, pulling it to his lips to place a soft kiss on my palm. I was too stunned at the transition to pull away and felt the flush of pleasure creep into my cheeks. I hadn't blushed in years. As a natural redhead, when I blushed, it was with my entire body. I thought I'd broken that habit years ago. Yet, a simple gesture from Lucien had me reacting as if I was a teenager again.

I studied Lucien, holding his gaze, ruby embers still burning in the depths of his green eyes. His power was a palpable thing. I wondered if he could possibly protect me but immediately rejected the idea. I couldn't think like that, and I wouldn't think like that. No one since my parents had protected me, and I had always learned to protect myself. I'd never needed a man to do anything, and I would not start with Lucien.

He glanced out the window and stood, his frame seeming to fill the space. I stepped back as he towered over me, having forgotten how *large* he was. "Ah! We've landed."

Lucien refused to relinquish my hand, grasping my rucksack and go bag with his free one. Bast jumped down to follow us as the flight attendants lowered the stairs. I hesitated again at the top of the steps, a shiver of foreboding going through me as I looked at the ground. By staying in one place for an indefinite amount of time, I was painting a giant target on my back with the words: *COME KILL ME.*

If the Council came for me, I would be helpless and at their mercy without my powers. I refused to allow that, not again, never again. I had to get these cuffs off, even if I had to cut my hands off to do it.

The well-dressed vampire deplaned first, and we followed, Lucien still clutching my hand. The sun was low, the time difference making it morning once again.

Lucien smiled brightly up at me from the lowest step, pulling his sunglasses on. "Welcome to Bucharest, Phoebe." I knew I would never forget the image of Lucien's smile as he looked up at me with an expression I was afraid to name.

Romania? I was in Romania? I had never left the country before without using a rift and the sudden sensation of jet lag dragged on my mind. Exhaustion weighed on me, even though I'd slept the entire plane ride. How did people do this? Lucien took my first stuttering step down the stairs as consent and pulled me along after him. I really needed to stop allowing him to do that. I was not docile. Well, at least not usually.

Another black SUV idled nearby for us, a couple of mortals waiting beside it. They bowed to Lucien when he approached. I rolled my eyes as the three of us got into the rear of the vehicle. I got that Lucien was *royalty* or whatever, but the bowing? It was a little much in this day and age.

Once we were settled in the SUV, I thrust my hand toward the well-dressed vampire. "I'm Phoebe."

Instead of taking my hand and shaking it as I expected, he shot a sly look at Lucien and pressed a kiss to the back of it. His voice was even deeper, and his southern drawl, smoother, losing its creole twang. "Elijah Jackson, ma'am."

Lucien's head swung toward the other vampire, his eyes narrowing at him. He snatched my hand away when Elijah held onto it longer than necessary, kissing it in the *exact spot* Elijah had.

I yanked my hand away, rubbing it along my jeans. "Was that necessary?"

Lucien smirked at me. "Completely."

The countryside sped by, and I pressed against the window to catch sight of it. Picturesque farmland rolled out in front of me. People walked along the side of the street as we approached the city center, soaking in the rising sun and crisp air. The cobbled streets rocked the SUV as we drove, the old buildings of Bucharest towering around us, passing by too quickly for me to appreciate them fully. We departed the bustling town, moving farther from the cluster of people.

Lucien shifted closer to me on the seat, leaving me no room to back away. He pointed out various sites as we traveled. His pleasure at showing me his home was reflected in the way his accent deepened. His scent flooded my senses when he leaned over me, brushing against me each time he pointed out historical landmarks and remarked on his own history with the city. I crossed my arms over my chest, trying to make myself as small as possible, avoiding touching him as much as possible. The smell of him was driving me insane. The more he flooded my senses, the more I forgot why I needed to be plotting my escape.

"We're almost home, Phoebe," he murmured into my ear, his breath on my skin making me shiver. What was it about Lucien that frayed my nerves?

"*You* are almost home," I snapped. He frowned but refused to back away. I needed distance, and he refused to provide it, pressing on me until I wanted to scream. I just needed to think, clear my head, focus. But I could do none of those things when he was close. I could barely remember my name when his hands were on me. He had kidnapped me, and worse, he bound my powers. I needed to remember that.

New Rule No. 1: Trust No One. Especially Lucien.

The trees parted after an hour of ascending a steep mountain road. I caught sight of the castle and couldn't help but gasp. It was *hideous. A gargantuan eyesore*, and the only access to it was from a single stone bridge supported by massive arches that sunk deep into the ground. Carved of midnight stone, it occupied the whole plateau. Its towers reached into the sky like monolithic sentinels. As we drove closer, I noticed the turrets actually spiraled, making the castle seem even more twisted and dangerous. Each one came to a tight point, seeming to pierce the sky. The entire building appeared to jut from the mountainside. The drop from the edge of the ramparts was almost a mile into the valley below.

It looked more intimidating and foreboding than I could have dreamed. The longer I stared at it, the harder I shook. The absolute darkness of the stone made it even starker against the bucolic countryside, the only light coming from the rough cut-outs retrofitted with glass. A sparse copse of trees lined the grand entrance, the only other color against the ominous black.

"You grew up here?" I asked, unable to stop the question.

I couldn't imagine growing up in such an imposing place. My home had been full of warmth and magic. We did everything as a family, from homeschooling to magic lessons to playing with toys and fawning over celebrities. Gods, how I missed them.

"Yes, it was my mother's gift to me for my coronation. She thought the king of the vampires should have a home that displayed his strength." His voice rang with disdain. At least he didn't sound overly proud of the imposing structure.

"It's so big. Who lives here with you?" I couldn't take my eyes off the monstrosity as we continued our ascent.

I tried to imagine a little Lucien running through the halls of the enormous structure. My brows furrowed, and I bit my lip. Lucien was so powerful and imposing it was a struggle to picture him as a child, but when I focused a little harder, I imagined a little boy with my eyes and his looks.

Where had that thought come from?

I shook myself, unable to afford fanciful thoughts like that. I had zero plans to stay with Lucien. The second I got these cuffs off, *boy, bye.*

Rule No. 5: Abandon Everything at a Moment's Notice, even Lucien. No, especially Lucien.

"You mean besides you?" he quipped. I shot him a withering look, and his smile died. "There's a whole passel of servants, and vampire nobles filter in and out every couple of years. You can invite anyone you like to stay with us."

There was no one to invite. Any friends I'd once had turned against me when I blew up the Council, and my family was dead. I only had myself to rely on. I couldn't even rely on Lucien. For all his talk about our supposed *bond*, he'd still bound my powers, the worst possible thing you could *ever* do to a witch.

As we drove across the bridge, I noticed several groups of people awaited us near the entrance. I could tell most were mortal, though a group of about fifty vampires stood in the shade away from the sun, and one young blonde woman stood pacing in front of them all. Every time she walked back and forth, she stopped, looked around as though surprised by her location, then continued on.

The car pulled to a stop, and I allowed Lucien to help me from the back this time, my eyes still on the castle. The mortal servants stood straighter, but the vampires looked bored. It was the blonde woman who drew my interest away from the massive structure. Even with my powers bound, I could sense the magic rolling off her. She wasn't a witch. We gave off a very specific energy, but she was different. Her energy wrapped around her, constantly shifting and frenetic. It made my head spin just to be near her.

"Lucien!" the young woman called, launching herself into his arms, forcing him to drop my hand. I smothered the immediate annoyance I felt when he spun the blonde bombshell around, laughing with her before settling her back on her feet.

Lucien smiled down at the blonde fondly. "I have you to thank for the audience?"

I ignored the taste of metal on my tongue, waiting for Lucien to let go of the woman. I was most definitely *not* jealous. You need to want someone to be jealous, right? Since I didn't want to be with Lucien, I *wasn't* jealous. Nope, not at all, no jealousy here.

I was tempted to dismiss them both and continue into the castle, not because I was jealous, but because they bored me. Yes, I was bored, not jealous. Maybe if I kept lying to myself, I might even believe it.

When I took a step back to storm into the dark castle, Elijah stopped me with a light hand on my arm. I frowned at him, and he smirked, his bright white teeth sparkling against his dark skin. I decided all vampires are high-handed pricks, especially the one who finally seemed to realize I was still here and turned to introduce the blonde. "Phoebe, Elijah, I'd like to introduce my daughter, Cassandra."

Daughter? The title sent my thoughts spiraling. An immortal male could only have children with his fated mate. If Lucien had a daughter already, I couldn't be his queen. I glanced down at my cuffs again. I couldn't be that stupid. Was this all a ploy to turn me over?

Cassandra elbowed Lucien in the side and added, "Adopted daughter. He took me in when I was young." She shot me a strange look, her eyes going dull and far away, the blue closer to a stormy grey. It almost appeared, for a single fleeting moment, her entire iris was going *white.*

Elijah bowed to Cassandra. "It's an honor to make your acquaintance."

Cassandra smiled again, but her eyes remained a vacant, stormy grey. "It is an honor, I know. Gifts and sacrifices would not be amiss."

I smothered a laugh at her response and Elijah's look of confusion. Lucien moved back to my side, retaking my hand. The vampires across the courtyard gasped at the action, followed by a shocked inhale, when he announced, "I would like to introduce my consort, Phoebe Silvano, Queen of Vampires."

My mouth dropped open in shock at the introduction. That high-handed son of a bitch. The inhale of shocked silence continued, and then suddenly, everyone was tripping over themselves to bow or curtsy to me. One of the vampire nobles bowed too far out of the shade, letting out a pained yelp before jumping back to safety.

When they finished, they locked eyes on me, waiting for something. My palms started to sweat at the attention, and I tried not to let my nerves show, even as Lucien squeezed my hand reassuringly. I had no idea what they were waiting for, a speech or something? Cassandra looped her arm through mine, drawing me away from Lucien and heading toward the castle, ignoring the fawning vampire court. I tensed immediately at the blonde's grip, rule one blaring through my head yet again.

Arm in arm, we strolled casually forward, or rather, Cassandra did. My every step felt like a death knell, each footfall bringing me closer to doom. The castle's massive doors swung open, revealing that an even darker interior matched the black exterior, though thankfully retrofitted for electric light. Cassandra pulled me past the gaping vampires, who didn't dare come any closer. They merely watched me closely as I stepped inside Lucien's castle. I tried to yank my arm from Cassandra's as we passed through the threshold, but the other woman merely held on tighter.

Inside, the castle appeared even colder and emptier. The black stone ceilings and floors had sucked up any warmth and sense of home. I couldn't believe this was where Lucien grew up.

"Did you grow up here?" I asked Cassandra.

The other woman hummed a discordant tune under her breath, continuing on as if she hadn't heard the question. She showed me into what I immediately recognized as Lucien's room. It was just so...*royal.* The dark stone of the castle was slightly lighter in here, and a large black crystal chandelier hung from the vaulted ceiling, lighting up the massive space. An area rug of silver and grey partially covered a design built into the stone floor and kept the cold from seeping into my shoes. Everything in the room seemed to revolve around the huge four-poster bed. The entire room reeked of *the king.* The only surprise was the color of his bedding. I quirked a brow, not having guessed he would be a fan of lilac.

My gaze caught on the seal hanging above the bed. It was a wooden circle painted silver and black, depicting a forest with the moon shining brightly from above. The cut of the dark castle into the mountainside, outlined by the moonlight, made me shiver involuntarily. The castle looked so lonely, reaching for the moon forever out of its reach.

I yanked my gaze from the seal, focusing again on the bed. I stared at it before flushing with realization. *My eyes.* The bedding was the same color as my eyes. I didn't belong there. I was no one, just a witch with a body count, not someone's queen. I pulled away from Cassandra, crossing my arms over my stomach and taking a step back. "I'm not staying here."

Cassie was dusting imaginary lint from her shoulder, but my words finally drew her attention. "You know he won't let you leave."

Bast walked past us and jumped onto the bed, stretching before curling into a ball. I frowned at my familiar as she watched me with a bored expression. The normally particular feline was already at home in her new surroundings.

Cassandra clapped in delight at the cat, cooing to it, "Aren't you just the prettiest thing? Yes, you are!"

To my surprise, the finicky familiar loved Cassandra, rolling over to let her pet her belly. Familiars were often used to focus a new witch's powers, but Bast always seemed like *more.* The feline often sensed my moods, and sometimes I could swear that the cat observed me as if expecting something.

"Cassandra, I'm not staying in this room with Lucien. He's taken much from me," I said, highly conscious of the constriction of the cuffs.

Cassandra ignored me, and I looked down at my hands again, flexing my fingers, still reaching for my magic. My head snapped up at the sound of Cassandra's voice vibrating with power.

"Poor little lost witch, confronted with such a destiny. She doesn't even know it's possible to be what she is. So much agony in the past, and still more to come." The other woman spoke so softly that I thought she was still speaking to Bast for a second.

"What does that mean?" I demanded, trying again to place the strange glow of magic I sensed from the other woman. It was so potent that even with my powers bound, I could see it.

The color leeched from Cassandra's bright blue gaze, turning white again. She was drifting away from me. Her eyes remained empty but filled with tears as she dropped her hand from Bast. The voice that vibrated with power a moment before was suddenly shaking. "So much to remember. People, places, things, queens, dragons, wolves. How will I remember them?"

I reached out, gripping the other woman's upper arms, turning to face me.

"Cassandra? Can you hear me?"

I snapped my fingers in front of her several times, watching in relief as some color returned to her eyes. "You have to be ready, Phoebe. Will you be ready?"

I opened my mouth to respond, but the other woman suddenly twirled away from me. Her eyes returned to their normal bright blue, her voice back to being lilting and cheerful.

"If you don't want to stay in here, there are tons of other rooms you can use. Follow me," Cassandra called, spinning out the door and forcing me to follow. Bast remained on Lucien's bed, looking bored.

Traitorous familiar.

Cassandra led me down two flights of stairs, three different hallways, and into another sumptuously designed room. I peppered her with questions about what she'd said earlier, but she claimed to not understand what I was talking about. The new room wasn't nearly as big as Lucien's, but it was much nicer than the apartment I'd left behind in New Orleans. I needed the distance from Lucien and time to figure out my next move, to find a way out.

I wasn't ready to be someone's mate, much less a *queen*. I could barely keep myself alive, let alone be responsible for an entire species. There had to be a way out of these cuffs. But if I ran, I wouldn't have him. I hated the treacherous thought whispering through my head. Besides, I didn't have him now!

I felt the delayed release of jet lag come over me but refused to fall asleep without having it out with Lucien or at least making *some* headway on my escape plan. My first step would be to learn my enemy's strengths and weaknesses to use them against him. I needed to have a plan for getting out of the castle if I couldn't get the cuffs off and rift away.

Cassandra had silently departed after showing me the bedroom, and I'd lost my only guide through the massive labyrinth. I forged ahead anyway, wandering through the hallways, hoping to stumble across a library or something similar. I needed anything that could help me learn more about the area. The castle's many switchbacks, dead ends, and identical passageways made it impossible to navigate. It was as if someone had deliberately designed it that way, and I realized they probably had.

It took me almost an hour of wrong turns to find the library. I opened the large doors and couldn't stop my gasp at the enormity of the room. The shelves were carved from the black stone and stretched to the cavernous ceiling. Books and manuscripts in hundreds of different languages covered every inch of the room. I wondered if Lucien knew them all.

I trailed my fingers lovingly over the spines. Despite what the other witches might have said after I lost my grimoires, I revered knowledge. Though the loss of the books had been freeing in a way. Without the strictly regimented spells laid out to me within their pages, I was forced to come up with my own, branching outside the dictates of the Council. For me, no longer was it Aegis studies battle and Margaux studies healing.

The longer I was without those tomes, the more I realized how truly ridiculous the Council's edict of power segregating was. If each familial grimoire contained the only spells allowed by each line, we were weak separately and strong together. It made sense that the Council would want to keep individual lines weaker than the collective whole, but it made us unnecessarily vulnerable to other species who preyed upon us.

We should be sharing grimoires, ensuring that knowledge spread throughout the lines to prevent any type from dying out. As an Atreus descendent, I studied battle magic to lead our armies into war should it ever come to that. However, I was a healer on my mother's side, the Margaux. Her line was responsible for all those who came to me with their wounds. Why couldn't I be both? Why did we have to choose? No one, including my parents, had been able to give me a satisfactory answer. If those witches in New Orleans had learned shield magic, they might still be alive. So why hinder us? Why not spread that kind of knowledge to all witches? Not just some?

My finger snagged on a black leather-bound tome with silver writing etched on the side, pulling me from her musings. *The Vampyr.*

Rule No. 2: Use your enemy's strengths against them.

Lucien was still an enemy, right? Maybe it would be prudent to learn more about my captor. I knew I was lying to myself. In truth, I was dying for more information about Lucien.

The binding on the book groaned as I cracked it open, and I glanced around guiltily, afraid someone might have heard it. When no one appeared from behind a column to accuse me of *liking* Lucien, I pulled a chair closer to one of the massive windows. I curled up on the seat, tucked my legs under me, and began reading.

Most of the book detailed the various factions inside the Vampire species. I didn't doubt that no matter the strength of any group, they would fall to Lucien's power. The way he easily discarded those two vampires in New Orleans spoke to his power and strength. I still shuddered to recall it and couldn't imagine a foe who could truly defend themselves against him.

What about the Council? Could he protect me from even them? No! I had to protect myself! Just like I always had! Like I would always have to, forever round and round, running and hiding. I tried not to feel disheartened and weary at the thought. It hurt when I reached for my power instinctually, only to feel its absence like a missing limb.

Finally, I came upon the renderings of Lucien. I traced an etching of him astride a massive black steed in ancient armor, charging into battle, his army of vampires at his back.

Lucien Silvano, King of Vampires, charged against the Death Demons. He and his army forced the horde back when they attempted to conquer the realm and extinguish all mortals.

The Demons of Thanatos tried to conquer Earth? When had that happened? Descendants of the Daemon Thanatos, the first death daemon released by Pandora, grew stronger with each kill. Their skin turned a ghostly white when enraged, growing pale wings and horns. I glanced at the date in the sketch's corner, and my eyes widened. Seventy-five hundred years ago?! How old was Lucien?

Having beaten back the demons, King Lucien struck a deal with the head of the Death faction of demons, Aidan the Forsaken. Lucien promised to entreaty the gods on their behalf for the creation of a demon realm, where all daemons and their descendants could exist in peace without fear of persecution.

Holy hells! Lucien was responsible for the creation of Pandora, the realm of demons? The realm was supposedly a demon paradise, where all the original daemons, those first released by Pandora, lived. However, no one knew for sure.

I flipped through the book to another battle image, this time fighting against lycans, wolf shifters. The etching portrayed him killing the Lycan King, and I read the description below.

King Lucien ended the decade-long battle with the lycans by beheading their bloodthirsty king, allowing Prince Erik's ascension to the throne.

I'd heard rumors about the current Lycan King, mostly that he was sex on a stick. My friends—*former friends*, I mentally added—had once whispered about how the werewolf had only to glance at a woman before she dropped her panties. Lucien was responsible for that kingdom as well? He had been busy in the last...however many millennia he'd lived.

I flipped through more pages and noticed the fae queen from Tír nAill shaking hands with Lucien, the date at the bottom was less than a decade ago.

King Lucien brokering a truce with the fae, aiding in eliminating slavery from the Realm of Tír nAill.

Was there anything the vampire hadn't done? I flipped to the most recent entry. The final etching was of him sitting alone in what I assumed to be the throne room of this very castle. Idly tracing a finger over the image, I noticed how his shoulders hunched, and he appeared lost in thought. Did the artist recognize how lonely he appeared?

Next to the entry, I read, *King Lucien awaits his fated mate, the Queen of Vampires, to relieve the unending years that stretch ahead of him.* My stomach knotted.

I was that fated mate, and the images of his past, the wars he fought, the miracles he'd wrought, made me more conscious of the fact Fate had very much fucked up when it had chosen me for him. I had done absolutely nothing close to heroic in my immortal life. He'd helped create realms, installed kings. I'd killed my kind.

I closed the book, tossing it away from me. I hated when I thought of that night, of how my fury and my magic became too intermingled. It had built inside me like a volcano, erupting when I'd lost control. Magic had whipped from me, destroying everything. I'd blacked out from the release of so much power, coming to hours later before any of the survivors could.

Flashes of that night still haunted me. The ashes of the witches I'd killed coated my throat, cloying and suffocating. So many dead, all because of me. The looks of accusation from those who'd survived, their disbelief at my power, had driven me away. I had run, escaping like the coward I was, leaving so much destruction and death in my wake. My mystical concussion to erase their knowledge of me was more of an afterthought, only taking root in the memories of those remaining because of their weakened shields.

I struggled to calm the torrent of tears that threatened to wash me away, becoming more determined to escape from Lucien. I couldn't face him

when he realized I was utterly unworthy of being his
queen.

XIII

I HAD FORGOTTEN HOW TIRESOME the vampire nobles could be, each hoping to pull me into conversation as Cassandra led Phoebe away. No wonder I left this place behind for Tír nAill. I couldn't stand their scraping and fawning. After ten thousand years, *everything* gets old, especially the tireless, *thankless* job of being king. You would think they would be grateful that under my eyes our people have flourished and blossomed, but no. They always wanted *more*. My eyes lingered on Phoebe's plump ass as she strutted away. It took everything in me not to follow her.

I needed to relax. She was home, and she was safe. I'd have her to myself soon. She was upset with me, but there were stolen moments when she reached for me, looked for me, and allowed me to touch her. I heard her heart racing when I was close. I saw the way her nipples hardened. She wanted me, and if I had to seduce her into accepting her new role, so be it. My hands itched to hold her, to discipline her smart mouth and distracting ass until she couldn't sit without thinking of me. But I wanted more. When I awoke in the plane with my arms empty, I imagined all the horrific things that could have happened while I slept. Things I'd done to my enemies' mates in the past

Mates were a favorite target for warring immortal factions. There was no worse torture for an immortal than losing a mate. She was running, and despite the small tidbit about her parents on the plane, I knew nothing about her. An unknown enemy was chasing my queen, and I didn't know how to keep her safe.

The list of people I cared about was extremely short by design. I hid my connection to Cassandra for the same reason and trusted my one friend to take care of himself. Now I had Phoebe, and she was the perfect way for my enemies to eliminate me permanently.

Each species dealt with the loss differently, but it always ended the same. When a vampire lost their mate, it destroyed us. We became lost to the frenzy, flying from rage to rage, and that was assuming we didn't greet the sun first. As king, it fell to me to execute those lost souls, a task I found particularly distasteful. The look of despair on their faces, their relief when I swung my sword were images that haunted me. Those memories swam through my dreams constantly. I hadn't understood their pain, even though I'd recoiled instinctively at the sight of it, but I was starting to. When I imagined a life without Phoebe, my fingers curled into my fists, and my claws cut into my palms. The sun wasn't even an option for me, to truly die, I would need to be beheaded. Yet there was no one to wield the sword, or to inherit the crown. I inhaled deeply, trying to regain my control.

Something I never struggled with before now was constantly flitting out of reach. Even now, the madness danced at the edge of my mind. It would just continue to grow until Phoebe was mine completely. A lesser vampire would already be insane. I was the oldest born vampire in existence, and I was being brought low by a red-headed witch.

The vampires followed me like ducklings as I stomped into my throne room. A pang of disappointment hit me when I saw both obsidian seats empty. I knew she would not stroll into Întuneric, see her throne, and forget everything I'd done. Was I that fucking *lost* when it came to my queen? I frowned at her empty throne and sat heavily in my seat, waving the first vampire noble forward.

Elijah remained on the outskirts of the throne room, watching the proceedings. I wondered if the other vampire noticed that not a single of the preening nobles wore a sun ring. Outside of the Elders, Elijah was the only non-royal to have one. I trusted Elijah. My gut told me he would be a staunch ally, and I didn't doubt my instincts. Except with Phoebe, she was the exception to ten thousand years of rules.

"My king, it is with great happiness that we welcome you home. Especially now that you've brought your queen with you, after all this time," one noble announced cheerily, though I could hear the strain in his voice.

I wondered what Phoebe was doing and wished Cassie had cleared out the castle until I could solidify things with my queen. I'd seen how their eyes lingered on the cuffs she wore. If I sent them all away now, it would only draw more attention to the unstable nature of my relationship, bringing the Elders down on us faster. I couldn't introduce the Elders to their new queen when she refused to stay in the same room as me.

The rumors had already begun, hinting at my weakness, my failure with her. *The king was spurned by his fated queen!* My nerves were already shredded, but I forced it down. I need to be a king first. I would be the unpredictable, mate-deprived, unstable vampire, on the verge of setting a new record for beheadings, second.

"I would like to plan for Phoebe's formal coronation as soon as possible. Make it a spectacle worthy of the name. I trust only you," I said, gesturing to all the vampires present with a negligent wave of my hand, "to see this done." The faux praise made them preen like peacocks. They rushed to obey my order, talking to each other fervently as they exited the throne room.

Elijah was the only one who saw me shift wearily on my throne at their exit. The vampire approached, placing a comforting hand on my shoulder in a silent show of support. "Well played," he said.

I sighed. "If only Phoebe were so easily handled."

Her continued absence only meant one thing, she was rebuilding her walls back. That is if she wasn't already trying to escape me again.

Elijah grunted. "But would a queen who bent to your every wish, obeyed you in all things, be someone you would truly want?"

No. That would be boring.

Phoebe already challenged me where most beings cowered. She let me know her mind, unafraid I was going to hurt her when she displeased me. She made no secret of her intentions of running and had already slipped through my hands *twice.* I had no doubt she was likely planning to try again. I tried to recall anyone who incited my anger so blatantly and came up blank. Yet, I knew that my fury would do nothing to deter her. With her exceptional power, my little witch would never bow to my dictates unless we were in bed, which was the only time we seemed to be of the same mind.

Cassandra came skipping through the doorway at that moment, yanking me out of my thoughts. When I noticed Phoebe was not with her, alarm bells blared through my head. Had she already vanished? *Already left me?*

I bolted to stand, recalling how easily she'd slipped from the alley in New Orleans. All the logic I needed to reassure myself that she couldn't escape Intuneric with her powers bound was absent. We were hours from the closest city, and the only way off of the castle grounds was across the narrow bridge.

"She's not used to the time difference yet and passed out," Cassie chided, reading my concern. Even if we'd barely seen each other in the last two millennia, she knew me too well. Cassandra saw a side of me that no one else did.

I fell back onto my throne, scrubbing my hand down my face. Since only Elijah and Cassandra were present, I admitted, "I don't know how to handle her."

Cassandra came closer, a frown lining her face. "She went from having no one, to having a ten-millennia-old vampire king insisting they belong together. She needs some space."

I recoiled. Even now, I could only think of getting to her, breathing in her scent, and exploring her body at my leisure. Yet, Cassandra said she needed *space?* I could barely tolerate the distance between us now!

Elijah seemed to sense my disquiet, offering another solution. "You *could* try charming her. Aren't you famous for that?"

Charm her? I ran a hand through my hair, sighing loudly. I was so out of sorts around her and didn't even know where to begin. In the past, I used my good looks to get people into bed but never concerned myself with convincing them to stick around afterward.

I stood again, determined to at least *try*. I headed out of the throne room, leaving my two pseudo advisors behind. A vampire noble and his daughter waylaid me the moment I stepped through the doorway.

"Sire, if I might have a word?" the vampire asked, preventing me from continuing on my search. I struggled not to snap at the other vampire, ignoring the voice in my head that whispered, *wouldn't the noble look spectacular without a head?*

I nodded and gestured with my hand for them to continue. "What is it?"

"We were curious about what species your queen is. We noticed she is not a vampire."

They were already probing for weaknesses between us. I gnashed my teeth to keep from killing them. My lip curled back from my fangs, but I held onto my patience, barely. Normally, I would have amused myself with the possible motive for such a question, but that was when I was in complete command of my actions. It was a different situation when I was so unpredictable, so volatile. The longer I went without claiming Phoebe, the harder it would be to control my temper.

"She's a witch. Anything else?" I said harshly.

There was a loaded glance between father and daughter. "The reason we ask, sire, is that we are worried she could have placed a spell on you to make you believe she is yours. Witches are untrustworthy."

I burst out laughing. I couldn't help it. The idea that Phoebe had cast a spell to make me believe she was my mate was so outlandish I could barely believe they felt the need to bring it up. "Rest easy. She has cast no spell on me. Her cuffs prevent all such magic."

I shouldn't have let that slip, but I couldn't call the words back, and the two vampires slunk away before I could explain. I almost wished she had cast an enchantment on me, that she wanted me like that.

I headed straight for my bedroom, a thrum of excitement coursing through me at the thought of Phoebe in my ancestral bed. So many nights, I lay awake, dreading the future, trying to distract myself from the aching emptiness and loneliness hounding me. I knew there was nothing but more of the same ahead of me. The same cycle of loneliness and distraction, round and round and round it went.

I swung the door open, immediately noticing the bed was empty except for her black cat, curled up on her pillow. No! She could not have escaped. Cassie said she was sleeping. I took a large, calming breath before starting my search and caught her lingering scent in the halls. She must have paced through the labyrinth, leaving numerous paths that led to many destinations.

I was too frantic to find the freshest, most recent one. Had she done so on purpose to confuse me while she escaped? I wouldn't put it past my clever queen. I needed to get control. With yet another calming breath, I reassured myself that she hadn't escaped. I continued looking for her, though the calm I needed to zero in on her scent was absent.

"Sire, if I may?" The housekeeper tried to stop me. Yet another delay. Was the universe conspiring to keep me from her?

I nodded to the woman, throwing doors open, continuing the search for my mate. I didn't break stride, but she kept pace with me. "We've had varied attire brought in for your new queen, but Lady Cassandra mentioned your mate is a witch, and I was wondering if there's perhaps more she might need to practice her craft."

I hadn't even thought of that. If I removed Phoebe's cuffs, she would no doubt want to continue honing her magic. I bit back my instinctive need to say she would never use her powers again. If she learned more magic, would it make it easier for her to leave me? I would have to take the cuffs off first. If she were free, she would require all the things a witch used to commune with their magic. My mind and emotions were in such turmoil, I answered without thinking, "She won't be practicing any magic. There's no need to accommodate her."

Could I ever truly allow her to practice her dangerous magic with complete trust? Trust she wouldn't disappear on me one day, leaving me lost and alone? I shook off the sense of foreboding, waving the housekeeper away.

Still, I searched, flinging open doors in pursuit of Phoebe. I looked for hours, becoming more frantic with each passing minute. Had she found a way to leave me? Madness banged against my skull as others waylaid me multiple times. Staff, my nobles, asking my opinion about the time for the coronation, prompting me to give a date two weeks into the future. Two weeks to win Phoebe, two weeks to convince her to stay. Again, the feeling of despair crashed over me like a wave. Why would she stay with me? She hated me.

Where the hells was she? My panic quickly escalated to fury the longer I searched. It was hours before I finally found her huddled in a corner of the library, cuddling an enormous book.

"Phoebe," I growled, half in reprimand, half in relief, pulling the book from her hands. A flash of hurt went through me when I saw the title. *Architecture of Întuneric Castel.* She was looking for an escape route. She was looking to leave me, just like everyone else.

XIV

I CRADLED HER GENTLY IN MY ARMS, carrying her toward our room. She turned to me in her sleep, seeking comfort. While her mind may hate me, her body searched for mine. I could take a little solace in that. Could I work to coax her from her anger? Coax her into giving us a chance?

Back in our room, she stayed asleep as I gently laid her on the bed and undressed her. I tried not to ogle her as I put her into a nightgown left by the housekeeper. It was difficult, but I wanted to take care of her, keep her safe, even from my own desires.

I stripped off my clothes to join her, leaving my briefs on. Normally, I slept naked, but I'd already pushed her enough by putting her in bed with me. I didn't need to be naked when she woke up as well. I pulled her into my arms, stroking her hair softly, gently tracing the furrow in her brow as she dreamed. Her scent flooded me, relaxing my muscles, soothing my mind enough for my eyes to close.

I could only have been asleep for a couple of minutes before I felt her tossing, muttering under her breath, "No! Please! I didn't know!"

I pulled her back against me, brushing her hair away from her face. "Shh, *vrăjitoare*, I've got you. You're safe," I murmured, calling her an enchantress in Romanian, the endearment tumbling from me. Slowly, she relaxed into me, clinging to me. "I've got you. I won't let you go."

She drifted off again, and I quickly followed when her breath evened out. I awoke to her nightmares twice more, repeating the process till she relaxed and fell back asleep. She wiggled from my arms each time I drifted off. It seemed she was constantly hoping to escape me, even in sleep.

When the sun slowly rose over the horizon, her dreams became more violent, causing her to toss and turn, a stray punch bloodying my lip and waking me again. The injury healed almost immediately, but my concern over the contents of her nightmares would not. I rolled over her, pinning her to the bed, pressing her wrists to the mattress above her head. "Wake up!"

Her eyes opened, but she stared at me blankly, still trapped in her nightmare. "Lucien?" she questioned, her voice breaking a little. "Don't let them take me!"

"Never. I will never let them take you."

I pressed my forehead gently to hers, letting her fully come awake. She stiffened in awareness and yanked her hands away from mine. She pushed at my chest, forcing me to move off of her. I fell to my side, immediately mourning the loss of having her beneath me.

She vaulted out of bed. "How did I get here? What am I wearing?"

Maybe I shouldn't have dressed her in such a transparent negligee.

"You're in my bed because that's where you belong," I muttered harshly, coming to a stand. She belonged in my arms. I could soothe her nightmares. She needed me. I reached forward, gently grasping her arms, forcing her frantic eyes to meet mine. "Who's after you? You made me promise not to let them get you."

"What? When did I make you promise that?" Her face was still pale, and she was visibly shaken from her dreams, her eyes darting away from me. So many secrets hid in her eyes. I needed her to share them with me.

I glared down at her, noticing she deliberately sidestepped the question. "When I woke you from another nightmare." I gentled my hold slightly, though it went against every instinct I had. "I can't protect you if I don't know what's coming."

She pushed against my chest, my words returning the flush to her cheeks and her eyes sparking. "You want to protect me? Take these off!" she yelled, holding the cuffs up between us. "Then I can protect myself!"

She wrenched even farther away from me, pacing back and forth along the wall, muttering under her breath. Part of it was in English. I caught *asshole, high-handed, dickweed,* but the other half was in a language even I didn't know.

I grabbed her again, snapping her out of her tirade. "You would disappear the second I turned my back!"

Images of me trusting her enough to remove the cuffs and her rifting away in an instant played before my eyes. That future taunted me. If I trusted her completely, only to face her betrayal, it would devastate me.

Phoebe didn't deny it. She was so eager to leave me. The madness that danced at the edge of my mind seemed to grow. If I claimed her, she would bend to my will. I could seduce her into seeing things my way. If I did that, I knew I would earn her eternal hatred. It had to be her choice. There must be trust between us first, and it had to be her choice. I would risk insanity to keep her. I would risk *everything* to keep her.

My fangs dropped into my mouth, blood pounding in my ears as I roared, "Let me protect you!"

"Release me!" she shouted back, standing toe to toe with me. I couldn't remember another immortal ever daring to incite my anger like this. Even Cassandra would have backed down by now. Yet Phoebe demanded her way, refusing to submit. If I wasn't so enraged, I would have felt admiration for her fearlessness.

"You stay with me!" My grip tightened, likely leaving bruises. "Accept it!"

Her head snapped back, her fiery brows furrowed. "You intend to keep me prisoner?"

My laugh was cold and mocking, even to my own ears. "No, my little *vrăjitoare*. This is your *home*."

She shoved against me, forcing me back a step, making my hands drop from her in surprise.

"And you expect me to trust you?" she scoffed.

"You are my mate. Trust *that*, at least."

An immortal male would never let harm come to their mate. It was something she could trust even if she couldn't trust me yet.

What if she never trusts me?

Her vivid eyes scanned mine repeatedly, pursing her lips, visibly debating my words. I could tell the instant she decided to tell me *something*. She sighed in defeat, and I checked a look of victory at the small measure of trust. It shored up my hope that she might trust me completely one day. *Baby steps.*

"I-I-um—" she struggled to begin.

I cupped her face tenderly, pushing back her hair and checking another look of triumph that she didn't immediately flinch away from my touch. I could win her, but I had to go slow.

"Start from the beginning," I coaxed, reaching out to lead her back to the bed.

Phoebe frowned down at her hands locked with mine. She didn't pull away, and some of the tension in my shoulders relaxed as we sat back down. I reluctantly released one of her hands and placed a finger under her chin, lifting her eyes to meet mine. I could only hope she saw my desire to protect her, to keep her safe. "Whatever has happened, nothing will change the way I see you."

Her entire body softened, leaning into my touch. I held my breath, praying she would share her burdens with me.

"I made a mistake. I trusted someone I shouldn't have, and I paid dearly for it." The pain in Phoebe's eyes nearly shattered me, and I covered a wince, knowing I'd only reinforced the idea that people were untrustworthy when I cuffed her. *Fuck me.* "The people after me, they want me to pay," her voice broke, "with my life." She shivered even though it was not cold. I pulled her against me, watching the emotions cross her face. She let out a deep sigh. "I did something horrible, Lucien."

"You're wanted by the Witches Council?" I asked, noticing the way she recoiled when I referred to the powerful group. There was only one entity that could sentence a witch, and they did so often. There was no shortage of fugitive witches on the run, though they rarely survived for long. I felt her nod against my side. She lifted her legs and wrapped her arms around them but didn't move away from me. "That's why you thought I was turning you over for execution."

Running and hiding from the most powerful witches in the world was supposed to be impossible. They touted their scrying as all-seeing and all-knowing. In my head, I listed the necessary precautions I needed to install at the castle to protect my witch from any who would dare harm her or take her from our home. I needed to make a few calls and burn some of the millions of favors I'd accumulated over the years.

"When was this?" I asked.

How long was she on the run? How long was she alone? Her own kind was hunting my vulnerable mate while I was dying of boredom in this very castle. I wished I'd found and protected her sooner. I'd been selfish, only thinking of my boredom, my needs. If I was more like Erik, I would have scoured the globe for my mate and then searched other realms. But I didn't, and she had suffered because of it. She had been alone and vulnerable. And I? I was mulling over a war or conquest in some pleasure den, hoping my boredom would not grow into true detachment.

"I was twenty-one when they sentenced me. It's been a long ten years."

Born immortals stopped aging when we were at the pinnacle of strength. Though the event that triggered the stop was different for each species. I'd stopped aging at twenty-nine, Cassandra at twenty-four. We were born with some of our race's

164

characteristics, but we didn't blossom into our full powers until we were at our prime. It was rumored that witches didn't gain their immortality or even their entire magical arsenal until some sort of strange initiation before the Council.

"So young." I kissed the top of her head. "I wish I could have been there for you."

She glanced up at me, her lips parting slightly. "What would you have done?"

"Killed them all for you." Her bright eyes shimmered with emotion. My fangs filled my mouth at the thought of her being in danger. The tension returned in a rush, and the need to hunt and kill her enemies was foremost. I could taste their blood in my mouth and feel it dripping down my throat. I would make them say her name, so they understood the reason their lives would end.

My mind played the brutal images on a loop, and I blinked in surprise when she placed both of her hands on my cheeks. She turned me toward her, distracting me from the rage. She must have released her legs while I was imagining the various ways I was going to torture those that pursued her. Her soft touch on my face soothed me instantly, allowing my fangs to retract and the madness banging in my skull to recede. Her effect on me was swift and powerful.

Phoebe placed a soft kiss on my lips, almost unsure. "Thank you," she whispered and kissed me again. She wrapped her arms around my neck and licked along my lower lip, deepening the kiss. I moved my hands to her waist, just barely stopping myself from yanking her on top of me. My fantasies of death and destruction quickly flipped to all the ways I was going to fuck her.

"For what?" I managed to ask between kisses.

She pulled back to look at me again, and I got lost in the lilac glow of her eyes. "I've never had anyone who made me feel even the slightest bit safe. Though we have things to work through," *subtle* jangle of the cuffs, "thank you for making me feel safe."

She shifted uncomfortably, as if annoyed at having revealed so much to me. Before she could withdraw, I kissed her forehead, both eyelids, nose, and ears. "You are always safe with me, *regina mea.*"

I was resisting going further, but she pulled me on top of her on the bed. She pressed her lips against mine urgently, snagging her tongue on my enlarged canine. At first, I thought it was an accident until she repeated the action, letting me suck the little droplets of blood from her tongue.

"Your blood is like a drug," I said, hovering over her. I looked down at Phoebe, wondering again at this beautiful woman that fate declared was mine. It was humbling being mated to such a bewitching female. I would guard her with utter ruthlessness.

Phoebe's hands slipped beneath the waistband of my briefs, but I stopped her, circling her wrists with one of my hands. "I will not claim you, Phoebe. Not until there is trust between us."

I could barely believe I had the strength to utter the words. Everything in me was screaming for me to claim her, that she was mine. It took far more willpower not to take her than I cared to admit. Especially with the way her eyes were glowing and her breasts were barely concealed in the gown. My cock was like steel, and I wanted inside her, *needed* inside her, but I couldn't. She needed to trust me. I couldn't let this mean nothing, and I knew she thought our coming together now would just be an exchange of pleasure. I couldn't let it be that. It needed to be more.

She pouted. "What does trust have to do with sex?"

I cradled her face again, letting my lower body imprison hers, her hands bound by one of mine above her head. She was at my mercy, her body begging for me, my hardness lining up with her softness. We fit together seamlessly. "It would not be *just* sex between us."

When I claimed her, I would sink my fangs into her neck while pounding into her body, our scents morphing, changing, becoming one. Most vampires would be able to identify her as their queen by scent as if me being at her side wouldn't be clue enough. There would be no going back for either of us. It was not a decision to be made lightly or impulsively.

Her lips pressed into a line of suspicion, her voice deepening. "Are you hoping that I'll become so desperate that I'll beg for it?"

I groaned at the idea, already picturing it, preferably on her knees, with a collar around her throat. She would spread her legs slightly, rocking her hips, pushed past all control, begging for my cock.

"As arousing as the image of you begging for my cock is," I said, punctuating my words with another groan. "We must wait. You must be sure."

She tipped her head slightly, biting her lip in that maddening way. "Sure about what?"

I pressed a sweet, lingering kiss to her lips. "That you want all of this, that you want to be queen." *That you want* **me**.

Phoebe frowned, and I kissed her down-turned lips again. I couldn't stop touching her, kissing her, reassuring myself that she was here. "That doesn't mean we have to live like monks in the meantime."

She licked her lips, and her eyes sparkled as she whispered, "Oh? And what did you have in mind?" Her entire body blossomed for me. She arched her back, wiggling her hips beneath me. I knew she felt my cock when she gasped and then tried to rub herself against me.

My hold on her wrists remained. With my free hand, I grabbed the silk tie from the nightstand, looping it around her wrists and anchoring it to the bed. I needed to be able to think, and I couldn't do that if she touched me. I expected her to balk at yet another binding, but she purred, her eyes glowing brighter. It was obvious that she liked it. If there was any doubt that she was my mate, it was put to rest. She was a perfect female. I took a step back from the bed from the moment, my cock clearly outlined in my briefs, and her eyes fell to it. She bit her lip, rocking her hips again.

Since she submitted so sweetly, I would reward her with a glimpse. I hooked a finger in my briefs, drawing them slowly down my legs, feeling her gaze on me. I stroked myself, watching as she licked her lips again, arching toward me with a soft moan of need. The sound of her hunger threatened my control. I leaned over and, using a single claw, I sliced down the gossamer material of her gown, careful not to touch her. The silk slid from her body and pooled beneath her. She struggled slightly against the tie, wanting to reach for me.

"Put your knees up and spread your legs," I ordered, moving to the base of the bed, lightly touching myself again.

She paused for just a moment before doing as I commanded, allowing me to catch sight of her perfect pussy.

"You are dripping for me," I growled.

She moaned, lifting her hips, spreading herself more for me. "Please, Lucien..."

The sound of her plea made my cock throb. I used two fingers to spread her lips apart, making her more vulnerable to me, her needy clit begging to be touched. She whimpered and clenched as I kept her clit exposed to the air and slowly slipped a single finger inside of her. "Your pussy wants to come. I can feel it squeezing my finger."

The words caused her to further drench my hand. I rocked my finger in and out of her while feathering lightly across her clit, not rubbing the way she so desperately needed. She pushed forward against my hand, and I added another finger, twisting them inside her. She dug her heels into the bed and lifted, trying to get more friction.

"Make me come, baby. Please," she begged.

I thrust my fingers inside her faster, harder, making her breasts bounce. "I love watching your tits when I have my fingers inside you." Phoebe moaned, and I finally added the friction she needed on her clit. Her entire body tensed and then began to shake as I felt her come around my fingers, screaming my name as she orgasmed. When I felt her relax and her body go languid, I pulled my fingers from her pussy, licking them clean. Gods, she tasted amazing.

My cock was rock hard as I kneeled between her trembling thighs, positioning my shaft against her wet folds to rub myself against her. I imagined the ways I would fuck her and thrust jarringly against her. She locked her ankles around my waist, unable to do more with her hands bound. She rocked her hips up and down, yanking me higher up the bed. Every time she dragged her clit over my piercings, I choked on a moan, my eyes rolling up at the feeling. I could feel her edging toward another orgasm, shoving me at my own.

"*Fuck!*" she moaned.

I panted, and my lips parted to expose my teeth. Phoebe tipped her chin up and leaned forward, trailing her neck along my mouth, nicking the delicate skin of her throat. A drop of her addictive blood landed on my tongue, her flavor exploding in my mouth. I licked over the small wound, my eyes glazing over at her taste. Gods, she was amazing.

I sank my fangs into her neck, and she hissed, rubbing harder against me. She circled her hips frantically and moaned, her second orgasm ripping through her. She screamed as she came against my cock, and my release quickly followed. I pulled my fangs from her, panting at the force of my climax, feeling the heat of my cum against her belly.

My body felt boneless, but I nearly hardened again as I untied her from the bed, and she grabbed me, covering my face with kisses. I massaged her arms, making sure the blood returned to them. She was such a wicked female.

My smile turned sinister, tempted to play with her more, but she slid out from under me. She cuddled close to my side, throwing her leg over mine, and resting her head on my shoulder. I kissed her head affectionately, a deep feeling of contentment coming over me. Had I ever felt such satisfaction, even after a long night of debauchery? I threaded her soft fiery hair through my fingers, luxuriating in the silky texture. Both of us were breathing hard, still riding hard from our orgasms.

"I will always protect you, Phoebe, but know that I intend to earn your trust," I murmured into her hair.

She looked up at me, her lilac eyes unreadable. "Lucien…" she began, but she glanced away, pulling away from me. I immediately mourned the loss. However, she was already withdrawing from me, and the madness delightedly returned.

She can't wait to leave, just like everyone else.

Phoebe couldn't wait to leave, just like everyone else. First my mother, then Cassandra, now Phoebe. She didn't speak again, heading for the closet to pull on clothes. I remained where I was but pulled the sheet over myself and sat up, my back against the ancient headboard.

She returned wearing tight jeans and a white blouse, still glowing from the pleasure of her orgasms. I growled at the sight, hardening again for her. Would I ever get enough of her? Instead of returning to bed, she headed for the door. "Where are you going?" I demanded, tempted to stop her, but I remembered my plan of baby steps and stayed where I was.

"I need… I just… give me space, Lucien," she murmured, the door clicking shut behind her. I bit my tongue to keep from roaring.

XV

THE REALM OF MORTALS.
ÎNTUNERIC CASTEL, ROMANIA.

"Aunt Caroline!" I cry, the sound muted by the persistent ringing in my ears and my makeshift mask. I scramble to her side, trying to remember the spells for healing, but I don't know them. They're in my grimoire, the stolen grimoire.

Still, I have to try. I close my eyes and focus all my energy into my hands, hoping to force it from my body into my aunts. My palms warm slightly, and my tear-filled eyes open, expecting to see my aunt's wounds healing.

I ESCAPED THE BEDROOM, knowing I might already be in too deep with Lucien. I admitted to feeling safe with him. Even if it was true and I felt protected for the first time in a decade, even if I imagined staying, it gave him a major advantage in their constant battle of wills. I couldn't let it happen. I had to find a way to escape. My hands absently tugged at the cuffs, reaching for my connection of magic just out of reach.

I meandered through the halls again, looking for Cassandra or Elijah, anyone to distract me from my own thoughts. But I couldn't find anyone, not even one of the lingering vampires who shot venomous looks at me when I first arrived. I couldn't find anyone. My arms wrapped around my stomach.

I did not know how long I was lost. There were no clocks or even windows in this part of the castle, nothing to tell me how much time had passed. But something was calling to me. How had I gotten here? The corridors must have changed. The very hallways morphed, delivering me to another area of the fortress. As if the massive stone labyrinth wasn't hard enough to navigate normally, was it also spelled?

I glanced around, disconnected voices suddenly echoing through the hallways, making my hair stand on end. *Okay, what the actual fuck?* I started sprinting down the dark corridor, hoping to put some distance between me and the approaching sounds. Despite the distance, the whispers only grew louder. They were overlapping hushed murmurs, but nothing I could understand or decipher. I tried to cover my ears to block them out, only for them to become hushed screams that sent me running down the dark hallway, attempting an escape.

I saw the familiar library doors and rushed forward. I pushed them open and was shocked that they did not lead to the library but into my childhood home.

A step back, and I was in the ominous hallway of the castle. If I stepped forward, I would be in the only home I had ever truly known. My eyes filled with tears, emotion clogging my throat. Like shades, transparent outlines of my parents and I flickered before me, moving at an almost invisible speed. My hand shook as I stepped further into the past, reaching out to touch the intangible, ghost-like shapes of my mother and father. As my foot fell, the scene solidified, playing out before me.

My mother was singing me to sleep. Her bright red hair shone in the low light as she hummed, the words lost. I looked down at myself, my brows furrowed, trying to place the moment. I was so young, likely around five or six.

My father waited for my mother, leaning against the doorjamb, his lilac eyes taking in the scene. His midnight hair was windswept, and lines of stress showed around his eyes. My eyes closed, listening to my mother humming, a tear slipping down my cheek. My mom stopped singing, kissed my head, and joined my father in the doorway. Instead of remaining in my bedroom, I followed them. As they softly closed the door behind them, I absently noticed Bast trotting along behind my father. They whispered to each other, and I struggled to hear them over the roaring in my ears. They were here and alive.

"She's already too powerful, Michelle," my father said. "Soon, the Council will know the truth."

My mother placed a gentle finger over his lips, hushing him. She pulled him into the living room, shutting the door to the hallway behind them. "They will kill her!"

Kill me? What could they have wanted with me at such a young age? I hadn't hurt anyone...yet.

My mother broke off at the sound of knocking on their front door. I could see the dread cross both my parents' faces as they went to answer it. My father's hands lit with battle magic, preparing to defend our family with spells that only

*he knew as a son of Atreus. Unspoken words vibrated
between them as my mother opened the door, my father
looming behind her, prepared to attack.*

*An elderly crone stood on their doorstep, hunched over
with age, her hands gnarled, clutching a cane to keep her
upright. Her hood was pulled down low over her face,
tendrils of snow-white hair escaping. My parents stepped
back, their mouths gaping, the magic in my father's palms
flickering and then dying.*

*"May I come in?" the old woman croaked, holding
herself over the cane.*

*My father nodded, bowing his head in respect. "Norn,
you honor us."*

*A Norn? An Oracle? The old woman shuffled into the
room, her bones creaking as she sat in the chair offered to
her.*

*A visit from an Oracle was an enormous deal. They
were so rare, and they did not visit people. Why hadn't they
mentioned this to me? My parents always talked about being
honest with me, sharing the good and the bad. Was that all a
lie? Was anything in my life true?*

*My father sat in the armchair, my mother perched on
the arm next to him. The scene was so familiar it made my
heart ache. I missed them so much.*

*"I'm here to discuss the girl." The norn's voice crackled
with age and power even I felt.*

Wait—what was she here to talk about?

*My father shifted in his seat, his elbows on his knees.
"Her power is growing each day. Soon we won't be able to
hide her anymore," he said, his voice conveying his worry.*

*"She is the one who will set it all to rights. The centuries
of lies will end. But...you will not be there to see it," the norn*

176

continued, her blue eyes becoming hazy as she stared at a point over my parents' shoulders.

My mother gasped. "I would never abandon her!"

The oracle sighed. "You will not have a choice."

My parents gazed at each other. A look of understanding flickered between them before morphing into one of determination.

Tears flooded my eyes, falling heedlessly down my face as I watched the scene. I wanted to reach out and touch my beloved parents, but I was only a spectator of the scene, not a participant.

"The gods have decreed her to return the balance. They set her destiny. All you can do is prepare her."

What balance? What destiny? I wanted to scream, but my parents just nodded gravely. They were content to die for me? My heart ached anew at the loss. They hadn't even hesitated when the oracle explained they would die. The tears continued to fall as the Norn stood to leave, her body spry for her age.

On her exit, she stopped at the door, and in a voice not loud enough for my parents to hear, whispered, "You're not supposed to be here."

I looked over my shoulder to see whom the norn was addressing. There was no one. She was speaking to me in the present day, though the moment spanned years. For a second, a film of ash seemed to fall over her, and I recognized the familiar swirling eyes behind the guise. Cassandra?

The realization threw me out into the hallway, and I landed on my back in Întuneric, the impact with the hard stone making me lose my breath. A sharp pain radiated through my chest as I struggled to breathe. The door in front of me slammed shut, closing off my view of the past, and slowly disappeared before my eyes. The blank wall was left behind as if the entrance had never existed.

I coughed as the air returned to my lungs, the hacking sound echoing in the empty hallway. When I could breathe normally, I rested on the floor, trying to piece together what I'd just witnessed. My parents knew they were going to die. They had constantly talked about preparing me and how I needed to hide my ability to rift. I thought they were just overprotective. But could it have been more? Were they trying to prepare me for whatever destiny Cassie hinted at?

My parents had taught me magic instead of sending me to spell school with other young witches. I'd never suspected they were concealing me from the Council, believing they wanted to take care of my education themselves. It had isolated my parents. They had only left me behind when they had full Council meetings that required them to attend.

Why the need to hide me? Why the visit from Cassandra? Why? Why? Why?

I lifted my head off the ground when I heard footsteps approaching. Cassandra was coming closer with her hands stuffed into her pockets. I sat up, my eyes narrowing on the oracle. My throat is clogged with tears and emotions, and I wrapped my arms tightly around my drawn-up knees. It was like my parents had died all over again.

"Is it my fault they died?" I whispered.

Instead of answering, Cassandra laid on her back on the floor next to me, singing softly, "Twinkle twinkle, little snitch, mind your business, you nosey

178

bitch." She finished the rhyme with a double middle-finger salute at the ceiling.

I looked up at the blank, black ceiling. Wasn't it still morning? My brows furrowed, and I glanced back at Cassandra. It was the fate of oracles. If they survived into immortality, the persistent nature of the future made them lose their grip on reality. After another moment frowning at Cassie, I lay down next to the blonde and silently let the tears fall.

"I was the one who found them." I reached up to wipe away the tears from my face, eventually giving up on stemming the flow, letting them continue their silent journey down my cheeks. "I remember the silence." The silence had been so complete. I could still hear it, that yawning, aching, haunting *emptiness.* "Our house was *never* silent. My parents were always singing, bickering, or casting spells. Never silent." I pushed back my hair from my face, my arms barely supporting their weight as I glared at the ceiling, the tears endless, emotion clogging my throat as the memories played in my mind. "The Council said it was demons, that my parents had found something they wanted and got in the way when they'd tried to take it. They never gave me a name."

No name, which left me alone. Just me. Me and the silence. If I closed my eyes and focused, I could see it. There had been so much blood. The white shiplap walls were coated in it, a macabre display of viscera. I remembered slipping on it when I opened the front door, finding my mom reaching out sightlessly for my dad, destined to never make it to him.

"It wasn't demons," Cassandra said distantly.

My tears dried at the statement, the silence dimming in my mind as I turned to look at Cassie. "What?"

The oracle's eyes were a swirling molten white. All traces of the vibrant blue had vanished. The white consumed everything, iris and pupil. Did she see the future as she lay on the floor of the castle with me? Her voice was layered, three unique tones merging and becoming one. "It was never demons."

I turned on my side, facing her. I waited for her to continue, but she didn't. Did Cassandra hold all the answers to my questions? Would she answer them if I asked? Or would she only create more questions?

I opened my mouth to ask, but Cassandra bolted to her feet. "I'm starving, and so are you," she declared. She pulled me to a stand with a powerful grip on my hand, yanking me down the hall.

I dug my heels in, forcing her to spin to face me. I grabbed Cassandra's arms, demanding, "Who was it?"

Her eyes were blue and blank. "Who was what?"

Did she really not remember, or was she playing me? I scanned her face, looking for some hint that she was lucid enough to answer my questions, but found nothing. I would have to wait for another lucid moment to question her more. That meant I had to stay here until I did. I released Cassandra, and she took my hand again before turning away, guiding me through the labyrinth. An infusion of pleasure hit me at the idea that I now had an actual excuse for postponing escape.

Cassandra led me into the massive castle kitchens, and my eyes shot wide to see that the human staff was in a flurry of activity, preparing a massive feast. I shifted uncomfortably when the cooks paused in their duties to curtsy to me before resuming their duties. I wasn't sure what to do about that, unfamiliar with being the focus of anyone's attention. Cassandra ignored it, moving forward to the massive wooden island where various snacks were laid out. She slid onto one stool and patted the seat beside her for me. I took it gingerly, my eyes tracking all the strangers in the room, trying to prevent my heart from racing in my chest.

Overwhelmed by the buffet of choices, I watched Cassie from the corner of my eye, prepared to follow her lead. I wasn't sure what I expected her to grab to eat, but the Red Vines were most definitely not it. She crossed her legs and placed the massive tub in her lap, eating the red candy tubes with almost alarming speed. So following the oracle's example was out.

I studied the offerings, feeling the pointed gazes of the various staff members watching and waiting to see what I was going to pick. I made a big show of sampling various plates, *oohing* and *ahhing* until everyone returned to their various duties. Once the focus was off of me, I sighed in relief. Being the center of attention went against Rule No. 4. I hunched my shoulders, trying to make myself smaller and more dismissible.

A dour-looking woman with a large key ring hooked to her waist approached us and curtsied. "Princess, my queen, my name is Adelaide. I serve as the housekeeper for Întuneric Castel."

I followed Cassandra's example and nodded politely, waiting until the human stood. "Please call me Phoebe."

Adelaide's mouth opened, horrified at the suggestion. "I could not, my queen." The woman appeared so offended. It was like I'd suggested that she strip down and run through the halls of the castle naked.

I sighed heavily, imploring the housekeeper, "Why not?"

Adelaide huffed. Her dark black hair was wound so tightly at the top of her head. It was shocking that she could show any emotion at all. "It's not the way we do things here."

The housekeeper curtsied deeply again, and I smothered an annoyed groan. This was already getting to be a pain. Fuck these formalities. It is 2022, right?

I glanced over my shoulder as I heard another pair of footsteps approach. Elijah took the seat on the other side of me as a member of the staff poured blood into a goblet for him. I narrowed my eyes at his profile. He was a vampire and probably hadn't seen the inside of a kitchen since he'd been turned. *Which meant...*

"Lucien sent you to spy on me, didn't he?" I hissed at Elijah, making him choke on the blood. I allowed him a moment to compose himself but glared at him, waiting for his response.

Elijah cleared his throat after a moment, carefully putting the goblet back on the island before turning to look at me. He lifted a white handkerchief from his suit pocket, dabbing at his lips.

"He sent me to check up on you. He would have come himself but said that you needed space." His formal tone was light with amusement.

I rolled my eyes at him, scoffing. "This is his idea of giving me space? Sending you to spy on me?" The man did not know the meaning of the word.

"You're the mate he never expected to have. Can you blame him?" Elijah asked, which was an *annoyingly* great point. "Vampires are already arriving *en masse* to catch sight of the immortal who brought him to his knees." Elijah smirked, making his bright white teeth flash.

The longer I stayed, the higher the chance the Witches Council might send an emissary to see the new Queen of the Vampires. Immortal kings didn't just stumble across queens every day. It was kind of a *thing*. If I had a seat on the Witches Council, I would have come. You had to know your enemy to know their strengths. Knowing the enemy was part of rule two. I had to get out of there.

"I haven't brought Lucien to his knees," I grumbled.

"You will," Cassandra said, her annoyingly cheery voice drawing my gaze. A bubble of laughter formed in my throat when I looked at the all-powerful, all-seeing immortal.

Cassandra's lips were stained bright red from the Red Vines. Lucien likely had the candy imported to Romania just for her. An act Cassie obviously appreciated by the way she demolished the sugary treats. Her fingers were red, and she left little fingerprints on her own cheeks.

The sound of my laughter was startling to my ears. Gods, when had I last laughed? Elijah seemed determined to take advantage of my good humor. "Most vampires are hoping to find Lucien following you around like a lovesick puppy. The odds are in favor of you leading him on a merry chase."

My smile widened at the image of the legendary vampire king being led around by a barely immortal witch. I could understand the appeal for any under Lucien's rule to witness such a sight.

How could I deny the people?

XVI

THE REALM OF MORTALS.
ÎNTUNERIC CASTEL, ROMANIA.

My palms are glowing, but nothing is happening. Tears fall down my cheeks as I try again, summoning every ounce of energy I have. "Work, damn you!"

No, no, please, not again. The glow flickers in my hand, then dies. "No! No, no!"

I curl my hands into fists and let out a piercing wail. I pull my aunt's corpse into my lap, tears dropping from my face to hers.

DON'T FOLLOW ME. I don't need my powers to cut off your balls while you sleep."

Elijah seemed to take my stern warning to heart. He swallowed hard, and his complexion lost all semblance of color. Of course, it also could have been that I grabbed a nearby melon baller before disappearing down a dark hallway.

Free of my immortal shadow, I further explored the depths of the castle. My plan for escape on the back burner, I noticed things I had overlooked earlier. Some areas of the castle were modernized, like the bathrooms and kitchens, but it was still *ancient* in others. I hadn't spotted a single piece of technology— not a camera, television, or laptop, nothing. It was barren, cold, isolated, and lonely.

If someone, definitely not *me*, wan*ted* to make the castle welcoming, they could. There were little traces of life throughout the labyrinth, a discarded pile of books in a corner, three mismatching pairs of shoes in Cassandra's size. There was even a section of the black halls that had faded pink paint on the walls. I tried to picture Lucien and his vampires painting the walls of the castle and came up short. I trailed my fingers along the stone and thought back on how my life had changed over the last twenty-four hours.

The way Lucien dropped into the alley in New Orleans and dispatched those two vampires still made me shudder. He had been ruthless, heartless, and cold. But also kind of…awe inspiring? If I was honest, it kind of turned me on. I couldn't remember the last time I had seen a male worthy of admiration, and none came close to Lucien. If the stories were true, he was a man deserving of his title and throne, something I hadn't thought possible. Men with power rarely deserved what they had, at least in my experience.

I had to stop these thoughts. It was not a good idea to soften toward him, no matter the pull I felt. I hated that even as I wandered this castle, I was wishing he was next to me, guiding me, touching me. His presence was soothing and stirring at the same time. I squeezed my eyes shut, shaking my head to deny the longing. The slight rubbing of the metal on my wrists made my eyes flash open and cooled my obsessive thoughts. He'd bound me and kidnapped me. He took what was mine. I relaxed, much more comfortable now that he was once more the villain in my mind. The lack of my powers stung, a phantom limb I wished to scratch. He knew that, and still bound me.

I turned a few more corners and heard the clash of steel against steel. Instead of just aimlessly wandering the halls, the sound gave me direction and led me to a sparring room. Various weapons and arms decorated the walls, from swords to guns, from daggers to maces. The floor was covered with a black exercise mat, bolted at the edges and softening the stone floor. Of all the rooms I'd stumbled into, this was the first that looked well used, and it was by far the most modified.

Elijah and Lucien faced off against each other, two blurs of immortal speed. I could only catch the flashes of silver as blows were exchanged and their swords met. I tracked Lucien by his eyes, the green intense as he fought. Elijah's glowed red, and I took a step back out of habit, knowing how unpredictable vampires could be. I took a step back but didn't leave the room, knowing that Lucien would never let Elijah harm me. I huffed in disgust at the unwelcome thought, ignoring the rush of warmth that filled me. The men came together like titans clashing, exchanging heavy blows. Lucien swept his leg out, taking Elijah to the floor, Lucien's sword at his throat.

"You're still telegraphing your hits," Lucien corrected the other vampire, who swatted his king's sword out of his face. Finally, I caught an uninterrupted sight of Lucien looming over the other vampire. His body was still long enough for my breath to whisk out of my lungs and set my heart to hammering.

Oh. My. Gods. He was dressed only in a pair of loose, black sweatpants, with the slightest sheen of sweat on his chest, his muscles on glorious display. I'd seen him shirtless in Tír nAill, but had convinced myself there was no way he could be as hot as I remembered. I had told myself it was the ambrosia—you know, the ambrosia, I did *not* drink—that made him seem so attractive. So wrong, I had been wrong.

My breath caught in my throat, and my cheeks burned as I pressed my thighs tightly together. I tried to control myself and failed miserably, desire flooding my body. Oh, how I wanted him. I could still feel the way he had touched me and the spike of lust when he had tied my hands to the bed. I never knew bondage could be so freeing.

Lucien caught sight of me standing in the doorway, and a wide grin split his face. Well, that was just rude. He wasn't allowed to be even more attractive. It wasn't fair, especially to me. The smile made his hard features soften, and my heart thudded in a completely different, *dangerous* way. For a moment, I could have sworn he was actually *happy* to see me, and it made my stomach flutter. *He thinks I'm his mate. Of course, he's happy to see me.* The butterflies died a brutal death, making my lips tug down.

My frown made his smile slowly die, and I felt a flash of guilt. I was a captive here, not a guest, and shouldn't feel bad for making my warden realize the reality of the situation. I would not think about the fact that it was the first time since I met him I'd seen his smile reach his eyes.

He bowed formally to Elijah before grasping the vampire's hand to pull him up. "It looks like we will have to postpone. My *queen* needs to speak to me."

A growl caught in my throat at his statement. Elijah bowed to Lucien, his hand over his heart as he did. "My king." He took a few steps toward me and paused, repeating the gesture. "My queen."

"I'm not—" I sputtered, but Elijah didn't wait for my response before passing by me and disappearing down the hallway.

Fucking vampire. I was *not* his queen. I wasn't *anyone's* queen.

Lucien slowly returned the sword he'd used against Elijah to its place on the wall, the muscles of his back flexing as he did. I barely stopped from licking my lips at the sight, concentrating on not drooling.

Phoebe! Rules!

Right, my rules, the rules that kept me alive for a decade…what were they again?

"If I had known I was putting on a show for you, I would have dragged it out." His eyes drifted down my chest to where my nipples showed through the cheap cotton of my shirt. I willed myself not to cover them, but my arms went up, crossing over my chest.

"Yes, I'm attracted to you. In other *breaking* news, water is wet."

He crossed his arms over his chest, brows furrowing a little, again displaying his mouth-watering muscles. I wanted to trace my tongue over every grove and dent. I ached to touch him, my fingertips tingling with the need. No! Why was I so weak when it came to this one man?

He noticed my focus, his smirk returning. I forced my gaze away, stepping deeper into the room, pretending interest in the weapons lining the walls. I needed to think about anything but the way he touched me earlier, how *exposed* I'd felt. I couldn't give in to the part of my mind that wanted to cling to him and let him shelter me.

"Quite the collection you've amassed here," I croaked out.

He reached for a towel and wiped some of the sweat from his face and chest. I would not be jealous of a towel. I absolutely refused. He didn't put a shirt on, coming back to stand far too close. I forced myself to plant my feet and not move away. Every nerve in my body was aware of him, every follicle and muscle urging me to spin around and jump him. This was a struggle I couldn't afford to lose.

"Have you used them all?" I squeaked. The scent of him surrounded me. My mind went blank for a moment.

"Most."

His voice sounded off, and without thinking, I glanced over my shoulder. His eyes weren't lingering on the weapons, but locked on me. He slowly trailed his tongue over his lips.

"Which one is your favorite?" I asked breathlessly, though I couldn't care less.

"None," he responded, shocking me a little out of the daze of lust.

"None?" I repeated. I turned to face him, finding him even closer, and just stopped myself from taking a step back. He was just a guy. I'd dealt with guys before. He was just like them, a normal guy looking like he was just waiting for the opportunity to swallow me whole.

Lucien shrugged, his wicked smile making my heart thud faster, which I knew he heard as his grin grew. But the smile didn't reach his eyes. That warmth from earlier was gone. "If you're constantly using *your sword* or *your ax*, you miss the opportunity to turn your enemy's own weapons against them."

Did he just quote rule number two?

I tilted my head, fascinated. "You go *unarmed* into battle?" That couldn't possibly be true.

He nodded. "Only until I meet my first opponent. Plus, I'm never truly unarmed." He flashed his fangs to demonstrate, and heat speared through me. I felt my cheeks flush again.

"I've never even held a sword," I murmured, hoping to conceal my arousal.

"Never?" he asked. Swords were the weapon of choice for most immortals. Modern weapons could cause painful injuries, but a beheading was the only sure way to kill every immortal. Though each species had other weaknesses, like witches were vulnerable to fire, lycans to silver, vamps to sun, a beheading was the end for *all of us*.

"Why would I need to?" I held up my cuffed arm, which caused him to look away. "With barely a thought, I can incinerate my enemies."

It was only a brag when you couldn't back it up.

"Truly?"

I wondered if I had impressed him. I hated to admit that I flushed at the thought of him in awe of my power. No one had ever been anything other than *terrified*.

"If you removed the cuffs, I could show you." I smiled teasingly at him. Lucien rubbed his palm over his chest absently, his eyes returning to mine. "Are you okay?" Did Elijah get a lucky shot in when I wasn't watching?

"I'm fine." He smiled brightly, making my heart skip a beat.

Blindly, I pointed to a sword on the wall, seeking a distraction. "Will you teach me?" Because hand-to-hand combat with him was *such* a smart idea, but I was too proud to call the words back.

"You want to learn?" Another stunned question from the vampire. I was enjoying surprising him, especially since he was at least twenty-five hundred years old, based on the library etchings. It was good to knock the fossil off his axis.

"I guess Elijah could teach me…" I goaded, noticing his eyes flash red for an instant before cooling. I blinked in surprise at how quickly they changed. During his fight with Elijah, they never wavered from their enigmatic green.

"No other male is teaching *my queen* to fight."

I winced at the title but nodded and lifted one of the two swords they'd used earlier from its hook on the wall. The weight of the sword fell into my hand, and I fell back a couple of stumbling steps. I tried to balance it, but instead, I hit the ground. The weapon landed across my chest, its weight pinning me to the mat.

Lucien's laugh echoed through the sparring room, and I shot him a venomous glare. "You could have warned me they were so heavy."

He shrugged and smiled down at me. "You seemed *so* determined."

Easily picking up the sword, which was almost crushing me, he placed it back on the wall effortlessly. Did he have to be so strong on top of everything else? It was unfair. He pulled down two wooden swords, each well-worn from training. Though not as heavy as the metal one, it provided an unfamiliar weight on my arm.

"You sure you want me to teach you?" He smirked, likely knowing my arm already shook from holding up the unfamiliar weight. I clutched it even tighter, gritting my teeth.

I sent him an answering smirk and said, "Bring it on, Father Time."

He gave me no quarter, and within an hour, my muscles collapsed from the unfamiliar use. "Mercy!" I begged, falling onto my back on the floor, unable to stand straight anymore. "I hate you," I muttered without heat, especially as he leaned over me with a smirk.

He poked me in the side with the wooden practice sword. "Giving up so easily?" he teased.

I huffed, my limbs spread across the floor, doubting I would be able to move from that spot for a while. "I demand a rematch with my powers."

He scoffed, "Such a sore loser."

"You're damn right I am."

He returned the wooden swords to their spot on the wall before reaching down to help me to my feet.

When I wobbled, he swept me into his arms and carried me back to his bedroom. He went straight into the massive en suite bathroom. The shower was large enough to fit ten, the bathtub sunken and carved out of the obsidian rock.

Lucien set me on my feet, and when he fiddled with the controls of the shower, I realized he wasn't planning on leaving. I shrugged and stripped off my soiled clothes, pretending like he wasn't there. When he turned around, likely to announce the water was hot, I strutted past him fully naked.

His jaw dropped as I closed the glass door of the shower, leaving him on the outside but fully able to see me. His eyes were glowing red with lust, but I turned my back to him. I noticed that he'd already placed my shampoo and conditioner on the black tile floor. My lips twitched at the presumptive action. He just thought he was *so* irresistible, didn't he?

I heard the door squeak open, and his voice rang with rage. "What forces do you play at?" His accent was heavier than ever.

I whipped around, not even remotely surprised to see him naked. I might just combust if I couldn't touch him.

"What do you mean?" Imbuing my voice with as much innocence as I could muster. I wanted to demand that he fuck me, beg him to get inside me. I needed more of what we'd done earlier.

He pushed me against the wall, the cool tile shocking against my heated skin. Too many males thought I was fragile and needed to be handled with care. All I wanted was someone so out of control that

194

tempering their strength was impossible. I glanced at Lucien's glowing red eyes and thought, *Ding! Ding! Ding!*

"You're provoking me on purpose." His face was an inch from mine and my entire body quivered with anticipation. I had been aroused before sparring, but naked and this close to him, I was a mass of quivering need.

"Maybe I'm testing your restraint," I whispered huskily, licking my lips slowly, drawing his gaze.

His eyes went an even brighter red, and he grabbed my wrists, pinning them above me in one hand. His touch was light over my curves, my back arching for more. He smacked my breast, the sound startling loud. I knew he'd likely left a red handprint on the delicate flesh.

"You're testing my restraint? I'll punish you for it."

I recalled the last time he'd punished me, and the thought made my thighs clench and moisture fill my core. His nostrils flared, and he growled, "You like when I punish you?"

I moaned instead of answering, his hand drifting down to palm my ass, pulling me against his hardness, forcing me to feel every inch of him.

"If you agreed to stay, I'd be so deep inside your pussy that you couldn't breathe without me feeling it."

"You know I can't," I murmured.

His palm left me and slammed into the wall, cracking the tile. "Why not?"

I glanced away, aware of my vulnerable position. "I can't tell you," I bit out.

Rule No. 3: Don't Tell Anyone Anything. Ever. Even vampire kings, who look at me with possession and desire.

His jaw tightened as he ground his teeth. "Won't tell me," he corrected, releasing my wrists and stepping back. Was he just going to leave me turned on to the point of pain?

Without thinking, I reached down to touch myself. He was in front of me, with my arms pinned above me again in a blink. "This is your punishment. You are not to touch yourself. Ever. Every time you come, it will be with me, or not at all."

He was planning to leave me like this? I whimpered. "But…"

Lucien's hand lightly collared my neck, not hurting but reminding me. "Agree," he demanded.

"Fine," I puffed out. I would just wait until I was alone…

"And don't think of hiding and getting yourself off. I'll know." The way his eyes narrowed made me believe him. "If you disobey me, I'll punish you longer."

More time in this state of painful arousal? I nodded in defeat.

He sped through his own shower, leaving me alone in the glass stall after a few minutes. My skin felt wrong, oversensitive, and every touch caused a rise in awareness. I rubbed my arms as I showered, the feeling of loneliness crushing me.

I shouldn't feel guilty about keeping things from Lucien, but I did. I recalled how the look of delight on his face when he realized I was watching him spar had died at my frown, and it sent a pang through me. He'd looked so hopeful, and I'd killed it.

As I finished my shower, it was so tempting to get myself off when I ran my soapy fingers between my legs, but I didn't. I could do that for him. There was no way I could stay with him, but I could resist. I stepped out of the shower, quickly toweling off, my body still feeling wrong.

I strode into the massive dressing room and gaped at all the clothes delivered for me. It was filled with gowns, jeans, sundresses, shoes, accessories, and everything I could ever need. When I'd arrived at Întuneric, half of the closet was empty. My meager belongings had filled three hangers on one side. But it wasn't mine, would never be mine, unless I decided to stay.

I purposefully pulled on my own worn jeans, a long sleeve shirt to hide the cuffs, and my own shoes, refusing to touch any of the new clothes Lucien had bought me.

My stomach growling, I stormed back to the kitchen. Elijah sat at the round cook's table by himself. He stuffed his cell phone into his pocket when he caught sight of me. I pulled out the seat next to him, grateful that he wisely remained silent.

XVII

THE REALM OF MORTALS.
ÎNTUNERIC CASTEL, ROMANIA.

"Please, not again, no, not again. C-Come back. P-Please."
Streaks of water cut through the black ash on her familiar face. She
would never smile at me again or huff in exasperation at my
millions of questions.

Why are there rules? Why can I only learn one type of magic?
Why does my bloodline define my life? Define all of our lives? Why
can't I bring them back?

I HAD JUST FINISHED AN AMAZING BLT, brushing the crumbs from my fingertips, wishing for another, when I heard voices echoing down the hall. Several of them sounded almost like *growls*, and I stood, turning to face the newcomers, preparing for whatever was about to come around the corner. *What in all hells was it now?*

Elijah moved to stand protectively in front of me as they approached. I peeked over his shoulder, and my mouth dropped open at the sight of four gorgeous, rough - will growl and scratch you in bed sort of - men enter the kitchen. All of them were laser-focused on the feast. So that was why they were preparing enough food for an army.

Their eyes blew wide, and they descended on the chef's table, moving faster than I could track. Chairs flew out and back in. I watched in fascinated horror as they tore into the food with their hands and *claws.* The men all stopped and focused on something just behind me. I jumped when I saw Adelaide at my back. I was certain the housekeeper had not been there a second ago. She cleared her throat, indicating Elijah and me with her eyes. The men didn't take the hint. Instead, one jumped up and fake chased the unimpressed woman around the kitchen. Adelaide swatted at him, though she cracked a hint of a smile.

"Now, Addie dear, when are you going to leave the leech king behind and come work for us?" he teased, his voice hinting at an accent.

The housekeeper smacked him hard on the arm, but it didn't deter him. She sniffed, turning on her heel, leaving Elijah and me alone again with the men. They ate until they'd decimated the food. Satisfied, several of them leaned back in their chairs, patting their stomachs.

I shoved at Elijah's back to get him to move from in front of me. The vampire stumbled to the side, and we finally drew the attention of the new arrivals, their eyes locking on me. A single moment of silence pulsed between us. I gulped nervously. Maybe this wasn't such a good idea, especially with my powers locked down. Even here, under Lucien's protection, I was vulnerable. What if one of them was a bounty hunter? Fuck, being in this castle was making me lose my edge. I held my breath, waiting for them to make the first move.

Seductive smiles slowly spread across their faces. There was one outlier who appeared more interested in the food in front of him than anything else. His eyes were locked on the plates as he continued to plow through what remained of the feast.

One male, several braids twisted in the mass of blonde hair hanging in shaggy waves past his shoulders, was all charm. His smile was predatory, and his grey eyes flashed at me. He approached me with feral grace, his feet stepping over each other without stumbling. *Okay, seduction was not a normal bounty hunter tactic.* I pushed Elijah away when he tried to step in front of me again. I could do this. Seductive men were not a challenge for me. Well, except for Lucien.

The big man stalked closer, his electric steel eyes predatory. I expected my heart to race at being the center of a gorgeous man's focus, but there was *nothing*. My body didn't react at all.

"Now, who might *you* be, gorgeous?"

"Phoebe." I grinned, my smile as predatory as his. His eyes widened before becoming hooded in interest. What was it with immortal males and challenges? They couldn't resist.

"The name is Leif, beautiful." Hmm, Norse name. That explained the accent and his appearance of a Viking of old. If he was from Norway, it narrowed down his species significantly. But my experience with immortals touched by the Norse Pantheon was *limited.* Witches were from the Greek Pantheon, touched by our goddess, Hekate. Each immortal species hailed from a different pantheon, touched by a god from a time before record.

200

My eyes darted to the other two immortals who closed in on me, another blonde and a brunette. The man still sitting at the table was also blonde. They looked like an advertisement for a Baltic cruise. *Come away with us! Escape to the land of Vikings!* Too bad I preferred Romania. Wait, no I didn't! I was completely neutral, like Switzerland. I was Switzerland. *Why did that sound familiar?*

The other blonde smiled at me. "Don't settle on Leif, pet. His bark is worse than his bite. Me, however? My bite is *better* than my bark." An abrupt laugh escaped from me as he pointed a thumb at his chest and said, "Thurston."

The brunette stood next to Leif and said in a deep, rumbling voice, "Don't listen to these two pups. You want a man who will make you howl? Look no further. I'm Viggo."

The three men formed a semicircle around me. Normally, I would have scrambled away from those kind of odds, but I didn't want to hint that I was powerless. It was definitely *not* because I knew Lucien would never allow a threat to me into the castle. More than all of that, I instinctively knew the only danger I faced from these men was their charm.

Viggo's brown curls came down to his shoulders, his dark eyes dancing as he snatched my hand to lay an exaggerated kiss on the back of it. My nose scrunched at his show of affection, and I politely pulled my hand away. Viggo didn't even appear to notice. Seduction came as easily as breathing to them.

I shot a glance at Elijah, my eyes narrowing on the skittish vampire as he edged closer to the door. I wasn't about to let Elijah ruin the most fun I'd had in years.

Despite the three of them pressing in on me, I couldn't help but smile at their over-the-top attitudes. Their easy familiarity with me was refreshing. It was almost like we were friends.

I glared at the vampire, freezing him in his tracks. "Don't even think about it, Elijah."

In a blink, all three of my new friends formed a wall of muscle between the vampire and me. "Is he trying to hurt you, pet?" Leif growled.

Aww, they thought to protect me. It was adorable that they thought I needed protection. I could take care of myself. I glanced down at the cuffs. Well, I could normally take care of myself.

I placed a hand on Viggo's and Leif's shoulders, gently nudging them to the side. "No, boys. Ignore him. What brings you to Întuneric?" I asked with a bright smile. The fourth man stood from the table, apparently done eating, and joined our little group. His eyes were more cautious and analytical of me than the other three. He tipped his head back and inhaled deeply, his eyes glowing amber. "You don't smell like a leech." He gestured to himself and added, "Gunnar."

"That's because I'm not." I tilted my head at them, trying to place their species. The amber eyes were a hint, prodding at a memory. An enhanced sense of smell was attributed to many species. Thankfully, it wasn't one of my abilities. Regular body odor was bad enough. I couldn't imagine catching a whiff with enhanced senses. *Ew.*

"Our king is here to talk to the leech," Viggo answered.

Oh great, there was *another* immortal king at Întuneric? With my current run of luck, I'd end up being his mate, too. I recoiled inwardly at the idea. The thought of anyone but Lucien touching me was abhorrent. When the hell did I become so attached?

"Oh? And which king would that be?" I asked. I watched as they sniffed the air and frowned at each other in confusion.

"King Erik Wulfric of the Lycans," Thurston finally answered.

Lycans? Wolf-shifters? That explained the strange way they kept sniffing me. With the bindings, I doubted I smelled like magic, so they must have thought I was some other immortal and were trying to figure it out. I resisted the need to place a hand over the cuffs on my wrists.

Wait, King Erik? As in the super-hot one?

My brows furrowed, recalling the passage about Lucien's war with the Lycans. Gods, he had dealings with kings and gods, I couldn't even be in the same room as another witch. My stomach rolled, and I crossed my arms, trying to mask some of my disquiet. I forced an inviting smile onto my lips, dropping my arms to my sides.

"Phoebe..." Elijah warned, his eyes hinting toward red.

"Run along now, Elijah. I'll be fine here."

I smirked at his murderous look. I could tell he wanted to say something, but he just shook his head before disappearing from the room in a blur of speed. That left me about ten minutes before Lucien came in, guns blazing. It was more than enough time to cause some trouble.

I glanced back at the four werewolves and smiled again, but this time, it was diabolical. "Now, which of you boys wants to see if he can drink me under the table?"

XVIII

THE REALM OF MORTALS.
ÎNTUNERIC CASTEL, ROMANIA.

I GOT THE NOTICE THAT ERIK HAD ARRIVED less than an hour after Phoebe disappeared somewhere in the castle. She needed space. The one thing I couldn't give her. I was constantly fighting the compulsion to seek her out, to be in her presence, to listen to her voice, to inhale her scent, and to watch her mind at work. I knew she wanted space to put that devious mind to work, figuring out how to escape me and our bond. She didn't want me, she was going to leave me.

The arrival of the messenger snapped me out of my dark musings. I ordered him to alert the kitchens, knowing that Erik traveled with a posse of lycans. Their appetites were especially huge because they burned so much energy during their shifts. The last time Erik had visited Întuneric, I'd needed to send servants out hourly for food.

I met Eric in the courtyard, clasping my friend's forearm in greeting. I tried to smile but it was probably closer to a grimace.

"What brings you here, Erik?" I inquired, skipping the pleasantries. Originally, the plan was to invite the wolf to Phoebe's coronation in two weeks, not now when things were still so unstable. Not when she still hated me.

Erik smiled. "I came to meet your queen. Your Oracle invited me. I'm guessing she didn't tell you?

I shook my head, but a genuine smile tugged at my lips. It was good to see Erik, no matter the circumstances. Just seeing him made me feel more like myself, balanced and grounded. The wolves who accompanied Erik immediately departed for the kitchens, bowing their heads respectfully when they passed me. Well, that was an improvement. If my mind wasn't so scattered, I would have wondered about their new attitude. But at the moment, I could barely breathe, and it took everything in me not to follow them and search for Phoebe.

The wolves shoved each other and roughhoused as they rushed off. Lycans were always physically affectionate with each other, especially with their mates. I saw a look of longing flash in Erik's eyes as he watched his pack mates. *Did he miss being one of the pack instead of their king?*

Unlike me, Erik experienced three centuries as a prince before becoming king. Three centuries to believe that, barring an extremely unfortunate incident, he might *never* be king. No one could have predicted the war between vampires and werewolves or how it would end. Immortal kings tended to remain in power *indefinitely*. I'd been king for ten thousand years. I knew kings who had worn their crowns long before me, though most resided in other realms.

Erik slapped me on the back, and the two of us strode side-by-side into the throne room. I couldn't hide my wince when I saw the empty throne beside mine, and I knew that Erik had noticed when he said, "So, tell me about her."

I gestured him into my office and closed the door behind him. This was where I preferred to hold my more intimate meetings. It was one of the few modernized rooms in the entire castle. It had been a forced upgrade as I clung to the ways of the past as much as possible. I despised technology, truly anything that I couldn't wrap my head around. WiFi? Social Media? Pass. What was wrong with sending a letter?

"Well, as much as it pains me to admit this, Erik, you were right. The woman on Tír nAill was my mate." I grimaced at the look on the lycan's face and the bitter taste left in my mouth at uttering the words *you were right* to another. People usually said that *to me.*

I poured us each a drink from the sideboard, vodka for me, brandy for Erik. Erik took the glass, and we toasted in solidarity. He sat in a chair before the desk while I took the one behind it.

When had Erik become a friend? He understood the burdens of being king, how every move you made needed to keep an entire *species* alive. Immortal regents had made the wrong choices in the past and been reduced to figments of myth and imagination, wiped from all realms. The power some of those kings and queens once held boggled the mind, but still, they were decimated.

Erik took a bracing sip of the brandy and let out a refreshing breath. He leaned back in the chair, his bright blue eyes scanning me. I shifted uncomfortably before catching myself. All the control I usually had over my emotions, actions, even *breaths* was gone. His lips twitched into a smirk, and my fists clenched. "Did you catch her name this time?"

My eyes narrowed on my old friend, picturing how fantastic he would look without a head. "Wait until it's your turn, my friend. You'll fuck it up even worse."

Erik raised a tawny eyebrow. "Is that even possible?"

I hissed at him, my grip tightening on my glass, tempted to throw it at the chuckling werewolf. Instead, I sighed and swirled the vodka, watching as it hit the sides of the crystal, letting the hypnotic rhythm lull me into some kind of calm. "Her name is Phoebe, and she's a witch."

Erik's surprise resonated between us. Matings outside of species were rare and often fraught with problems. I looked up as Erik slowly set his glass on the desk. Erik had dealt with the spell casters in the past. They came in handy when his wolves turned in public. The Witches Council was excellent at wiping memories and altering the perceptions of mortals. I relied on my fearsome reputation to keep my vampires in line. That, and my *other* projects.

"A witch? No wonder you look so fucking miserable. What bloodline?" Erik inquired.

Fuck, I didn't know.

"What does it matter? Her name is Silvano now," I snapped. A witch's bloodline was everything, each specializing in a single form of magic. I couldn't pin down a single magic she seemed to favor. She'd used a shield in the alley of New Orleans, battle magic when the vampires first appeared, and then her rift. Then I'd bound her. She had so many secrets.

At Erik's penetrating stare, my eyes darted away, and I pinched my nose. "She can create and close rifts." The wolf's gasp of shock kept my eyes down as I

208

continued, heat burning its way up the back of my neck. "I…I bound her powers to keep her from running."

There was a litany of curses from the lycan so foul that even my head came up in surprise.

"You know what that does to a witch!" he hissed, standing and slamming his hands down on the desk between us.

I stood in response, my mouth opening and closing, trying to find something that could explain my actions. I came up short because I knew there was no excuse. Instead, my desperation colored my words. "Rifts, Erik! At will! I could turn my back, and she could be in Etrebeus!"

Etrebeus was the realm of darkness from which all shadows originated. It was home to the Erinyes, female spirits of vengeance with shadow wings. They were the judge, jury, and executioner for immortals they perceived were escaping justice. It was a plane no one ever escaped from.

Erik winced, sitting back in his chair again, running a hand down his face. "Are you sure she would run?"

"Yes," I answered resolutely, falling back into my chair, glaring up at the ceiling. She hated me and wanted to run. She didn't trust me to protect her. "Phoebe makes no secret of her plans to escape."

I threaded my fingers through my hair, tempted to rip the strands from the roots. I rolled my head to the side and dropped my hands uselessly, looking back at Erik. The lycan stood, refilling both our glasses, holding mine out for me to take. I barely felt the glass between my fingers. When had I finished mine?

"I'm just so fucking *lost* with her, Erik. The more tightly I hold on to her, the more I feel her slipping away. It's like trying to catch smoke." I threw back the drink, not even feeling the burn against the back of my throat.

"You need to trust her, Lucien."

That was easier said than done. "Could you, Erik? Could you trust her?"

Erik glanced away, unable to admit that he could. Mates were everything to lycans. Once found, a wolf would do *anything* to keep theirs. Erik had been searching for his queen for the last millennia. The lycan must despair of ever finding her, and Phoebe just *landed* in my lap. Fuck, I was an idiot.

Elijah burst into the study, saving Erik from responding. The vampire's eyes were wide and frantic, his dark skin waxy, but he took the time to bow to each of us despite his obvious urgency. Elijah was a traditionalist.

"My king, if I may?" Elijah's shaky question made my nerves stand on end. I'd tasked the vampire with keeping an eye on Phoebe. It wasn't one of my prouder moments. Though I don't think I'd had a single one of those since meeting Phoebe.

I gestured for Elijah to proceed, knowing Erik was hanging on every word. "I was spy-watching over Phoebe, as you asked." Erik's gaze seemed to bore into me, and I swore I could feel his judgment. "Well, the lycans," he continued, gesturing to Erik, "seem to have taken an *interest* in her."

Oh, had they? The sound of roaring filled my ears, and my fangs dropped into my mouth. A flood of liquid emotion scalded me, and I knew my eyes had turned red. She was mine! If one of them dared to touch her... The glass in my hand shattered as I bolted to my feet, the chair slamming against the wall behind me. *Mine. Mine. Mine!*

My mind whirled with images of dead werewolves. All that breathed in her direction would meet their demise. I made it to the throne room before Erik slammed into my side, tackling me to the floor. I bared my fangs and hardly resisted the need to rip out the werewolf's throat.

"No! Lucien, think!" Erik grappled with me, pinning me to the floor. "You want her to trust you? Show you trust her!" I cracked my forehead against the lycan's, throwing him off. Erik rallied and took me to the ground again. We rolled across the stone floor, exchanging blows. Or rather, I pummeled Erik. The lycan blocked them, never returning a strike. He was only trying to keep me from killing his pack members, not injure me. Though his eyes were glowing amber, and his fangs were extending and retracting as he tried to control his beast, he was resisting his need to shift. Once the change began fully, Erik would not be able to stop it.

In the most logical side of my brain, which was admittedly very, *very* far from the surface at the moment, I knew Erik was making sense. But the thought of another touching Phoebe…

Mine. Mine. Mine!

The more overpowering the need to get to Phoebe, the more savage I became, and Erik was powerless to block the brutal hit to his jaw. The werewolf shook his head repeatedly, allowing me to shove him off. I got to my feet, preparing to continue my race to my mate. I could taste the werewolves' blood in my mouth, dripping down my throat as I strung them up by their entrails, making them watch as I played with them.

"Damn it, Lucien! You'll lose Phoebe if you do this!" Erik shouted at my back, and it was those words that penetrated the thick fog of possession that claimed me.

Lose Phoebe?

Never.

Frozen at the doors to the throne room, I shut my eyes tight. I forced away the images of another with her. Instead, I remembered the healthy sheen of sweat on her face when we sparred. I filled my mind with the way she cuddled against my side after I'd pleasured her, the way her smile lit up her face, the sound of her laugh. I hissed out calming breaths through my clenched teeth, repeating her name over and over in my mind. It took a few minutes of teetering on the edge of control before my fangs receded. The rage was still running through me and likely would continue until I caught sight of her, but at least it was leashed.

"What do you suggest, Erik?" My voice was guttural and unrecognizable. I kept my back to the lycan, unsure if I could maintain the control if I moved.

"If you offer your trust now, she will be more likely to offer hers in return." He paused before continuing. "Do you believe she would encourage one of my men's affections?"

No, I didn't. I remembered the way she spoke about her parents' marriage, and I heard the envy in her voice. She was loyal to those she trusted. With that realization, the rage eased.

Erik sighed as he came to my side. He hit my shoulder again and said, "Now let's go see what trouble they've gotten themselves into."

XIX

THE REALM OF MORTALS.
ÎNTUNERIC CASTEL, ROMANIA.

IT TOOK EVERY OUNCE OF CONTROL I possessed to force a calm I did not feel. My skull was pounding from the need to slaughter, to *kill*. My fists flexed as I struggled to maintain my sanity. I did not think Phoebe would *encourage* their affections, but I didn't want someone gaining any kind of goodwill from her, not when she still hated me.

Erik forced me to walk when I wanted to sprint through the halls, making the trek torturously slow. What horrors awaited me? What if she convinced them to help her escape? Or *worse*? As we closed in on the kitchen, we could hear raucous singing echoing against the stone walls.

"For Norway, birthplace of giants, we this toast will empty!"

What in all hell? We turned the corner, and my jaw practically dropped to the ground. Two of the wolves were drunkenly bellowing, extremely off-key, slumped against the wall by the doorway, several dishes of half-eaten food on the ground between them.

"And when we first get our blood in a boil, we sweetly of liberty dream."

I shifted to take in the rest of the kitchen. Some of the staff were deep in their cups, whispering behind their hands, forgetting about the enhanced hearing of immortals. It didn't matter, as most of the words were slurred beyond recognition, anyway.

"Though we will someday wake up and break chains, ties, and force."

The two still upright lycans were at the round dining table with Phoebe, locked in a battle of extreme concentration. I counted eleven empty shot glasses sitting in front of each. The two empty spots only contained nine. I shot a look at the two werewolves on the ground. Nine shots, and they were down for the count? What the fuck were they drinking?

I watched in amazement as Phoebe and the two lycans threw back their twelfth shot. One of the wolves swayed in his seat. Phoebe and the other survivor watched him carefully, waiting for him to topple.

"For Norway, birthplace of giants, we this toast will empty!"

He slid from the chair onto the floor in a boneless heap. Phoebe cheered, high-fiving the remaining lycan, though she missed and smacked him hard in the face. What the fuck had happened here?

I leaned against the doorway, taking it all in. Of all the horrible scenes running through my mind during my tortuously long walk down to the kitchens with Erik, I couldn't have even guessed at the one playing out. Erik had tested my restraint by delaying us, and when I wasn't torturing myself with scenarios, I'd passed the time by imagining ways to kill him.

The newly collapsed werewolf joined the other two for their drinking song. Though he remained on his back, his limbs spread out on the floor.

"Each brave hero, among cliffs born, we will drink to his honor!"

I cautiously stepped forward into the light of the kitchen, Erik at my side. The human staff that could still stand fled at the sight of us, but the werewolves didn't even flinch at the presence of their king. The remaining lycan battling against Phoebe noticed us and shoved her roughly, gesturing to Erik and me. Phoebe's head swung toward us, and I held my breath, waiting to see how she would react to my presence.

"Lucien!" she screamed with delight and threw both her hands in the air. Well, that was unexpected. If only she always greeted me in such a way. If I'd come in here, determined to destroy these wolves, I wouldn't have had that reception from her. Erik was right, not that I would tell him. Once was enough for a lifetime.

I smiled, her flushed face making her almost youthfully exuberant. I stood behind her and placed my hands on her shoulders, kissing the top of her head. She leaned her head back against me, giving me a drunken smile. My stomach fluttered, but my nostrils burned at the smell of the liquor on the table. What the hells were they drinking?

"Did these lycans challenge you to a battery acid drinking contest?" I asked, scrunching my nose at the smell.

She smirked, looking back at the remaining wolf. "I challenged them! Couldn't resist."

Phoebe closed one eye and looked at the last shot before carefully picking it up. She held it in front of her, waiting for the wolf to do the same. It took him three tries to get his hand around the small glass, then together, they slammed back the liquid. A minute later, the lycan slumped forward in defeat, and Phoebe leaned her head back to look at me in triumph.

"I tolds 'em you shouldn't challenge a southern belle to a moonshine fight." Phoebe hiccuped, and I couldn't stop the smile that stretched across my face at the picture she made. She was just so...*adorable.*

Phoebe wobbled in her chair, noticing Elijah and Erik for the first time.

"Elijah! Did you *tattle* on me?!" she yelled. Elijah hunched over, hiding behind Erik, fearing his queen's wrath. I masked a chuckle. Elijah was smart to hide from her.

She shut one bleary eye and pointed at Erik, though her finger was off by several feet. "And you're the wolf king? The super hot one?"

Erik gaped at her question, his eyes dancing with laughter. "I guess I am."

Her eyes trailed up and down Erik. I gritted my teeth until she scoffed at the lycan, "My king is *way* hotter than you." She tilted her head up to look at me again. "Aren't you?"

My ire instantly cooled. "It only matters that I'm hotter to you, *vrăjitoare.*"

I helped her to stand, but she stumbled, falling against my chest. She didn't even pull away when I wrapped my arms around her, keeping her close. "You are the hottest of the hottest to me. Like Vesuvius hot. What does vrajshfut mean?" she said, butchering the endearment.

She twirled her fingers along my chest, drawing little designs. Did she know she drove me mad with even such a simple touch? Even drunk, her effect on me was swift and powerful. Gods, she was addicting.

"Enchantress," I whispered, stroking the hair falling into her face, brushing it behind her ear. Her eyes glimmered at the endearment as she reached up to touch my cheek. I held my breath, not wanting to scare her. I did not want this moment, this precious, *fragile* moment, to end. This is what our life together would be like if she stayed.

Then she wobbled, and the moment ended. I chuckled and scooped her into my arms. She rested her head on my shoulder without protest, trusting me to keep her safe.

"Did you enjoy drinking those wolves under the table?" I asked, pressing her closer against me.

She giggled and nodded, the innocent sound striking a chord in me. I needed to hear more of it. I needed to see her smile and hear her laugh every day.

"I figured their burly man bodies wouldn't be able to handle it." She imitated the wolves' accents when she spoke, forcing a bark of laughter from me. The wolves grumbled their protests as I carried her out of the kitchen, leaving Erik to take care of them. I maneuvered the dark labyrinth easily, heading for our room.

"It's good I found you then. Who knows what kind of trouble a drunken witch could get into?"

She scoffed, tapping my chest lightly. "No trouble," she said, jangling the cuffs. I stiffened, prepared for her to rage at me. Instead, she laughed. "Might be a good thing. The last time I outdrank a bunch of immortal males, I almost rifted into a stone wall afterward."

Phoebe snorted at herself, settling back against me. Not wanting to release her, I used my foot to open the door to our bedroom. I stepped through, kicking it closed before placing her gently on the bed, expecting

218

her to pass out. I should have known better. When did Phoebe ever do what I expected?

She sat up and swung her legs off the mattress, trying several times to come to a stand but failing. I moved to her side of the bed and kneeled in front of her, taking off her shoes. I frowned when I noticed they were the same ones she'd worn in New Orleans and not any of the new pairs I'd purchased for her.

The sounds of the wolves still shouting their loyalty to their homeland grew louder as they came closer, making their way to their own beds to sleep off the alcohol.

"Each honest Norwegian, who chains broke, will forever be loved!"

Phoebe covered her mouth, giggling again. She gave me a wobbly smile when I removed her socks, tucking them into her little boots. How did one so powerful have such tiny feet? She grabbed my shoulders to keep from falling back on the bed. The moment she touched me, I forgot my reasons for getting her into bed. She already owned me, just one touch, and I was lost. I needed a distraction.

"How did you out drink them like that?" It shouldn't have been possible. Lycan metabolism was accelerated even among immortals. I'm pretty sure that was the first time I've ever seen a lycan trashed.

She smiled brightly at me, her hands moving up and down the sides of my neck. "It's all about the alcohol. Moonshine and I go *wayyyy* back, but those not used to it," she pulled away, making a slamming motion with her hands, "you're on your ass with just a few sips."

Phoebe pushed me back and stumbled to a stand. She tore at the buttons of her jeans, huffing in frustration when she failed.

"Let me do it." I chuckled, efficiently peeling the denim off her legs. She fell back on the bed, kicking off the pants with a flurry of pale limbs, missing my face by an inch. Once free, she balanced on her elbows, shooting me a heated look. She licked her lips slowly, and I swallowed a groan. "Don't even think about it, Phoebe."

She pouted at me. "But I want to!"

A hoarse laugh escaped my lips. "Another time, when you're not off your rocker."

She collapsed back on the bed, clad only in a t-shirt and underwear. She shouldn't have looked so alluring, but she did. Everything about this female pulled me in. I even found it endearing she plotted to outdrink four lycans and succeeded. She'd brought more life back to Întuneric in the last twenty-four hours than I had in the last ten millennia. She was bringing me back to life.

"They were the first real werewolves I ever met. How'd I do?" she asked the ceiling.

"The wrathful guard's crackling guns, most likely explains Norwegians' grievance!"

"I have a feeling you'll soon be a legend among them." There was nothing a werewolf loved more than a mystery, their animal curiosity a powerful force. "Under the covers with you."

"You're so bossy," she whined, even as she obeyed, crawling under the covers and giving me a lopsided smile.

220

I chuckled again, rising to tuck her in. "You like when I'm bossy," I whispered huskily.

"Only when we're in bed, or on the floor, or on the balcony…" she trailed off, a loud snore vibrating from her.

I placed a soft kiss on her forehead as her familiar jumped on the bed and curled up at her feet. I didn't recall seeing the cat the night before. The fickle feline was likely wandering around the castle. Absently, I reminded myself to order the staff to leave doors open so she didn't get locked into an abandoned room.

I stood to leave, but she grabbed me, her lilac gaze holding me in place. "Stay? Till I fall asleep?"

I nodded, shucking my jeans and shirt as I came around the bed. I pulled on sweats to make her more comfortable. This was the first time she was prolonging contact with me in a non-sexual context, and my heart thudded against my ribs. It gave me hope.

She looked so innocent and vulnerable as she reached out for me. Fate had brought us together, and I was already coming to realize Phoebe's presence was the key to my future. There would never be another for me. Now I just needed to work on keeping her.

She pulled me closer, resting her head on my chest. We lay like that for a few moments in companionable silence as I stroked her silken hair down her back.

"Is Întuneric mystical?" she asked drowsily.

"No. Why?" I muttered into her hair.

She sighed, snuggling closer. "No reason."

XX

THE REALM OF MORTALS.
ÎNTUNERIC CASTEL, ROMANIA.

Her nose scrunched with distaste. "You are a Margaux and an Atreus. You will learn battle and healing practices. Is that not enough for you?"

No. It was never enough. I needed more power, more education. I needed more.

I WOKE UP TO A POUNDING HEADACHE and the taste of dryer lint in my mouth. Even more irritating was Lucien smiling down at me. Couldn't he look like shit when I was so hungover? It was only fair. I blinked slowly for a moment, trying to focus on him, but the room kept spinning.

"Good morning!" he yelled.

I groaned in pain, clutching my ears. His voice pinged around my brain in a painful samba. *Asshole*, I mouthed at him.

He smirked, enjoying himself. Then, he kissed me softly despite being able to taste my breath and it reeking like a garbage bag left out in the NOLA heat.

"You started quite the legend last night. Erik said you should have been one of their mates, and fate got its wires crossed when it picked you for me," he commented, his voice amused with none of the anger I expected.

I raised my eyebrows, trying to sort through my memory of the night before. There was some moonshine...*a lot* of moonshine. I groaned, covering my face with my hands. "Please tell me they feel as bad as I do." The only thing more miserable than being hungover was being hungover alone.

Another smile stretched across his lips. "Even worse."

I smiled weakly at that and groaned as I sat up, putting a hand to the side of my head. Lucien reached out to help me stand as I threw my legs over the side of the bed, but I pushed him away. He laughed softly but didn't try to help me a second time.

I stumbled to the bathroom, absently noticing all my toiletries intermingled with his as if we were a real couple. His high-handedness should agitate me, but I was too hungover to care.

I struggled through brushing my teeth four times to get the lingering taste of moonshine out of my mouth before moving to fiddle with the shower. When the water turned hot, I stepped beneath it, letting out a wistful sigh.

The scalding heat relieved some of the aches in my muscles and made my head slightly less foggy. I looked down at myself, frowning at the appearance of several bruises on my legs. Was a night of drinking complete if I didn't wake up with mysterious bruises? It didn't help that being a natural redhead guaranteed they would show up at the slightest bump.

After a luxurious forty-five minutes, I turned off the water and exited the glass stall, feeling somewhat more human. There was a pile of clean clothes on the counter. Lucien must have brought them in. The action was so normal. I almost teared up. It was like we'd been together for years. I could not let myself get any more attached to this man.

Lucien had selected a pair of yoga pants and a black tank top with some of the raciest lingerie I'd ever seen. There was the Lucien I knew. I blushed as I fingered them. The bra was a series of straps and black elastic that would cup my breasts, barely covering my nipples. The bottoms were a thong, also black elastic, that would snap against my skin. They felt utterly wicked as I slid them on with a shiver, my headache lessening as I became more turned on.

"Phoebe, what are you doing in there?" Lucien called at the door, a smirk in his voice.

I blushed. Damn his stupid vampire-enhanced sense of smell. "Nothing!" I shouted back, but my voice cracked.

I yanked on the rest of the clothes, trying to calm my lustful thoughts. I had to stop thinking about him taking off the lingerie! With his teeth! Bad! His voice was next to the door when it came again. "You sure?" he asked smugly.

I whipped the door open, tempted to punch him in the face. "Yes."

He was still smiling as I brushed past him, but Lucien stopped me by grasping my hand. He pulled it to his lips for a brief, sweet kiss, then walked in step with me toward the kitchen. I flushed at his tender gesture but kept my gaze averted, remaining silent for the walk. When we stood together in the kitchen doorway, I pulled my hand from his, wishing I didn't see him frown at the loss.

Every trace of the previous night was erased. There were no lingering bottles or shot glasses. It was like a dream, except for the four miserable werewolves sitting at the breakfast table. A breakfast buffet was laid out. The plates were set off to the side, and even an espresso machine. If only the sight and smells were not giving me the immediate urge to hurl.

Gunnar, who was the first out last night, pushed away an untouched plate of food, slightly green at the sight. Viggo and Thurston were staring deeply into cups of coffee as if the answers to all the world's questions lay within. Leif, who lasted the longest against me, had his head on the table and had covered it with a pillow, attempting to muffle all sounds.

Erik was deliberately clanging his silverware and plate as he picked from the buffet, an evil smile on his face the entire time.

Gunnar was the first to catch sight of us lingering in the doorway and croaked, "I didn't expect to see you among the living, *völva*."

I recognized the word as Old Norse for *witch*. He started calling me that somewhere between the third and sixth shot. When I'd pointed out how much it sounded like *vulva*, a smile cracked his grim face, and the others had been unable to conceal their shock at the sight.

The other three men groaned, and a smile spread across my face. Even as my head pounded, I masked my hangover, refusing to show any signs of discomfort. I had a reputation to uphold, after all. I strutted forward to the buffet, filled a mug with glorious coffee, and piled a plate full of food. Lucien took a mug of blood for himself and swiped my plate. He put both down on the table and pulled a chair out for me, refusing to give me the option to sit elsewhere without causing a scene. Damn it! Why did he have to be sweet and thoughtful on top of being high-handed and controlling?

I sighed heavily and sat down. He took the seat next to me, bringing mine as close as possible to his until our thighs touched. Even that small amount of contact had me blushing and tucking a lock of my hair behind my ear. I was just going to pretend there was not a pack of lycans watching this exchange with blatant curiosity. I focused on my plate and nibbled on my bacon, trying not to taste or smell it.

Lucien was glaring at his own breakfast, blanching at the blood in front of him. If I didn't know better, I would think his mug was full of that other life-giving liquid—coffee. Lucien took a sip and shuddered.

"Has it gone bad?" I murmured. Did blood go bad? He shook his head, taking another sip, his lip curling back from his teeth. "You don't have to drink it, Lucien."

"It's fine," he snapped.

Okaaay. That was the last time I worried about his diet.

Determined to ignore Lucien while he was acting like such a dick, I looked around the round table at everyone pretending they hadn't heard the terse conversation between us. "Where's Cassandra?" I asked.

A harried-looking Elijah burst into the room, clutching something in his fist. "She's gone. She left a note for you, my queen."

I brushed off my hands, reaching for the scrap of paper Elijah held out. The parchment was old, wrapped around a handful of...Red Vines? Thank the gods that immortals couldn't get cavities, or Cassandra's teeth would have fallen out already.

I unfurled the note, my brows furrowing as I read the words written in precise script.

Little does the new moon comprehend,
The era of false rulers is at its end.

What in all hells? I turned the sheet over, looking for something to explain the bizarre message. There was nothing but a small scribble on the back: *Eat the Red Vines and perish.* I gave the note to Lucien, who then passed it on to the wolves. Everyone seemed equally puzzled by it.

Lucien read the note once more before handing it back. "Best hold on to it and the Red Vines. You never know with Cassandra."

Gunnar lowered one of the Red Vines he'd raised to his mouth. Lucien looked back at his mug of blood, swirling it with a grimace, dismissing the note and message. Unable to resist my natural curiosity, I asked, "How did you find her?"

He shrugged and then flinched when he took a sip of blood. "By accident. I was in Thrace, fighting some war, I can't remember which. I stumbled across some tribe attempting to sacrifice a newborn babe in the forest. They believed that the sacrifice was necessary. They were going to spread her blood around the fields in order for something ridiculous to occur, like the growth of fertile crops or some other lie. I couldn't let them kill a newborn, and so I snatched Cassie and brought her here to grow up."

"You didn't know what she was?"

Oracles were born to humans and experienced their first vision of the future when they were around six or seven, later transitioning to full immortality. As far as I knew, there was no discernible pattern. It was a complete guess as to which mortal child would spout prophecies.

Lucien shook his head. "Not until she was a little older. She was already a hellion, and then she added in predicting the future."

After reading about him, I was already nursing a bit of hero worship for Lucien. Who wouldn't be impressed by him? But hearing what he did for Cassandra made me look at him in a new light, as if he could...protect me.

Adelaide appeared out of nowhere, and I startled, nailing my knee on the table. "Where in all hells did you come from?!" I exclaimed, nearly jumping out of my chair. Not a single immortal besides me appeared surprised by her sudden presence.

Lucien laid a calming hand on my shoulder, pushing me back into my chair. I rubbed my now sore knee with a wince. "Announce yourself, Adelaide," he said.

The housekeeper nodded solemnly, handing the huge scroll she carried to Lucien. "My apologies. I need your approval for the coronation invite list, sire."

"Whose coronation?" I inquired, tilting my head to the side. A beat of utter silence followed, during which the wolves glanced at each other with shocked eyes, prompting a feeling of dread to course through me. With my teeth gritted and my hands gripping the table, I hissed, "Whose. Coronation?"

Without another word, Erik disappeared, his men following close behind. Elijah pulled Gunnar, who hurriedly scooped some breakfast into his arms. In a single minute, we were alone in the kitchen.

"Now, Phoebe…" he entreated, resting a hand on my shoulder.

I shoved away from the table and from him. "Are you planning a coronation for me? You're going to *force* me to become queen, no matter what I have to say about it? What about my choice?"

He was taking away my decisions again! When would I learn? For all his sweet words about mates and forever, I was still a prisoner. I was being controlled again! First the Council and now Lucien. I was always being made into someone's puppet.

Lucien stood up, his green eyes hard. His fists were tight at his sides, the knuckles white. "You don't get to choose! You are my mate! My queen!"

My head snapped back at his words. "So you think you'll take away my freedom? Again?" I threw up my wrists, showing him the cuffs. He winced slightly at the sight of them, but his face hardened. "Were you planning on showing your queen off to your court with her powers bound?"

"No! I hoped…" he broke off, his face paling. His eyes were bright with emotion, but I was too angry to read him.

"Hoped for what?" I hissed.

"Hoped you would stay…with me." He glanced away, his fists relaxing at his sides.

My anger dimmed slightly, though I desperately clung to it. I needed every defense against him. "How can I choose anything without my powers, Lucien? Were you planning never to take them off?" My magic was like a phantom limb, aching just out of reach. Not to mention, I was utterly vulnerable to my enemies.

"How can I trust you not to rift away if I do?" he snapped. He whirled around, giving me his back.

If. If he does. Bastard.

The fury returned, scorching me. My nails dug into my palms, my emotions in turmoil because somewhere deep down, I was thinking of *staying.* That couldn't be right. I knew so little about him, except that he'd protected a mortal baby, and later a powerful oracle, from those that would harm her for no other reason than it was right. He'd entreated gods to create a home for demons to end a war, helped end fae slavery. Most of all, I felt *safe* with him, and that was by far the most dangerous realization of all. I needed to escape and run. I was almost in too deep, and soon it would be too late.

"So, you can't trust me without the cuffs, and I can't trust you with them. Where does that leave us?"

Desperation gnawed at me, only heightened by my fear. I was so afraid I was already so far gone on this male that I *wouldn't* leave given a chance.

His shoulders slouched in defeat. "I don't know," he muttered.

I had to escape now. I couldn't wait any longer.

XXI

THE REALM OF MORTALS.
ÎNTUNERIC CASTEL, ROMANIA.

I HEARD HER FLEE FROM THE KITCHENS but didn't turn around, shame burning its way up my neck. *Why couldn't I do anything right by her?* My hands fisted at my sides. I wanted something to throw, someone to punch, anything to release this boiling rage inside me, scalding me. Yet, for all the anger coiled inside me, I knew nothing would help. Not when the real enemy, the one truly responsible for everything, was the one that looked back at me in the mirror. My fists relaxed, and I took a deep breath. The relief would be fleeting. The only genuine relief was with her.

She hated me, and with good reason. Reasons I kept adding to every time I open my cursed mouth. I sank into the abandoned chair, burying my head in my hands, trying to release some of the tension in my muscles. Every fiber was drawn tight, my stomach turning with upset, though that may in part be the vile mug of blood.

I'd barely managed to get it down. Yet, I swallowed it, forcing every revolting drop down my throat, rather than reveal how dependent I was on her already. I didn't want her to stay because she felt forced. I wanted her to stay because she wanted to and because she wanted *me*.

Did I really think she was going to want to stay with me after everything? After I bound her powers?

After forcing responsibility onto her shoulders until they broke from the weight? How could I expect her to so readily assume the crown I still struggled beneath every day, even after ten thousand years?

I tunneled my hands into my hair, gripping the strands, tempted to yank them out at the roots. The memory of her eyes when I didn't answer was an image I couldn't banish. The way the light in them flickered and died, the vivid lilac dulled.

Why couldn't I stop pushing her even further away? I hoped to draw us closer, and for a moment, a single breath, I'd felt it. But then, I'd ruined it. I longed for her, constantly looking for her, needing her, yet she couldn't wait to leave me.

Phoebe made no secret of her plans, which only made my chest ache more. If she escaped, I would...what? With her powers bound, I could track her down, but if she got free of the cuffs, I would never find her. I squeezed my eyes shut, grimacing. That was the crux of it, wasn't it? Phoebe would never return if she left.

I heard Erik approach but didn't bother to lift my head to look at the wolf.

"I'm assuming that it did not go well?" the lycan mused, settling into a chair.

I grunted noncommittally, not looking up. "She thinks I plan to keep her bound forever."

I almost wished she'd slapped me as I so richly deserved, but she hadn't, and that was so much worse.

Erik sipped at his now lukewarm coffee before asking, "Well, didn't you?"

My head snapped up to gape at him. "No!" I flinched slightly at the vehemence in my voice. "No. I wouldn't want her to feel like she is less than who she is."

But the state of affairs between us was bleak, and someone needed to make the leap of faith toward trust. Her eyes had flashed with hurt when I didn't answer, and that failure would be a lifelong regret. Her thoughts had been obvious as her eyes flickered. She believed I'd planned to keep her bound forever, and I *hated* that part of me was tempted to.

When she asked, images of my mother and Cassandra flashed through my mind. At that moment, I couldn't differentiate between what was past and what was present. She would leave me behind, just like all the others. I was doomed to chase her forever, to want a woman that didn't want me.

Insidious thoughts clouded my mind, and I banged my fists against my skull, hoping to clear it. We couldn't continue on this way. I was only widening the gulf between us instead of bridging it. I squeezed my eyes shut as Erik continued to sip his coffee while I evaluated the best strategy for winning over my mate. Fuck the baby steps. It was time for the leap, and I had to make it.

My eyes shot open, and I stared at the table. I dropped my hands, took a deep breath, and leaned my head back on my chair, looking up at the ceiling. Could I forget a millennium of feelings of abandonment to have Phoebe? *Yes.* I would do anything to have her.

My head throbbed, and I pinched the bridge of my nose as a migraine formed. I'd bound her, kidnapped her, and forced her to accept me. The next step needed to be mine, and it needed to be big. It needed to be...*fuck.*

There was only one avenue open. I had to take them off, give her the power to leave me, and pray she stayed instead. I sat in pained silence with Erik sipping his coffee for several minutes, dredging up the resolve I needed to remove Phoebe's cuffs.

"What if she still leaves?" I whispered.

"If she does, there's no rule that says you can't try to change her mind," Erik said. My head came forward, and I gaped at Erik. He just grinned slightly and shrugged.

When my mother and Cassandra had left, I didn't beg them to stay, though I secretly longed to. With Phoebe, I couldn't hesitate. She had already come to mean so much to me. She challenged and surprised me, inflamed me with desire and rage.

"How would I find her, though?" With her power, she could be worlds away in a blink.

Erik shrugged again. "How did you find her before?"

Cassandra. How did I forget about her? There was no realm where Phoebe could hide, which Cassandra could not see. She helped me find her before, which meant she wanted us to be together, but I was never sure what the oracle would do. I would track her across all the realms. I took heart in that and stood up from the table, slapping Erik's shoulder roughly. "Thank you, my friend. I'm happy you're here."

Erik nodded, finishing his cup. He smirked at me, his smile showing his extra-long canines. "Good hunting."

My lips twitched at the old werewolf farewell and headed for the library, where Phoebe spent most of her time at Întuneric. Empty. Maybe she was in our room instead? Empty. The first tendrils of panic shot down my spine. Where was she?

Her scream pierced the air, and my blood turned to ice when the sound suddenly cut off.

Phoebe!

XXII

THE REALM OF MORTALS.
OUTSIDE ÎNTUNERIC CASTEL, ROMANIA.

I close my eyes, sucking in a shaky exhale before opening my eyes. I look around at my surroundings, my eyes almost fully healed.

The Witches Council chamber is a shadow of its former magnificence. The shining white marble is covered in ash. I glance up at the sky, blinking when one fleck of ash falls into my eye again. The ceiling is gone. There is nothing left of the massive dome but a half-charred wooden beam. The full moon shining through the chambers allows me to take in more of my surroundings.

I choke back a gag from behind my mask and cover my mouth, realizing only part of the ash is from the building. The rest is from the bodies.

I DIDN'T WASTE a moment before sprinting from the castle, not even surprised Bast waited for me outside the kitchen door. The familiar sensed my moods, likely feeling the crushing sense of panic almost suffocating me. My determination to escape redoubled. I had to escape before I believed the truth and admitted he could protect and safeguard me from all threats.

I ran, ducking and darting through the hallways, avoiding lurking servants. Thankfully, I'd taken the time to memorize the labyrinth, just in case. I made it outside in moments, avoiding the garage. He was too paranoid not to have trackers on all his vehicles.

My eyes scanned the landscape in front of me. The arching bridge that attached the castle to the mountain path was too long. I would never get across it without Lucien catching up to me. With that out, I needed another route. I panted and shoved my hair out of my face, catching sight of a narrow dirt trail off to the side of the entrance. I sprinted toward it. It started wide but soon narrowed until I gripped the side of the mountain to keep from falling. Bast led the way, twitching her tail and easily balancing on the small outcropping. She turned back every so often to look at me.

Rule No. 5: Abandon everything at a moment's notice.

The path thinned the farther I went, till I clutched at the cliff, doubts gnawing at me. I should turn back. Yet, I couldn't. Internally, I went back and forth in my head. Should I continue to move forward or go back? I couldn't stop thinking about the fight with Lucien.

Rule No. 4: Never attract attention, mortal or otherwise.

He never planned on taking the cuffs off. I hated that the knowledge made me ache. When did I get in so deep? The way he treasured me and pleasured me made me forget everything, including all the rules that kept me alive.

Rule No. 3: Don't tell anyone anything, ever.

He seemed to value me, tempting me to hand over my safety to him, something I would have never considered before. You learn to depend only on yourself when you're on the run. Trust was a luxury I could never afford.

Rule No. 2: Use your enemy's weaknesses against them.

I knew the stories, the battles and foes he'd fought. Could I ask for anyone better to keep me safe? I froze at that insidious thought. Would I have trusted Lucien to protect me if I wasn't on the run? Yes. I couldn't imagine a more stalwart immortal to help me fight off my enemies. Would *everything* be different if I wasn't on the run? I wanted to rip out the part of my brain making excellent points and let it splatter on the floor of the valley below.

Rule No. 1: Trust no one.

I slipped and barely grasped for another handhold in time, my breath coming in short, uneven bursts. I had to forget about Lucien and focus. My heart thudded as I glanced back along the path from which I'd come. A part of me hoped to see Lucien standing there, and when there was no one, I felt a stab of disappointment. I shook the feeling off, knowing I had to run. I could never count on anyone. Rule No. 1 was number one for a reason, but going back to constantly looking over my shoulder for the newest threat sounded so wearisome. I would love to rest, to trust my safety to someone else, even if just for a moment.

The feeling of being watched persisted. Bast was back at my side, hissing and her tail bristled to make herself appear larger. It was something she only did when there was *imminent* danger, something she never did with Lucien.

Oh shit.

I spun on my heel, dreading what I would find. I pressed my back against the mountain, maintaining my precarious grip. A giant flock of birds were circling right behind me. At first, I thought it might be geese, but they were larger than any I'd ever seen, and their beaks were full of pointed teeth. I gasped when I realized what they were. They never came this far north. Stymphalian Birds were monstrosities with sharp fangs that feasted on human flesh. These creatures usually preferred Greece, especially the old region of Arcadia. Their wings turned to knives, to pin their prey down as they tore it apart.

When one swooped toward me, I screamed, which startled the bird enough for it to miss my face. I shuffled quickly back down the path, hoping to reach the castle. It was my only exit, besides a fall into the valley below. The cuffs prevented me from fighting back, so running was my only option. The birds descended on me, clawing and ripping at my flesh. Every time my hand landed on them to hit them away, their lethal wings cut me. I felt blood gushing down my arm but didn't dare to look.

A massive roar momentarily stunned the birds, and they scattered. I opened my eyes to see Lucien storming toward me, Bast trotting at his side. When had the cat slipped away? Lucien was more vampiric than I'd ever seen him, his eyes glowing blood red, his fangs out in full force. A bird swooped at him, its own fangs bared, but he merely punched it toward the ground. It fell into the valley below, incapacitated.

"Lucien!" I cried, reaching for him, trying to make my way toward him. I stumbled on the ledge, slipping but continuing on. Even now, under threat, I knew he would protect me. I needed to get to him.

Another bird took a bite out of my arm, and I screamed in pain, cradling it to my chest as spots formed over my vision. Lucien reached my side and stepped in front of me, putting my body between him and the mountain. He jerked multiple times as the birds clawed and bit at his back, making himself their only target.

Even through his pain, he made sure no part of my body was exposed. His arms and legs caged me, his hands trailing gently down my arms, despite how the birds ripped at his flesh.

He whispered, "I'm so sorry, *vrăjitoare*. For everything."

Lucien kissed the side of my temple and reached down to position himself against the mountain. His hands gripped the rock face, making new handholds with his strength. He pulled his legs up under him, leveraging himself against the mountain like a coiled spring. Finally understanding his plan, I screamed, "Lucien, no!" I tried to grab him, to yank him back, but it was too late. He launched himself backward off the path and into the fray. He fought the birds midair, taking them down with him as he plummeted.

I watched helplessly as he fell, my hand shaking as I covered my gaping mouth and tears filled my eyes. I wanted to look away. It took me a moment to recognize the familiar feeling of my magic coursing through me through my shock and fear. It was like a beloved family member had enveloped me in a long-awaited hug. My hair whipped around my shoulders, the power making my entire body come alive. Electricity scaled down my arms, and I pulled my hand away from my mouth, looking at my wrists.

He'd removed the cuffs. They sat on the edge of the cliff next to my feet. I let out an astonished laugh, delighting in the familiar feeling, then narrowed my eyes on the birds. *Those flying fucks didn't stand a chance now.*

I called forth my magic, freezing Lucien's descent into the valley with a wave of my hand. He had passed out from blood loss, and my heart ached with fear for him. I twisted my wrists together, muttering the spell I needed to conjure a cradle of air to protect him from any more attacks.

The birds bounced off the shield. Frustrated at their failure, they clawed at the air, shrieking. As Lucien hovered closer, I winced, seeing they'd pecked out his eyes. His arm hung limply, his forearm missing, and those were only the most obvious injuries.

Unhappy with the loss of their prize, the Stymphalian Birds turned on me. I brought up my own protections, incinerating any who got close enough. The shield caused a flag in my energy, but the magic had been building within me the entire time I had worn the cuffs. Days without magic left me with power to spare. I was going to kill these fucks so good.

Once Lucien was close enough, I moved him higher so he wouldn't get caught in the explosive crossfire. The barrier protected me, but I needed to be *smart.* I only had so much energy, and I needed to use it wisely. My first priority had been saving him. Now it was time to deal with the birds. I stepped off the narrow path into midair, buoyed by my magic, creating solid ground beneath my feet where there was none.

I glared at the Stymphalians. "You messed with the wrong witch," I said, my tone deadly.

I chanted under my breath, releasing the spell building inside me, and exploded. Molten magic, destruction burst from me, a lethal wave that consumed the Stymphalians, incinerating them. The horde of birds drifted to the ground as ash. My injuries, combined with the use of such powerful magic, threatened to drag me into dark oblivion. I needed to get Lucien to safety before passing out. I had to protect him. *He sacrificed himself for me.*

I pulled Lucien closer and scooped Bast up. I made a swirling motion with my hand to open a rift. The magic felt as if it was tearing pieces of me with it, but the air rippled in front of me, showing me Lucien's bedroom in Întuneric.

I pulled us all through, barely able to rest Lucien on the bed before my vision flickered toward black. With the last of my strength, I yelled, "Erik!"

I'd poured desperation into my tone and hoped he'd make it to us before it was too late. I fell onto the bed before the lethargy overtook me, finally passing out on Lucien's chest.

XXIII

THE REALM OF MORTALS.
ÎNTUNERIC CASTEL, ROMANIA.

STYMPHALIAN BIRDS THREATEN MY CONSORT!
The thought blared through my mind as I came to,
and I prepared to fight to protect her. My muscles
coiled beneath me, my shoulders tense as I readied. I would go
to Pandora and back to keep her safe. *Wait, was I in bed? Had it
all been a horrific dream?* My fingers traced the familiar silk
sheets beneath me, though I didn't open my eyes. My lids felt
glued shut.

Something soft brushed my chest, bringing back more of
my memories. The feeling of my flesh tearing from the beaks
of the enemy, their screams shattering my eardrums, all of it
was nothing compared to the terror coursing through me
now. I dreaded opening my eyes. *Was she already gone?*

Echoes of soft voices hovered around me. I recognized
Erik and my housekeeper Adelaide, but I didn't hear *her*.
Prepared for the worst, I gritted my teeth and pulled my
eyelids back. I blinked several times, trying to clear the hazy
film. The fucking birds had gone straight for my red gaze, and
they must still be in the process of regenerating.

My vision slowly focused, and I scanned my
surroundings. Erik was pacing in the corner, all four of his
men in various states of relaxation on the stone floor. When
had Erik become such a loyal friend? I'd

killed the man's father, for gods' sakes, but couldn't seem to shake him.

I blinked slowly and saw my housekeeper flitting in and out of the room, carrying out used, bloodied bandages. Were those from me? A black blur drew my attention, and I watched Phoebe's cat darting between the wolves. *Could that mean...?* The flare of hope burned brightly, and I glanced down at my chest.

Phoebe.

The breath I didn't know I was holding hissed from my lips. Her head was laying against my chest, her fiery hair tickling my side as she idly traced her fingers across my skin. The cuffs were gone from her wrists, and yet she had stayed with me. *Unbound.*

I raised my hand, catching the fingers tracing patterns on my chest. She tensed for a moment before her head snapped up, her eyes wide. "You're awake!"

Her exclamation brought the attention of the other immortals in the room. Erik stopped his pacing and stood next to the bed. "You gave us a scare there, old friend."

I struggled to sit up, and Phoebe retreated, allowing me to brace myself against the headboard. As she moved even farther away, I grabbed her wrist almost instinctively, bringing her back to my side. She took the invitation without even hesitating, burrowing against me. I wrapped my arm around her back, squeezing her. I breathed a little easier with her there.

My voice croaked as I asked, "What happened?"

Phoebe remained silent at my side, resuming her idle petting on my chest. The simple touch relaxed me, making my eyelids heavy.

"You've been out for four days. When I heard Phoebe yelling, I thought we might be too late." The wolf visibly shuddered. "You were both in rough shape. We've been waiting for you to wake up."

Erik crossed his arms over his chest with a loud huff, his blue eyes shining slightly. Instead of soothing the ruffled haunches of the werewolf, I turned to Phoebe. I traced my hands over her, searching for injuries.

"You're alright?" I asked, my voice low and raw, aware of our audience. I could almost feel the massive smirk on Erik's face. *Smug werewolf.*

Phoebe nodded, then playfully smacked my chest. I covered the flinch the affectionate movement caused. I'd gladly be flayed alive so long as she kept touching me. "Don't you ever do anything like that again! Watching you fall took years off my life," she admonished.

I captured her hand in mine, kissing her palm, then the inside of her wrist, pressing my cheek into her hand. She had stayed. I'd leapt and was rewarded. She could have run. She should have run. I would have continued my plummet to the valley below. Though the fall would not have killed me, it would have taken days, even weeks, to regenerate from those injuries. Phoebe's trail would have gone cold.

I wasn't able to take my eyes off of Phoebe, not even when I heard Erik and his men shuffle out of the room. Thankfully, they could tell I needed a moment alone with my queen. I cradled her in my arms, inhaling her cherry blossom scent. Her silken hair was loose on the bed, and her soft breaths made my stomach tighten.

I remembered the feeling of her skin beneath my hands as I touched the cuffs, breaking the mystical lock. Her screams echoed in my ears when I let go. I'd known the moment the cuffs were off that she would run. She had no reason to stay. I'd given her no reason to. I wanted to squeeze her to me, to crush her with my strength.

Would she leave me now? My mind raced, all euphoria at her presence dying under an onslaught of panic. *Was this the calm before the storm? Should I shore myself up for more anguish?* My breath quickened, and my grip on Phoebe tightened.

I took a few deep breaths, Erik's words ringing in my head. If I was too controlling, I would lose her. I couldn't lose her, not again. The desperation that coursed through me earlier was simmering right beneath the surface.

"Why did you stay, Phoebe?" I blurted hoarsely, dreading the answer. Empowered for three days, and she hadn't disappeared. Could this powerful witch, with the strength to tear reality, to be across the world in a second, have *possibly* stayed for me?

She trailed her fingers along my chest, hiding her face. With a touch, I brought her chin up. Her eyes were flashing, but I was too agonized to attempt to interpret. Was she as lost as I?

"You sacrificed yourself for me, Lucien. I've never had anyone do that for me before. I couldn't leave you after that."

Still nothing about staying.

"Are you going to leave now that I'm healed?" I steeled myself for her response. I didn't want to get my hopes up.

"Do you want me to?" she whispered, worry lacing her tone.

"No!" I yelled, sitting up, so we faced each other. Every movement was agony, but this could be the most important conversation of my immortal life, so I endured with gritted teeth. I traced my fingers along her freed wrists. "I had planned to take the cuffs off, but..." I sent her a pointed look, and she had the decency to blush.

"I thought you wanted to keep me powerless forever," she admitted.

I considered it.

"I fucked it up," I muttered, the truth spilling from my lips. "I have trouble with logic around you, Phoebe. All I can think about is you, and when you said you would leave me, I—" I broke off, just the memory stealing my voice. She placed her soft hands on my face, cradling it, stopping my mad inner ramble. As long as she was touching me, the madness was muted.

"I...leaving you...it... It's just that the people after me are powerful, very powerful, and staying in one place for a prolonged period..." she trailed off, her hand on my chest shaking slightly. "I realized as I was climbing along the mountain that I didn't really want to leave." She buried her face against my chest more, but I could feel her cheeks warm against me. "I have been running for so long it's hard to stop. To be *still.*"

"Will you tell me what happened?" I asked, sensing a delicate bridge of trust was growing between us. When she hesitated, her body tensing, I rushed to add, "You don't have to." I couldn't push her. I had to remember I was taking baby steps.

"I *really* want to tell you, Lucien, but I'm not there yet. I'm agreeing to stay with you for the...foreseeable future. Can't that be enough for now?" she entreated, desperation ringing in her voice and her eyes shining up at me. When she looked at me like that, there was little I wouldn't give her. I bit back a sigh, hating that she included the qualifier. She still didn't trust me, not fully. I leaned back, pulling her tightly against me. I needed to feel her breathing against me.

"For now," I agreed, though I was desperate to understand her, to know absolutely everything about her. "Just give me till the coronation." Two weeks to win her. "If I fuck up, you'll talk to me instead of running."

My tone was harsher and more commanding than I meant it, but this was too important for me to be gentle. She glanced back up at me, one red brow raised, and asked, "You are still going to throw a coronation for me? Even though I haven't fully committed?"

I nodded. "Yes, I am. Because even though you have not fully committed to me," the words tasted like acid, "I hope that seeing the event—"

"Might change my mind," she murmured, laughing softly. The feel of her soft body against me was awakening other parts of my battered body. My erection was already tenting the sheet between us, which she noticed with a smile. "Seems another part of you is feeling better," she murmured, her eyes going hooded with desire.

"Always," I growled. "You need only breath for my body to be ready for you."

"We should probably wait till you feel better." Her hand patted my chest, sitting up more. "You need to feed again." She reached for a mug of blood that was sitting on the bedside table, handing it to me. The smell almost made me hurl, but I needed to be healed to resume *activities* with Phoebe.

I threw back the blood with a grimace, closing my eyes and bracing myself for the taste. But I couldn't keep it down, choking as I coughed the small amount back into the mug. Phoebe turned to rest on her knees, worry crossing her face. "Is something wrong? You didn't have a problem earlier."

That was because I was unconscious, but with her this close, my body refused to take blood that wasn't hers. I sighed and passed the blood back to her so she could place it on the side table.

Her brows drew down over her bright eyes, her teeth catching her lower lip. "Do you need fresh blood?" Then, like an offering conjured from my darkest desires, she tilted her head to the side, offering her neck to me. From some unknown well of strength, I resisted the need to sink my fangs into her neck, turning away from her.

"I don't want you to offer it to me because you feel you have to," I muttered.

She tilted her head to the other side. "I'm not. Do you not want to drink from me?" she asked, her voice laced with hurt.

"Phoebe, the only thing I crave more than your blood is your body. I don't want you to feel compelled to offer either." I swung around to face her, wincing as I did. Her pale cheeks were tinted pink, and the color only deepened at my gaze.

"I like when you drink from me," she whispered, her voice going husky. It was all the permission I needed.

I groaned. Already hard for her, I could barely contain myself as I sank my fangs into her neck. She gasped and then moaned. Even over the intoxicating smell of her blood, her arousal was perfuming the air. I was an animal around her, driven by pure instinct. Despite the pain it caused me, I pushed her back onto the bed, wrenching down her top to free her breasts. She moaned as I roughly pinched each nipple, and I dug my fangs deeper into her neck in approval. I wasted no time in ripping open the jeans she wore and delving into her heat. Phoebe was wet and ready for me. I moaned against her neck at the naughty things she whispered as I fed my fingers into her.

"My pussy has missed you. It aches for you."

Wicked female. When I wasn't able to move inside of her as I wanted because of her jeans, I ripped them from her with my claws. Once she was free, I thrust my fingers in and out of her, grinding my palm against her clit.

"Please make me come!" Phoebe begged.

With two fingers wedged inside her tight sheath, I vibrated my palm, making her squirm as she frantically sought more friction against her clit. I made a beckoning motion with my fingers, and her hips slammed up to meet my touch. I would have done depraved things to be balls deep in her at that moment. I screwed my fingers inside her, bringing forth her orgasm right as I released her neck.

The look on Phoebe's face when she came was my new favorite thing, and I didn't want to miss a moment of it. She threw her head back, screaming as she came almost violently around my fingers. I could picture how she would feel wrapped around my cock.

When I wrung every gasp from her, she collapsed in a sated heap. I pulled my fingers from her, grasping my own length and using her wetness to lather my cock. "I'm going to come on your tits, mark them as mine."

She frantically nodded in agreement, pushing her breasts together to prepare to catch my falling cum. I roared as it shot from me, decorating her chest and dripping from her luscious tits. As she'd done before, Phoebe trailed her fingers through my release and brought it to her lips. She sucked my cum from her fingers lovingly. Gods, she was fucking amazing. My wounds were healing rapidly, and my entire body felt wired with power. I rose to fetch a washcloth, her eyes sparkling up at me as I cleaned her up. I didn't think a male had ever been so lucky.

"When you agree to stay forever, I'll claim you." I hadn't meant for the resolution to slip from me, but I couldn't call the words back.

She softened. "What will happen when you claim me?"

"When?" I smirked, catching her slip.

"If," she corrected.

I sighed. "When I claim you, I'll bite you, and part of my scent will imprint on you forever. Any immortal with an enhanced sense of smell will be able to tell that we are mates."

"What would it mean for your vampires to have a witch as their queen? Our species don't exactly get along," she murmured as she rose to change into yoga pants and a loose tank top. I really needed to stop shredding her clothes every time we touched. *I'd just buy her more.*

"They will be your subjects. Any changes you want to make are up to you." I shrugged nonchalantly.

Phoebe tilted her head to the side. "If I made feeding on witches outlawed?"

I considered it, pulling her back onto the bed to cuddle her in the shelter of my arms, yawning in exhaustion. My body was tired from healing. "Maybe outlaw it by force, still allowing consensual feeding. I would hate to be a hypocrite."

She laughed and wrapped her arms around me, pulling me close. "You might have a point there."

"Will you still be here when I wake up?" I whispered.

She nodded, fitting herself against me. "I'm not going anywhere for a while, Lucien."

I kissed her forehead and allowed myself to drift off, clutching her to me.

XXIV

THE REALM OF MORTALS.
ÎNTUNERIC CASTEL, ROMANIA.

The rest of the Council members are in varying states of disintegration. The slight breeze from outside is lifting the skin off their corpses and mixing in the air. I press my hand harder to my mouth, my stomach churning as I look down at myself.

I brush some of the ash from my aunt's cheek, a cough drawing my attention. I'm not the only survivor! There is someone else who knows what happened. They can explain this to me. I don't know what could have possibly gotten through the layers and layers of spells built into the Witches Council chamber. The building dates back to the witch trials and has never been breached.

WHEN LUCIEN FINALLY WOKE UP AGAIN, it was hours later, but I remained by his side. He had saved me, sacrificing his life for me. I still couldn't wrap my head around it. The way he launched himself off the cliff and into the fury of birds still made me shudder. I hadn't even *considered* leaving before he woke up. I was *overflowing* with magic, but every time I thought about calling up the power necessary, I stopped.

I just *couldn't* leave him while he was unconscious, lying there, helpless. I could not say no when he begged me to stay for a couple of days. I had one week to decide whether or not to trust Lucien. I had no delusions he might let me go after the coronation. If I stayed until then, I was essentially declaring I was staying forever. I could give this a chance...for a little while.

When he next awoke, Lucien bolted forward. His eyes were wild, searching the room until he caught sight of me. I was getting used to his weird moments of waking up.

"I thought I dreamed you," Lucien blurted, relaxing again. He slowly rested back on the bed, careful not to look away for a second. Was he really that scared I would vanish?

"I told you I'm not going anywhere." Did he not trust me? When had I ever given him a reason not to? Well, other than trying to run at every opportunity. There was a flash of guilt at that, but he always seemed sure and confident. I never thought he would be as unsure or as confused as I was.

He grabbed my hand, bringing it to his lips to kiss the palm, holding it to his chest so I could feel his heart racing. I loved when he did that, the little things he did, deepening our connection without words. They showed me we might be more than a fated pairing.

"Just making sure," he answered, holding my hand tighter. He seemed to hesitate before continuing, "I don't have any experience with this. I've never wanted someone to stick around so badly. I'm a little lost." His mirthless chuckle broke my heart a little.

I cleared my throat to relieve some building tension in the room. "Okay, if I'm going to be sticking around for a while, there are some things I need to survive."

He tilted his head, a small smile tightening his mouth. "Like what?"

I began listing things off on my fingers. "WiFi, a TV, Netflix, Disney+, etc. A PlayStation would not be unwelcome. I need technology, Lucien."

He smiled brighter. "Anything you want. Tell Adelaide, and it will arrive within the hour."

Since he'd brought up the mysterious housekeeper, I said, "I can't figure out what she is or how she appears out of nowhere all the time."

Lucien laughed, the sound prompting a feeling of warmth to seep into my soul. "I'm not surprised. She's a shade."

Shades were shifters between life and death. They could turn invisible and intangible, and some had telekinesis. "How did you wind up with a shade as a housekeeper?"

He shrugged. "She served my mother. She's been around for as long as I can remember."

As if powerful immortals were just something one inherited. I would have to investigate more about Adelaide. There had to be more to the story.

I gently extracted my hand from Lucien's and stood. "I should leave you to sleep some more."

"No," he responded, crossing his arms over his chest. His denial stopped me short.

"No?"

"I don't want to let you out of my sight." His brow got that stubborn look, and I rolled my eyes.

"You know you can't boss me around anymore? I have my powers back." I called magic into one palm, letting it dance. With a flash, I was under him, my arms pinned above my head. His body kept me pressed to the bed, and his knowing grin was insufferable.

"I believe you said I could boss you around in bed, or on the floor, or in the shower, or on the balcony…." Each location earned me another kiss on my face, one to my forehead, each eyelid, and my nose.

"This is blackmail," I murmured half-heartedly, already softening.

"I will use every tool at my disposal." He planted a long, drugging kiss on my lips. "Now that you have your powers back." Another mind-scrambling kiss. "I have to make sure it's an even playing ground," he added with a laugh, rolling off and releasing me. I sent a teasing frown at him.

"Now, what was it my queen said about a television?"

The television arrived within an hour, along with several mortal cable men, whose mouths gaped at the sight of the castle. They spoke in lightning-fast Romanian to each other, and Lucien stifled a laugh from where he stood by my side.

I raised an eyebrow at him. "What are they saying?"

He leaned closer to answer directly into my ear, and I didn't even bother to hide my shiver. "They're wondering if they should have brought garlic with them to fend off the vampires."

"They know what you are?" I hissed.

He shook his head. "No, but apparently, there is a myth in the village that Dracula lived here at Întuneric instead of where everyone else says he lived. Not that I would have allowed him here. Tepes was a prick," he casually added, then shot off rapid Romanian to direct the men to the room.

Erik came up next to us, raising an eyebrow at the commotion. "Finally updating Întuneric, eh?" he asked, seeing the giant flat-screen being wheeled in.

His men came up behind him, all breaking into grins at the television. The werewolves loved sports, and I'd caught several of them streaming soccer on their phones as they huddled on the floor of our bedroom while Lucien was healing. I'd shushed them multiple times when they shouted at their small screens.

I sent them a wink. "I told Lucien that if I was going to be staying here for a little while, he needed to make some changes."

Lucien slung his arm around my shoulders, pulling me close, unabashedly adding, "Anything to get you to stay forever."

I sent him a fake frown, trying to smother the butterflies in my stomach at the prospect of staying with Lucien at Întuneric. Would it be so bad to be sated and spoiled by this legendary vampire king?

I was saved from responding as we followed the cable men to the room close to the library. Thanks to the five burly werewolves and two vampires I'd enlisted, it was already cleared of the outdated and antique furniture. The cable men continued to whisper to each other, and I caught the word *Mina* being repeated several times.

We retrofitted the room within a few hours, complete with a 144-inch TV, surround sound, and a Netflix subscription. It was all the essentials.

The Romanian cable guys were still working on the WiFi, but I could breathe easier knowing the castle was slightly more welcoming. If I stayed, I could make this place a home rather than just a cavernous shell.

A furniture delivery arrived, including a massive sectional, big enough for all the lycans and vampires. I raised an eyebrow at Lucien at that delivery, and he shrugged. "In case you want to invite...people."

I glanced away quickly. There was no one to invite. The feeling of isolation seeped in, escalating further when Lucien handed me a brand new phone. He had already programmed in some numbers. I pushed away the sappy warmth that filled me when I saw he had saved his number as *Sugar Fangs*. He had put in Adelaide, Cassie, and, in case of emergencies only, Erik. The lycan's number was saved as *Overgrown Chia Pet*.

I smiled sadly, realizing there was no one else to add to it. My parents were dead. My ex had betrayed me. My friends had turned their backs years ago. The cable guys' rapid muttering became louder as they packed up their tools.

"What are they whispering about now?" I asked, hoping to distract myself as Lucien came up behind me and kissed my head, wrapping his arms around me.

"They think you're being held against your will. They keep calling you Mina, like Dracula's bride." His voice held none of the suppressed humor from before.

I turned to face him, placing a soft hand on his cheek, drawing his eyes. "I'm not here against my will, remember?" I emphasized my bare wrists and couldn't resist adding, "Not *anymore,* at least."

His lips twitched in a ghost of a smile. "Cheeky female."

I pulled Lucien in for a long, lingering kiss, giving them no doubt that I was there *voluntarily*. When I moved away, he yanked me back, plundering my mouth, sweeping me into the kiss with little effort. When he finally released me, I felt a little dazed, forgetting my original intention. His forehead touched mine, and a smile of male satisfaction lit his face. I pushed away from him and shot a look at the two men who were trying to appear over-interested in their work.

I smirked at them, then back at Lucien, who was still smiling. "What?"

"I'm happy you're here," he answered, and I froze, unsure how to answer.

The cable men saved me from having to respond when they announced the *vifee* should be working. They shot cautious looks at Lucien, still hesitant around him. I wondered if they sensed his...power.

Some mortals were more sensitive than others. The men hesitated, sending more tentative looks at us. Lucien's eyes flashed red, and they sprinted out of Întuneric, screaming in Romanian.

I snickered and smiled up at him, his eyes green. "I suppose you had nothing to do with that?"

"Who me?" He gestured to himself. "I would never do such a thing." He couldn't stop the smirk. "Now, what does my queen want to watch on her new system?"

I bit my lip in thought and came up with the perfect choice, but I had to make sure not to laugh before I pulled up Netflix to pick out the show.

"*Buffy the Vampire Slayer*? Absolutely not."

I burst into laughter and ignored him, starting the first episode. "What? She's one of my favorites."

He stuck his lower lip out. "There must be something else."

"Hmm, we could watch *Vampire Diaries.*"

He sent me a quelling look. "Not a chance."

"*True Blood?*"

He didn't even dignify that with a response.

"Give *Buffy* a shot. You can point out all the inaccuracies!"

He huffed, pulling me against his chest. "Fine. But note this sacrifice I'm making for you, my queen."

I smiled sweetly up at him and said, "I'll add it to the list."

We cuddled together and binged through the first season, Lucien demanding to know, "Why the hells would a vampire's face get wrinkled when he was about to attack?" I had no answer for that, but I admitted to having a major crush on David Boreanaz, which offended Lucien. He eventually settled back in when I patted his arm and assured him he was a much better vampire.

Erik and Gunnar filtered in and out. Unsurprisingly, the younger lycan was a huge *Buffy* fan. When Lucien widened his eyes in surprise, he shrugged and said, "I've got a thing for powerful women."

Cuddled into Lucien's side, I drifted off somewhere toward the end of the first season, his chest too warm and comfortable to resist.

Suddenly, I was back in front of the room in Întuneric that led to the past. Would I see my parents again? I pushed against the door, eager to see them. The thought of seeing them again was compelling, but this time, when the wooden door swung open, it was to somewhere new.

It was a moss-covered cathedral, the bones of the once magnificent structure left to the wilds. A cloaked figure was pacing frantically across the room, her steps echoing on the stone, a bundle tucked in her arms.

I moved closer and saw that she was cradling a small, swaddled infant in her arms. A brief glimpse beneath the hood left me with the impression of dark hair and lilac eyes, far too similar to my own. Was she an ancestor of mine? The woman continued forward and back, the child not letting out a whimper of protest at the movement.

262

Another cloaked figure appeared directly behind me, calling out, "Majesty."

The woman turned, and I caught full sight of her face. Was she wearing a golden circlet? As far as I knew, the Council had always controlled the witches. Was that a lie?

The woman's tears fell silently down her face, but she didn't acknowledge them, her steps sure as she approached the new arrival.

"You are sure she'll be safe?"

"Yes, my queen, only you and I know she is from your line. We'll conceal her with another family. No one will know. They believe her to be from a distant relative, orphaned and alone. Not even she will know the truth." The man's voice was confident and reassuring but did nothing to stop the woman's tears.

"My sweet daughter, the future of our kind rests on you flourishing and surviving," she murmured to the bundle before handing the baby off to the man. She brushed back the hair that had fallen into the infant's face, her touch so filled with love it was nearly reverent. My heart broke for both of them. She muttered under her breath, and I recognized the spell as a glamour.

Without taking her gaze from the babe, she said to the man, "I hope that by the time the little one has a child, our people will have long forgotten the significance of it."

Of what? The eye color? Did my eye color mean something? I knew it was rare, but unique eye colors were not exactly uncommon in the world of immortals.

As the man turned to leave, the woman kneeled next to the small familiar at her side I'd previously overlooked. The woman's tears still flowed from her eyes as she petted the small black cat with eyes identical to hers. "You'll keep her safe, won't you? Until it's time?"

The familiar nodded, darting after the departing man.

Before I could puzzle through the meaning, I bolted upright out of the dream. Lucien had carried me back to our bed and was asleep beside me. As the implications of my dream—*vision?*—wore off, I looked at him uninterrupted. I delicately traced my fingertips across his lips and felt my heart thud in my chest. I was all too easily forgetting the rules that had kept me alive.

New Rule No 1: Trust No One...except maybe Lucien.

I pulled my hand back, hoping to shore up my emotional walls. It was just three more days. I could do three more days without succumbing to his allure, to the desire to put down roots here with Lucien. My mind shied from the thought of leaving him. I squeezed my eyes shut as if I could force the thoughts from my mind and feelings from my heart. I could *not* afford to fall in love with him. Malcolm's betrayal had devastated me, but I survived. I wasn't sure I would if Lucien did the same.

XXV

THE REALM OF MORTALS.
ÎNTUNERIC CASTEL, ROMANIA.

I AWOKE THE NEXT MORNING, the now familiar panic that Phoebe had disappeared during the night seizing my heart and lungs. The fear eased when I felt her resting on my chest, her breaths even and deep.

I pulled her closer and slowly relaxed as I watched her sleep. Her brow furrowed, and she murmured. I soothed her with soft words in Romanian, as I had before, wishing I could take the nightmares. I hoped one day soon she would trust me enough to reveal the secrets that haunted her. Demons hid in her eyes, plaguing her day and night. I would fight them for her if only she let me. Eventually, she settled, allowing me to gaze at her and memorize every slope and dip of her face.

I twined a lock of her fiery hair around my finger, rubbing the silky curl against my lower lip. She had stayed, and that reality eased some of the cloying panic in my chest. It gave me enough hope to wonder what it would be like when I finally claimed her. When she was totally and completely mine.

Though my body ached and I was weaker than normal without our bond in place, I didn't regret the decision to postpone the official claim. I was desperate to have her and know what it meant to be inside my mate finally. If I made love to her and she still left, it would kill me. It was better only to take that step when knew she would stay, even if I became weaker by the hour.

Phoebe snuggled closer, slowly coming awake, her bright eyes gazing up at me. "Hi," she murmured softly.

Unable to resist, I pulled her in with a long kiss, and she mumbled something against my lips I didn't catch. She broke away, blushing slightly. I liked that she still blushed. Despite her often brazen attitude, some of her innocence was still there. The monotony of eternity hadn't yet scraped it away.

She cleared her throat and asked, "So, what are our plans for today?"

"Hmm, let's see, first on my agenda is making you climax at least three times before lunch, then some conference calls, followed up by another three orgasms for you."

She slapped my chest lightly. "Who do you have conference calls with?"

I sighed. She would focus on the least interesting part of my day. "I have to speak with some of my COOs about research and development. They're not as far along as they should be."

"You have COOs? For what?" she asked, resting her chin against my chest and raising an eyebrow.

"I own several medical research labs. I'm hoping to invent a synthetic blood that vampires can survive on. In the age of smartphones, I just know some dumbass vampire is going to get caught feeding on someone, and it'll go viral. Less need for blood means it is less likely one of them is going to fuck up." I couldn't control everyone, no matter the stories of my legendary acts of retribution.

"That's very forward-thinking of you."

"Just because I was born ages ago doesn't mean I can't see the writing on the wall." It just usually took longer for me to notice it and even longer to *act* on it.

"This coming from the man who needed me to ask for a television?" she asked archly, a smirk lighting her face.

"Well, I used to find other ways to occupy my time without it," I replied huskily.

She arched a brow. "Oh, I'm sure you had no trouble *occupying* your time."

I pulled her closer. "You're the only way I want to occupy my time now."

A flash of emotion flickered across her face. "For how long?"

"For as long as you'll let me."

She sighed, pushing back slightly. "But you're geared to want me."

I shook my head. "You don't know much about vampire mates, do you?"

She shrugged. "Before you, I would have never thought I needed to."

I pinched a soft red lock of her hair, luxuriating again in its texture. I took another heavy inhale of her cherry blossom scent, the only thing leashing the madness that played at the edge of my consciousness. How much to tell her? Now that she was free, I didn't want her to stay for some misbegotten belief that I couldn't survive without her, even if that was the truth.

I needed to tell her just enough, but not so much she would run again. "Fate does not push us toward random pairings. It pushes us toward the only person we could make a true life with. It does not make me desperate to have you like I would kill to have any part of you. That's all you."

Her eyes darted away. She often did that, trying to hide her feelings from me and conceal the thoughts hiding in her lilac eyes. She had so many secrets.

"We recognize vampire mates when we first scent their blood." Recalling the first time I'd scented Phoebe's without the clouding scents of Tír nAill, had me hardening beneath the sheet. "The Elders call it *cântecul sângelui lor* or the song of their blood. I think my mother worried her bloodthirsty creations would kill their predestined mates without a neon sign pointing them out."

She brought her eyes back to mine, curiosity brightening them even more. I could so easily get lost in their depths. "Tell me about your Elders. I find it strange that a man of your history has to answer to anyone." She smirked as she added that last bit.

"Oh? And what do you know of my history?" I asked, arching a brow.

Phoebe sighed, realizing her slip. "I may or may not have found a book in the library with all your feats listed." So she had researched me, had she? "I've meant to ask, how old are you exactly?"

This time, I shifted uncomfortably. I didn't want the ages I'd lived to become yet *another* stumbling block between us, but I didn't want to lie.

"I'll be somewhere around ten-thousand in the summer." I paused, bracing for her reaction.

"Really?" She moved off my chest, resting on her elbows on the bed. "How cool! The oldest immortal I've ever met was only five-hundred." She pulled the sheet tighter around her, using her fists to prop her face up. "You're like a walking history book!"

My mouth gaped, and she giggled. "You're pleased? I did not expect you to delight in our marked age difference."

"I've always loved history, and with immortals, time's all relative." She shrugged, waving away the ten millennia difference between us.

Every time I thought I had a grasp on how she would respond to something, she surprised me. "I'll tell you all about it another time. I believe you asked about the Elders?"

She nodded with a pout. "For now."

I propped my back against the ancient headboard. How many times had I lain there and dreaded the coming years? With Phoebe beside me, I was excited at the chance to experience them with her. I hoped to lie exactly like this for the next millennia.

"*Elders* is a bit of an oxymoron. All but one are younger than me, but I hand-picked them all as advisors, should I need them. They've brought me great council over the years."

"All but one?" she queried, her eyes bright. I *could* only hope to live up to what she saw in me.

"My father's brother, Ambrogio. He was the second turned after my father." I concealed all emotion in the statement. There was no affection between my uncle and me. The man was cold and unfeeling. A block of marble had more emotion.

She must have heard something in my lack of inflection and cuddled up to me, draping a leg over mine. Before I could distract her with more interesting activities, a loud bang came on the door.

"Get out of bed, you dick. Not all of us have mates to lose ourselves with," came Erik's shout through the thick wood.

I groaned. I'd promised the wolf yesterday that we would spar, and Erik was holding me to it. "I swear I should ban all other immortals from Întuneric for the next hundred years, just so I can be alone with you."

I kissed her before she could respond, hoping to take her scent with me as I got up to dress. To my surprise, she followed me into the closet, wrapping her arms around my waist. "But then I wouldn't get to watch how you and Erik interact or out-drink unsuspecting lycans." She pressed a kiss between my shoulder blades before releasing me.

I dressed in a black tank top and black sweatpants but decided against shoes. By the time I turned around, Phoebe was wearing a sports bra and a pair of the tiniest exercise shorts I'd ever seen. My mind blanked for a moment.

"You are not wearing that," I ordered, just the sight of her skin making me lose control.

She raised an eyebrow at my command. "What is wrong with what I'm wearing?"

"Phoebe, I can barely restrain myself from shoving you against a wall and feeding my cock inside you now. I would really hate to make an enemy of Erik by killing his men for staring at your ass or luscious tits."

I hooked my finger in the sports bra and yanked her forward, the elastic snapping. I shifted my hold to grab her ass, those perfect handfuls, and pushed her against my aching length.

"Erik's waiting for you," she murmured, her eyes lingering on my lips.

"Fuck. Erik." I growled, swooping down to kiss her. Her lips were like a honeyed wine, and her taste addicting. It was everything I remembered. She gasped, allowing me entrance and gifting me with her submission, yielding to me so sweetly.

I easily pulled her with me as I sat on the massive ottoman in the center of the dressing room. Without breaking the kiss, I arranged her until she was straddling me. She rocked her hips back and forth, dragging her heat along my length.

Phoebe pushed lightly against my shoulders, forcing me to lie back on the ottoman. I could taste the passion in her kiss, and before I understood what was happening, we were levitating. Her magic pulsed around us, lifting us from the ground.

I started at the unfamiliar sensation, but she shushed me. "Happens sometimes when I get really aroused. Occupational hazard." She shrugged but bit her lip, a flash of insecurity showing on her face. "Does it weird you out?"

We drifted back down to the ottoman, my back meeting the softness of the cushion. "Not at all. I was just surprised."

Still desperate for her, I stood and rid her of her top and shorts. I shrugged quickly out of my own clothes and sat back down. My lips took hers in a deep kiss as I pulled her back on top of me. I was unsurprised when we started floating this time but broke away from her to chuckle in wonder.

Without letting go of her, I flipped her until she straddled my face, and her mouth perfectly aligned with my aching cock. I gripped it. "Suck. I want to feel your wicked mouth on it."

She groaned, and I looked into her perfect pink pussy. "Gods, woman, your fucking pussy is heaven."

I leaned into it and blew cold air directly inside her, making her jolt. Her mouth released my cock as she wiggled her ass toward me. I smacked her rear to remind her to resume her job while I did mine.

This time, when I blew on her aching bud, she was prepared and grew wetter as I watched. Her tongue was making swirling motions on my tip as she fit me into her mouth. The piercings hit along her teeth, the bite of pain arousing me more. I flattened my tongue and teased it around her aching bud, not yet giving her pressure where she needed it most. She moaned around my cock, vibrating the piercings.

"That's a good girl. You suck on me like you were born to do it," I groaned.

Phoebe wiggled her hips again, and I stiffened my tongue, mimicking the movements of sex. I pressed as deep as I could get. Oh, how I wished I could be inside her. I took her needy little clit into my mouth, sucking hard on it until she came apart in my arms. Her magic surrounded us, and we floated higher.

She swirled her tongue around me again, and my heels dug into the air, desperate to be fucking her mouth. I felt my semen climbing, unable to resist her wicked little mouth. I feasted on her, timing her next orgasm to mine. She screamed and came on my tongue as I warned, "Drink me down, *regina mea*."

As I filled her mouth, the magic fled, and we were falling. I took the brunt of the fall, landing on the soft ottoman. Its legs immediately gave out from the unexpected weight slamming into it. I lay on my back and laughed at the sight we must make. The regents of the vampires going at it like teenagers until we broke furniture as old as me. Phoebe threw her leg over me, closing herself off. She sent me a glare, which only made me laugh harder.

"Stop laughing!" she demanded, though a smile spread across her face. "How are we going to explain this to Adelaide?"

I shuddered at the thought of trying to explain the need to replace the furniture to my dour housekeeper. "I'll leave that to you, my queen."

Phoebe smacked me playfully and rose to dress. She didn't say anything but added a flowing workout top over her sports bra and yoga pants. I was so caught up in watching her I was still naked. Once she was ready, I swatted her ass and said to her, "Tell Erik I'll be right with him." She sent me a smirk before flouncing off to do so.

XXVI

THE REALM OF MORTALS.
ÎNTUNERIC CASTEL, ROMANIA.

Slowly, I move my aunt off my lap, stumbling back to my feet.
They'll have answers! Were we attacked?

I limp forward and see the falling ash gathering on the clear
outline of a mystical shield, sparing the handful of people inside. I
lift my hand, pressing against it, looking at the survivors within.
They are still unconscious from the force of whatever attacked us,
but the shield had saved their lives. My brows furrow as I look over
my shoulder, assessing the scene.

I STRUTTED FROM THE DRESSING room,
satisfaction humming. The ease with which he took
my powers in stride during sexual activities made me
even more comfortable with the idea of sleeping with him, of
staying with him.

Possible Rule No. 6: Never leave Lucien's side. Rules 1-5 are
now obsolete.

I smiled brightly, almost floating to the sparring room,
unsurprised to see Erik and the wolves waiting

there. Erik stood in the center of the room, his blonde hair sweeping over the side of his partially shaved head. He wore only black joggers and a t-shirt, the three scars on the side of his face flashing under the light. I caught myself staring, and I blushed, murmuring, "Lucien will be right along."

The other four wolves lingered on the benches next to the mirrors, all of them in various stages of relaxation. Leif and Viggo elbowed each other, and I noticed money swapping hands. I refused to look any of them in the eye as I sat on the bench next to the most stoic wolf, Gunnar. His jaw was like granite, his face barely moved, but his eyes *watched*. I could feel him cataloging every breath each of us took, each microscopic twitch of our expressions. The other three were fun-loving, carefree, and wild. They were everything I'd heard about lycans, but Gunnar was different.

When Lucien arrived, his hair was slightly out of place, a smug smirk pasted on his face. He stretched his arms from side to side, wiggled his jaw, and twisted his long body. Erik just growled and threw a sword at Lucien. He caught it easily, barely glancing at it. The first sword hit released a wave of energy throughout the room, making my hair stand on end. Gunnar had tensed at Lucien's arrival, and he hadn't relaxed.

"You don't trust him, do you?" I asked, taking my eyes off of the fight and tilting my head to stare at Gunnar.

Gunnar paused, his jaw tightening and relaxing. "I regretfully did not for a long time, not until just before we arrived here."

"Regretfully? So, something has changed your mind?" What could change a distrust that likely spanned centuries?

"Understand, *völva*. I watched him," he said, gesturing to Lucien, who still battled Erik, "kill our last king. For a long time, I thought he was just biding his time to do so again." Gunnar must be at least a thousand years old himself if he'd been present when Erik's father was killed.

"Why bother to install Erik as king if he was planning on killing him?" I queried. I didn't understand what motive Lucien could have to replace the Lycan King, to let him grow in strength and age if he only planned on killing him later.

"You sound like Erik. I warned him you could never be sure they weren't just waiting for a moment to strike."

Lucien knocked the sword easily from Erik's hand, but the wolf dodged the next swing, jumping to swipe a mace from the wall.

"But you still didn't trust Lucien?" I asked.

Gunnar shook his head. "No, I did not."

"What changed?"

"Erik finally told us everything about the war," Gunnar answered.

Erik struck a hard blow to Lucien's side. He went down but merely rolled from the impact, picking up Erik's discarded sword as he rose, twirling them both.

"What do you mean?" I asked, though my focus was back on the two kings. They clashed against each other, neither gaining ground.

"We didn't know the truth about Erik's father, our last king. Erik finally explained before we came here." Like a blur, Lucien twisted with the two swords, keeping Erik at bay. Erik dropped the heavy mace and grabbed a loaded crossbow, shooting a bolt without seeming to aim. Lucien dodged before it could meet its mark.

"Why did Erik wait until you were coming here to explain?" Erik reached for a broadsword and wielded the massive piece of metal with two hands, catching Lucien's next strike against it.

"Because of you," Gunnar replied. I turned my head toward him in surprise.

"Me?"

"He wanted to make sure that none of us would think about using you against Lucien. That you were to be protected as if you were our own queen." Gunnar's eyes tracked the fight, but besides the clanging of steel, my focus was on the wolf next to me.

"What was it?"

The wolf sighed, taking his own eyes from the fight to glance at me. "Lycurgus, Erik's father, was not a good man or king, but we lycans are loyal to a fault. During the last battle between our two species, we thought Lucien mercilessly took his head only to subjugate the werewolves. Erik told us the truth, and it was a harsh truth." Gunnar gulped, shuddering to recall it. "Lycurgus was planning to sacrifice his youngest child, Alaric, to the gods. He believed the babe's death would ensure his victory. Lucien stopped the blade before it struck and took Lycurgus's head in a rage."

I inhaled sharply. "Why did they keep it a secret?"

Gunnar sighed. "Lucien knew if anyone realized what had almost happened, Erik would have to fight for his right to rule for the rest of his immortal days."

I glanced back at the fight. Lucien had lost both his swords and was now using a bo staff against Erik's broadsword.

"Because of what his father almost did?"

Gunnar nodded. "There is no greater crime than killing an unarmed babe. If revealed at a time of such upheaval in the lycan court, I don't know that Erik would still be king now." He paused before continuing. "And he's a great king. The best we could ever hope for."

When a hit of the broadsword split the staff in two, Lucien smiled and twirled the two pieces of wood around his wrists. I rolled my eyes at his display. It seemed that even ancient vampire kings were prone to showing off.

I sent a mischievous look at the wolf next to me and leaned in to whisper, "Should we remind them who has the actual power here?"

Gunnar's smile was slow to form, but when it did, the grim lines aging him disappeared. "Go for it, *völva*."

With magic glowing in my palms, I yanked the weapons from their hands. The broadsword impaled itself in the wall behind us, and the staff splintered uselessly against the floor. When both kings sent looks of surprise at me, I widened my eyes and pointed at Gunnar, stage whispering, "It was all him."

Lucien's bright smile caused my foolish heart to skip a beat, and to my surprise, he gestured me forward. "I believe you swore a rematch with your powers."

I nibbled my lip and slowly stood, my steps unsure. "Against both of you? At the same time?"

Erik glanced at Lucien, then back, his bright eyes studying us both. Lucien was watching me intensely, his emerald eyes searing me, infusing me with confidence. "Yes, *vrăjitoare,* both of us. I believe I promised you an even playing field."

I shrugged, crouching down into a fighting stance like I saw them both do. The kings collected short swords, and Erik took a half-hearted lunge. My hands came up in a defensive position, and his sword froze mid-air, held still by my magic. Erik's eyebrows went up.

You ain't seen nothing yet, werewolf.

With a shove, my shield launched Erik across the room. He hit the ground with a loud thud. All present looked at me, their mouths dropping in unison. Lucien gazed at me with something that looked suspiciously like *awe.* I could get used to that look.

"Are we going to spar or what?" I smirked as Erik came to his feet, rolling his shoulders.

Lucien and Erik glanced at each other, and moving like twin trains, attempted to land a hit from each side, hoping to catch me off guard. They failed. I fell backward, using magic to slip between them. Their swords met. They looked surprised at the clash of steel, not registering how I'd moved so fast. With two pointed fingers, I controlled the swords, wrenching them from their grips. I sent the weapons flying, Leif and Viggo ducking as they flew toward their heads.

I felt the flag of exhaustion, better to end the fight sooner rather than later. With another surge of power, I threw both men back, denting the walls where they landed. I smiled as they groaned in unison, but I wasn't able to stop the faltering step I took. Lucien was by my side in an instant. He smirked, covering my power drain, pulling me against him, and twirling me around. His brows came down in worry as he whispered against my ear, "Is something wrong?"

I waved off his concern. "I usually use a single spell to annihilate my enemies with one move."

Erik came to a stand, bowing to me. "I've never seen a witch move like that before."

"I doubt you've ever seen a witch do any of the things I can do," I added. Though exhaustion weighed on me, I refused to appear weak before them. As long as I didn't use more magic, I would be fine. I needed to rest. Despite that, I gave more of my weight to Lucien.

"I doubt he has," my vampire boasted, making me feel a little niggling of something like *warmth* around my heart. "Now, I believe I promised you an afternoon of history."

I kissed him softly, uncaring of our audience. "Lead the way."

XXVII

GODS, HER POWER WAS HUMBLING. I led her toward the library with her hand tucked into mine. When we were out of sight of the wolves, I swooped down to pick her up in my arms. "You should have told me magic wears you down. I wouldn't have encouraged the fight."

"And look like a weakling in front of the wolves? Never." She smiled brightly, lightening some of my guilt. "If all our enemies knew they only had to last through our spells until we collapsed from exhaustion, they wouldn't take us very seriously."

"At least you can count vampires out as enemies," I said, settling into an armchair with her in my lap.

Phoebe raised an eyebrow at that, but I only shrugged. "If you don't put the fear of the gods into them at your coronation, I will."

Her eyes shimmered. Even that slight sign of affection between us made my heart soar. She cleared her throat. "Tell me about your coronation, so I can know what I might expect."

Might not *will.* She still might leave me. I forced the thought away and sighed, recalling the ceremony. "It was bleak. Many of the vampires who are now Elders felt I was too young. They had made their objections to my uncle, who suggested taking it up with my mother." I laughed hollowly. "No one dared do so. How do you tell the Goddess of Vampires that her son is not fit to lead them?"

"But you still made them your advisors?" she asked.

"I did. I believed, and still do, people who questioned my rule were more likely to question my decisions. I knew they would speak up and prevent me from acting rashly." I kissed her forehead. "They usually only come once a century to report on the vampire population, or before a Great Event, like a war or…" Her eyes connected with mine before I finished my thought, "finally, placing a queen on the throne next to me."

She visibly gulped before glancing away, tucking an errant red lock behind her ear. "Did they help advise you after your mother left?"

"They did. The second the crown touched my head, she vanished without a word."

I tried to conceal my bitterness in remembering the moment, but it leaked into my voice. I had turned my head, hoping to see something other than the cool detachment in her eyes. My foolish heart had hoped for something like pride from her. But found nothing but empty space where she had stood.

Phoebe grimaced at that, tracing a finger over my cheek. "I'm sorry, Lucien. That must have been hard."

It was. Harder than I'd realized. I hadn't thought of it in ages, foolishly believing I could move on without it affecting me, that the abandonment of my mother hadn't left lasting scars.

I coughed to cover the way my throat clogged, thick with emotions. "I… I didn't understand why she'd left so suddenly. The only reason I even knew she'd gone to Ethereal was that one of the Elders told me."

Phoebe pressed more firmly against me, as if she could physically ease my pain. "When I first found my parents, I remember closing my eyes repeatedly, praying that eventually, I'd open them and the scene before me would vanish. It never did." I stroked a lock of her hair, kissing her head. "It's the silence I still remember, the emptiness of my childhood home. In a single moment, the house turned from my haven into my darkest nightmares."

"The Council could not figure out who did it?"

She shook her head, her eyes far away and haunted. "They couldn't find a reason for anyone to want to harm them. The killer, or killers, could still be out there."

"I can help you figure out what happened," I carefully suggested.

"Really? You would do that?" Her eyes gleamed. My chest ached at how beautiful she was at that moment, with hope shining from her.

"Anything for you, *regina mea.*" She blushed at that statement and glanced away. A shot of despair went through me as I realized she was still trying to throw up walls between us. "What would you have wanted if your parents had lived?"

She bit her lip at the sudden redirection, making my body stir. "I wanted what my parents had. A husband who loved me and kids to spoil."

Little girls with her eyes and powers, boys with my strength and speed. The image already played behind my lids, and a dream of our future together formed. I cleared my throat and asked, "What was it you wanted to know about my past?"

She raised an eyebrow at my segue. "Fine, tell me about your favorite historical figure you've ever met."

I tapped my chin in thought. "Alexander the Great."

Her mouth gaped, "You met Alexander the Great?!"

"Met in the loosest sense of the term. I was there when he faced the Gordian Knot."

"What makes him your favorite if you didn't talk to him?"

I laughed, remembering. "The Gordian had stood for centuries, intimidating all other conquerors with its supposed magic. A fiction invented by powerless people, but it had deterred conquerors in the past. *Whoever can undo this knot will rule all of Asia*, the keeper of the knot announced when Alexander approached. Alexander looked at the knot, then back at the keeper, who was sure that the legendary general would turn his back on it and return to Macedonia. Then Alexander saw me and raised an eyebrow, nodding in respect. I was shocked because he knew what I was. He returned his gaze to the keeper of the knot, and without looking away, slid his sword from his waist. With a single slice, he cut the knot in half." I chuckled again, remembering the astonished looks on the faces of the people present. "I don't think I've ever laughed so hard in my life, especially as he made sure that his entire army walked through the posts and remains of the knot before ruling all of Asia."

"Wow," she breathed, clearly fascinated by my story. "You didn't take offense that he was so arrogant?"

I laughed. "Not at all. I had immense respect for him and was saddened to hear of his death. I had considered turning him into a vampire before deciding against it. He deserved his place in mortal history. I didn't want to take him from those books by making him immortal."

Terrible things happened to immortals who risked exposure. The powers that be would wipe the slate clean, and an immortal would vanish, or worse.

"Who else have you met?" Her eyes sparkled in fascination. I loved her curiosity. The word sent a bolt of shock through me. Shit, I was falling in love with her. Every moment I spent with her, I was falling ever deeper for my beautiful queen. I coughed to cover my revelation. "Trust me, *vrăjitoare*. I have met many fools throughout the years. I have stories to keep you interested for a century, at least."

She looked at my lips and said, "I look forward to making new memories of our own." She glanced away immediately after the statement, and my heart froze in my chest. It was the first time she'd given weight to the possibility of staying, speaking the words into existence.

Please stay, Phoebe. Please, I silently begged. I didn't give voice to the plea, hoping she would stay because she felt the same, but maybe that was a foolish dream.

XXVIII

THE REALM OF MORTALS.
ÎNTUNERIC CASTEL, ROMANIA.

I'm the only survivor without a shield. My eyes trace over the survivors, and the reason I was summoned before the Council roared through my head.

They knew about my plan to break the cardinal rule of being a witch: don't ever resurrect the dead.

OVER THE NEXT SEVERAL DAYS, I spent every available moment with Lucien. We continued practicing our sparring, increasing my stamina of non-lethal magic to the point that I no longer felt the immediate need to pass out. Each witch was like a battery. Some were low-powered and could last for years without fail, while others burned their power quickly and constantly needed charging.

I fell into the latter category. I was increasing my experience with daily battle magic so that *maybe* I could fight without killing.

After sparring, Lucien cuddled and read to me, allowing me the afternoon to shore up my strength. He made comments as he read from history books and accountings of immortal battles and wars. My sides often ached from laughter by the end. Stories of how Charlemagne had some of the worst breath he'd ever smelled or that Ben Franklin often greeted his guests nude for no apparent reason.

If I were honest, I was already in too deep with Lucien. I couldn't help the thoughts that danced in my head, but they didn't come with the bone-jarring panic like they had before. Rather, a kind of contentment, a feeling of warmth and familiarity. Roots were growing like ivy along the black walls of Întuneric, twisting around me, locking me in place. *Shit, how did that happen?* Lucien snuck past my defenses, and I would need to break every rule that kept me alive for years.

I was wandering the halls of Întuneric and realized I was *somehow* lost again in the ancient castle. Despite being here for several days, and memorizing the architecture, I was still constantly getting lost. I could have sworn the sparring room was this way, but I definitely didn't remember this room. I stepped over the threshold, expecting another vision of the past, but nothing happened.

My breath was fogging the air, and the wall next to me seemed to flicker. I reached out to touch it and felt the surge of magic, an illusion blocking off a portion of the room. I doubted anyone else would notice, especially those who couldn't see the runes carved into the floor. Even though I was not familiar with them, I could tell they were ancient. I reached down to touch the carvings, only to flinch back at the power I felt coursing through them.

I muttered a spell to reveal hidden objects, and a whiplash of corresponding magic flooded back, throwing me against the wall. I landed with an uncomfortable humph and a burning pain in my side. What in the hells kind of magic was that? My curiosity piqued, I brushed some lingering dust from my jeans and pulled out my phone. I planned to text Lucien and tell him to come and explain this strange anomaly in his castle, but my screen blinked once before going dark. I'd just charged it, but the battery was dead. So much for that plan.

I crossed my legs on the dusty floor, flurries erupting as I sat to stare at the illusion. I pondered it, wondering what could have sent me flying across the room. Damn, I still need Lucien's help. If I left, I doubted I'd be able to find this room again, and Lucien was in his office all day. I decided the safest thing would be to pull him through a rift. Without standing, I began the circular motion with my hand, but heavy mist-laden lands appeared instead of the throne room office I meant to conjure. *What in the hells?* I stood up to close it, concerned about what might stumble through. But no matter how I tried to banish the rift, nothing happened.

I tilted my head, weighing the options. I could enter the rift and risk it snapping closed behind me or sit there like an idiot until something invaded the castle. My choice made, I cautiously took a step through the opening. The tear in reality leading back to

Întuneric remained open. With a sigh of relief, I decided I would figure out why the rift opened here.

The farther I trekked from it, the heavier and colder the fog became, my breath puffing out in front of me. I felt heady magic but could see no source. I saw a glimmer of metal and pulled battle magic into my hands, preparing for a surprise attack.

"Hello?" I called out.

The moment the word left my mouth, I was filled with self-disgust. It was as if I'd learned nothing from every scary movie ever. The girl who calls out hello always dies. I glanced back and noticed the rift still shined on my periphery, the sight of it calming me. I could make it back to Întuneric if I needed to, back to Lucien.

I stepped farther into the mist and saw the shine again, but realized it was just a reflection off of the marble surface of a temple. The black stone had golden veins glowing through it. The colonnade jutted over me, and the enormous steps leading to the interior were far higher than normal.

I cautiously journeyed up the stairs to the temple's entrance, traveling above the layer of mist. I glanced around me, seeing numerous other revival temples in the distance. They were of all different pantheons, including Norse, Greek, Roman, Celtic, Egyptian, Chinese, Japanese, and more, but I was drawn to this one.

The Corinthian columns towered above me, and I continued through the opening. When I saw the statue that greeted me, I relaxed even more. Hekate the Goddess of Witchcraft, *my goddess.* The three-faced goddess had a crescent crown adorning her head, and the statue was truly a work of art. There were flickering flames in the two torches in her hands. They were lit but dim. A large black dog stood sentry at her side, but her second familiar was oddly missing from the ensemble. The goddess's eyes appeared to be closed, and I couldn't recall ever seeing a statue of her with her eyes like that.

A flash of light from behind the statue lured me further into the temple, so I ventured within. There were veins of magic flowing through the marble walls, flashing brighter as I came closer. My mouth gaped open when I understood I was looking at ancestral lineages. Carved meticulously into the walls were the ancestral names of every witch in existence. The lines of the first witches, those five hundred women and men touched by the goddess millennia prior, were written here.

I came closer and realized with a flare of sadness why some glowed gold and pulsed with magic while others were dull and dark. The lines that had died out had died here too. Only fifty of the names remained bright with magic. I trailed my fingers over them, realizing how much magic we had lost over the years because of persecution. I affectionately traced the surname *MARGAUX*, noticing it was still pulsing with magic. It was my line on my mother's side.

There were others I recognized. Witches learned our lines the way mortal children learned the states. By the time we received our grimoire, each of us could easily recite them all. I faced the wall and grimaced. We could only do so because what started as a legion was

290

down to a handful, five hundred lines down to fifty. Yet still, the Council persecuted and executed our own.

I studied the glowing names, looking for my father's line, frowning when I noticed it was absent. I saw the first name closest to the back wall was lit up. That must be Atreus.

I traced my fingers over the wall, moving closer to the isolated name that pulled me like a beacon, passing by those first picked by the goddess. My stomach dropped when I saw there were more dark names than bright ones. I finally reached the first and saw it was lit up, but it wasn't mine.

REGINA.

I'd never even heard of that line. My gut twisted as I looked closer. Directly below it, darkened and dead: *ATREUS.* That was impossible. I was the last of the Atreus line, and I was most *definitely* not dead. There must be some kind of mistake. In shock, I reached out to touch it.

I didn't hear the growl until it was too late. A dark shape plowed into my side, throwing me against the wall. I barely managed to roll out of the way of the next assault, and I caught sight of long, sharp teeth snapping at me.

The black shadow formed into a snarling dog, fangs dripping. I attempted to call on my magic, but the shadow dog lunged at me again. I dodged and shot a frantic beam at the animal. The shadows merely absorbed the magic, the creature reforming without incident.

I rolled out of its way and ran out of the temple, throwing beams of magic behind me to dissuade the pursuit of the shadow dog. My stomach dropped at the sight of my portal shrinking. My heart raced as I sprinted forward, the sound of growling and snapping following me. I dove into the closing rift, stumbling on the other side as it snapped shut, keeping the shadow dog from following me into Întuneric. I panted and collapsed on the ground, the dust of the chamber coating me. My mind whirled as I stood up to pace, struggling to process.

Lucien's voice echoed off the stone halls, becoming more frantic each time he called for me. The man would never believe I would not disappear the second he turned his back. As I strode into the hallway, the door to the mysterious room slammed shut behind me. It disappeared into the wall, and any sign it was ever there evaporated before my eyes.

"Over here!" I called. He whipped around the corner, not stopping until he was yanking me into his arms and kissing me deeply. I could taste his fear, anxiety, and desperation. Of all the things a ten-thousand-year-old immortal king might have, abandonment issues were the last I would have expected. It only endeared him to me more, making him more attainable, more human.

Lucien tore his mouth away and said, "I was worried you disappeared again."

I stroked his cheeks gently, pulling back to better look into his eyes. "How many times do I have to tell you I'm not going anywhere anytime soon?"

"Until I believe it," he admitted.

"How about I make it abundantly clear if I'm about to disappear on you?" I smiled unrepentantly, even as he smacked my ass in reprimand.

"Sassy," he said, his voice going husky.

I pulled him down for a long, drugging kiss, pulling away just enough to ask against his lips, "Race you to bed?"

"Challenge accepted, my queen."

XXIX

THE REALM OF MORTALS.
ÎNTUNERIC CASTEL, ROMANIA.

But...but I hadn't technically broken the rule yet. So there is no way they could have carried out the sentence just because I thought about it. Right?

My eyes catch the things I missed before, the remnants of the pyre they tied me to, the scent of accelerant and smoke still lingering in the air. Slowly, memories of the flames heating my feet and burning the soles of my shoes flicker through my mind. I remember the feeling of being torn in two and something breaking free from me.

THE DOOR TO THE PAST AWAITED ME. *I stood once again in front of the door where I'd first seen my parents and later my ancestor. No matter how hard I had searched, I hadn't been able to find it in Întuneric again.*

I hesitated before pushing open the wood panel. What would I see this time? My parents? The heartbroken woman giving away her child? More memories that weren't mine? More questions and no answers? Could I handle more?

My heart pounded as I shoved it open, the bright light behind it momentarily blinding me. I held my hand up to block it, allowing my eyes to adjust, again stunned by what I saw.

A war-torn beach with crashing waves colored red from the bodies claimed by the tempest. Spears and swords were strewn everywhere, small fires raging as corpses burned around her. A single girl stood at the center. Her clothes singed from battle. She wore a dented breastplate and was bleeding heavily from one side, her hand pressed against the wound to stem the flow of blood.

There were several male warriors surrounding her, their spears poking at her, mocking her injuries. Then time slowed. The young girl watched fascinated as a white-robed figure appeared, her skin glowing, her eyes a bright lilac. In my bones, I knew at first sight who the woman was. It was Hekate, Goddess of Witches, and at her side were her two familiars. The large black dog and small black cat strode over the battlefield, their gazes focused on the girl.

"Poor girl, why did you fight? They outnumbered you," Hekate said.

The young girl showed none of the deference to the goddess I expected. "A fate far worse awaits those who don't fight. I refuse to submit to that without doing everything I could," she spat.

Hekate approached her, reaching out a shining hand to touch the warrior's face. The girl flinched, but she continued to glare up at the goddess.

"You could have surrendered, given up to them."

"Become one of their slaves? One of their whores? Never," she said, yanking her head out of the goddess's grip.

"Why pray to me? Why not Athena or Ares?" Hekate asked, her head tilted.

"I knew they wouldn't come. I thought you might, but you didn't." The woman glanced around at the bodies of her fallen comrades. "Too little, too late, goddess."

"They didn't pray to me. You did," Hekate said, waving away the dead as if they were inconsequential.

"So, you waited until I was about to die to intervene?" The girl spat blood at the goddess's feet. "I should have prayed to one of the others."

The goddess didn't appear offended, only amused. "But you prayed to me. I will not have such a smart woman killed by these savages." She pointed at the males still surrounding them, frozen by her power.

The woman's brown eyes glimmered with hope, but she dropped her gaze again. "You will only spare me? What about the others?"

I noticed for the first time she wasn't the only female fighting off the invading horde. There were others frozen.

"Some fallen are claimed by other gods, I'm going to let you save whoever is left."

"Me?"

"You will be my instrument. You will channel my powers as if they were your own, and you will be the first witch. The First Ancestral Line. I will establish so many more, but you will be the ruler of them all."

Ruler? There was no ruler of witches, only the Council. As far as I knew, it had always been that way.

"Why me?" the young girl asked, still trying to stem the blood leaking down her side.

"Because you prayed."

Without giving her the chance to say yes or no, the goddess grabbed her. The golden light within Hekate leeched down her arms and coursed into the body of the girl. The

296

*girl's veins lit with golden light as the power climbed up her
arms, pulsating from within her. When the girl glanced up
again, she had the same eye color as the goddess.*

*The girl collapsed on the ground before Hekate, missing
how the goddess swayed. Hekate reached down to her side,
petting her black cat absently. "You'll stay by her side, won't
you? Guide her?"*

*The cat gazed back at Hekate, its bright eyes oddly
familiar.*

Thrown from the past, I sat up in bed. I was
unsurprised that Lucien lay next to me or that he came
awake when I bolted upright. He always slept so
lightly. More than once, I'd woken up in his arms, with
him murmuring soothing words to me and stroking
my back, coaxing me from a nightmare.

I threw myself into his arms. I clutched him tight,
burying my face into his side. He didn't hesitate,
pulling me close and murmuring, "I will always be here
when you need me."

I believed him enough to fall asleep in his arms,
trusting him to keep the nightmares at bay.

When I awoke the next morning, Lucien had
vanished, likely called away. He usually woke me up
with a sweet kiss and told me he was leaving or left a
note behind. There was nothing this time, but I figured
it must have slipped his mind. Vampires and his staff

were always seeking him out, even more frequently the closer we got to the coronation.

Inside our dressing room, I trailed my hands over the formal gowns that had arrived for the ball. Apparently, following the actual crowning portion of the coronation, a massive ball would take place. Music, light, and laughter would flood the castle. *Life in the hall of the dead.*

I recalled trying on the various gowns to show Lucien, but we barely got through one option before he was pushing me against the wall and making me scream. He growled, telling me the sight of me preparing to accept my new title made him eager to claim me. I was forced to try on the rest of the gowns when he was absent.

There was an extra box in the dressing room today, a large black square tied with a bright red bow. I pulled the card from the ribbon, shock filling me when I read it.

To my dearest daughter,
My gift to you and Lucien is this and many years of happiness.
Your Goddess-in-Law.

Holy shit, Lucien's mother, the Goddess of the Moon and Vampires, sent me something. She was resting in the Ethereal Realm but woke up to send me this?

Carefully removing the lid of the box, my breath caught in awe at the contents. Nestled in red velvet was a crown made of onyx. It was more delicate than the one I saw Lucien wear and featured a half-moon cut from a single diamond, nearly as big as my fist. I held

298

my breath, just touching it, afraid that someone was about to jump out and tell me there was a mistake. I wanted this, and I wanted Lucien, but he had to know everything before I could have him.

I sighed in envy and placed the crown back into the box before changing into a white sundress with small purple flowers sewn into the hem. I glanced at myself in the mirror, preparing myself for the conversation I needed to have with him.

"You can do this. You're a badass witch."

It was time to break the rules which had kept me alive. I tried to convince myself that I could move on if Lucien looked at me differently after he knew everything. *Could I survive if he realized fate had fucked up, pairing a legend-inspiring vampire king with a blood-soaked witch who hadn't stayed in the same place for over three months in over a decade?*

"You can do this," I muttered.

I turned away from the mirror, my stomach in knots, mentally preparing myself for the conversation I was about to have. I glanced at the clock. Lucien would likely be in the throne room office, going over various financial statements from his companies or on the phone with his COOs.

I strode in that direction, noticing that another group of vampires had arrived and were waiting for Lucien to allow them to enter. I froze when I noticed one vampire standing off to the side. When he saw me, he paled to the color of my dress and stood rooted to the spot. Malcolm. *No, no, no.* Why was he here? Why now? Before I could process any of those questions, or my emotions surrounding them, Lucien opened the door. He ignored the group of vampires when he caught sight of me, pulling me into his arms and pressing a kiss into my hair.

"Waiting for me?" He smirked.

I nodded, but his attention drifted to where my gaze was locked. Malcolm stared back at me, neither of us able to look away. I cleared my throat, suddenly unable to speak. Lucien's smile turned lethal as he focused on Malcolm, jumping to his own conclusions. Lucien gripped my hand and jerked his head toward his office door before leading me and the other vampire into the throne room, locking out the others who were watching in fascination. Purposefully stomping toward the dais, he gestured for me to take the throne next to his. I sensed Lucien's anger and slid into the obsidian chair. It was the first time I'd sat there, and it was happening while Malcolm was watching.

I glanced warily at Lucien as he sat, his face carved from granite. He indicated the vampire in front of him with a lift of his chin. "Malcolm Shaw, born 1969, turned 1992 by Daniel Arturo in Dallas, Texas. Now that's out of the way, how do you know my queen?"

Lucien didn't look to me for a response, but I'd managed to compose myself after the initial shock at seeing Malcolm in Întuneric and provided one.

"Malcolm is an ex-boyfriend, Lucien. It surprised me to see him here in Întuneric," I whispered, my voice cracking over the statement.

Lucien glared at the other vampire. His glowing red eyes narrowed as they assessed Malcolm, who fidgeted under his king's intense gaze. There was complete silence between us as we waited to see what Lucien would do.

Then, as I watched, Malcolm seemed to come undone, as if he could not keep the information in. "They had my sister! I had no choice but to betray you, Phoebe. I loved you."

Lucien hissed, no doubt irritated at the other vampire's past with me. The knots in my stomach intensified. This was the first time I'd seen Malcolm since my life went to shit, and it looked like he was already making a mess of my newest relationship. I planned to reveal everything to Lucien, but never like this.

"So, you stole my grimoires and disappeared on the orders of someone else?" I asked.

I assumed he had done it of his own will, that he had merely waited until I'd received my grimoires to move against me. Grimoires were valuable on the black market, and I'd despaired of ever finding them again.

"They got in touch with me right after you showed me the grimoires, Phi." *Phi.* It was his old nickname for me. When he made to step toward me, his hands out in supplication, Lucien growled, forcing him to step back again. "I thought Mia was dead, but they showed me they had her. It was your grimoires for her life," he muttered, shame coloring his tone.

That he'd betrayed me to save his sister did nothing to lessen the fact that he left me at the mercy of the Witches Council. "You couldn't have told me this? I would have helped you get your sister back." I would have done anything for him at the time. He'd been there for me when I'd lost my parents.

Malcolm visibly gulped. "I couldn't risk you saying no."

His eyes kept going back to Lucien, looking like he was about to piss himself from fear. He was afraid of what his king might do, as he should be.

Lucien allowed his burning gaze to bore into Malcolm a moment longer before saying, "So let me see if I understand this. Some group who claimed to have your sister approached you. They informed you that in exchange for her life and freedom, you had to steal and turn over Phoebe's grimoires. You did so, knowing the Witches Council would sentence Phoebe to death because of it." Malcolm glanced down at the floor in shame, bowing beneath the weight of his cowardice, but Lucien wasn't done. "And then, you left her to face the consequences alone?"

I couldn't help but fall even more in love with him. Lucien's voice was harsh, and his jaw clenched as he growled, "Phoebe?"

Without words, I knew what he was asking. I'd imagined Malcolm's death hundreds of ways over the last ten years. Now, with revenge right in front of me, it felt stale. Lucien would execute him, giving me everything I thought I wanted, but I wasn't able to give the command.

"Let him go," I answered. "He'll have to live with the mistakes he's made." I rose, coming to stand face-to-face with the cowering vampire. "One thing before you leave—who was it?"

Who destroyed my life, making sure I remained on the run for the next decade?

"It was eight members of the Witches Council," he whispered, and my head snapped back as if he'd struck me. Why would they set me up? "I only saw two of them, Hans and Monteux, but I smelled the rest of them. They were all witches."

My eyebrows went up in shock at the names of two of the highest-ranking members of the Council. I knew both had survived my little *explosive* episode.

"Leave. Before I ignore my queen's wishes and paint this room with your insides," Lucien bit out. With a rush of air, Malcolm disappeared from the throne room, his tail between his legs.

Slowly, I turned to face Lucien, bracing myself for his reaction. His eyes were still a violent red, and he was barely holding himself together.

"Did you love him?" The words were little more than a growl, garbled by his fangs and fury.

I shrugged. "I did at one time."

The arm of his throne disintegrated as it broke away in his fist. He lunged to his feet, pounding at the wall in frustration. Dust flew into the air, his strength forcing the stone to yield to his fury. I'd never seen him so angry, but I felt no fear that he would lay hands on me. I knew no matter his mood, he would never touch me in anger. He whirled back to me, still seething.

"Do you still?" he spat the question. Was he seriously more enraged about me loving Malcolm than about what he'd revealed?

"No," I answered resolutely, and some of his anger seemed to ease. I ran a hand through my hair in frustration. "I had planned on telling you everything today, but not like this, never like this."

I stood and walked to the massive window, gazing out through the tempered glass. Lucien was breathing hard, but I didn't look back at him. "There's more, Lucien. After they found out about the grimoires, they brought me before the Council to answer for what Malcolm had done. Loss of a grimoire is a death sentence. There are no exceptions." He came up behind me, but I did not turn back to him. I couldn't. "When they sentenced me, I...I lost control. Magic seemed to force its way out of me in waves, like an explosion. Before I knew it, there was ash falling from the sky, ash from their corpses." I choked back the memory but knew I had to get it all out now, or I might never leave. "I killed a good portion of the Witches Council that day. Those who survived, I placed a memory charm on. They each recall different people when they think of me."

Lucien was at my shoulder, and I closed my eyes, bracing myself to turn around and see how his face had lost that glowing look of pride. He placed a soft hand on my shoulder, forcing me to face him, but I kept my eyes closed so I didn't have to see his disgust. He placed his finger under my chin, tipping it up.

"Is that what you've been dreading telling me?" His voice was light and amused. "That when faced with death, you fought to live?"

My eyes snapped open in surprise, meeting the green of his. They were compassionate, almost understanding. "I killed so many witches that day, Lucien." I felt the tear slide down my cheek at the memory. He caught it on the tip of his finger and flung it away.

"Did a single one of them speak up in your defense, vote against you being put to death under some archaic law?" he softly asked. His hands framing my face, he continued. "Did anyone explain how you were being sentenced to death because of the actions of another?"

I wanted to glance away, but he held me fast. "No. They did not."

His eyes searched mine. "Then every single one of them deserved their fate."

I gasped in surprise. "Why do you say that?"

"Because they were planning to execute you, a young woman who'd recently lost her parents, for a crime she was not responsible for." He said it so reasonably like it was impossible to draw any other conclusion.

I wanted to collapse in relief at the fact that Lucien's gaze hadn't changed in the slightest when he looked at me, even knowing everything. I was falling hard for the legendary king and didn't want to fight it anymore. At that moment, I realized with a jolt that I was staying. I was staying with Lucien.

When the Council came for my head, and they would, we would fight them together. I would trust Lucien with my life and my heart. Somehow, he'd wormed his way past any defenses I had, and there was nothing left but him.

I threw myself at him and kissed him hard, pushing him back into his throne, desperate for him as always. He caught sight of my fevered eyes, his own turning red with lust and his fangs descending into his mouth.

Lucien moaned as I dropped to my knees between his spread thighs, cupping his length through his pants. I murmured, "Every time I've seen you sitting here, all I could think about was sucking you off while you sat on your throne."

He gulped, a tremor of anticipation shivering through his body. "Gods, you're perfect," he groaned as I slowly unzipped his jeans, freeing him from their confines. I glanced over my shoulder at the door.

"What if someone comes in?" I asked, one eyebrow raised.

"They won't if they want to live," he growled in response. I took him into my hands, and the muscles of his thighs went stone hard. My eyes locked with his when my tongue first lapped at him. I tortured him slowly, licking over the crown, pre-cum beading on the head. "Take it into your mouth," he ordered.

I ignored him, enjoying how the tables had turned. Though I was submissive to him in bed, and I knew he was allowing it, I was enjoying taking control for once. I ran my tongue from base to tip, and he shuddered when I finally took the head into my mouth. His glowing gaze shot to the ceiling, then immediately came back to watch.

My lips wrapped tightly around his shaft, and I flicked the piercings with my tongue, feeling him throb in the wet heat of my mouth. I began a slow rhythm, moving up and down, taking as much of him as I could. Lucien's knuckles went white as he gripped the throne, the stone groaning beneath the pressure of his grip. He muttered half in English and half in Romanian. I increased my pace until his hips thrust up, his cock pushing deeper and his balls tightening, preparing to come.

"Going to come on your tongue. Swallow me down," he commanded.

Lucien came with a yell, and I obliged, swallowing every drop of him. I licked him clean, giving one last loving drag of my tongue before pulling back and smiling up at him. He looked blown away, utterly decimated, and the expression of wonder in his eyes had my heart thudding. He was still looking at me as he always had.

He reached for me, but I dodged him, a massive smile lighting my face as I turned to exit the throne room. He caught me and pulled me back against him. "And where do you think you're going?"

His tone made me shiver, and my good humor lit up my voice. "You have vampires waiting to speak with you."

"Fuck my vampires. I want to make you come," he whispered, biting my ear playfully, his hands taking an extensive tour down my body.

"Later, Lucien. Finish with them, and then you can make me come as many times as you want. I'm a giver like that." The smirk I gave him earned me a slap on the ass, but he released me. He walked me toward the door, trailing his fingers down my back.

"You can count on that, my queen. Wear something sexy." He growled, swatting my ass again before opening the throne room door to let me out. I noticed the various wide-eyed stares of the vampires present, but I ignored them. I knew Lucien would make his meetings as short as possible.

My stomach was once again in knots as I headed for our bedroom but for a different reason this time. I was going to ask Lucien to claim me, and I was *nervous* but not exactly sure why. I'd wanted to sleep with him since our first night in Tír nAill. Finally, I was getting my wish, and it filled me with anxiety. Part of me wanted him to blow off all the waiting vampires and head straight for me. He had a way of calming me down.

I stood in the dressing room, biting my lip and glaring at the various lingerie that Adelaide had purchased for me. Tonight was special, and I didn't want the mundane or hooker light. Bast came up behind me and rubbed against my legs, sensing my disquiet. I scratched the cat's ears, the feline purring in delight at my touch. "What do you think, Bast?"

The cat tilted her head and blinked at me. Though witches and familiars had a special bond, often used to steady their magic when they were younger, I wished Bast could give me actual advice instead of her usual stares. The cat disappeared through the hanging clothes, spreading her scent on the fabric. The familiar often spent nights curled between us, even cuddling up on Lucien's chest a couple of times.

Bast let out a long meow, calling to me. I drifted farther into the closet, finding the cat clawing at a box wrapped with a bow. Was this another gift from Lucien's mother? I pulled it out and looked for a note but found none. My smile turned wicked when I lifted the lid and caught sight of the contents.

Lucien will have no idea what hit him.

XXX

THE REALM OF MORTALS.
ÎNTUNERIC CASTEL, ROMANIA

I WAS GOING TO STRANGLE the next individual who kept me from Phoebe. My rage and lust were still running high after her ex's appearance in Întuneric. Rage practically blinded me, and my nerves vibrated inside my skull, making my vision narrow. It was impossible not to imagine the boy's hands on her, and when she said she'd once loved him, a haze of red had fallen over me. The crowd of vampires in front of me took a deep breath at my glowing eyes. My subjects knew to bolt, people usually died when it happened.

Why had she never mentioned she'd dated a vampire before? When I reflected on our time together, I realized for the first time that she never made a fuss over drinking blood, even offering her own without hesitation. It was familiar to her.

At the thought of the boy drinking from her, my jaw tightened and my muscles primed. I was a breath away from unleashing everything boiling within me. An inferno, magma hot and scalding, was about to blow, and I'd take down everyone, *everything* in my proximity. He had sampled her blood, her body. He got affection, even *love*, from her. The unbroken arm of my throne came away like dust in my hand. Shards of stone slipped through my shaking fingers. For ten thousand years, the throne of the vampire king had sat on that pedestal, and in less than an hour, I'd rendered it into nothing but an armless hunk of rock.

I muttered to myself madly, the words unrecognizable even to my own ears. I didn't even notice the vampires vacate the throne room, Erik standing in their place looking grim. Where did the werewolf come from? In my mind, I shoved past my old friend, storming to my mate, losing myself in her writhing form. Instead, I settled heavily into my armless throne. "What is it, Erik?"

Erik's eyes made me shift uneasily. They were sky blue and vibrating with a pulse of amber through them. The wolf was surfacing within Erik, fighting to take control. His golden hair was falling in all directions, and the white of the scars on his face were stark. His voice shook when he said, "I heard from the Witches Council."

Fuck, I'd totally forgotten about the bounty. Phoebe distracted me so much I couldn't think straight. When I thought back on the night in Tír nAill, I didn't think about meeting with Erik. I thought about her scream of pleasure and the taste of her lips.

"And?" I asked, waving the wolf on imperially.

"It's Phoebe," Erik whispered, his voice breaking.

"What is?" The hair on my arms stood on end, a shiver shooting down my spine. My mind was recoiling. I couldn't be one of the bounty hunters she so dreaded. I couldn't be the source of her nightmares, the reason she ran.

"The bounty. It's her," Erik answered, paling even more.

I jumped up, grabbing him by the shoulders, shaking him. Desperation was an icy dagger in my gut, twisting. "Please tell me you didn't take the bounty."

Magical bounties were utterly binding. There were no exceptions, not even mates. If the Witches Council requested I hand over Phoebe, I wasn't sure what the mystical contract would make me do. I had to tell her. I had to explain. Would she listen? Or would she run? I just felt the bridge of trust growing between us, a major milestone when she confessed her past to me. But this would destroy us.

"I'm so fucking sorry, I-I didn't know," Erik muttered. I knew the wolf was fond of Phoebe. She had a *way* with people. Erik had searched for his queen for over a thousand years. I knew he understood the gravity, but it didn't do anything to change the truth.

I paced back and forth, my mind turning over repeatedly. The ragged edge of madness taunted me. What if Phoebe ran? She hadn't asked me to claim her. What if this was what pushed her away forever? My stomach rolled at the thought.

"I have to talk to her, have to explain," I muttered, having trouble controlling my chaotic thoughts. My mind was a maze of half-formed expressions and impressions. I couldn't get a grip on any of them. Everything slipped through my fingers like a silk cascade, my mother, Cassandra, Phoebe.

"I'm going to search for something to get us out of this. I swear to you," Erik vowed, but his voice was barely audible over the rushing in my ears.

I wanted to say something, but I couldn't respond. I released Erik, staggering to find Phoebe to fumble my way through an explanation. Am I just another vampire betraying her, another person turning their back on her?

I knocked on our bedroom door before pushing it open. "Phoebe?"

The breath left my lungs on a hiss, all the blood rushing from my brain to my cock. She was my every fantasy made flesh. She was bent over at the waist, tying on sky-high heels. The midnight corset she was wearing barely contained her breasts, the luscious orbs threatening to spill out. I struggled to remember why I had rushed up here.

Phoebe straightened, glancing over at me. Her eyes were hooded and almost glowing with desire. She raised a single brow at the erection outlined in my jeans. She wasn't wearing panties, just garters hooked into the corset, leaving little straps down her thighs and ass. I wanted to snap those little elastic bands so she would feel me for days. Any logical thought went out the window. Anything I could have said, needed to say, devolved into *mine.*

I bolted forward, grasping her hips and groaning at the sight of her curves tied up in such a delicious package. My brain was blank, driven by desire and instinct for her. Everything since I'd first turned to see her in Tír nAill, had led to this point.

I was so mentally fogged with desire that she had to repeat herself twice before I understood.

"I want you to claim me."

They were words from a dream. I shook my head, trying to clear the fog in my mind. Was I hallucinating, or had she said she wanted me to claim her?

"Are you sure?" I croaked. The idea of sliding into her, making her mine in truth, was a dream I barely dared believe could be true. My life before her had been lonely, empty, shallow, and cold. Spending a day spooning her, watching a show about a *vampire slayer*, brought me more satisfaction than any erotic encounter in my past.

She bit her lip in that maddening way, making my cock pulse with need. "I'm sure. I—I trust you."

Those were powerful words for her. She'd been betrayed by her first love and her own people, and trust was a massive step for her. I couldn't wait any longer, but didn't I need to tell her something?

I snapped the garter that lay over her ass. Phoebe jumped, and her eyes went heavy with desire. "I like you in this. My wicked queen," I growled, snapping the other garter, the sound of it hitting her flesh loud in the room.

I grabbed her hair, clutching it in my fist before claiming her mouth. Our teeth clashed with a frantic need for each other, our tongues dueling. My hands traced her bodice before I grabbed her hips, forcing her to jump and lock her legs around my waist. Her heels dug into my back as if she were spurring me on, but I needed no prodding. Our kiss became more desperate, ragged, punctuated by pants. We landed on the bed with me over her, almost crushing her.

"Must get you ready..." I muttered, barely able to marshal a coherent thought.

Thank the gods she had the foresight to forego panties, leaving nothing between us. My hand trailed down her front, snapping both garters again. I dipped my fingers between her thighs, unable to hold back a low moan. "You get so wet for me. You love to come."

I teased her clit, rubbing it languorously and unhurried, though everything in me was clamoring to be inside her. The mad side of me wanted to fuck her into the next century. The need howled at me to take her. It demanded that she could quiet the madness, but I would not hurt her. I was bigger than most, and I would take everything she had to give. I needed her dripping for me.

I slipped a single finger inside her and felt her clamp down hard. "Your greedy little pussy wants me to fill it?" Slowly, I picked up the pace, my finger ducking in and out. She squirmed, trying to get more of me. I was finally going to be inside her.

"I need you, baby. Please. No more waiting," she whimpered.

She wiggled on my finger, and I added another, widening them, preparing her. I was finally going to be inside my mate. Some part of my mind was waiting for the other shoe to drop, for something to rip her from my grasp. She was so slick, but tight. She needed to be out of her mind with desire for me to fuck her without causing her pain.

"I'm going to be inside this pussy tonight. Everyone will know who you belong to."

She drenched my hand, her arousal increasing the more I talked to her, the more controlling I became. She was so responsive, shivering and moaning as my other hand came down to snap her garters again. When I could finally get a clear thought through my head, I was going to show her all the dark things she would beg for. This was just the beginning.

"These tits, this ass, this amazing pussy. They all belong to me."

I picked up the rhythm of my fingers, my other hand playing with her clit, taking her toward her first orgasm.

"Gods!" she screamed without a care who heard.

Her back bowed, her breaths coming in short pants as her orgasm began. She screamed my name as it crested and then collapsed bonelessly onto the bed. I was tempted to push her toward another, but didn't think I could last. I wrapped my arms around her and flipped us over. She straddled me, her cheeks flushed and her lilac eyes glowing. The slickness I felt on the tip of my cock nearly made me lose my control, and I fought the need to thrust up into her pussy. I would be damned if I acted like an untried youth and came before I was in her.

Without saying anything, she braced her hands on my chest and rocked herself on the tip of my cock, teasing me with shallow thrusts inside her. I was so close to the paradise awaiting me. I had to get inside of her.

"No more teasing, Phoebe. I need to be inside you. Work yourself down on me." My muscles bulged with strain, actively resisting the instinctive urge to plunge inside her. She continued her short, shallow thrusts, taking more of me each time. "More!" I growled.

She whimpered, slowly easing herself down on me, the crown of my cock just breaching her. I was so close to where I would kill to be. She had taken maybe an inch, almost two, when she moaned, "Gods, you're filling me up."

"More!" I growled, my claws digging into her hips, tempted to wrench her down and force her to take all of me. My fangs filled my mouth, needing to bite her, to claim her.

"Don't want to hurt you," I bit out, my voice unrecognizably rough.

"You won't. I trust you," Phoebe murmured, taking in more of me.

At her words, my control frayed and snapped. My claws dug into her hips as I slammed her down on me, forcing her to take my length. She yelped and then panted as she cautiously rocked her hips back and forth on me. Her body welcomed mine with a rush of liquid heat around my cock. She moaned as she slid up and down on me, and that was all I could take.

I flipped us over and laid on top of her, thrusting inside her, frenzied and out of control. She came again around my cock, but I didn't let up, didn't pull back, continuing my punishing pace inside her. I grabbed one of her legs, throwing it over my shoulder, widening her hips to take more of me, continuing to grind inside her. She tossed her head as she submitted, unable to do much more than allow me to do whatever I wanted.

Mine.

I was frantic for her, fucking her pussy for all I was worth, and she was wild for it, her nails and heels digging into my back. The tension in my body increased, knowing I was on the verge of coming, and I glanced at her throat, at the pulse beating there.

"Need your blood."

She didn't even hesitate, just lifted her chin and offered her throat. I sank my fangs into her neck, making her scream as another orgasm ripped through her. The taste of her blood sent me soaring toward my own. I kept thrusting, the feeling of being inside her indescribable.

If I wasn't already lost for her, this moment would have sealed it. I pulled my fangs out of her and rolled so she rested on top of me. Her strong cherry blossom scent was now tinged with my own. She was mine. She couldn't ever leave me. I clutched her to me, kissing her forehead, nose, eyelids.

"Mine. Forever," I growled.

Forever. I'd claimed her forever. Phoebe was finally mine. Already the persistent banging of the bloodlust in my head had receded.

"Yours," she murmured. Her eyes twinkled as she kissed me rough and deep, making my shaft stir again inside of her. "Mine," she growled, imitating my accent, forcing a smile from me. She wiggled her hips and squeezed my cock with her inner muscles, making me harden again. My queen was insatiable. I was going to need every ounce of my immortal resilience to satisfy her. It was the first time I'd looked forward to the years ahead of me. I knew it would take every one of them to satisfy the need for my mate.

XXXI

THE REALM OF MORTALS.
ÎNTUNERIC CASTEL, ROMANIA.

I didn't fight. Until the very last second, I expected them to pull the plug on the whole thing and announce to everyone that I'd learned my lesson. You can't execute someone for thinking about committing a crime.

I didn't fight, so I burned, just like all the other witches who came before me, just like my ancestors. Time passes, but nothing ever changes.

HOLY SHIT, I thought for probably the hundredth time as I sprawled across Lucien's chest, every molecule of my body sated. We made love five more times until I begged for a slight reprieve. His stamina was impossible to keep up with, even for me. *Mated and sated.* I guess the old sayings were true. I always thought sex was just...well, *sex.* But when Lucien's eyes locked on mine and he first moved inside me, I felt an almost soul-deep connection snap into place. Now, I felt altered, as if there was a pre-cataclysmic-sex-Phoebe and a post-apocalyptic-sex-Phoebe. And this was only our beginning.

I sighed and glanced up at him. His eyes were hooded, and his hand was idly tracing patterns on my back. I shivered at the intensity of his gaze and asked, "Do I smell different?"

Lucien leaned closer, taking an exaggerated sniff of my skin before licking my neck, making me giggle.

"Only slightly." He inhaled deeply. "Cherry blossoms tied with a splash of citrus." He dug his nose into my hair, breathing in more of my scent. My lips stretched into a goofy smile.

I almost wished I had enhanced senses so I could experience it. With magic, I could make it happen, but it would constantly wear down my energy. My daily power level would reside at an eight rather than ten. Plus, not all immortals smelled as good as Lucien. I nuzzled my nose against his neck, only able to smell his familiar scent of lemons and olive oil. "You still smell the same to me." I pouted at him. "How are all your old conquests going to know you're off the market?"

His lips twitched, his hand twirling a lock of my hair. "How could they not? I think my glaring, *jealous* queen at my side would be an excellent hint."

"Oh, and I'm the *only one* with jealousy issues?" I pinched him, eliciting another laugh from him. I'd seen the way he wanted to tear apart Malcolm.

Lucien chuckled again, the sound warming me. He didn't do enough of that. "That boy would be wise to vacate this realm as soon as possible." Though his tone was teasing, I could feel the tension in his body and knew some part of him wasn't joking. He'd spared him for me. I'd asked, and he had complied.

I frowned and traced a pattern across his chest, hoping to calm him. "It doesn't make any sense. Why have Malcolm steal the grimoires? Why frame me?"

He tangled my hair through his fingers. His body was tight with anger, and his voice dangerously low when he said, "They wanted an excuse to kill you."

"But why go through the trial? Why not just kill me?" I questioned, my brain struggling to figure it out. Why had my parents felt the need to hide me? Was it because there was something more to it? Why bring up resurrection? How did they even know about that? I never even told Malcolm. "I feel like I'm only seeing half a picture. It's infuriating."

He cupped my chin, forcing my eyes up to his. "I won't let them touch you," His eyes shimmered with sincerity, but there was a flash of something unidentifiable there, disappearing before I could analyze it. "If they strike at you, they make an enemy of me."

If even half the stories in that book were true, Lucien was a formidable enemy. I kissed his bare chest and snuggled closer, though I was still lost in thought. They didn't know I could create rifts. *So why me?*

"They won't give up. I couldn't live with myself if you got hurt protecting me."

"Phoebe..." He dragged my name out.

"I know you're this legendary king that's fought every war since the dawn of time." I hushed him when he opened his mouth to protest. "But this is the *Witches Council*. They would come at you in a way you'd never expect." *A way I would never expect.* My stomach rolled at the thought. "What if they killed my parents?"

320

He pulled me closer. "We'll figure everything out. Together we can do anything."

His confidence was so factual, so reassuring, that it actually helped ease some of my worries. What *couldn't* we do together?

Tired of the worry and the constant circling of my thoughts, I shifted until I straddled him, teasing myself along his hardening shaft. Maybe I wasn't as exhausted as I thought. Lucien's eyes flashed red, and he threw me off him and onto my front. With rough, urgent hands, he positioned me on my knees with my face pressed into the pillow. Impatiently, he fed his cock into me, sliding in easily. I bit the pillow beneath me as a loud moan ripped from my throat.

He forced my arms back, gripping my wrists and pinning me in place as he pounded frantically inside me. "I'll never get enough of this pussy," he moaned, rotating his hips to enter me more deeply. I screamed at the sensation, unable to do anything but take it and submit to him. He bellowed as he started to come. "You are mine!"

I screamed as a violent orgasm tore through me, but he didn't stop. He seemed desperate for something. "You belong to me! Never will I be parted from you!"

His thrusts slowed, my body still gripping at his cock as aftershocks of pleasure rippled through me. He moaned as he slowly withdrew, pulling me back into his arms, both of us panting.

As I drifted off, I swore I heard him whisper, "Don't leave me."

XXXII

THE REALM OF MORTALS.
ÎNTUNERIC CASTEL, ROMANIA.

WHEN PHOEBE DRIFTED OFF TO SLEEP, exhausted, I finally comprehended what happened. I claimed my mate. Phoebe was mine. My chest bowed with pride over satisfying my young queen so thoroughly. I knew she would feel me tomorrow. Soon, I'd show her the delights of bondage and obedience.

Phoebe's soft hair tangled around my fingers as I gently fisted it. Her face was still flushed from her orgasm, her body languid and relaxed against me. My hand paused on her hair, my entire body tensing. I meant to speak with her, but I'd lost my mind. My own words rang in my ears. *Together, we can do anything.*

My stomach knotted with fear. I had to figure a way out of the bounty. There must be someone who did so over the years, though I struggled to recall any stories I might have heard about it. Exhaustion settled in, and I sighed, letting my eyes drift closed with Phoebe cuddled against me.

I could only have been asleep for a couple of hours when a chill shot down my spine. The sensation was so unlike the warm, curvy witch I fell asleep next to that it dragged my eyelids open despite the force trying to hold them closed. I was standing half-naked, hovering next to the bed. *Did I sleepwalk?* I'd definitely never done that before.

I glanced down and realized I was standing over Phoebe. A feeling of warmth spread through me, especially when her modified scent hit me. I reached forward to brush a lock from her face, my stomach dropping at the sight of the cuffs I held in my hands.

I leapt back, hitting the wall, clearing the entire room in a single move. Where the hell had they come from? I dropped the silver bracelets as if they burned, the sound of them landing muted on the Aubusson rug. When had I retrieved them from the side of the mountain? I pulled my leg back to kick them across the room but stopped myself. If Phoebe woke up and saw me standing in the bedroom with the cuffs in my hands, she might run. I couldn't risk it. I snatched the hated metal off the floor and flew from the bedroom, almost colliding with Erik. He looked rather dazed, his eyes bloodshot.

"We have a problem." My voice cracked as panic suffocated me. I held the cuffs up for Erik to see. The wolf paled at the sight. "I do not remember retrieving these."

"That's what I was coming to tell you." Erik swallowed hard, trying to force the words out. "I found out more about the mystical bounties last night."

I felt a flash of guilt at hearing that. While Erik was gathering research on how to get us out of this, I was lost in a haze of desire with Phoebe.

The wolf looked haggard. His blonde hair was oily and falling all over his face. *When was the last time he showered?* "The longer we're in the bounty's presence, the more it's going to force us to complete it."

Force me to turn Phoebe over to the witches, the people who had already tried to kill her? *Never.* Then I realized I clutched the cuffs harder in my hands, the silver metal clanking softly. I felt sick that I might have just become the greatest threat Phoebe had known.

"Are you saying that I am a danger to Phoebe the more time I spend with her?"

We couldn't have gotten past everything else for this to tear us apart. Some part of me, the cowardly part, was happy that she forced my mind to a screeching halt last night. If I confessed the truth, she might have left.

Even now, with the bounty forcing my actions, I couldn't tell her. Her trust in me was still fragile, and if I even hinted at the truth, she would leave. She would see another vampire who betrayed her. She would hate me and leave forever.

"I don't know," Erik muttered, his face bleak. The three scars on his face were even paler with strain.

Historically, neither of us had failed to discover and capture or kill our target. I felt my stomach roll at the thought. How many had been like Phoebe? How many had been wrongfully accused? I ran a hand through my hair. What had I done? The quest for escape from the constant monotony of immortality might force me to lose the one thing I felt like I would die without.

She finally trusted me, and I might betray her because of some *parchment*? I couldn't stomach the thought. There had to be a way out.

"Tell me there is a way out of this," I pleaded, my voice cracking in desperation. "I can't lose her."

I was in love with her and on the cusp of losing her. Fuck you, Fate. I didn't bother hiding my emotions from Erik, even though the sight made the wolf wince in sympathy. "I'm going to petition the Witches Council to release us from the bounty. We'll tell them she's dead or something, anything to get us both out of it. Give me three days. I'll be back in time for the coronation."

With those instructions, Erik sped off. He left me standing alone in the halls of Întuneric with my terror at the thought of losing Phoebe choking me. I glared down at the hated cuffs still clutched in my hand.

This force thought to dictate to me? *Me?!* My fury rose, muting my despair. I stormed out of the castle, marching down to the location where I'd plunged from the mountain to save my mate. I was ten-thousand years old! A piece of parchment would not control me! I was stronger than any compulsion.

I pulled my arm back and threw the cuffs as far as possible, hurling them toward some point in the distance. A glimmer of hope flickered inside me as they sailed away, but it disappeared when the moon caught the silver, and they began their descent into the valley.

Unable to control my limbs, I sped into the valley below, locating the cuffs. I regained control once they were back in my hands.

No.

I tossed them again, farther this time, and the compulsion forced me to go after them again. I was mystically compelled to hold on to them.

No, no.

I desperately repeated the process, hoping that if I tossed them far enough, I wouldn't have to retrieve them. I wanted to return to Phoebe cuddled in our bed and make love to her again. On the fourth try, I fell to my knees, pocketing the cuffs in despair.

I clung to Erik's words. Maybe the wolf could get us out of this. I could be on guard for three days, three days to spend with Phoebe, three days to pray to every dark god for a way out of this.

With the hateful cuffs clutched in my fist, I trudged the miles back to Întuneric. My repeated disposals of them made the distance great. My head hung as I slowly made my way back to the castle. The wolf was ruthless, and he knew what was at stake.

The dark stone of Întuneric stood out against the rising sun, making the structure even more foreboding. Since Phoebe had been in residence, the halls had echoed with laughter and joy, no longer cold and empty. I viewed the castle as a home instead of just somewhere I slept, and I might lose it all.

It was just three days. I could do three days. I wouldn't sleep until Erik returned, being on guard against any possible compulsion moments. There was no choice. I had to do this.

XXXIII

THE REALM OF MORTALS.
ÎNTUNERIC CASTEL, ROMANIA.

"You...abomination," a broken voice cracks, making my head swivel back to look at the survivors. One of them had come awake during my inspection of what remained of my execution.

My eyes connect with Silas Cren's black ones, and the hatred living there makes me physically recoil. Abomination?

I STRETCHED LANGUIDLY AS THE morning sun shined through our window, highlighting the empty bed next to me. For a moment, I felt a flash of panic, but I could still smell him. His scent covered the sheets, and I curled into his pillow to get more. Goddess, preserve me. When had I become so pathetic? Oh right, that had happened just about the time I met the vampire king who made me orgasm to the point of blacking out. Yeah, I'm kind of drawing imaginary hearts with our initials in my mind. *Whatever.*

"Lucien?" I called, hearing the water running in the bathroom. *Hm, round of shower sex sounds like a good idea.*

I sat up, expecting to feel some soreness from our night, but I didn't have even the slightest bit of discomfort. Well, that just meant we would have to put more effort into it. I was nothing if not persistent.

Without bothering to cover up, I strutted naked into the bathroom. Lucien was in the shower, and I stopped to admire him unobserved for a couple of seconds. The water was sluicing over his muscles, playing with his gorgeous physique. His midnight hair was slicked back from his face, his hands rubbing along his tan skin.

Mine.

Every inch of him belonged to me. I was falling hard for him. Not that I would ever admit to it unless he did. I had some standards, after all. A lady never said *I love you* first. I was pretty sure it was in the rules of etiquette somewhere.

I pulled the glass shower door open, and Lucien whipped toward me, surprise and something that looked like trepidation flashing in his eyes. I blinked for a moment, trying to decipher the reason, then he noticed I was naked. Desire muted all his other emotions, his eyes quickly turning red.

"Phoebe," he growled, reaching for me. I dodged him, a teasing smile lighting my face.

"You weren't planning to hog all the hot water, were you?" I smirked at his groan when I made a big show of bending over to pick up my shampoo. He grabbed my hips, and I swatted at his hands. "No touchy."

Lucien leaned forward to whisper huskily in my ear, "Tease."

I shivered at his voice and smiled guilelessly over my shoulder. His eyes still glowed red with desire, and his cock was hard. I bit my lip to keep from reaching for it.

I began massaging my scalp with the rose-scented shampoo, but this time he swatted at my hands, taking over lathering my hair.

"You don't have to…" I started, but broke off on a moan. His fingers were firm as he kneaded my scalp, and my eyes drifted closed. This man was too good to be true.

"Believe me. I want to."

He took his task seriously, continuing until I stepped under the spray to rinse the soap from my hair. He looked hard to the point of pain, and I heard the click of his fangs when he spoke, but he was resisting. This mundane task was important to him. He reached down to grab my conditioner, pouring some into his hands.

I raised an eyebrow at him. "Have you done this before?"

He shook his head. "Never. There are certain things I've only ever done with you."

"Like what?" I liked Lucien sharing a part of himself with me and no other. I had never considered myself a jealous person, but he was *mine*. I didn't like sharing him with anyone, even those from his past.

"Like slept." He lathered the conditioner into my hair, focusing intently on his task.

"You've never slept with a lover?" I asked, shocked. "Not even once?"

He grabbed the loofah, squeezing some of my body wash onto it. He knew my shower ritual a little too closely, knowing I loofah before rinsing the conditioner from my hair. How long had he been studying my habits? "Not even once, not until you."

His hands traced my curves as he gently scrubbed the loofah over my back. "What else have you never done?" I asked with a sigh of pleasure.

"Thought about children," he admitted, though his voice was a little unsure. My heart stopped in my chest.

"Y-you want kids? With *me?*" I stuttered. I'd never thought of myself as *maternal* before. My past had demanded I become a kickass, name-taking fugitive. But I had never dared dream I would be a *mom*.

"Do you not?" Again, his voice was cautious, gauging my reaction.

"I did, but with everything with the Council, I haven't thought about it in years." Those dreams died that day, alongside the witches I'd killed.

I was a little happy that I was facing away from him, so I could struggle through my own thoughts. Did I want kids? My heart lurched as I imagined little fanged boys with a mop of dark hair running amok through Întuneric and tiny witch girls to teach.

"I think I want kids. With you."

I heard his intake of breath at my response. "I don't mean right away," he rushed to say.

I smiled at that. "I'm on witchy birth control." There was a tattoo on the back of my neck, laden with magic. "But if you want to, I'm game."

"When I can share you, we'll talk about it. I want you all to myself for a while."

Somewhere around my mid-back, the loofah had disappeared. Now, it was just his hands trailing down to my waist, exploring my curves. I once tried to diet away my butt, knowing that when I reached my prime, I'd be stuck with that shape forever. At that moment, I was glad I'd never taken to it. I moaned when he grasped my ass and squeezed. The steam from the shower was another caress on my overly sensitive skin, and I rolled my hips against him, seeking relief. Wasn't I supposed to be teasing *his* desire, not the other way around?

While I waited for him to spread my legs and slip inside me, he came closer to my neck to growl in my ear, "It's too bad you told me not to touch you…"

"Touch me, please touch me," I begged.

At my words, Lucien spun me around and hoisted me up. He wrapped my legs around his waist, centering himself right at my entrance. My back hit the tile so hard I heard it crack, the slight pain only escalating my desire. I moaned as he pressed the tip of his cock to my entrance and hovered there.

"Please, inside me." I tried to wiggle down on him.

"You're mine?" He groaned, thrusting hard inside me.

"Yours!" I screamed, trying to meet his frantic thrusts.

"Forever?" he asked, his hips pivoting to get deeper inside me.

"Forever! Please, Lucien!" I begged, needing more.

Then he pounded inside me. He braced one hand on the wall above my head, his claws digging in and cracking the tiles. I felt the sharp sting of his talons as he grasped my hip to hold me still.

My scream echoed in the shower as I came around his cock. My first release was followed almost immediately by another orgasm as he sunk his fangs into my neck. The pulls on my blood just felt too good, and I swore I saw stars.

He broke more tiles as he came inside me. When his eyes locked with mine, I felt the connection between us grow, and wonderment filled me. Our breaths were ragged, both of us panting, my heart practically bursting from my chest. We remained like that for a moment. He reverently traced his hand down my cheek, pressing his forehead to mine. "I don't know what I have ever done in my long life to deserve to be mated to you."

My eyes misted, and I wasn't sure what to say, so I kissed him hard. I tried to convey all my emotions with the touch of my lips to his. We both groaned at the loss when he pulled out and gently set me back on my feet. I never wanted him to stop looking at me like that.

What was I next to him? I covered my discontent with a smile and rinsed the lingering conditioner and body wash off. Lucien watched me as if fascinated and enraptured by even the most mundane things about me. My stomach tightened, but he was mine, and I would keep him.

XXXIV

THE REALM OF MORTALS.
ÎNTUNERIC CASTEL, ROMANIA.

TWO DAYS WITH PHOEBE PASSED IN A BLUR. Every second I didn't hear from Erik felt like a death knell. I checked my phone constantly. When Phoebe noticed, I admitted that Erik had left to take care of some wolf business, and I had hoped he would've been back by now.

Phoebe offered to rift to find him, and I quickly discarded the idea. I barely covered my slip by claiming I wasn't sure exactly where the wolf was. Phoebe could open rifts to places, not people, though I knew she wished she could think of someone and appear next to them.

The castle was bursting at the seams with vampires and various other immortals, all coming to glimpse the newest vampire queen. Every time she lit up at the sight of the gifts I showered upon her, the secrets I kept twisted inside me. I hadn't slept since the night Erik had left, and though I could normally go for weeks without rest, the guilt was making me weaker than usual. I just had to make it a few more days.

So many times it had been on the tip of my tongue to confess all to her. Maybe together, we could find a way out of this. She had the cleverest mind, and she enjoyed how often people underestimated her because of her age and beauty.

She was already earning the loyalty of the Vampire Elders after beating several at chess. I recognized the look of astonishment on their faces when she handily bested them all. I'd seen it often enough in the mirror. She was a witch who'd seen only a handful of decades, and she was outwitting vampires older than most fossils.

The oldest of Elders and my paternal uncle, Ambrogio, pulled me aside to discuss Phoebe. I was prepared to hear a list of all the things wrong with having a witch as a queen, but my uncle merely slapped me on the shoulder, stating we could not ask for a wilier queen. It was the first time he'd ever shown affection toward me.

Phoebe's musical laugh drew me back to her, like a moth to a flame. I noticed for the first time that she was making slight hand movements under the table as she played. I smothered a smile. My brilliant queen was cheating. I kissed the top of her head and bid the Elders good night. Back in our rooms, I pulled her into my arms.

"You are too competitive. You know that?"

"Why do you say that?" she asked slyly.

I kissed her softly, relaxing into her mouth, inhaling her scent. "You know, eventually, they are going to figure out you used magic to win."

She smirked. "And when they do, they'll respect me even more."

True. I was falling even more in love with her, but I wouldn't give voice to my feelings until I knew Erik had found a way out of the bounty. I couldn't let her doubt those words. If I told her I loved her and then was forced to betray her, she'd never forgive me. She would never forgive me if I betrayed her at all, declaration of love or not.

The compulsion was a constant pressure on my mind, only slightly alleviated by constantly carrying the cuffs in my pocket. I focused on the present, holding her in my arms, the sheets tangled around us. I tried to enjoy the moment without worrying about the future clouding it. She was tracing patterns on my chest again. She often did that after we made love and when she was deep in thought. Her lilac eyes were distant, her mind millions of miles away.

"Where are you?" I murmured, pulling her from her musings.

She smiled up at me. "I want to go somewhere before the coronation tomorrow."

That had my alarm ratcheting. I hadn't forgotten how easily she could leave me. A wave of her hand and she could vanish, leaving no trail to follow. I struggled to keep my voice calm and asked, "Where?"

Her eyes were bright but sad. "I want to go to my parents' graves, to finally say goodbye."

I gulped. She'd told me of the horror of discovering her parents in her childhood home and that she had trouble imagining the future without them. For her to move on, to take them into her heart, was huge. She was looking to a future with me, away from the past. Could I let her go alone for such an event and trust her to come back to me?

"I want you to come with me," she added before I could say anything. My breath left me in a silent exhale.

"Are you sure?" I asked, hoping she would insist.

She did. "I want you there. Will you come?"

I nodded. "We can go now."

Her smile touched me, making my chest warm. "Would that be okay?"

"Anything for my queen," I murmured before kissing her. She leaped out of bed before the kiss could become more heated and rushed to the dressing room. She knew me too well. I got carried away with her way too easily.

I pulled on the jeans I'd shucked earlier before joining her in our dressing room to grab a clean shirt and shoes. The cuffs felt like weights in my pocket, making every step a struggle.

Already dressed, Phoebe glowed with excitement as she watched me finish getting ready. She fit her body against mine and, between kisses, deemed me fit to travel. She swirled her hand to open a rift, and a vacant cemetery baking in the Texas heat appeared on the other side. I marveled anew at her magic. She had slammed together two points in space and held them there with nothing more than a fission of air between them. *Gods, her power was humbling.*

I stepped through first, sniffing the air before holding my hand through the rift for her to follow. She took it without hesitation, trusting me completely. It made me sick to think that her trust may be misplaced. I smothered the thought. There was still time for Erik to come through. The wolf had never failed me before.

Hand in hand, Phoebe led me deeper into the empty cemetery. She stopped at two isolated headstones, and I wrapped my arm around her, pulling her into my side. While she was gazing down at her parents' graves, I was scanning our surroundings. The oppressive humidity settled on my shoulders, making my jeans cling to my legs. Yet the hair on the back of my neck was raised, and a shiver felt close to shooting down my spine.

She squeezed me tighter, glaring sadly at the markers. "They would have hated you, you know."

I sputtered. I must have heard her wrong. "Hated me?"

She smiled down at the gravestones. "My father definitely would have hated you for stealing away his little girl. In his eyes, that would have been an unforgivable slight. My mother was more progressive. She would have secretly liked you but would have been openly hostile toward you to support my dad."

"Wow," I muttered. "You could have lied and said they would have loved me."

She smiled up at me, her beautiful eyes flashing with mischief. "But then I wouldn't be me, would I?"

"I suppose not." My mate was unusually forthright.

A circle of people suddenly surrounded us. They closed in like a veil had been dropped from our eyes. The witches must have concealed themselves and their scent to get this close. I grabbed Phoebe, flashing my fangs at them. "You'll be wanting to leave now."

As they circled closer, Phoebe's back met mine. Her palms came up bright with magic, her voice filled with menace. "What the vampire said."

I counted eight of them, all but one covered head to toe in cloaks. My skin crawled when I made eye contact with the one witch whose hood was down. His black hair was gelled back from his face, his eyes a fathomless black. The witches powered up their battle magic. All except the one who assessed me with an evil gleam in his eyes, a shiver of unease shooting through me. The compulsion was back, stronger than ever before.

"Phoebe, run." Even that warning was a struggle for me.

"Not without you," she answered, prepared to fight to remain by my side.

"Run…" I warned, falling to my knees as the compulsion became overpowering. The witch smiled at me. He knew, oh gods, he knew about the bounty. I could feel him in my mind, breaking the last links of my formidable control.

Phoebe whipped around when I collapsed, her hands coming down on my shoulders. "Leave him alone!" she yelled, not knowing that the fight was within.

The compulsion was forcing me, my actions out of my control, and it was too late. She was too close when I lost the battle against it. I was suddenly on my feet and facing her, the cuffs already growing on her wrists. For a second, her eyes held total confusion, as if she couldn't believe what she was seeing. She stared at me, still trusting me to keep her safe, trying to figure out what my plan was.

"Well done, vampire. Consider the bounty fulfilled. You can collect the reward at your earliest convenience. We will take the prisoner from here."

Her wide-eyed gaze searched mine, and when understanding fell on her, she took a stuttering step back. Still not free from the compulsion, I wasn't able to move forward to unbind her. I was forced to watch her, helpless before her enemies.

"Phoebe, no…" I could barely speak, barely move. I used every ounce of power within me to utter those words.

I reached out for her, and my heart almost tore from my chest as her eyes filled with tears. Betrayal was spreading through her gaze like a malignant fog, and I watched something fragile and precious in her break. I knew she would never forgive this.

"You said I could trust you," she spat, staggering back again, moving farther from me and closer to the witches. Every growing inch separating us sent a spear of agony through my body. I was losing her.

"You can…" I began, conscious of our audience, and as I watched, her eyes blazed with hatred. She thrust her hands up, emphasizing the bindings controlling her powers. I winced.

She whirled on the witches, facing away from me. "You can take me, so long as he does not follow," she ordered, refusing to look back.

The compulsion holding me in place released the second she agreed, the bounty fulfilled. I lunged forward to grab her, but one witch's hand flew up to place a shield between us. Everything in me strained to get to her. I pounded against the barrier, feeling it crack beneath my fists. Two more witches threw their hands up, reinforcing it, keeping me from her. She held her head high as tears fell silently down her face, breaking me. No! I couldn't lose her!

"Just let me explain!" I pounded harder on the shield, but she wasn't listening.

"Take me from here, leave him behind. You can have my head so long as he is not there to witness it," she declared, still a queen despite her bindings.

"No!" I roared, even as four witches created a rift. It took four of them to do what Phoebe could do as an afterthought. No wonder they feared her so. I tore at the magic, more savage than ever. She was mine! There were cracks in the shield, but not enough to break. Instead, I was forced to watch, *powerless*.

She shot me one last look before stepping through, and it tore at me. I did this to her. She looked utterly defeated and resigned. The rift closed behind her, the witches disappearing from sight.

She would never forgive this, and how could I blame her? I'd lost her. I fell to my knees in defeat. My worst nightmare had come true before my eyes, and I had no one to blame but myself.

XXXV

THE REALM OF MORTALS.
THE WITCHES CELLS,
SALEM, MASSACHUSETTS.

I take a step back, my heel hitting another body on the ground behind me. I look down at the remnants of another witch, horror seeping in, twined with gut-wrenching realization. I remember the feeling of being torn in two. My volatile, unpredictable power, the part of me I usually keep in brutal check, was unleashed.

I did this. I killed them. Aunt Caroline... The threat was never from outside the Council Chambers but within.

STUPID TEARS SLID DOWN MY FACE AS they led me to the dungeon. The cells held our most deranged enemies, and I was now among their number. None of the other witches spoke as they locked me in, which I was strangely grateful for. I couldn't stop the tears from flowing silently down my cheeks, but I would die before I broke down completely in front of them.

Once I was finally alone, I fell to my knees. I had trusted a man, and he had betrayed me to the Council again! Would I never learn?

Rule No. 1....

When those cuffs had first come down on my wrists, I hadn't understood. It had been so outside the realm of possibility that Lucien would betray me. I just stood there thinking he would never do that to me. He couldn't. I was his mate. I was his. But he'd bound my powers while enemies surrounded us. He sent me to my death. This was so much worse than Malcolm's betrayal. Malcolm was a young girl's fantasy. I was truly in love with Lucien. I guess I didn't learn my lesson after the first betrayal, so Fate sent me a second. *The vengeful bitch.* My stomach clenched with agony, and I wished I could rip my heart from my chest, anything to stop the feeling of it breaking.

"Looks like the vampire and lycan kings are as good as they say," came a familiar, hated voice. Erik was involved, too? Another betrayal I could add to the fucking list.

I dashed away my tears and stood as Alfonso Damian approached. Unofficial head of the Witches Council, he was one of the few who had survived my trial and the one who'd spear-headed my sentence. *Prick.* He was just as slimy as I remembered, his black hair greased back from his forehead, his beady little black eyes making my skin crawl as he looked at me appraisingly.

"What do you want, Damian?" I snapped, hoping he didn't notice the tears drying on my face. I hated appearing weak in front of him.

His smile reminded me of a shark, more predatory than when Lucien smiled with his fangs. I hid my flinch, even thinking his name sent a bolt of fresh pain through me.

"You always were a high and mighty bitch," he snarled. "Good to see you behind bars on your way to your execution, as your kind deserves."

"My kind? Are you not my kind?" I sneered back. I knew I wasn't exactly the Council's favorite, but I was still a witch.

Had something infested the Council to turn them against me? Was that why they dogged me so determinedly? Was there an interloper in their midst turning them against me?

"I am not of your line," he spat.

"Atreus?"

"Atreus! Your lying family has concealed the Regina line for a thousand years."

The Atreus line was dull in that temple, but the Regina line was lit up. Why hide a witch line inside another? None of this made any sense. I pinched the bridge of my nose, my head pounding.

I focused on the other visions I had at Întuneric, the other things I saw in the past. Hadn't Lucien said most immortal species had *regents*? Because if immortals had the chance to argue every issue to death, they would. Could that be why they'd hidden me? Was Regina the *royal* line?

I gave a bitter laugh, dropping my hand. "You've got the wrong girl. I've never even heard of the Regina line."

The Council erased our history, *my* history. They had tried to strike the royal line from memory. They must have killed all who remembered a time before the Council. I was never an Atreus, neither was my father. That dream with Hekate, that was the first witch, the first Regina. That's why Bast looked so familiar. She had protected my line for centuries, since the first.

Alfonso flew at the bars, gripping them in his fists, his eyes wide. True madness lingered there, far beyond what even Cassie's eyes held. I took a step back on impulse, but he didn't seem to notice. "Foolish girl! You think you can lie to me? I was there when we killed the last Regina! I felt her blood on my hands, and heard her heart stop!"

That must have been the woman I saw in the cathedral, the one who gave away her baby. She was the last witch queen and my ancestor. I was a witch queen on top of a vampire queen? I was quite the overachiever.

Well, I wasn't a vampire queen anymore, so I might as well take the witch queen title if it was up for grabs. I refused to give any hint of my thoughts to Damian, keeping my face blank and a bit bored. "Had enough of that queen bullshit. I'm good."

"We knew the last witch queen had a child she hid in the Atreus line. We just weren't sure until you were born."

I tuned out his rambling, his spittle hitting my cheek as he told me of the glorious battle that took place. The things I saw at Întuneric were all leading me to this. My parents hid me because Cassie warned them. They did it to save me, to bring me here, to this moment. These dominos had been falling for thousands of years.

"Did you kill my parents?" I snapped, interrupting his tirade.

Another evil smile answered my question. My hands fisted, rage making my body vibrate. "You were supposed to be home. We needed to find an excuse to execute you."

They made an example of me in front of the entire Council. Fury like I'd never known coursed through me, everything piling on top of me at once. I was drowning under the fury of my parents' murder, my trial and execution, my betrayal by Malcolm, by Lucien, by everyone. My skin burned, the cuffs binding my magic warping, and my vision was awash in red.

Alfonso was still crowing about his success and how he'd plotted to destroy me since birth, unknowingly signing his own death certificate. He had taken my parents from me. I remembered my mother's lullabies, my father throwing me into the air in delight. It was all stolen from me by the witch in front of me, the very dead witch.

I concealed my arms behind my back and let the anger free, melting the metal binding my powers. I would never be bound again. No man would ever take what was mine again, not Lucien, not the Council, *no one*. It was time to be the monster they all feared. If they thought me a threat before, they hadn't seen anything yet.

Once my magic coursed through me unimpeded, I shot a bolt of pure power at him. The cell door blew off its hinges, landing on top of Alfonso. He didn't even have a chance to brace himself, blindsided, just like me.

I strode out through the smoke, stepping on top of the door, pressing the heavy steel into his bleeding chest. He was still alive, but barely. Another powered-up kill shot glowed in my palm. I held it over his face, his skin blistering and melting from the heat.

"Who else was a part of this? Which of you conspired to kill my parents?" They were all dead, every single witch who took my mother's soft embrace, my father's furrowed brow. They were all going to die. This was going to make my trial look like a warmup.

He said nothing. Instead, his lips pulled back from his bloodied teeth, and he hissed at me, "You will never be queen. We will not bow again."

"I don't give a flying fuck if you bow." I launched the kill shot, leaving a smoldering crater right next to his head. He whimpered in fear when I powered up another immediately.

"This will not bring them back," he groaned, "they are gone. Forever."

"Yet, I remain. Give me their names."

His eyes flickered, and he leaned closer to me, his words a whisper almost lost in the cold, damp dungeon. With his last stuttering breath on the last name, I pressed harder on the door, making him scream. A part of me wanted to drag this out, to listen to his cries for mercy for the next millennia, but that would make me just like him.

"I want you to know that I would have never done this, never become queen, had you not killed my parents. I should thank you. You handed me my destiny. Now begins the age of the witch queen."

Witch Queen, Bitch Queen. All hail!

I launched my kill shot, and his body froze, slowly turning to dust. The door clanged as it hit the ground. *One down.* There had been eight Council Members who bound me. *Seven to go.*

I cracked my neck and glared at the entrance to the Council chambers, where I knew they were deciding my fate. No one decided my fate but me. My smile was wicked as I ascended the stairs. They had taken my family from me and stolen ten years of my life. There would be no escape.

The Council was in full swing, arguing over each other, no one able to get in a word as they debated my sentence. Several were against executing me, defending my actions on the day of my trial. They could live. Others were adamant that my death was necessary, or all witches would think they could defy the Council. There was absolute truth in that. The Council was a farce and had no genuine power.

Slowly, one by one, they noticed me standing on the floor and fell silent. I put my hands up, gesturing for them to continue their arguing. "No, no, don't let me interrupt. You were talking about how I'm evil incarnate and deserve nothing but death, blah blah blah."

The Council chamber was enormous, reminding me of the colosseum. Each council member had an allotted seat surrounding the center where they tried and executed witches for frivolous offenses. They must have rebuilt it after I blew it up.

I strutted to the middle of the chamber, smiling menacingly as each witch powered up their own magic. I held up a single finger, twirling it around, my arm lifted high. What did I have left to lose? Let's find out what exactly a witch queen could do. I was about to unleash all that power that once terrified me.

"I will give you all one chance to come clean. One chance to confess the sins against me by this Council."

There was a moment of silence before the first launch of power came hurtling toward me. On instinct, I threw my hand up. The bolt burned my hand slightly as I caught the magic for a moment before deflecting it. It landed on the ground a couple of feet from me and exploded. I pulled my magic into my hands, launching it back at the witch. I stopped myself from returning the lethal bolt. Instead, I pinned the witch to her seat and locked her power. I would not be like them. Damian was deserved, but I would not add to my tally of witch deaths.

I expected to feel some drag or energy drain at the spell, but I just felt invigorated. That was odd. With the kill strike to Alfonso in the dungeon and then a power bind, I would normally be on the ground, passed out. Yet, there was no flag in my power.

My rage burned through me, making my voice echo through the cavernous room. All the remaining witches' eyes locked on me. "Anybody? No? Nobody here wants to confess to the cold-blooded murder of my parents? Executed to prevent me from claiming a title I had absolutely no interest in?"

The next bolt of power hit me in the shoulder, making me spin in a tight circle. I stopped myself from falling, crouching to steady myself. My long hair fell forward to cover my face, allowing me to hide an unsteady breath before I flipped it back. I shot a lethal glare at the source of the attack.

Sankt Hans, patriarch of the Hans line, his name whispered to me by Alfonso.

One of the eight witches who planned my demise and killed my parents. I powered up a lethal bolt into my hand but stopped myself a second before I launched it. I would become no better than them. That was not the path my parents or my goddess would have me take.

My brow furrowed with concentration as I dodged the next spell and launched another power-binding spell at the Hans line. The other witches finally seemed to break free of whatever daze held them suspended, some wisely heading for the exits. I watched as the fleeing witches immediately flooded back into the chamber. The sound of growls echoed through the room as werewolves prowled forward, cutting off the exits. I easily recognized Erik and his wolves, though the hurt from his betrayal only made my anger burn brighter. I thought I'd found a new family, a new life, a new place to belong, but it was all a lie.

The remaining witches powered up, throwing multiple spells at me at once. I darted between the first couple, but the third hit me in the side, making me spiral midair. I landed hard on the ground, and my hands flew up, projecting my shield. Several bolts of energy hit it hard, and for a moment, exhaustion overtook me. Then an infusion of strength, *familiar* strength, flooded my body. Fuck, I was drawing on Lucien.

I gritted my teeth and threw both my hands out. My shield exploded, sending shards flying through the room, shorting out several spells. The wave of energy from within me shouldn't have been that strong, but Lucien was that strong.

"As of today, I'm destroying this Council and reclaiming my birthright as witch queen." There were several gasps of shock and outrage from around the room, some obviously not understanding what I was. They'd erased everything of my life, my line, trying to get rid of me. They wouldn't get a chance to do so again.

A scream of rage alerted me to the next attack. A witch launched over the railing, intending to take me down. With a step to the side at the last second, I tripped her before she could touch me. Who knew those lessons with Lucien would come in handy? Pain flashed at the memories, and I pushed them away. I wouldn't think of him.

"It was Alfonso's idea! We just followed his orders!" the Ellis witch screamed, afraid of my demonstration of power. They'd never seen anything like this before. I'd never seen anything like it before. I spun on my heel, launching another binding spell, trapping and gagging the witch.

They were right to fear me. I was their reckoning. No other young witch would cower when summoned before them. No longer would they use these chambers to conceal their crimes. This was justice for every witch they'd executed because they thought them a threat.

Like my mother, my father, and me.

"How many of you venerated Council members agreed to kill my parents? How many of you agreed to execute me for a crime I was innocent of?"

Not that I needed the names, but I wanted to make sure those innocent in this festering cancer of hatred and jealousy understood why my vengeance would be so absolute.

Several witches watched me warily, their eyes wide with fear at my awesome power and horror at what I was revealing. Many likely didn't know what the Council had done for years to maintain their power.

The lies ended today.

XXXVI

THE REALM OF MORTALS. OUTSIDE AUSTIN, TEXAS.

I **TUNNELED MY FINGERS THROUGH MY HAIR,** struggling through my thoughts. If I didn't get to her soon, they'd execute her. How did I get to her in time? I recalled the look of agony on her face when she realized what I'd done. I couldn't think about that. There would be time to make her understand once she was safe, but first, I needed to get to her. I tried to block out the memory of her words, how final they'd sounded. She thought I'd betrayed her. *Another vampire to add to the list.*

I had to stay focused if I was going to help Phoebe. The Witches Council chambers were in Salem. I'd never get there in time. *She was never going to forgive me.* If only I could rift like Phoebe, collapsing space to be by her side when she needed me.

I paced back and forth in front of the two gravestones, guilt ripping me apart. I did the very thing she feared. If I could just get to her, I could make it right.

"Well, you've made a real mess this time," a familiar voice said from behind me.

Cassandra's words had me lunging forward, grabbing the Oracle by her shoulders. I knew my fingers were likely leaving bruises, but I was unable to temper my strength.

"Why didn't you tell me not to take the bounty? You could have prevented all of this! They are planning to kill her!"

Cassandra didn't seem to fear me, though I wasn't sure what I would do in this state. To my shock, she head-butted me, forcing me to drop my hands while she swept her leg out. I fell hard, landing on my back in the grass. She stared down at me, dusting off her hands. Where had she learned that? The Oracle who left the halls of Întuneric had never held a weapon. She had changed so much since she left me behind.

"You were meant to take that bounty. You were meant to be moping in a graveyard in Texas while they imprisoned your mate in Salem, and she waited for execution."

"Why?" I asked, leaping to my feet. "Why was I meant to betray her?"

A spark of foolish hope flared within me. Had there been some outside force making me betray Phoebe? Maybe I'd had no choice in the matter. I discarded the idea as easily as it formed. There was no one here to blame but me. I should have told her about the bounty, about the compulsion to complete it. The words would now seem false and desperate.

"Have you ever heard of a witch's true mate?"

"Witches don't have predestined mates." It's why I had such trouble with Phoebe in the beginning.

"They've fallen to the status of myths. A witch's true mate shares more than just eternity with them. Their mating is an equal exchange. In a true mating, they can even share each other's *power*."

"But I'm not a witch. I have no magic to give her." If I had any, I would have forfeited it to her immediately, praying it kept her safe. She wouldn't forgive this. Her face when they took her, those tears falling silently down her face, had shredded me.

"No shit. But what do you have that she doesn't?"

I had speed, strength, and age. "Are you saying Phoebe is as strong as a vampire now? As strong as me?" Why wouldn't she just tell me how to get to Phoebe? How to fix this? I couldn't get the sight of her tears out of my mind.

"Not in the way you're thinking. A witch's powers draw from their very essence, draining them of energy when they do multiple powerful spells, but you have that in abundance. What's better for an extremely powerful witch than a ten-thousand-year-old vampire to draw energy from?"

"How does that help me now? I still need to get to her!" I was happy to let Phoebe protect herself, but I needed to be at her side when she fought them. My madness was returning with a vengeance at the separation.

"Men! So thick! Needing everything spelled out for them." Her tone became condescending. "What does she have that you don't?"

The ability to rift. Could I access that power through our bond? I kissed Cassandra's forehead. "Thank you for this, Cassie. You know how much I love you."

"I know." She turned away, saying over her shoulder as she strutted back through the cemetery. "I sent some reinforcements ahead for you, just in case."

As she disappeared among the headstones, I sat on the ground, trying to figure out how to call up Phoebe's power. I thought back to the times she'd used magic around me. What had she done? I concentrated and made a circular motion with my hand like she had when she opened that rift in New Orleans. Nothing happened, and already my frustration was mounting. I should be able to access her powers, but I couldn't. What if Cassie was wrong? What if I couldn't access her powers? What if they had found a way to cut her off from me? What if she was already dead?

No, no, no, I was not going there. When a vampire lost a mate, they went mad, unable to differentiate between friend and foe. Who would execute me if that happened? Who became king?

These thoughts were useless, and I had to stop and focus on my task. I closed my eyes, pulling up the image of Phoebe's face. I remembered the first time I saw her and the first time we kissed. The memory of when I claimed her nearly broke me. I held tight to how I felt at the sound of her laugh and how her eyes sparkled when her competitive streak kicked in. I inhaled deeply, imagining her scent, immersing myself in it. How she consumed me, frustrated, and fascinated me.

My eyes flashed open as a rift appeared, but it was the smallest one I'd seen. I bolted to my feet, reaching for it, but it was too small even to put my hand through. Phoebe was the key, as she was to most things concerning me. I closed my eyes again, thinking of how she hustled the vampire elders with magic at chess. The way she tricked me into obsessing about a show with a *vampire slayer*. My skin tightened at the memory of how she trailed her fingers on my chest after we made love. She made the future something to look forward to instead of something to dread. Barely opening my eyes, I saw the rift was larger but still not big enough for me to fit.

I remembered how I felt when I woke up and realized she had stayed after saving my life, how she submitted to me in bed but fought for her way everywhere else. How I loved her, how I couldn't imagine life without her. I would do anything to be at her side now. The sounds of voices raised in anger rang around me. The rift was large enough, and I saw Phoebe alone, facing the witches on the other side.

I threw myself through. My fangs bared at the Council members who threatened her. I stood by her side, where I belonged.

XXXVII

THE REALM OF MORTALS.
THE WITCHES COUNCIL,
SALEM, MASSACHUSETTS.

Silas Cren reaches over to another council member, shaking them, hoping to rouse them.

Tick-tock, Phoebe, tick-tock. This is my chance to run. The choice I should have made instead of trusting the Council to a fair verdict.

I RECALLED MY FATHER'S BOOMING laugh and my mother's soft singing. If they hadn't plotted to destroy me, would I still be in my childhood home in Texas, surrounded by my family? I would have never met Lucien and been betrayed by him.

I felt the fear radiating from them. They were right to be afraid of me. If they hadn't been so stubborn in their prejudices, maybe other witches would have bonded with an immortal battery.

"Who else?" I bit out, my teeth grinding with rage.

A torrent of magic that wasn't mine lit the room, and my palms glowed brighter as I prepared to fight this new threat. To my horror and my foolish heart's delight, Lucien stepped through the open rift, closing it behind him. Fuck, I'd gotten his strength, and he'd gotten some of my magic.

Before I could even comprehend that unprecedented shift, the door leading out to the street burst open. Elijah and several of the Vampire Elders burst in to join the lycans in preventing the witches from escaping.

"Who else was a part of the plot to kill my parents?" I yelled, trying to organize my chaotic thoughts. "This is your last chance to confess and survive, or I'll have the vampire force it out of you."

Lucien bared his fangs for effect, and several witches cowered. None stepped forward, yet two witches simultaneously shot spells at me, hoping to catch me unawares. My back met Lucien's instinctually, my shield coming back up. The two bolts of magic pinged off and hit the ceiling, raining dust down on us.

I snarled to Lucien under my breath, "This means nothing."

There was a pause, heavy with all the words I sensed brewing in him. "We can talk when we're not actively fighting for our lives."

The two witches who'd launched their spells gaped at us, even as two Vampire Elders suddenly appeared behind them, sinking their teeth into their vulnerable necks.

"Stop!" Lucien yelled, surprising me. "Don't kill them. Their fates are for your queen to decide."

His words raised my hackles again, recalling my rage. I pushed off of his back and let the shield drop. My magic pulsed from me as I fired off spells at the witches. I snarled at Lucien, "I am not your queen."

I glared at the remaining witches. There had been eight who bound me, and I suspected more of those present had betrayed my parents. "Shall we reveal why this Council condemned me to death? Why they killed my parents because they couldn't get to me?" I asked.

Another bolt of power came hurtling at me. My reflexes were too slow, but luckily Lucien was faster. He grabbed me, moving me out of the way, as a werewolf pinned the witch who'd launched the spell. I noticed that the canine merely growled, keeping the woman under his heavy paws, discouraging a repeated attempt.

I barely kept my voice from shaking as I faced the remains of the witches assembled. "Everything told by this ruling body has been a lie! They were all attempts to cover up the avarice and power-hungry cancer growing in our midst!"

"That's a lie!" another witch screamed and bolted for an exit. Elijah tackled her to the ground before she could get anywhere.

There was an eruption of murmurs at the announcement. I continued, my palms still glowing, ready for any more attacks. "When Hekate touched the first of us, she gave her a mission. She was to bring order to the chaos, to rule the others. She was to be queen."

"Impossible!" another Council Member shouted, but instead of launching a spell or attempting to run, he merely looked astonished.

"Very possible. We have a royal line, just like almost all other immortal species." I refused to glance at Lucien. "The memories of it erased, covered up, and extinguished by members of this very Council."

"You never deserved it! You still don't!" another witch screamed, and instead of a spell, threw a dagger. It flew with alarming speed, likely boosted by magic. Lucien again came to my aid, jerking me behind him and taking the dagger to his shoulder with a hiss.

Lucien's hands lingered on me. I deliberately shrugged them off, pretending not to see the flash of hurt in his eyes. In my head, I mentally crossed off the names Alfonso had moaned with his dying breath. With a deliberately evil grin, I swirled my hands. Multiple rifts formed simultaneously, dropping the witches who dared to strike at me into the cells below.

More murmurs erupted, and another witch called out, "What about the rest of us?"

"I'm getting to that. Is there anyone else who is going to have a problem with me? Speak now or forever hold your peace!" The witches remained so silent that you could have heard a pin drop. "Well then, I install myself as Queen of Witches and convert this Council to my advisors."

"This is the part where you bow," Lucien added. To my surprise, several of them did, likely out of fear for the vampire by my side.

"Meeting adjourned," I added for flair. The remaining vampires and lycans retreated from their posts, though they watched the remaining witches fleeing from the scene warily. To my surprise, several of the fleeing witches' faces revealed their relief at the proceedings. If it was relief that they'd survived or that the Council was no more, remained to be seen.

Assured that I was safe, the vampires and werewolves departed as well. Soon I was alone in the cavernous chambers with Lucien. I felt him move toward me and steeled myself for what I had to do.

"Phoebe—" he began.

I cut him off, unable to hear his voice. It reminded me too much of how I loved him, and that love tried to force me to forget how he'd betrayed me. He'd made me forget the rules that would have protected me from this. *From him.*

"You can go with your vampires all the way back to Întuneric, or to hell, whichever is closer." I made sure not to look at him. I didn't want to face the way my traitorous heart was begging me to listen to him.

What if he had a reason? My heart pleaded, but there was no justification for what he had done.

"Phoebe, you don't understand—"

Again, I was tempted to listen to him but knew I couldn't. "I understand just fine. You were one of the bounty hunters out for my life, and you turned me over to them."

Why did I forget rule number one?

Lucien grabbed me, forcing me to face him. My eyes drifted over his shoulder, refusing to make eye contact. "Look at me! Please, Phoebe, look at me!" he pleaded.

I wanted to scream that I couldn't. I kept my gaze away from him, wrenching out of his grip. His hands dropped to his sides, and I felt the loss of his touch as if it was a blow. "It's over, Lucien. It was over the second you took that bounty."

Stupid tears were welling in my eyes. I opened a rift to my old apartment and disappeared through it before he could see me cry.

New Rule No. 6: Never let a man see he made you cry.

He refused to remain behind, forcing the rift to remain open, using his new power to follow me through. I tried to push the tears back, but they filled my eyes. I gave him my back and said as calmly as I could, "You are not welcome here, vampire."

"I go where you go," he whispered.

"No matter what I have to say about it?"

"You're my mate. My place is with you."

That had me whirling around in anger. "That makes it so much worse! Don't you see? *You* betrayed your mate! *You* signed your precious mate's death warrant!" The tears began falling, and it only escalated my rage. "You told me to trust you! That you would keep me safe! Every time you begged me to tell you everything, you kept this from me! All along, I was in danger. From you!"

I took a deep breath and muttered, "Just leave me alone."

It was a pain like nothing I'd ever felt before. Still, I wanted to listen to him, to understand why. Yet, with betrayal, there was no explanation, no reason.

"Phoebe—" I refused to buckle at his tortured expression.

"For once, will you listen to me and leave me alone!" Tears streamed down my face. He reached out toward me but stopped midway, pain and regret so clear on his face. "You kidnapped me from here. You gave me no choice but to stay with you, no choice but

362

to accept you. For once, you can do as I ask and leave me alone!"

Just leave! Before I beg you to stay!

Before I beg for an explanation!

Before I forgive you!

He bowed his head, breaking eye contact, and retreated through the still open rift. He sent me a last agonized glance before it closed.

XXXVIII

THE REALM OF MORTALS.
ÎNTUNERIC CASTEL, ROMANIA.

PHOEBE WOULDN'T LISTEN TO ME, wouldn't see *me*, and the look she gave me as the rift closed kept me from pushing her. I hadn't given her a choice, not really. I could give her one now.

For once, will you listen to me and leave me alone!

Her words followed me back to Întuneric, haunting my days and nights. Three days of misery to understand what a complete failure I was and how I irreparably ruined things with my mate.

Her look of betrayal, her eyes bright with unshed tears. I lunged from the remnants of my throne, plowing my fist into one wall, the bite of pain doing nothing to temper my self-hatred. Since my return, I'd spent the restless energy organizing my businesses and sending my COOs into a tizzy of work. But nothing but her had occupied my thoughts.

You betrayed your mate!

I hit the wall again as her voice echoed around me.

You signed your precious mate's death warrant!

I put another fist through the wall, surprised it still stood with the amount I'd attacked it in the last three days.

The Elders had returned to Întuneric, shocked at the state I was in. My eyes hadn't stopped glowing red with madness for three days, my lips constantly bleeding from nicking them on my fangs. I didn't bother wiping them, just letting the blood dry on my face and throat. My clothes were still in tatters from the fight in Salem, but what did any of it matter? She wouldn't see me. She had left me.

They all remained in the castle, refusing to leave me alone, wary of what their king might do in this condition. When I heard my uncle order someone to find Phoebe and bring her to Întuneric no matter the cost, I nearly took his throat. I'd commanded that no one was to go near her, and no one was to bring her here. I'd loved her and lost her, just like the others.

I pummelled the wall again.

It was no use. The enemy I really wanted to strike at was me. I'd had her trust and betrayed both it and her. My claws dug into the stone, frantic for a mooring in this detached state. I was floating unfettered through the ether without Phoebe to ground me, despondent and lifeless. I had become the one thing I had once feared. The future was nothing more than a yawning abyss of more loneliness.

My heart ached for her. This was more than the typical madness that accompanied being away from one's mate. It was the realization that I had no one to blame but myself. Unlike my mother and Cassandra, there was no outside force fighting against me. This time I could have done something different to make her stay, but I hadn't.

Yes, the compulsion of the bounty had forced me, but I could have told her, warned her, instead of putting all my hopes on Erik's shoulders. I'd been too afraid to tell her, too frightened that she would leave and I would never see her again. I snorted at my stupidity and the self-fulfilling prophecy of it.

It had been fear that kept me from telling her, not the hope that Erik could find a solution. I'd been kidding myself with that. Deep down, I knew there was no way out. It was my own selfish desire to keep things *safe* between us.

"Lucien?" came a hesitant and familiar voice.

I whirled on the other vampire, and Elijah jumped back. I growled at him, barely able to form words. "What do you want, Elijah?"

"What's happened?" he asked.

You told me to trust you! Her words, her voice, wouldn't give me any peace.

"She's gone." I didn't need to elaborate on who I spoke of. There was only one thing that mattered.

"What? Why?" he asked, baffled.

You said you'd keep me safe! I hadn't, lying to her from the first word to the last, but I didn't know I should be protecting her from myself.

"I hurt her."

"You couldn't." Elijah didn't understand. He saw how affected I was by Phoebe, how I constantly searched for and obsessed over her, but the other man couldn't understand what had happened.

"I was in Salem. You fought by her side to secure the witches. We all expected you two to merge your kingdoms. Rumors have already started. They are calling her Phoebe Silvano, the Twice Crowned."

"Don't say her name!" It tore at me to hear about her.

All along, I was in danger from you!

Stubbornness glinted in Elijah's eyes, and he braced himself for a blow before saying, "No. You need to hear this. Phoebe is still in danger." I grabbed him and threw him against the wall. "She doesn't know who to trust in her new court!" he managed to choke out before my grip cut off his ability to speak.

My fingers tightened on his throat. I couldn't hear anymore. I loved her, and she wouldn't see me, wouldn't listen to me. *For once, will you listen to me and leave me alone!* I roared my anguish as the hated words echoed in my mind.

My Uncle Ambrogio appeared, throwing me off Elijah, who coughed as air returned to his lungs. "You need to help her. You'll sit here in your cold castle while your mate struggles, surrounded by enemies?" Elijah croaked, having to force the words past his bruised throat.

Did the much younger vampire sound *disappointed*? Did he not realize how close to madness I was? How close to death he was? With barely a thought, I could separate his head from his shoulders. Ambrogio stepped between us as I coiled to lunge for Elijah again.

"The boy is right."

Elijah straightened at the hated term but nodded at the Elder's support. I stumbled back from the pair, not able to face their condemnation on top of my own. "You think I'm choosing to stay here?"

My laughter sounded mad even to my own ears.

"Aren't you?" Ambrogio asked.

More insane laughter burst from me, the sound wholly without mirth. "She doesn't want me!" I roared, and it broke me even more to say it out loud. "She doesn't want me," I repeated, my voice breaking slightly.

Elijah's eyes softened with understanding, but my uncle's stance had not changed. The older immortal crossed his arms over his wide chest, frowning at me.

"You are a fool, Nephew." The first time he ever called me such, and it was a reprimand.

"What do you know of it, *Uncle?*" I sneered.

"I'm happy that my brother is sleeping, so he does not have to witness the mess his only son has made."

That had me lunging at him, but the Elder merely side-stepped. As the first-born vampire, I was stronger. Not even the older turned immortal could match me, but I was too infuriated and agonized to approach him with anything resembling skill.

"You think your father wouldn't give anything to be with your mother right now? Do you think she wouldn't give anything to be with him?"

I made another half-hearted lunge, but my interest in hearing the story of my parents made the effort less than satisfying. "There are worse things in this life than being told to leave by a mate. It is being kept from someone, someone you'd give anything to see again." His voice was morose, heavy with regret. How much did my uncle miss my father? Ambrogio once mentioned they were thick as thieves. "If you think that just because she said she doesn't want you means you have to listen to her, you are a fool."

"What are you telling me to do, Uncle? Force her back here?" I couldn't, not again.

My uncle rolled his eyes, exasperated. "A blind man could see how much you two love each other. She loves you, Lucien. Gods know why." Hearing that the feelings tearing at my chest might not be as one-sided as I believed eased my agony a bit.

"Love like that doesn't go away. I watched your mother destroyed when Zeus sentenced Endymion to sleep forever. For years she watched you grow, a shell of herself. You have the chance to be with your queen, the woman you love, and you're going to let some little thing like her refusal to see you get in the way?"

My mouth dropped open, surprised at the impassioned speech. "My mother... she loved him?" She had never told me that, only that she'd picked a vampire to create a royal line.

"She did. You really think Selene would have a kid with just anyone?" He made a good point. My mother was fierce and a goddess. "She used to say that she felt no warmth until she met him. He was the sun when she'd only known the moon. She never told you this?" Ambrogio asked, astounded.

I shook my head in answer, trying to rationalize this new information. "How does this help me with *her*?"

Ambrogio slapped the back of my head. "Fool! If your parents could make their limited time together work, then there is nothing, short of death, that you and your queen cannot conquer."

He was right. She never heard my side of the story. I could do so now. I could lay all my cards on the table and pray she took me back.

"Thank you, Uncle."

I turned away from Elijah and my uncle, striding toward my room. I couldn't call on the ability to rift with my mind so scattered, so I needed to arrange a flight. She would listen to me.

She had to.

XII

*THE REALM OF MORTALS.
THE WITCH CELLS,
SALEM, MASSACHUSETTS.*

I spin on my heel, yanking my hood up as my tears fall and I limp to the exit.

I have to run and never look back.

SINCE I'D CONQUERED THE COUNCIL, I often visited the prisoners, rooting out the remaining cancer. It was all too exhausting. So many witches feared my power, jumping to obey my every command. They were worried if they spoke against me, they would end up in the cells. The prisoners didn't pretend. Their open animosity toward me had become an almost refreshing change of pace. Even now, as I descended the steps into the cells and heard the hisses, I felt less out of my element.

"If it isn't the witch bitch come to admire her handy work," Sebastian Ellis sneered, calling out from his cell. Finally, something familiar, give me insults and sneers over fawning masses any day.

"Yes, my handy work." Then I tapped my chin as if in thought. "But wait, is this not your handy work? Was it not this group that plotted and schemed to kill my line? Were you not trying to extinguish all memory of the rightful queen?" I narrowed my eyes at the witches trapped in their cells and asked, "How many did you kill to erase all memory of us? It wasn't enough to just kill *her*. You had to kill all *memory* of her. How many witches burned in your pursuit of power?"

Silva Cren clutched the bars, madness glimmering in her eyes. "Hundreds! And we'd do it all again!"

I wanted to feel fury at the statement but couldn't. I was past any glimmer of anger. I was so filled with pain. There was no room for more. I felt frozen and afraid to thaw. To do so meant understanding that every day was one more day without waking up in Lucien's arms. I would truly have to face that he betrayed me. My heart begged me to forgive him with every beat, and I would have to endure the fresh stab of pain when I realized I couldn't.

Curious as to what my prisoners would think of my next proposal, I studied each of their faces and said, "I offer you a choice. I can strip you of all power and allow you to live out your days with no magic, or you may remain my prisoners until I feel you have adequately atoned for your sins. However long that may be."

No one jumped at my offer, and I wasn't surprised. When a witch was cut from their magic, it felt like a missing limb, something precious lost and always out of reach. I should know. It was something I had recently endured. I turned on my heel to exit but paused when one of them called out to me.

Silas Koyle said, "When do you plan on releasing us?"

"When I feel you have atoned and will never strike against me or mine," I responded, though I doubted I could tell when that would be. One year? Fifty? One hundred? I wondered if it would take me that long to get over Lucien.

How long would it take to not feel this emptiness and pain? Would it never cease?

I left the prison and climbed the many stairs to the room I'd converted into my new royal bed chambers. The tears refused to stop, and I wasn't sure when they had started. Sometimes it felt like I had cried forever. They dripped from my chin as I glared at the massive empty bed, knowing I would likely never see him again, never touch him, never kiss him. I wished the thought didn't hurt, but it did.

Memories of him were haunting me. I saw him everywhere. In the newly established library, where wayward spell books arrived, and all witches could make use of any tome. I saw him in a chair in the corner, flipping through a book as he read to me. In my dreams, I saw him waiting on the bed in my new bedroom, hands tucked behind his head as he reclined, hunger burning in his eyes. I swiped at the tears, trying to stop them, and they finally obeyed as I wearily sat in front of my new vanity.

Lucien often said that most immortal species had a royal line because they needed someone to make decisions. That was becoming more apparent the longer I ruled over the witches. I glared at myself in the mirror. I had to stop thinking about him. He betrayed me. He took everything I was and then handed me over. My eyes remained dry as I stared at my reflection.

I was four days into the life sentence that awaited me, four days of ruling alone, and I was trying to keep busy. The first thing I'd done was to demand all information relating to the Regina line be gathered and presented to me. There had been a single scroll. That was it. It was written with annoyingly familiar handwriting.

> *When the sun sets on the last Witch Queen,*
> *A new moon will arise from the same line,*
> *Stronger and harder than any before her.*
> *She will return the Witches to prosperity and peace.*
> *With her King at her side.*

There would be no king for me. Cassie messed up that part. I would be alone as I set the witches to rights. When I'd finally stopped crying at that, I'd issued my second order. To reform the study of witchcraft so no topics or magics would be off-limits no matter the line.

There was resistance, but there would be benefits of a well-rounded magical education. Why should every witch not know about healing spells or battle magic? Grimoires needed to be shared and new spells created, so knowledge couldn't be lost to time. Still, I felt lost, like a ship without an anchor, set adrift with no course.

I wandered away from the mirror, lying down on the massive bed. Bast, who had somehow appeared in Salem, cuddled next to me, sensing my disquiet. Now that I knew the cat was older than Lucien, a lot of the unexplainable things she did made sense. So many witches had black cat familiars. I never considered that there was one in each of my visions because the castle was trying to tell me it was the same one. Bast was the Regina familiar.

Alone with my silent familiar, I could give voice to my thoughts. "I miss him, Bast. I know I shouldn't, but I do."

The cat moved closer to me as if she could ward away the hurt that seemed to fester. I should be rooting out any remaining enemies in my court, not pining after him. Yet, I couldn't stop. I was completely in love with him, and he betrayed me. *What if he had reason to?* I snarled at that thought. What possible reason could he have?

Still glaring at the canopy of my bed, I thought of our bed in Întuneric—*his bed, not ours.* Another lance of pain shot through my heart. We would never again spend our nights making love. I would never again wake with his arms wrapped around me. When my eyes watered, I pounded my fist against the mattress, making Bast start in surprise. I had spent an ocean of tears on that man. I would not shed a drop more! The tears still welled, but this time they didn't fall. I took deep, stuttering breaths, and thankfully, they slowly dissipated. I fell asleep, emotionally exhausted, knowing that nightmares would likely plague my sleep.

XL

THE REALM OF MORTALS.
THE WITCH QUEEN'S CHAMBERS,
SALEM, MASSACHUSETTS.

I DIDN'T BOTHER KNOCKING BEFORE striding into Phoebe's new bedroom in Salem, prepared to fight to force her to listen. I wasn't expecting her to be asleep. Bast meowed at my entrance, jumping off the bed to rub against my legs. At least someone seemed happy to see me.

I scratched the feline's head, looking around the room. There were spells carved into the walls, fresh ones. There could only be one reason she was carving spells into the walls of her new home. Phoebe didn't feel safe here and needed protection.

Curiously, she hadn't banned me. Or maybe she just hadn't gotten around to adding that spell yet. She wouldn't get the chance.

It was tempting to tuck her beneath the covers, as I had done so many times, but I resisted. It was bad enough I'd showed up uninvited. I didn't need to add moving her around in her sleep when she was most vulnerable to my list of sins.

I pulled an armchair close to her side, resting my elbows on my knees. My gaze was locked on her as I went over what I was going to say. I'd agonized over it for the last twenty-four hours, but I could not come up with anything other than *I love you. I'm sorry. Please take me back.*

I hoped it was enough, prayed it was, but the insidious voice of my insecurities still whispered.

You loved your mother and Cassandra. They still left, and Phoebe will too.

Phoebe mumbled in her sleep, tears silently falling from behind her lids. She was having a nightmare. Unable to resist her haunting dreams, I sat on the covers next to her. I pulled her into my arms, murmuring to her in Romanian, as I had so many times before. I lay next to her and felt the first sense of calm since she'd left me. She still needed me, and I could be there for her. She relaxed into me, cuddling closer as she always did.

"Shh, I've got you. I'm not going anywhere." Not this time.

Her body stiffened as she began to wake, and I instantly mourned the loss of her pressed against me. "Lucien?" she asked groggily.

Unable to resist, I kissed her, clutching her to me. She became fully aware in the middle of the kiss and began shoving against my chest. I released her but remained sitting on the bed, wary of her anger growing like a tangible force in the room.

"What the hell are you doing here? How did you get in?" she spat out as she stood. She turned her back to wipe the tears from her face, hoping to hide that she'd been crying. How many days had she cried herself to sleep? The thought felt like a lance to my chest.

"I got in the same way most people do, through the door." I sent her a small smile, hoping to pull a laugh from her, but I failed.

"You need to go. Now!" She seemed frantic for me to leave, and a treacherous suspicion had rage coursing through me.

"Why? Are you expecting someone?" The jealous thought snuck out before I could call it back. I tried to calm the rage to a more manageable level at the thought of another moving in on my female, but again, I failed.

Her eyes narrowed on me. "Even if I was expecting someone," she started, and I exhaled with relief, "it would be none of your business."

"*You* are my business. Now and always."

She let out a cruel, short laugh. "Just like the bounty on me was your business?"

I winced at that and bolted to a stand. I came around to face her, leaving her no avenue of escape. If she departed from the room without hearing me, I sensed I would never gain her forgiveness. She needed to listen to me.

"I took that bounty before I knew who you were. It's what Erik came to see me about in Tír nAill." Her eyes fired at the mention of the wolf's name. "Will you please listen to me? I—" love you, can't live without you. When I close my eyes, I am haunted by visions of you, so vivid I reach for you, only to come up empty. But I couldn't say any of that. "I want to tell you everything. Will you give me five minutes, please? If you still hate me by the end, I'll leave, and you'll never see me again." It was hard to even utter those words, but I needed to convince her to listen. I'd say whatever it took for her to give me a chance.

"It's over, Lucien. You need to move on." Her eyes darted away when she said that, as if she couldn't take her own advice. I wondered if she had been suffering the same agony I had.

"I can't. Have you slept, Phoebe? I know I haven't," I whispered, knowing that her nightmares were probably back in full force without me sleeping next to her.

I was horrified at the possibility of having created new nightmares for her. I silently promised both myself and her I'd give her new memories, better ones, to block out the old if she'd give me the chance.

Her eyes blazed with anger and pain so poignant I almost fell back a step. "What do you care, Lucien? You gave me up. You handed me over to them, knowing what they would do." Her voice broke slightly at that, and I wasn't able to cover my flinch.

"I came for you," I added, though I knew that did little to remedy the damage done. I could only stand by her in victory, not in the battle. It was something I didn't think I would ever forgive myself for.

"Too little, too late. What if they'd executed me? Have you thought of that? If I hadn't been able to escape the cuffs?" I paled at the idea, my eyes turning an even more violent red, my teeth grinding.

"If they had harmed you, I wouldn't have left a single witch alive. Then I would have found my own end with open arms." My answer stunned her, her lips parting on a slight gasp.

"You would? Why?" The shaky nature of her tone lit the smallest flicker of hope in my chest.

"I couldn't live in a world where you don't exist." Even the thought of it stole my breath. I thought I knew pain, but these last few days without her had been utter torture. The true agony was imagining a world without her. "There is no future for me where you don't live."

"Hard to believe that after what happened. I...I trusted you, Lucien, more than anyone, and that hurts the most. You made me trust you when you knew you would have to betray me." Her voice was raw with grief.

She truly hated me, but there must be a way for me to fix this. I could not have lost her forever.

"That's not true!" I tunneled my hands through my hair, gripping the strands in frustration, trying to explain everything. "You can't truly believe that."

"What else am I supposed to believe?"

"I can try to explain everything. If you'd let me," I begged, past the point of caring how I might appear to her. I wanted her to know the truth. Even if it meant she wouldn't stay.

She nodded hesitantly, taking a seat in the armchair, gesturing me into the other.

XLI

THE REALM OF MORTALS.
THE WITCH QUEEN'S CHAMBERS,
SALEM, MASSACHUSETTS.

*L*UCIEN WAS HERE, AND HE LOOKED TERRIBLE. He'd lost a significant amount of weight. His eyes were a solid red, only flickering to green once since he'd appeared. They were bloodshot, and I knew he hadn't been sleeping. I could barely do so these days, not without crying for hours before.

I hated that I warmed at how awful he looked. Some part of me was happy he hadn't returned to his hedonist ways the second he turned me over as if *we* had never been. When I had awakened to the familiar warmth of his body, I was convinced I was still dreaming. When he'd kissed me, my heart leaped. Then I registered how the dream felt *too* real, realizing he was, in fact, cradling me in his arms.

It had taken everything I had to extricate myself from him. I was so surprised by his sudden appearance that I wasn't able to call forth the mental fortitude to throw him from the room. I didn't know why I'd agreed to listen to him, though some terrible, foolish part of me still yearned for him, still loved him despite everything. It was that part of me that nodded and waited for him to begin.

"When I first met you in Tír nAill, I didn't know who you were. Who you were to me." He glared at his hands in anger before fisting them closed as if he was resisting the need to touch me with all his might. "When Titania interrupted us, she mentioned Erik was there to see me. It was about the bounty."

Just the mention of it had me flinching in remembered pain. He looked tortured by that small reaction. I tried to remain impassive, still determined to send him on his way. "The bounty was vague, only listing the Atreus & Margaux descendent, with no physical description or anything. I thought it was intriguing." He laughed bitterly. "Erik claimed the witches suspected you'd glamoured yourself so many times that any description they could provide would be worthless."

"When I first escaped, I implanted distinct memories in the survivors' heads. They couldn't come to a consensus on what I looked like." The bounty should have been useless. No doubt, the Council hoped by some stroke of dumb luck Lucien and Erik would stumble across me. They'd been right.

"It was that same night that Erik pointed out my desperation to get back downstairs to you was a sign that you were my mate." He laughed again in remembrance, but it was still brittle. "I completely forgot about the bounty, focused only on finding you. It was the furthest thing from my mind."

He hadn't recalled the bounty when we met in New Orleans? I couldn't remember ever telling him my last name. He never knew my line was Atreus—when I still thought it was Atreus.

"When did you recall it?" I snapped, trying not to fall for his explanation, although it was making me forgive him, bit by bit.

Lucien hadn't realized the bounty target and his mate were the same, at least not at first. The brief space between us was killing me, my heart begging me to close the distance, but I brutally shut that thought down. I was attempting to fortify my resolve to show him the door when his explanation was over. I crossed my arms over my chest, preventing myself from reaching out to touch him.

"I didn't. Erik did," he admitted. His eyes laser-focused on me, his face observing every minuscule change in my expression, so I tried to maintain a blank look. "He came to me a couple of days before your coronation and told me he'd figured out the bounty from Tír nAill was you."

"How many days before my coronation?" I gritted out. I needed to know if he'd been aware before he slept with me.

He rubbed the back of his neck. "A couple..." The way he trailed off was damning.

I leaped up, my rage returning, muting other emotions. "You knew when I asked you to claim me, didn't you?"

He stood warily, his hands out in supplication. "I was on my way to tell you that day, but…"

I had seduced him. Could I truly blame him? I thought back to that day, recalling the glazed look of desire that had come over him. I'd never felt more powerful than I had at that moment. It was doubtful I could have resisted him if our roles were reversed. "Why didn't you tell me after?"

"I had hoped Erik would find a way out of it, but it was already too late." He turned his back on me, concealing his face. "I don't know how much you know about mystical bounties, but saying no is not an option.

After that first night together, I woke up hovering over you, the cuffs in my hand."

"What do you mean, you woke up? You don't remember retrieving them?" Had it *compelled him* to complete the bounty? I remembered the way he'd told me to run in Texas. Had he meant run *from him?*

He shook his head. "Not at all. I fled from your side, horrified that you would wake up and see me standing over you." His hand tunneled through his hair. "I knew you wouldn't stay and listen if that happened."

I felt a flash of guilt at that, knowing I likely wouldn't have. The sight of the cuffs was a bit of a trigger. I would have run if I'd seen him standing above me holding them. My survival instincts would have kicked in, and I would have left. He was right.

He had predicted my reaction and hidden the bounty from me because he knew he would lose me. He had told me so many times of his fear that I would disappear. There had been so many mornings he woke in a near panic, afraid I had snuck away during the night.

"I ran into Erik in the hall, and I clung to the hope that he would find a way out of it for us. I refused to let my guard down, refused to sleep until I heard from him."

"You should have told me," I said softly. He whipped around, and I started at the absolute agony on his face. I reached out to touch him but stopped, pulling my hand back. He noticed, and raw, unfiltered pain shone in his eyes at the action.

"I wanted to. I…I was so afraid." *He* was afraid? I struggled to believe that. Then I remembered the way he'd clung to me in the night and how he'd stormed through the castle searching for me. Had it been fear of losing me that made him so paranoid and not his lack of faith in me?

"Afraid of what?" I murmured, still struggling against the need to provide some comfort to him. It hurt me to see him in such pain.

He sighed, falling back into the chair and glaring at his hands, seeming to plan his answer. "Afraid that you'd leave me." He released a mirthless chuckle. "It was indeed a well-founded fear."

"I—" I broke off, realizing that if he'd told me about the bounty, I still would have left, despite my feelings for him.

"The thought of you leaving me…" he trailed off, running his fingers through his hair and gripping his head. "It eats at me."

I'd confirmed his deepest fears when I left. I tried not to feel remorse for that. "The thought of you being one of the bounty hunters I dreaded ate at me," I responded, and he laughed emptily.

"That day, when you took me to your parents' markers and we were ambushed, I tried to warn you to run from me, but the compulsion was too strong. I hated binding you, but the bounty was stronger than I was. I was too weak to protect you."

It had forced him to complete the bounty. For the first time, I saw the day through that lens. I remembered the tortuous look on his face as the bindings had come down, how he'd seemed to battle some unseen foe. I realized he had been waging war with himself.

"Why didn't you tell me after I imprisoned the Council members?" If I'd known, could things have been different? Could we have been in Întuneric for the last four days? I wasn't sure.

"You wouldn't listen to me," he said, his voice hoarse as he recalled it. "And I couldn't blame you."

"You weren't tempted to force me back home with you?" It wouldn't be the first time he'd done so.

"I couldn't do that to you again. I wanted you to be with me because—" He broke off.

My head tilted. "Because what?"

He turned his face away, muttering something unintelligible.

"What was that?"

"Because you loved me as I love you," he whispered. My heart stopped in my chest. Had he just said he loved me? He'd talked about fate and mates, kings and queens, but never about love before.

"You love me?" I asked, stunned. He sent me a look as if it was an obvious conclusion, one I should have been able to deduce from his actions. Sometimes even I needed things spelled out for me, needed the words.

"You know that," he said as if his reaction wasn't clear enough.

"How would I know that? You never said as much." I smiled and could have sworn I saw actual hope flourish in his eyes. I was going to forgive him because I loved him. Not that I wouldn't bring up the time he had hid the truth of the bounty from me every time we argued, but it was a start. It was a *baby step.*

"Do you think…" He cleared his throat as if speaking had suddenly become difficult for him. "Do you think you could ever feel that way about me?"

"Hmm." I tapped my finger on my chin, enjoying torturing him for just a little longer before I fessed up. "I don't think I could." His face dropped. "I *know* I could since I already do."

Cautious optimism sunk in, and he pulled me into his lap. "Do you mean it?" he asked, his eyes shining with emotion. I rested my hands against his chest, feeling his racing heartbeat under my palm. It felt like the organ was trying to burst from him.

"Yes. I love you, Lucien." I placed a soft kiss on his lips. He yanked me closer, deepening the kiss, and I felt his hands shake as they traced across my hair and face.

"You forgive me for being an unmitigated ass and almost fucking things up between us beyond repair?" he asked, cupping my face.

"I expect prolific apologies for at least the next hundred years before I consider it."

His voice dropped huskily. "Do you accept payment in the form of orgasms?"

I smiled, kissing him again. "I suppose I could be talked into a payment plan of some sort," I said, barely getting the words out before he tossed me on the bed.

XLII

THE REALM OF MORTALS.
ÎNTUNERIC CASTEL, ROMANIA.

IT TOOK SHOCKINGLY LITTLE convincing for Phoebe to move her Witch Queen residency to Întuneric. There was simply no possible way I was going to allow us to live on separate continents. When she was concerned about uprooting the witches to Romania, I explained we weren't just merging two species. We were creating a new future, one where vampires and witches could live in harmony.

Her first step was to replace our harsh and daunting thrones. She'd raised an eyebrow at my destroyed one. I gruffly admitted that I hadn't taken losing her well. She wordlessly created new custom thrones for each of us. Though black obsidian like they once were, the smooth surface was now littered with golden runes and spells. When we sat, golden crowns etched into the stone appeared to hover over our heads. I thought the effect *was a bit much,* but she winked at me and ignored my disapproval.

She took her role of decorator seriously and also redid our bedroom, filling the space with herbs, mortars, spell books, and enchantments. I would have found it disconcerting at one time, but as long as she stayed, I didn't care what she did.

With my help, Phoebe established a stable rift that led directly to Salem. It opened into the bowels of the castle, so both she and her advisors could come and go as they pleased.

Our efforts to merge the two species, to mix the magic of the witches with the strength and energy of the vampires, met resistance on both sides. However, the Vampire Elders were thrilled Phoebe had returned with me, and they were willing to try anything to make her stay. They even agreed to the outlawing of feeding on witches, except for mates or consensual feeds.

Most of the Elders departed for their territories to ensure others followed the new law, but my uncle remained. It almost appeared as if Ambrogio was waiting for something as if there was something more he wanted to happen, something he wouldn't reveal to us.

With the establishment of the stable rift, Phoebe worried about whom to let come and go. The rift allowed access both to our home and the very heart of the castle that protected the witches. We could not assume that all that crossed would be friendly. I offered to threaten death to any who dared approach. She rolled her eyes and decided on a spell to warn of someone's intentions when they crossed the boundary going either way. If an immortal tried to take her coven unawares or invade Întuneric, mystical alarms would alert everyone in both places.

I didn't mind the constant coming and going of witches through our home, so long as they knew better than to show anything but absolute loyalty to Phoebe. I hadn't even minded when she informed me that since witches didn't have mates or consorts. They didn't recognize me as her king. I didn't care, especially since I had a surprise for her. Well, I had three surprises, in fact. One weighed heavily in my pocket as I caught her coming out of the library and swept her off her feet.

"Lucien! You scared the life out of me," she said with a surprised squeal, letting me carry her to the throne room. I placed her delicately on her new seat. She smiled up at me and said, "I'm supposed to be sparring with Gunnar soon."

Gunnar had stayed on as a personal guard for Phoebe. The gruff and stoic lycan felt the need to protect her at all costs. I would have felt uncomfortable about another male hanging around my mate, but Erik pulled me aside, explaining that Phoebe reminded Gunnar of his lost sister. The lycan's need to protect her stemmed from his inability to do the same for his sister centuries earlier. I welcomed the lycan after that and was happy to have the extra security.

"Gunnar can wait. I have some surprises for you." I smiled and hoped it didn't betray my nerves. "Stay right there."

I sprinted to my office, pulling out the two boxes from where I'd hidden them, and was back in front of her in a blink. "I got some help from Erik for this. He said it was his olive branch to you for bringing me the bounty." I kissed her hard when she frowned.

"He's forgiven." She smiled, reaching for the gifts. I sighed at her but handed them over, holding my breath as she opened them. "Are these...?" Her eyes filled with tears.

"Your grimoires. Erik found them supporting a wobbly nightstand in some troll den." I thought I probably should have skipped that part when she started crying, but when she looked at me again, I saw the love shining there. She brushed the tomes off her lap and leaped into my arms, smacking loud kisses over my face.

"I love you so much. Thank you, thank you, thank you." More kisses on every place she could reach.

"You better not be thanking Erik like this," I warned, and she laughed, sliding down my body to inspect the two books. When she opened the Atreus one, she noticed the note I'd left tucked under the cover. When she glanced back at me, I was down on one knee next to her.

"Lucien?" she asked, still unsure, but tears filled her eyes again.

"Let me get this out. I know witches don't recognize mates like other species, and I wanted you to have everything you dreamed of before everything changed. I love you more than the air I breathe. Will you marry me?"

I flicked back the lid of the ring box that I'd pulled from my pocket, displaying the ring I'd picked for her. It was non-traditional, just like her. A massive black diamond sat in the center, surrounded by a halo of smaller white ones. Inside the ring, I'd inscribed *My Enchantress*.

I'd felt like a sap when I first purchased it, but the way Phoebe's face was lighting up now made it all worth it. She was staring at the ring but wasn't saying anything, and I was getting a bit nervous.

"This is the part where you say yes," I hinted.

"Yes!" she screamed, tears still falling down her face. She held her hand out, letting me slide the ring on her finger. Phoebe threw her arms around my neck, kissing me as I stood. Before I could spin her around, unable to contain my delight at her acceptance, the throne room doors burst open. Blood scented the air, and lots of it. I turned to glare at the intruders, pushing Phoebe behind me. Erik half-carried his younger brother into the room. Alaric was covered in blood, and his face was nearly gray.

"Please help us," Erik said, his voice pleading.

XLIII

THE REALM OF MORTALS.
OUTSIDE BUCHAREST, ROMANIA.
TWO HOURS EARLIER.

WHAT IN THE HELLS KIND OF TROUBLE had Alaric gotten himself into now? I scoured through Bucharest on the rumors that my younger brother was raising hell in the capital. Alaric always checked in, but it was over a week without hearing from him. I really should have my title changed. It shouldn't be Erik Wulfric, King of Lycans. It should be Erik Wulfric, Wolf Wrangler. It sounded a little too much like the Crocodile Hunter. Rest In Peace, Steve.

I growled in irritation and sent Leif and Thurston ahead, hoping they could track down my wayward brother. I was just like him at one time, wild and carefree, no crown weighing me down. Then everything had changed, first the war, then my ascension to king. Responsibilities dragged down my shoulders until I worried I might collapse beneath the weight.

I pushed away the memories of those three hundred years of freedom and stormed into another bar, looking around for my brother, a shiver of foreboding shooting down my spine. I couldn't remember Alaric, or any of my siblings, going this long without checking in with me.

Viggo sniffed the air, alert to any threats. I hated traveling with a posse, but the wolves refused to let me go to Întuneric alone, so I was stuck with them for the entirety of my sojourn to Romania. One thousand years old, and they still treated me like a child.

Viggo hissed next to me, "Leeches." He growled, indicating the two vampires sitting at the bar, their backs to us.

Unlike the vampires I usually kept company with, they smelled like aggression and blood, like death. My instincts screamed at me as my nostrils flared. I bolted across the bar, not even caring that several humans likely noticed the blur of movement.

I slammed one of the vampires against the wall and growled, "What have you done to my brother?"

My claws sunk into the leech, unable to control the wolf clawing within me. The blood I scented was Alaric's. Viggo grabbed the remaining vampire, discreetly telling the remaining visitors of the bar to fuck off unless they wanted to join the incoming fight. The room cleared in a matter of seconds.

The vampire struggled, his eyes turning a menacing red. "We only did what the other mongrel paid us to!"

"What did you do to my brother?" I demanded again, refusing to relinquish the squirming vampire, my grip grinding his bones together.

"We took him to the caves! He should still be there!" The other vampire shouted as Viggo displayed his own fangs to the vampire. I threw the second down, breaking his arm before grabbing the uninjured one in an uncompromising grip.

"Take me to him, now," I ordered, the wolf within me roused. The vampires hurried to obey when I felt my eyes turning.

Our drive into the mountains was silent except for harsh directions from the injured vampire. When we could go no further by car, I yanked them out and forced them to lead us to the abandoned network of tunnels hidden beneath an oil refinery.

I beheaded the two vampires without mercy. Nobody threatened my siblings. The wolf ripped through my skin, bones popping and breaking as the beast emerged. The pain was so familiar I barely felt it anymore.

Fully turned, I entered the cave and struggled to comprehend what I was seeing. Ten vampires circled an altar, my brother's broken and bloodied body atop it. They were bowing and chanting in a language even I didn't recognize. A vampire stepped forward and bit his own wrist, forcing the blood into Alaric's mouth. *No!*

I slammed into that vampire first, taking him to the ground and allowing my wolf to wreak havoc. My snarl was loud as I ripped the vampire's head from his shoulders before turning to tear at the followers. Viggo fought at my side, the other wolf relishing the bloodshed as we killed them all.

Must protect pack and Alaric is pack. My wolf and I were in agreement on that. No one touched my brother and lived, no one.

When there was nothing left to kill, I shifted back into human form to assess Alaric. My brother was in awful shape, covered in injuries. He had cuts that were seeping black foul blood and burns that hurt to see. It shocked me when he opened his eyes and gazed up at me. His lips twitched into a relieved smile but died when he saw the horror I was helpless to conceal.

My brother's eyes were glowing lycan amber, but blood-red encircled his irises. What had the vampires done to him?

"Erik…" Alaric moaned, blood bubbling from his mouth.

I slung my brother's arm over my shoulder and lugged his heavy frame toward the entrance of the cave. Viggo shifted back and retrieved my pants, handing them over to me. I stabbed my legs into them while Viggo supported Alaric. My wolf paced close to the surface, rippling under my skin, demanding more blood. The other lycan noticed Alaric's otherworldly, haunting eyes and sent a distressed look my way. I shook my head subtly, silently ordering Viggo not to say anything.

The other wolf nodded, finding his cellphone in the pocket of his jeans, dialing Leif to bring the car. Alaric passed out from the pain while we waited, his new eyes hidden behind his lids. Viggo and I stood in silence, both of us lost in our own thoughts and worry. When Leif and Thurston arrived, they helped us carry Alaric's gigantic frame to the car. Leif looked at me in a silent question as he settled behind the wheel.

"We have to take him to Phoebe and Lucien. They'll know what to do." They would help us. Heal him and then figure out what he is.

Our drive to Întuneric was disturbingly silent, only punctuated by Alaric's labored breathing. I counted each inhale and exhale, praying to whatever god was listening to save him. Once the lights of Întuneric were close enough, I didn't wait for the car to stop. I leaped from the vehicle and stormed into the throne room, begging, "Please help us!"

Phoebe reacted before Lucien. She waved her hands in the air, removing Alaric's weight from my shoulder and buoying my brother with magic. Alaric lay suspended in the air, and I could barely look at the injuries he'd sustained. I was supposed to protect him. What kind of king was I?

Lucien sniffed the air, his eyes turning red at the smell. "Erik..." he began.

"He cannot die, Lucien! He cannot," I snapped, knowing what Lucien scented. Death clung to my brother like a second skin. I couldn't fail my brother, not again. *Failure, just like always, boy.* My father's phantom voice rang in my skull. A thousand years and still, it plagued me.

Phoebe bit her lower lip, and her eyebrows came down over her vibrant eyes. "Get me the Margaux Grimoire." Lucien flashed to the throne and back, handing the tome to her. She frantically flipped through the pages, something like dread and indecision crossing her face.

"What is it?" I breathed, my voice cracking.

"I can save him—"

"Then do it!"

"But I can't reverse what was done. He'll be like this forever." Her words were devastating, and I gulped at the implications. Alaric would be the first and only lycan-vampire hybrid. What would he become?

Still, this was *Alaric*. "Do it." My voice was little more than a growl.

Lucien glanced at his queen nervously, placing his hands on her shoulders. My men finally caught up to me, Gunnar hard on their heels. He must have heard the commotion and come immediately to Phoebe's side. I couldn't blame the man. I knew the scars and burdens Gunnar carried.

My hair stood on end as Phoebe chanted, and potent magic filled the room. Her hands roamed over Alaric's injuries, healing the skin. The process was painful, making my brother whimper even while unconscious. I bit my tongue until it bled to keep from howling in response. He was my brother, my responsibility, and my failure.

The space was eerily silent except for my Alaric's pained growls. When those tapered off, I glanced at Phoebe, trying to force down the hope that boiled. "Is it done?"

"I healed his body, but his mind…" she whispered. "Erik, they did horrific things to him there. I wish I could take the memories from him." She likely felt every wound, even the ones I couldn't see or smell.

"I'll take care of him." *Always*.

"He should stay here, just in case," Lucien said, his tone surprisingly gentle.

In case he needs to be put down. Lucien didn't speak the words, but I could tell he thought them. I shook my head, not wanting Alaric to wake up in some unfamiliar room, not after he'd been trapped in that cave for a week. I wanted familiar sights, smells, and our family surrounding him, supporting him.

"I'm taking him home to Völsung," I ordered. My lycans moved forward to support Alaric as Phoebe gently lowered him into their hands. As they escorted him out, I could still smell the putrid scent of the caves on him, and his scent was different. It wasn't the one I grew up with, the one I knew as well as my own. What was this going to do to him and our people? Despite the friendship between Lucien and me, lycans and vampires remained enemies. I didn't know how they were going to react to Alaric, but he was alive, and that was all that mattered. A sigh of relief slipped from my lips.

Phoebe stepped closer to lay a comforting hand on my arm, and I caught the flash of the ring on her finger. I winced, realizing what I'd interrupted. I pulled Phoebe into a hug and kissed both her cheeks. "Congratulations. I'm sorry if we ruined the moment."

Marriage wasn't exactly a *thing* between mates because they could end. Would my queen want a wedding? That was just another unanswered question about my mate, one I'd likely never know the answer to. Lucien had waited ten-thousand years for his and oh how Fate had rewarded him. But I wasn't Lucien, and I knew I had done nothing to earn my mate. My crown was handed to me by Lucien, and I had failed my family time and time again. Agony tore through me as I imagined Alaric on that altar.

Phoebe smiled brightly. "It wouldn't be home if you didn't feel welcome, Erik."

I flushed at the sentiment. Phoebe was too warm and affectionate for an immortal. She was melting the icy castle, along with its king. "You both are welcome at Völsung." It was an invitation never extended to a non-lycan, not even Lucien.

Phoebe sent a glance at Lucien before saying, "I have a feeling we will find our way there."

EPILOGUE

THE REALM OF MORTALS.
ÎNTUNERIC CASTEL, ROMANIA.

I WAS BACK IN THE ROOM I'd discovered at
Întuneric, this time with Lucien at my side. The man
had not let me out of his sight for an instant, and I was
pretty sure he wasn't sleeping either. I kept waking up to find
him staring at me like he was making sure I wasn't a mirage or
something. I wouldn't admit that I was enjoying his attention.
It reminded me I'd made the right choice.

Within one of my newly recovered grimoires, I found a
spell to help me navigate the mystical part of Întuneric,
proving to Lucien that our home was very much enchanted. It
stunned him to realize that even though he'd lived there for so
long, the castle never spoke to him as it did to me. I comforted
him, pointing out that since we now shared power, the castle
might show him things too. When I'd winked and added, *just
remember, I'm its favorite,* my sass had gotten me a spanking we
both enjoyed.

"Okay, what do you see?" I asked, standing in front of the
annoyingly persistent and powerful illusion. It flickered, the
runes powering it glowing slightly. Even Lucien's library
could produce no translation for the symbols.

"I see the wall of a room I did not know existed," he
answered, pulling me into his arms and resting his chin on my
head. He was constantly touching me,

kissing me, and maybe one day I would mind. But it wasn't today.

"It's an illusion. There's more to this room." I extracted myself from him and, holding my hand up to the illusion, showed him how my hand froze, meeting unseen resistance. The illusion quivered and warmed but didn't break. "Lucien, I think there's something here."

His eyebrows rose, and he held his hand up next to mine. "All I see and feel is a wall."

Our power share only went so far. This illusion was powerful enough to trick even his senses.

"The last time I opened up a rift here, I ended up on another plane." I pushed against the illusion, trying to break it, but there was no give. "I found a temple, which had all the ancestral lineages carved into the walls. It was the first time I saw the name Regina."

"You went to another realm without me?" he murmured. "What if it trapped you there? Or you were hurt?!" His voice was low with concern, but I waved away his worry. It was best not to tell him a shadow monster chased me out. Some things should remain secret.

"I was fine. Queen of Witches, remember?" I reminded him, but his dark brows remained down over his emerald eyes. Despite being able to incinerate immortals with my mind, Lucien still treated me like I needed protection. I loved him for that. I also knew he wouldn't stop me from kicking ass if the occasion called for it, so long as I brought him with me. He was my roots, and I could finally grow with my vampire at my side. "The realm was shrouded in mist, and there were a ton more temples nearby."

"The temple you were in—was there a statue in it?" he whispered, paling more than I thought possible. There were lines of strain around his mouth as it tightened.

"Yes, of Hekate. Why?"

"It was not a statue. You were in Ethereal."

I'd stumbled into the land of the gods? I'd stood before my goddess? "Why would a rift open to Ethereal? I thought that was impossible."

The land of the gods was supposed to be closed to visitors, especially accidental ones. The gods were vulnerable as they slept, which is why the realm was created in the first place.

"You said you saw runes on the ground. Can you draw them for me?" he asked. His frantic vibe was making a chill of unease shoot down my spine. The only other time I'd seen him like this was in the cemetery. Even now, a flash of hurt at the memory shot through me.

I nodded and conjured fire with a short chant, drawing the runes for him, leaving them suspended in the air. "Do you recognize them?"

"I—That is my—" He gaped, his mouth opening and closing as if trying to find the words. "The reason you cannot break those runes is that they were made by the one thing with more magic than you."

"What does that mean?" I was the most powerful witch ever; *no one* had more magic. Except... "The illusion...the gods made it?" The rift opened to Ethereal and Hekate's resting place, where she still slept, conserving her power because she was powering the illusion.

He grabbed my hand, trying to pull me from the room. I dug my heels in, but it did little good. "If there is an illusion here, you are not breaking it."

"You're not curious? What if it's dangerous?" He stopped, trying to pull me away, turning back to face me.

"When it comes to the gods, you do not meddle." He grasped my shoulders, his emerald eyes shining. But I felt the call. Whatever summoned me here, showed me this room, and sent me to Ethereal was still here. I could feel its power humming in the air expectantly, waiting for something.

"I think I'm meant to break this illusion, Lucien. I think...I think it's calling to me. What if we need to break the illusion?" He still didn't look convinced, so I went to my toes, pressing my lips to his reassuringly. "This is the first time I've been down here since we bonded. I want you here with me when I break it."

I could see the way his mind worked through the words I left unsaid. *I will do this without you if you try to stop me.* I may be his mate, his queen, but I am no one's subject. Lucien empowered me to be who I truly was without fear, and I loved him for it.

"I'll never be able to deny you anything, *regina mea*," he said with a huge sigh as he caved, but I could still feel his worry and reluctance.

I clapped delightedly and shooed him to the side of the room as I chanted the spell I created for the occasion. Okay, in all honesty, I was planning to do this no matter what Lucien said. Magic built more than I'd ever used at once, but there was no flag in my energy because of my ten-thousand-year-old battery frowning in the corner.

I sent him a wink before throwing the ball of magic at the illusion, hearing it crack and splinter. Pieces fell from the illusion in a cascade of broken magic, the force throwing me back. Lucien was faster, snatching me out of the air before I could collide with the wall, taking the impact with the stone against his own back.

"Well, shit," I murmured, the dust from the magical collision slowly settling.

Was that a coffin? The tomb was cut from the same black stone as the caste and seemed to jut out of the floor, big enough for someone as tall as Lucien. Why was there a tomb hidden in Întuneric behind a god-powered illusion?

I struggled to my feet, Lucien stopping me from striding forward. "You broke the illusion. Now it's my turn."

I nodded, gesturing for him to go ahead of me. "Did you know this was here?" I asked.

He shook his head, cautiously approaching the tomb. I initially thought the top of the tomb was as solid as the rest of it, but it was actually translucent. A golden lightning bolt was carved into it, stretching from its inhabitant's shoulder to his thigh. I came closer and used my cellphone to light up the inside. We need to see what had been hiding there. I nearly dropped my phone when the dust cleared enough for me to see.

It was Lucien. At least, that was my initial thought, but when I looked closer, I saw a scar bisecting an eyebrow. This man also looked slightly older than Lucien, with streaks of grey at his temples.

I gaped at him. "Lucien, I think this is…"
His lips lost all color as he muttered, "My father."